The Gravediggers Series 5

A PUNK ROCK DEMON STORY

Matthew R. Miller

Copyright © 2022 by Matthew R. Miller

All rights reserved. No part of this book may be reproduced or used in any manner without the written permission of the copyright owner except for the use of quotations in a book review.

Matthew R. Miller

Email: matthew.miller.writer@gmail.com

Facebook: https://www.facebook.com/Matthew-Miller-Horror-Writer-100169618967966

Instagram: @matthewmillerauthor

The Book's Savant Talent

Content Editing by Leoneh Charmell

Cover Art by Elvins Acurero

Interior Design by Avril Acurero

https://thebookssavant.com

Sigil Illustration by Anthony Noble

FIRST EDITION

Disclaimer: This is a work of fiction. Names, characters, places, and incidents either are the product of the author's imagination or are used fictitiously. Any resemblance to actual persons, living or dead, events, or locales is entirely coincidental

TABLE OF CONTENTS

Make the Children Pass Through the Fire 1

Oy Vey! 6

Take a Hint, Punk 13

A Sigil Signal 22

Bad Religion 26

Walk the Fire for Me 31

Eldritch Horrors 42

Break the Circle 49

Suffer the Little Children to Come Unto Me 59

The Circus Tent 64

Mourning Exorcise 76

Slick Oil Lamp 83

A Drink of Djinn 92

Always Room for One More 100

Fly Me to the Tomb 111

Sweet Kolkata Rain 116

Best Wishes 123

Goth Chicks Rock	131
Siesta Fiesta	139
Past the Expiration Date	151
In the Houses of the Unholy	156
Ten Little Indians	165
Who Needs Some Exorcise?	170
Sex Pistol	180
Dry Run	184
Wager Danger	189
Paul's Addiction	196
Well, That Blows	203
Man's Best Friend	207
The Last Temptation of Paul	211
Gag Me	216
The Call of the Ancestors	223
Grave Danger	228
The Ashes of Ushaville	232
Punk Resurrected	237
The Clash and the Crash	253
A Deal with the Devil	261
An Alley and a Roofie	263
Who's Afraid of the Big Bad Demon?	277
Ooh, Baby, When You Cry	287
Eat Me	291
Roch Hard	300
Bottle Up Your Feelings	305

Torch of Love, Porch of Betrayal 311

Fly by Night.. 319

We Walk the Streets at Night; We Go Where Demons Dare 322

Police Truck 328

Idol Hands Are the Devil's Workshop 337

Old Punk... 341

A Load of Bull 351

En Garde! 359

I'm Gonna Get You, Sucker! 369

Hey Little Girl, I Wanna Be Your Husband 374

CHAPTER 1

Make the Children Pass Through the Fire

Thou shalt not suffer a witch to live. — Exodus 22:18

Jerusalem, Damascus Gate
The month of Nisan, in the reign of King Solomon the Wise.
The trial of Abijah of the house of Elihu, recorded by me, Elisha the scribe.

Elder 1: "Abijah of the house of Elihu, you have been brought before the Elders here at the Damascus Gate, being accused of sorcery. Do you understand this charge?"

Abijah: "Yes, Elder, but…"

Elder 1: "You will have your defense! Silence for now."

Abijah stopped talking and looked down at the dusty ground.

Elder 2: "Judah of the house of Koresh, Machla of the house of Peleg, and Noach of the house of Shaul, you have brought this most serious accusation of sorcery against your fellow Hebrew. As Moses has taught us, *a single witness shall not suffice against a person for any crime or for any wrong in connection with any offense that he has committed. Only on the evidence of two witnesses or of three witnesses shall a charge be established.* You are three; thus, these charges will be heard and judged by us, the Elders."

Elder 3: "Tell us, Judah, Machla, and Noach, did you truly witness the accused, Abijah, performing sorcery, as you have said?"

Judah: "Yes."

Machla: "We did."

Noach: "It is so."

Elder 1: "Very well. The testimony of three eyewitnesses has established the matter. We will proceed. Abijah, you have been accused of sorcery. Give the glory to God, son. Tell us what you have done."

Abijah: "Elder, I did not intend to practice sorcery. Rather, I sought an answer from God for my troubles."

Elder 1: "What are your troubles, my son?"

Abijah: "My harvest has failed, and my family has nothing to eat. I only sought God for help."

Elder 1: "How did you go about seeking God?"

Abijah paused and looked at the ground, thinking carefully of how to answer.

Abijah: "Elder, I went to the shrine of God in the valley Geh-Ben-Hinnom, at Tophet."

Elder 1: "Abijah, you have gone to the place of evil! That valley is good for nothing but demons and trash! Which shrine did you visit?"

Abijah: "The shrine of God!"

Elder 1: "And what did this *god* look like to you, son?"

Abijah: "The god of the shrine has the body of a man and the face of a calf, Elder."

Elder 2: "Blasphemy! The Lord God has no such form! Never has a man seen the Lord God!"

Elder 1: "Abijah, you describe the god Moloch, the abomination of the Ammonites. You know that Moses has taught us never to worship the abomination Moloch. Did you offer him a sacrifice, Abijah? Give the glory to God, and tell the truth, son!"

Abijah looked at the ground again, then burst into sobs.

Abijah: "I did! I did, elder!"

Elder 2: "And what was that sacrifice? Tell us now!"

Abijah: "I offered my firstborn! It is the highest sacrifice to God—"

Elder 1: "That is not the Lord our God, who would never ask the sacrifice of our children! You have done wickedly, Abijah! You have broken the commandment of the Lord our God and Moses in the worst way, giving even your own son to the devil Moloch! Moloch requires fire sacrifice! Did you burn your son? Did you?"

Abijah fell to his knees in the dirt and pulled at his hair in grief.

Elder 1: "Oh, Abijah, son. Do you know the penalty for such wickedness? Moses in the Law has made it clear we must stone to death anyone giving his son to Moloch, the abomination of the Ammonites."

Abijah: "Mercy, Elders! Mercy!"

Elder 1: "There is no mercy for those who sacrifice their children to Moloch. Judah, Machla, and Noach, is this what you saw? What do you say?"

Judah: "There is more, elder. We witnessed Abijah take his son down into the accursed valley and into that ancient, abandoned shrine, yet he

HELL´S BELLS: A PUNK ROCK DEMON STORY

is lying still! He did sacrifice his son to Moloch the abomination, but he did not do so to ask for a good harvest. For, when he returned home that night, we saw that the demon Moloch did truly appear to Abijah in the flesh, as a great beast, a devil, and Abijah did bow down to him and worship him and ask for great wealth!"

Elder 1: "Abijah, is this true? Is it as Judah says?"

Abijah tore his shirt, pulled on his hair, then fell prostrate before the elders and cried, "May the Lord my God have mercy on me! I have done wickedly! I have been tempted with wealth and riches, and the priests of Moloch assured me that Moloch would grant me my wishes! Did not King Solomon himself construct the shrine to Moloch at Tophet, in the Geh-Ben-Hinnom?"

Elder 1: "Do not speak of the king in such a manner, Abijah. You have already blasphemed against God; do not add to your iniquity by doing so against the king! Your confession is proof, and your own words testify against you and condemn you. Therefore, we, the elders, pronounce you guilty of sorcery, of blasphemy, and of murder, and we do condemn you to death by stoning, as Moses has instructed us in the Law."

Abijah: "Mercy! Have mercy! What will my family do without me?"

Elder 1: "As you showed no mercy to your firstborn son, so shall the Lord our God show no mercy to you. Judah, Machla, and Noach, take Abijah to the Place of Stoning, outside of the Jaffa Gate, and bind him, and we shall announce to the people what is happening.

Abijah did not resist as Judah, Machla, and Noach took him by the arms and led him through Jerusalem, then through the Jaffa Gate outside of the city proper, then to the barren Place of Stoning. They sat him on the ground as the elders went through the city and announced the coming event. All the people rushed through the Jaffa Gate to the Place of Stoning. The men surrounded Abijah, and the women stood apart and watched.

Elder 1: "Let it be known to the people that Abijah of the house of Elihu has confessed to the sins of sorcery, blasphemy, and murder, as witnessed by Judah of the house of Koresh, Machla of the house of Peleg, and Noach of the house of Shaul. According to the Law, as given to the people from God to Moses, we are bound to stone Abijah to death without mercy. Abijah, have you anything to say?"

Abijah: "May the Lord my God have mercy on me and forgive me!"

Elder 1: "As is our custom, the three witnesses shall cast the first stones!"

I, Elisha the scribe, did then witness with my own eyes the following:

Judah, Machla, and Noach each took a large stone in one hand, and at the nod of the elders, they threw them at Abijah. Two stones struck the man in the chest, and one in the head. After the witnesses had thrown the first stones, the rest of the men joined the stoning.
Abijah: "A curse on you all, you cruel men! Moloch shall avenge my death!"

He then gave up the ghost.

CHAPTER 2

Oy Vey!

"Look," said Paul Junk Roy in the grand parlor of Lâmié Chasseur's mansion, on St. Charles Avenue, in the heart of the Garden District of New Orleans, "if you two are gonna make out on the sofa, then I need a fucking drink. Not that I care, but it's kind of gross. At least wait until I get back from the corner liquor store, will you?"

Isabella Marcello giggled and replied, "Fine, Paul. Fine. Me and Varco will wait until you come back."

"Gross?" asked Varco incredulously. "Well, you think you and Mary are any better when we hear you at night, you know, *doing it*?"

Mary gasped and blushed. "What? That's…I…we…oh my God!"

She pulled a pillow over her face. Paul grinned proudly.

"Say, Lâmié mate, when're we gonna go see that priest dude and check out the scribbling on the wall?" asked Paul.

"Father Woodrow said he has time tomorrow. He hasn't moved or touched anything 'cuz he wants us to see for ourselves. *Die Gravediggers!* isn't the most comforting or welcoming message to appear on a church wall under a cross that flew across the room, is it?"

"Ghost or fraud," replied Paul. "I don't trust them religious types."

"*Those* religious types," corrected Mary. "You should read a book sometime, Paul. You might pick up some basic toddler English."

He stuck his tongue out at her.

Isabella's parents had decided to spend half of the year in Monaco. They had left her in their house with the staff to look after her, but she and Varco had quickly decided to move into Lâmié's mansion with the others.

After all, they were now freshmen at Tulane University, and though the two teenagers still *officially* lived at Isabella's house, they spent so much time with the gang at Lâmié's that they had seen no reason not to move in. So they shared a bedroom, and the others just turned a blind eye to their cohabitation, despite the disapproving *tsks* of Yarielis.

After the goblin massacre, Judy Felix had also remained living at the mansion, mainly because she been traumatized and did not want to be alone anymore. The same trauma had led Erin Drasiedi and little Grimbil to move in along with Evelyn Fogelberg. In addition, Siofra Fay had decided to remain in New Orleans to teach another year at the high school, and so she had also become one of the housemates.

Overall, Lâmié's spacious, ancestral home was currently occupied by Paul Junk Roy, Scary Mary Gambino, Mucky Matt Moulin, Isabella, Varco, Zoë, Detective Pace Barillo, Yarielis, Judy, Evelyn, Titania, 'Tit Boudreaux, Siofra, Erin, little Grimbil, and the two furry friends, the cats Baozi and Pidan. This made for seventeen humans and two feline housemates.

The house overall had more than plenty of room, but since everyone enjoyed congregating in the grand parlor, that particular room was continuously packed with laughter, sarcasm, good food and drink, and the not infrequent bodily noise from Paul.

"Any booze requests?" he asked as he stood up and headed toward the hall.

"Good beer, not watery crap," said Matt.

"Could you possibly buy some decent red wine, Paul?" asked Siofra.

"Um...yeah, but I don't know good wine from cheap plonk."

"Something French, Italian, or Spanish, and ask for a recommendation, please," she instructed, and Paul just shrugged and nodded.

"Oy vey, you expect me to remember all that?" he asked.

Mary said, "Wait, *oy vey*? The fake English accent isn't enough,

Paul? Now you're pretending to be Jewish?"

"What, a guy can't say oy vey?"

Mary just shook her head.

Paul stepped onto the sidewalk under the glorious oaken canopy above St. Charles Avenue, took a deep lungful of the warm, sultry New Orleans air, and grinned. No vampires, no werewolves, no zombies, no goblins, and Ophelia had gone back underground into hiding. They would re-open The Gutter Bar, and, as Paul hoped with all of his being, they would return to playing (bad) punk music. Nothing supernatural would bug them anymore, and the memories of the horrible things they had endured would simply fade over time.

After all, weren't they going to see the priest the next day, the priest who claimed that an invisible hand had written their deathwish on the church wall? *Hell*, he thought, *it was probably just a hoax or a leftover from the goblins*.

He saw a young woman walking toward him...*well, not walking precisely; maybe more like crawling?* Paul thought, because this woman was upside down on all fours.

"For fuck's sake," he muttered. "Hey lady, are you drunk or high? Maybe practicing for a gymnast competition? Hey, watch it!"

He slid laterally out of the way as the woman crab-walked right toward him, quickly skittering like a grotesquely-oversized insect. She was murmuring something in an unrecognizable language and a deep, throaty voice.

"Same to you, lady!" huffed Paul. "Might wanna get to rehab."

In English, but in the same gravelly, baritone voice, she replied, "Paul, Paul, we will sift you like wheat and burn the chaff!"

"Huh? How the fuck do you know my name? Go chaff yourself!"

He weakly kicked at her, then sidestepped her and continued down the sidewalk as she persisted with the babbling. The strange woman did not follow him, and he eventually reached the corner liquor store.

Paul opened the door and walked inside to the luxuriously crisp air conditioning. He scratched his head and looked around, then saw the new clerk who had replaced Evelyn.

"Ahh!" yelled Paul with a jump.

"Ahhhh!" yelled the man behind the counter with a jump of his own.

"Sorry, mate! Geez. Scared the hell out of me," said Paul sheepishly. "Just not used to seeing, you know, well, um..."

"Hasidic Jews. You can say it, friend," said the man warmly in a thick Yiddish accent after he had calmed down from the startling entrance and Paul's strange clothing and Mohawk hairstyle.

"Um, yeah, that. I didn't mean anything by it, mate. Sorry, then."

"I'm Uri, Uri Horowitz. Pretty Jewish name, eh?" he said with a chuckle.

"Couldn't be Jewisher," agreed Paul. "I'm Paul Junk Roy."

"That sounds vaguely familiar," said Uri.

"Well, I sing for a crappy local punk rock band called The Gravediggers. We suck."

"Oh, I love punk rock!"

Paul cocked his head in confusion. "You're allowed?"

"Oy vey, always with this question!" said Uri. "We Hasidim believe in joy and mystery. We can enjoy life, you know! So what? Are we supposed to be grim and somber all the time? Most goyim don't know that about us: we formed our group originally to *get away* from the strict asceticism that was popular at the time."

"Asceti-what?"

"Oy. Nevermind. Nice to meet you, Paul."

Paul perused the store, looking at a few brands of beer that he had never before tried. The air conditioning buzzed from above, and the fluorescent lights flickered, giving the cases of beer the look of an old-fashioned movie.

"You like punk, you say?" said Paul after thinking for a bit. "Well, if you like listening live, mate, we own a bar too. It's called The Gutter Bar, and it's just around the corner. Heard of it? You should stop by sometime. Lots of punk shows there, if you like live, that is.

Uri frowned and said, "Have I heard of it? Everyone's heard of the bar where constant massacres happen."

"Er, *constant* might be a bit of an overstatement, but yeah, that's us."

Uri nodded, his curly *payot* shaking from beneath his *hoiche* hat. "You know, and I hope this doesn't sound like bragging because I can assure you it's not, but I happen to play the bass guitar."

Paul opened his mouth in silence for a moment.

"You what, mate? *You*? You play the bass guitar? You know, you're kind of the opposite of a Hasidic stereotype, Uri."

Uri laughed heartily and said, "Yeah, I guess I am. That's also why my parents and my congregation call me too liberal. They're not too happy about it, although, to be honest, the tales I could tell you about the other guys that hide their sins better!"

Paul could not help but think about the former, tragic ends of their bassists, and how they needed a new one. Would there be any harm in asking Uri to try out for the Gravediggers? After all, they were weird to begin with, and having a Hasidic bassist might be just the thing to make then stand out among all the other punk bands in town – their crappy music sure wasn't the secret to success.

"Say, mate," said Paul, "we've had some, um, bad luck with bassists, and we need a new one. Wanna try out with us?"

From somewhere in the depths of the beer cooler in the rear of the store, a cricket chirped and Paul wrinkled his nose. He hated insects.

"Oh, would I! I thought you'd never ask!" squealed a delighted Uri.

"Don't get your hopes up. We suck, like I said. By the way, are you even allowed to work in a liquor store?"

Uri shrugged and replied, "Again, my family's not too happy with me. I'm not saying I'm having a crisis of faith, but I'm having a little crisis of faith. We can drink, you know, but we're not supposed to interact with goyim like this. But hey, what? Am I supposed to *not* work and just starve to death? Feh to that!"

Paul placed a couple of cases of Bass Ale on the counter, rubbed his chin as if trying to remember something, then said, "Oh, yeah, I'm supposed to get red wine, too. No idea what's good."

Uri blew through his lips and replied, "Outside of Mogen David, I don't either. All I know is this stuff here is sort of expensive, so it's probably not too bad."

"Alright, I'll take three bottles of that," agreed Paul. "Here's our address," he said as he scribbled down the directions to Lâmié's mansion. "It's literally just right down the street. Tomorrow, around three in the afternoon?"

"I'd be honored, Paul. Playing with a band will be fun, even if you don't like my music or accept me."

"Honestly, if you can even hold a bass guitar, you're in."

"Nice to know I've got such high standards to meet. Sheesh. Alright, Paul, I look forward to it. Nice to make a new friend, even a goy. I grew up in such a strict and closed community that we were never really allowed to make friends with goyim. I'm learning that I missed out on lots growing up Hasidic."

Paul grinned and said, "We'll open your eyes to the world, mate."

"I'm not sure if that's good or bad!"

Paul headed toward the door just as a man entered—another Hasidic man, this one a bit older than Uri. Paul could not help but observe as the two men began to speak in Yiddish. The conversation seemed friendly enough, but Paul could see that Uri had tensed up and was not the same smiling, happy guy he had just been a few minutes before.

The volume and pace of their words both began to increase in direct proportion to the range of motion of their arm and hand gestures. Then, in just a matter of seconds, they were both screaming at each other and flailing their arms wildly, like a drowning man trying to swim. This continued for another minute, and then the man huffed off out of the store with his face bright red from the argument.

"What the hell was that about?" asked Paul.

"Oy, that was David, my older brother. He's extremely pious and observant, and he hates that I work here. He came to invite me to a prayer meeting tomorrow, but I told him I'm auditioning for a band. He did not like that at all. I'm sure you picked up on that."

"Shit, I don't wanna come between family!" said Paul.

"Feh, it's nothing. That was a normal conversation. You should see us when we're upset!"

Paul just chuckled, then walked out of the store. His arms being full of cases of beer and bottles of wine, he could barely see ahead of himself. He had made it almost all the way to the front porch steps of Lâmié's mansion when he tripped and fell but managed not to break the beer and wine bottles.

"Shit!" he said, then noticed why he had tripped. The creepy crab-walking girl had skittered in front of him right as he was walking.

"You again! Watch where you're going, you crazy girl! You need to get to the psych ward!"

He watched her defensively, expecting another weird assault. Instead, she just stared up at him with a maniacal, frozen expression of pain and anger on her face.

"Paul," she growled. "We're coming for you!"

He sighed deeply and shook his head. His arms were beginning to shake from carrying all the beer and wine, and he was becoming quickly frustrated with the crazy woman.

"Shit, this again. Don't come for me, baby. You'll be

disappointed. Go come on yourself, and be sure to piss right off, you nutter."

She hissed at him, and scurried off down the sidewalk. Even in weird New Orleans, people looked at her strangely as she did the crabwalk past them.

He strained against the beer and wine and walked inside the house. As he put the alcohol in the kitchen, opened himself a beer, and sat in the grand parlor drinking it, he told everyone about the crazy woman and about Uri, the bassist.

"Yay about Uri," said Mary. "Boo about nutter girl. Let's just ignore it and hope it goes away. The last thing we need is more supernatural crap in our lives." Just when she finished pronouncing those words, like a bad omen, a crash came from the kitchen, causing Mary to jump and squeal. "Christ! What the hell was that?" she cried.

Paul stood up and walked into the kitchen.

"Shit!" was heard by everyone in the parlor.

They rushed into the kitchen and saw that one of the wine bottles had been smashed against a wall, and the other two had been delicately stacked, one on top of the other.

Paul examined the stacked wine bottles. The tannic smell of the spilled wine filled the kitchen, causing him to sneeze.

"Look at this!" Matt exclaimed. "These bottles are stacked and perfectly balanced, but nothing is really holding them together. It's the balance!"

He picked up the top bottle, then tried to replace it on top of the other one, but he could not balance it well enough to make it stay.

'Tit Boudreaux stepped into the kitchen and, after marveling at the broken wine bottle, grabbed a broom and mop and began to clean up the mess.

"Supernatural, alright," said Matt.

"Oh, for fuck's sake," said Paul.

Chapter 3

Take a Hint, Punk

Paul, Mary, Matt, Lâmié, and 'Tit Boudreaux decided to see Father Woodrow at St. Louis Cathedral in Jackson Square. Isabella and Varco begged to tag along, and they indeed agreed, making a total of seven misfits. After all, they reasoned that too many of them would overwhelm the priest.

They arrived just as the midday mass was over, and the congregants were filing out and shaking Father Woodrow's hand. The priest recognized the Gravediggers and their friends. "Oh, hi, everyone!" he began. "Thanks for coming. I'll be with you in just a sec. Have a seat in a pew if you'd like."

They walked inside the church, and Paul ducked as he passed through the doorway.

"What was that?" asked Mary.

"I was just expecting to catch on fire as soon as I walked in."

"Dude, it's not like *you're* a vampire."

They sat in the first pew and looked up at the enormous, intricate crucifix affixed to the front wall above the altar. The Christ stared down accusingly at Paul.

"What?" he said. "What'd I do? Why's he staring at me?"

Mary giggled. "I think he's telling you to cut back on your drinking."

"Well! They serve wine here for Communion, right? So, I can't win!"

"Alright, sorry about that delay. Thank you all for coming. First thing, I hope you are all doing alright while you mourn the loss of your friends."

They all noticed that Father Woodrow had removed his priestly robes, leaving him in simple slacks and a polo shirt.

"Yes, Father, thank you," answered Lâmié. "It's hard to lose several friends at once, of course, but I guess only time heals those wounds."

"Time and God," said Woodrow. "You know, you are always welcome to come to Mass and pray with us. Are any of you Catholic?"

Isabella and Varco raised their hands.

"Most of us went to Catholic school," explained Lâmié, "and Isabella and Varco are graduates of Our Lady of Perpetual Sorrow. I can't speak for everyone, but I think we're mostly, well, sort of agnostic these days. No offense, Father."

Father Woodrow chuckled and said, "If that offended me, I'd be in the wrong business. Yes, having faith is hard these days; I can understand that. Just know that I am here if you ever want to talk. Speaking of talking, let me show you what happened in my office. The day it happened, I closed and locked the office door and have not been back in since. I wanted you to see it *in situ*."

"In what?" asked Paul.

Mary slapped his arm and said, "It means in its original state," she explained.

"Let's go this way," said the priest, and they followed him around the altar, into a side room, a hall, and then into his large, comfortable office. With soft, red carpet; oak-paneled bookshelves built into the luxurious paneled walls; and a high, vaulted ceiling; it seemed more like a mansion than a priest's office.

"Over there," said Father Woodrow, pointing to the far wall.

"Whoa!" said 'Tit Boudreaux.

On the floor in front of the wall was a large gold crucifix. They could see where it had hung on the wall because it had left a faint imprint, much like paintings do after hanging on walls for years.

"The crucifix was secured very well with stout nails," explained Father Woodrow. "It would have taken a strong force to pull it off like that."

Underneath the crucifix's former hanging spot, smeared large onto the wooden panel of the wall in bright red, were the words, *Die Gravediggers!*

"Maybe the ghost is German, and it's just saying, *The Gravediggers!*, like, it's a fan," suggested Paul.

"Don't think so, dude," said Matt. "Fans usually don't vandalize crosses."

"Yes, the message seems hostile and threatening to me," said Father Woodrow.

Varco walked to the wall and looked closely at the writing. "Is it blood?" he asked. "May I take a sample, Father? I brought a Ziploc bag just in case."

"Be my guest!"

Varco used a small pocketknife to scrape some of the red substance into the plastic bag, then sealed it. "I think Barillo will let us use his lab resources, at least to see if it's blood, yes?" said Varco.

"For sure," agreed Mary.

"What's your take on this, Father?" asked Lâmié.

The priest rubbed his hands together and chose his words carefully before replying. "Well, I'm in a bit of a dilemma. I am torn between official Church doctrine and my own experiences and beliefs. So, the Catholic Church teaches that the supernatural is real, of course. God, Satan, saints, angels, demons—they all exist, and I agree. The problem is that the modern Church will only recognize and acknowledge the paranormal, the supernatural, in extreme circumstances. Even an exorcism is very difficult to get approved these days. The Church looks first, and looks hard, for natural explanations for everything, which I find ironic, but anyway. The Vatican would look at this incident here and argue that it is a hoax, a natural phenomenon, or something like that. They would not accept it as paranormal."

The others listened carefully, and Lâmié was even taking notes.

"Now, as for me? Barry Woodrow, the man, and not the Vatican representative? Well, I've seen ghosts, and I am sure of it. I attended seminary in France in a building that was hundreds of years old. Three times, while I was awake and sober, I saw a full-bodied apparition, a definite human being walking around, but transparent, just like you'd imagine a ghost to be. So yes, off the record, I fully believe in the paranormal."

Paul walked to the wall and felt the writing with his hands. "Say, Padre," he said, "this ain't a ghost. Pretty sure ghosts float around and look scary. But, whatever did this had the power to move things around physically, and can spell and write."

"A Poltergeist, then?" replied Father Woodrow. "I don't know much about those, but aren't they supposed to be ghosts that can manipulate the physical world?"

"Yes," answered Lâmié. "Mainstream theory—well, I guess none of this is really mainstream—but most paranormal investigators believe that a Poltergeist is indeed a human spirit that has severe unresolved issues and is angry, and that anger gives it the ability to move things. The word *Poltergeist* in German means *rumbling spirit* or *noisy ghost*."

Father Woodrow was listening and nodding, then he asked, "I've heard of that, I guess. So you say mainstream theory: what's the alternative theory?"

"Well," continued Lâmié, "a minority of ghost hunters, for lack of a better word, believe that no disembodied human spirit could have the sort of power that allows it to throw things around, and that Poltergeists are actually demons disguised as human spirits in order to deceive people."

A slight, chilly breeze puffed through the room, causing everyone to look around.

"Oh, hell," said Paul. "I know you lot felt that."

Everyone nodded.

"Well, that's frightening," confessed Father Woodrow. "The demon theory, it's sobering, isn't it?"

Mary leaned against Paul. He noticed that she was shivering a little, so, in a comforting gesture that he only showed toward her, he put his arm around her shoulders.

"What are demons, anyway, Padre?" asked Paul.

"Well, official Church teaching is that they are fallen angels. They are real, spiritual beings with a personal agency who desire to steal, kill, and destroy. In other words, they want to cause as much harm to people as possible. They can only do what God permits them to do, though."

As soon as he uttered the last part, everyone heard a faint growl coming from somewhere around them. The office curtains billowed, as if something were walking behind them, sneaking and trying to remain hidden.

Everyone in the room felt the pit of their stomach falling like a roller coaster as they tried to deal with the fact that they were directly experiencing something both supernatural and hostile.

Mary's face began to sweat, and poor Father Woodrow was shaking and shuddering. His face had gone pale, and he was quietly whispering frantic prayers.

The office lights flickered, and a zapping electrical sound seemed to come from the thin air right under the ceiling. Another growl, threatening and unearthly, roared more loudly than the first one.

"Alrighty, that's my cue to leave," said Paul as he stood up in a flash. "The rest of you are welcome to stay and find the source of that growl. I'll be at home drinking beer. No offense, Padre."

The others also stood up hastily.

"Yeah, I think we'll all head off, Father," said Lâmié nervously, his hands shaking.

"I'll walk out with you. I think I'll also head home for the day!" confessed Father Woodrow as they all speed-walked out of his office and did not look back.

·+·+·+·

Back at Lâmié's mansion, Varco gave Barillo the sample, and the detective agreed to run it through the crime lab.

Paul, Mary, and Matt went to the studio room that Lâmié had allowed them to set up in one of the back rooms on the first floor. The room had once been a servant's bedroom in the days when families had kept staffs of live-in servants. Uri Horowitz was set to arrive at three o'clock that afternoon for the tryout, and the three Gravediggers needed to set up and make sure the equipment was in working order.

After the sad loss of both Janine and Mortimer as both friends and house cooks, 'Tit Boudreaux had taken over the role, although his repertoire mainly consisted of hearty, rural Creole dishes. The few dishes he cooked were delicious, but he worked every day to try to learn something new. Some of these experiments came out delightful. Unfortunately, others ended up in the trash.

Knowing that Uri was Hasidic and therefore certainly a strict observer of Kosher food regulations, 'Tit Boudreaux had decided to make a traditional shakshuka. He had timed it so well that just as Uri knocked on the front door, 'Tit Boudreaux was cracking the raw eggs into the small pouches he had made in the spicy and fragrant tomato sauce so that they would be perfectly poached but not overcooked.

Paul answered the door.

"Uri, you came, mate. Come in."

"Nice house, Paul. I didn't know punk paid so well."

Paul laughed and said, "House belongs to our rich friend Lâmié Chasseur. If I had to live off our music, I'd be in a cardboard box in Pirate's Alley."

"Wait, Lâmié Chasseur?" asked Uri. "The ghost hunter?"

"Yep."

"What are the chances? I love his show! I heard he's going to reboot it."

"We tried," said Paul, "and it was a massive fail. We're going to try again soon. Come on, mate, let me introduce you to the gang."

As usual, all of the housemates were sitting in the grand parlor talking. But, when tall, Hasidic Uri walked in, a few of them jumped a little.

"Hi, everyone! I'm Uri! I know my appearance probably startled you, but I can assure you that we Hasidim only bite latkes, not people. And Lâmié, I'm a big fan of your show!"

His good nature and humor seemed to calm everyone, and before they knew it, they were all eating shakshuka and talking like they were old friends.

"Uri," said Matt, "I gotta ask, and I don't mean this in any bad or offensive way…"

"Ask! Ask! I'm not easily offended!"

"Alright, so, surely you know it's unusual to see a Hasid playing punk rock, yes? Isn't klezmer more your style?"

Uri laughed and replied, "Yes, yes, it's true. We're not known for punk so much, right? I already told Paul that my friends and family are a little sore with me right now because I work in a goyim liquor store and like punk rock. But hey, think about it. What is punk if not returning to the simple basics of rock and roll and being yourself despite society? Paul wears a Mohawk, and I wear payot and a hoiche. Neither of us fits in with mainstream society, and neither of us wants to. We're not so different after all, are we?"

They thought about his words for a moment.

"Damn, you're right," admitted Matt. "That's pretty damn punk, Uri!"

Uri just smiled and shoved a large bite of shakshuka into his mouth. "Marcus," he said after swallowing, "this shakshuka is first class. Are you a *member of tribe* or something?"

'Tit Boudreaux laughed and said, "No, just a Creole coonass. I just like to cook and learn new recipes."

"Well, I won't say it's just like my bubbe's shakshuka because that's a sin for a Jew, but I will say it's right up there with some of the best I've had."

'Tit Boudreaux looked at the ground in embarrassment. Finally, they finished eating, and 'Tit Boudreaux served them coffee.

"Uri, it's kosher. I got it in a little store near the Touro Synagogue, and the guy assured me it's kosher for Hasidim. Just water and coffee beans, nothing else."

"Very thoughtful!" said Uri as they drank the coffee.

"Alright," said Mary, "y'all wanna play some songs?"

"Oy, I'm nervous!" said Uri.

"Dude," said Paul, "you haven't heard us play. If you have a pulse, you're in."

Paul, Mary, Matt, and Uri walked out of the grand parlor, down the hall to the back of the house, and into the studio room. Uri opened his bass guitar case and pulled out an old, beaten-up Squier Classic Vibe.

"That thing looks like it's seen a hard life," noted Matt, and Uri chuckled nervously as he plugged it in and performed a quick tune.

"You know Dead Kennedys' *Kill the Poor*?" asked Matt.

"Know it? It's one of the first songs I learned!"

"Let's do it!" said Paul.

They all poised in position, and Paul counted them off. Matt began slamming his drums, Mary blasted out the chords in her guitar, and Uri began to slap and pluck his bass masterfully. Paul screeched the lyrics made famous by Jello Biafra.

As they played through the song, Uri thrashed around, jumping vertically and spinning in a circle like a mad dervish. He managed to leap over his guitar's cord like a girl playing jump rope, avoiding the almost-inevitable entangling that would have tripped ordinary people. He jumped higher than an NBA basketball player, spinning fully around on each jump until he was almost a blur of spinning beard and curly locks. Through it all, he played the bass line perfectly, even adding his own triads and arpeggios. Finally, they finished the song, and Uri threw his bass across the room and fell to the ground, exhausted. There was silence for several moments.

"Holy shit," said Paul.

"Language," said Uri between deep, panting breaths.

"Um, that was…unexpected," said Mary. "I mean, badass, but

unexpected."

"You play really well, Uri," said Matt, who yawned when he saw Uri lying down relaxing. "As far as I'm concerned, you're in if you want it."

Uri stood up and brushed off his black slacks and jacket.

"Really?" he said. "I can be a Gravedigger?"

"Um, hell yes," said Paul, and Mary nodded in agreement.

"Fantastic!" exclaimed Uri. "I'm a punk rock bassist! So when's our next show?"

Paul, Mary, and Matt looked at one another hesitantly.

"Well, you see," explained Mary, "our bar, The Gutter Bar, it's a little, um, out of order at the moment since there was an *incident* again."

"Yes, the massacres," said Uri. "I know all about them. Don't worry. I already told Paul."

Paul shrugged and said, "We need to clean it up and do some repair work. And we really haven't been playing any gigs anywhere else but Gutter. But, on a positive note, it's a crappy dive bar anyway, so it won't take too long to get back in shape."

They put up their instruments, turned off the amps, and then returned to the grand parlor.

"Well?" asked Lâmié.

"Welcome the newest Gravedigger, poor bastard," said Paul.

Everyone clapped.

"Oy, you're embarrassing me!" said Uri. "Now, I apologize, but I need to run, as my mother is cooking tonight for the extended family. If you know anything about Jewish families, then you know I'll be excommunicated and executed if I miss it. I joke! I joke! But seriously, I can't miss it. This was really fun, and the shakshuka was delicious. Keep in touch, yes? Let me know when you clean up The Gutter Bar. I insist on helping."

Lâmié walked Uri to the door, and as Uri stepped onto the porch into the steamy New Orleans air, Lâmié said, "Uri, come over anytime. All those crazy people are my housemates, and there's always someone here, and something is going on."

"Sounds like a Jewish household!" said Uri with a chuckle.

Lâmié smiled and said, "And if you get hungry, I'll make sure 'Tit Boudreaux learns some more kosher dishes! So take care, and…whoa! What the hell is that?"

Uri spun around to see what Lâmié was pointing out and saw the man across the street that had given Lâmié pause. The man was staring at them on the porch, and his arms were straight out in front of him like the mummy in the old monster movies. More unusual was the man's color: his skin was a greenish-red, and his eyes were almost glowing red.

"You, man of God! We know you! We will sift you like wheat in the sieve!" The man's voice was gravelly and hoarse.

"Um, I'd better get home quickly. That can't be a good thing," said Uri, licking his lips nervously. He looked up and down St. Charles Avenue to make sure that the weirdo was a one off.

It was still late afternoon and the street was populated with pedestrians and cars, and Uri seemed to be looking for escape routes just in case the man rushed him. The birds and squirrels in the web of oak branches seemed none the wiser; they continued their chirps and barks and chitters.

Lâmié, who was visibly shaken, said, "Want to stay here tonight? Want me to walk you home?"

"Feh, it's alright," replied Uri. "I'll take the back way. Lots of crazies in this city, after all." His brave voice was not convincing.

CHAPTER 4

A Sigil Signal

"*Ki Adonai hu ha Elohim, bashamayim mi ma'al, v'al ha'aretz mitachat. Ein od,*" prayed David Horowitz, Uri's father, at the conclusion of the extended family gathering and meal at his home. His wife, Abigail Horowitz, had directed the women of the family in an all-day, extravagant cooking marathon, and as the aunts, uncles, brothers, sisters, cousins, grandparents, and the entire extended Horowitz family had sat around the enormous dining room table and relished the countless homemade dishes, they had talked, laughed, argued, and enjoyed the familial fellowship.

The one guest who had remained a bit shy and quiet was not family but still welcome. His name was Abe, and he was new to the synagogue. David had introduced the young man as being from New York City but having spent the last several years in Israel studying.

"Abe, I hope you enjoyed the food?" asked a beaming Abigail.

"Oh, Missus Horowitz, it was just amazing. Just delicious. I think those latkes were the best I have ever tasted, including in Israel."

She blushed with pride.

"Say, Missus Horowitz, may I use your restroom?"

"Of course, dear. Turn right down the hall into the next hall, then the third door on the left."

After a while, several rounds of goodbyes were said as the guests made their leave, including Abe. Once the house was cleared of people, Abigail and Uri's little sister Elizabeth set to cleaning up while David sat at his desk to study the Torah. Uri went to his bedroom to practice his bass, unplugged, of course, to avoid his mother's wrath. The Gravediggers had given him a list of their songs along with the .mp3 versions for him to learn.

"*Do you have the sheet music?*" he had asked.

"*Uri, look at us. Do you really think we can read music?*" Paul had answered.

Uri played his way through the songs and then paused for a moment. Had he heard a rustling outside his window? Like most Hasidic families in the Touro neighborhood of New Orleans, the Horowitzes lived in a lovely old home with a surrounding garden behind a fence. It was not unheard of for an animal to get inside the garden and make a little noise, but what Uri heard was decidedly loud and *human*, for soft, padding footsteps accompanied the rustling sound.

Uri froze. It could have been anyone, even someone from his family. Still, sometimes a person's reptilian brain forces a primal hunch, a deep and ancient evolutionary memory, that warns of something perilous, uncanny, something that is just *wrong*, and that was what Uri was feeling at that moment.

He knew he should peek through the window, but he was terrified to do so.

He sat for several minutes while the footsteps faded away from outside of his room, and then he stood up and walked into his father's study.

"*Abba*, sorry to bother you."

"Sit, Uri. What's going on, *meyn zun*? Wasn't today fun?"

"It was," agreed Uri.

"You know, Uri, you should start attending more prayer meetings. Everyone's worried about you."

Uri blew air through his lips in frustration. "I know, but not now. Someone was outside my bedroom window. I heard clear footsteps."

David wrinkled his brows and said, "Hmm. I already locked the front gate; that could mean trouble. Let's go take a look."

He stood up, but Uri held his arm. "Wait, Dad, that could be dangerous."

"God is with us, son. And we can always call the police if we have to. Who knows? Maybe it is a stranger in need of help."

Uri knew that it was no use arguing with his father. If his dad was going to go outside to investigate, then at least Uri would go with him to protect him.

"Abi," called out David, "we're stepping outside for a moment."

Father and son walked onto the small front porch of their beautiful, centuries-old home and felt the hot, sticky New Orleans evening air. The sounds of the city—honking cars, laughing people, the tinkling of silverware on plates and wine glasses being toasted—seemed so familiar. Yet, there was an acrid tang in the air as if something were off. The faint odor of rotten eggs wafted past them, and they wrinkled their noses.

"Come on, Uri," said David as he walked down the steps into the front garden and then started around the side of the house. Uri followed him nervously.

They tiptoed around the back left corner of the house, peeked into the small backyard, and saw no one. It was empty, except for the neighbor's two cats, who liked to visit occasionally.

"No one's here, Uri."

"Wait, Dad, just a moment." Uri walked around the garden, looking at the ground. "Here!"

David walked over to where Uri was and saw what his son had seen: unmistakable human footprints leading from the back fence to near Uri's bedroom window. Apparently, someone had jumped the fence. They followed the light trail of footprints to the side of the house near Uri's window, and both gasped.

It was dark outside, but with the glow of the street lamp on the other side of the fence, they could just make out that someone had drawn something on the outside wall of the house. It was scribbled in red, probably paint and not blood because of the sheer amount of it.

"Oy! What is that?" asked David loudly.

"I dunno, *Abba*. It looks creepy, that's for sure. Is it some sort of secret symbol? Like, from a secret club or cult or something?"

David ran his hands over the symbol, then leaned in and sniffed it. "I don't think it's blood. More like red paint. But why? What would some secret cult want with us? What, they want to recruit us? They like your mother's latkes that much?"

"Dad, be serious for a minute!" chided Uri. "This could be bad. Like, what if they're marking our house? What if it's a psycho death cult?"

"Feh!" said David with a light slap on Uri's shoulder. "A death cult? What would a death cult want with us? Let me tell you something, son. When you're Jewish, especially Hasidic, you get used to people messing with you. I mean, it's the whole story of our people! Whatever this symbol means, whatever the intent behind it, whoever did it, I've learned that the best thing to do is to simply ignore it."

Uri raised his eyebrows and protested, "Dad, how can we ignore something so sinister?"

"They meant it as a message, Uri, to shake and intimidate us. I'm not going to let them do that. First thing tomorrow, I'm painting over it. A hundred times can they paint it, and a hundred and one times I'll paint over it. Come on, son. Let's go back inside. I'm ready for a snack!"

CHAPTER 5

Bad Religion

Rabbi Shlomo Cohen was the last to arrive at the Wednesday lunch meeting of the New Orleans Interfaith Council (NOIF). As soon as he entered the establishment, he saw that his friends were already at a table. They had decided to try out the relatively new Magic Forest Café, so enchanting was its colorful and whimsical exterior, with its windows of diverse geometric shapes, the glass of each a different pastel color, and all of the little charms hanging here and there above and around its door, which was designed to look like a tree trunk.

The Catholic priest Father Barry Woodrow, the Baptist pastor Reverend Don Malbrook, and the Muslim Imam Mohamed Riyad were seated at a round table waiting for the rabbi.

"Right on time as usual!" teased Reverend Malbrook.

Rabbi Cohen laughed and replied, "Yeah, yeah. So sue me."

Cohen, being Hasidic, would usually not spend much time with the leaders of other religions. Still, he always kept an open mind and wanted to show goodwill to the city of New Orleans. After all, his people had suffered so many times throughout history at the hands of false accusers, and he wanted to show that he was harmless.

He had grown to genuinely like the three other men and considered them friends. Although each leader's religion taught wariness about becoming good friends with people outside the faith, the four men, while very orthodox in their own practice and piety, nevertheless felt that some traditions needed updating, in particular, openness and friendliness outside of the fold. In fact, Rabbi Cohen, the founder of NOIF, had hand-selected each of the other three men for that very quality. Most importantly, each one had a good sense of humor and did not take himself overly seriously.

A tall, thin, pale woman with snow-blond hair and icy blue eyes seemed to almost float to their table.

"Welcome to the Magic Forest Café. I'm Titania, the owner. The worker over there at the other table is Evelyn. We consider our customers like family, so feel free to call us over if you need anything. Now, let me guess what you're hungry for today. I'm pretty good at it."

Reverend Malbrook smiled and said, "Alright, I like a good challenge. What do you foresee on my plate, Titania? I'm Reverend Malbrook, by the way."

Titania pursed her lips and looked him up and down.

"Reverend, I bet you're a sucker for a delicious club sandwich."

"Ha! It's my favorite! Could I also get a—"

"Coke?" she interrupted.

"You *are* good!"

They all chuckled.

"Alright, Father, you strike me as a large bowl of vegetable soup and a bottle of Evian kind of priest."

"Wow!"

"Imam, we have a delicious, certified-halal lamb sandwich and perhaps a Lebanese iced tea?"

Imam Riyad opened his eyes in surprise.

Titania looked at Rabbi Cohen and said, "And Rabbi, I just learned a certified-kosher shakshuka recipe from a friend. How about that, and a nice cup of coffee? Coffee's kosher, too."

"This girl is amazing! It's almost magic!" declared Cohen.

Titania just smiled, winked, and whisked herself away.

The four men small-talked for a few minutes until Titania reappeared with their food. The beautiful presentation of it all, combined with the tempting aromas and colors and the whimsical, multi-colored interior decoration, produced a distinct feeling of calmness and warmth, of an almost halcyon succumbing to all of life's worries and troubles. As if the air itself were perfumed with opium, the four religious leaders were lulled into a happy, smiling state of tranquility, a sentiment of safety and belonging. On top of that, the food was delicious.

"Wow! I can see us returning to this place many times in the future!" declared Cohen to the agreement of the other three.

"Alright, gentlemen," began Reverend Malbrook, "what's on the agenda for today?"

They looked at one another in silence.

"Doesn't seem like too much!" interjected Cohen.

"I actually have something," said Father Woodrow. "So, I may be thinking too big here—"

"God is big, my brother!" said Riyad.

"Ah, yes, yes, good point," agreed Woodrow with a nod. "I'll just get into it, then. How do you three feel about setting up some sort of interfaith street fair? I envision booths from all faiths who wish to participate, offering information and discussion. We could hold it at Jackson Square, and we could also have a fair-like atmosphere. You know, like food, some games for kids, that kind of thing."

Cohen finished a bite of his shakshuka and said, "I like the concept. What would be the ultimate purpose?"

Woodrow took a small bite of vegetable soup and then answered, "The purpose, as I see it, would be threefold: to promote goodwill among the faithful of New Orleans, to offer information about our individual faiths in a relaxed and fun environment, and to show the people of New Orleans that we can get along even if we have different beliefs."

"Sounds like you thought that one out," said Malbrook. "As for me, I like it."

"Me too," agreed Cohen. "Mohamed?"

The imam nodded with a mouthful of lamb sandwich.

"Alright, then it's agreed," said Cohen. "I suggest we each come up with detailed plans, and then we can compare them next week or the week after."

Agreeable grunts sounded from mouths full of food.

"Alright, what's next on the agenda? Does anyone have anything else?" asked Malbrook between swallows of Coke.

Cohen raised a finger as he chewed and swallowed the last succulent bite of shakshuka.

"Actually, friends, I have something a bit more serious. It's not really related to NOIF, but I wanted your opinions and knowledge. It's something, well, something *odd* that happened to one of my congregants."

As everyone had finished their lunches, Titania seemed to almost apparate out of thin air, so quietly did she walk to the table.

"Gentlemen? I hope everything is good?"

"Delicious, Titania," assured Rabbi Cohen. "We will certainly be back. We're just sitting around talking at this point."

"Of course!" replied the nymph-like girl. "Please, stay as long as you'd like. Consider this your home!"

They smiled as she cleared their table and almost floated away.

"You were saying, Shlomo?" prodded Riyad.

"Yes, well, one of my congregants, David Horowitz—his entire family are congregants too—his son heard someone shuffling around outside his bedroom window the other night. So David and Uri, the son, went outside to investigate, and they found some faint footprints in their backyard, and someone had painted a symbol on their house." He pulled out his iPhone, opened up the picture he had taken of the symbol, and showed it to his three friends.

"Whoa," said Reverend Malbrook. "Shlomo, I hate to say, but that looks Satanic to me."

"My first thought, yes," agreed the rabbi. "I mean, I know about Jewish demons through the Kabbalah, but it's not like we study their symbolism and all that."

"May I?" asked Riyad, taking the phone to get a closer look.

"It certainly seems magical or demonic or something," said the imam. "We have *djinn* in the Islamic tradition, sure. They are basically comparable to the demons of your faiths, with some differences. But as for this symbol? I have no idea."

Father Woodrow took the phone and squinted his eyes at it.

"I can give you some information," he said to Cohen. "It's a demonic *sigil*."

"A what?" asked Cohen.

"The idea comes from Medieval superstition in the Catholic Church. Yes, I admit that we were a superstitious lot back then! So the deal is that a sigil is the demon's personal signature in the demon language, whatever that may be. So when a person would make a deal with Satan or another demon, the human would sign his name in blood on the contract, and the demon would sign its sigil."

"Oy!" exclaimed Cohen. "A demon's signature?"

"Don't get too upset," explained the priest. "Most of this stuff appears no earlier than the Middle Ages, and it comes from *supposed grimoires,* which were journals kept by witches and sorcerers. There's a whole field of study called *demonology* that deals with this stuff, but in my opinion? It's all superstitious invention from the Middle Ages."

"Alright," said Cohen after a sip of strong, dark, New Orleans coffee, "so how would someone in the modern day know about Medieval superstitions?"

"My guess is Luciferians," said Woodrow. "Satanists these days don't really worship the literal, biblical Satan; they're more about freedom of agency and self-expression. But Luciferians actually do. They believe in the literal, biblical Satan and his demons, and they worship him in exchange for things like power and money."

Woodrow handed the phone back to Cohen, who asked, "So, what does this demonic sigil mean? Whose signature is it?"

"No idea," admitted Woodrow. The other two also shook their heads.

"Can you text me that photo?" asked Woodrow. "I have a section of my library that deals with demonology. I'll do some research. Have David and his family been threatened otherwise?"

It being late afternoon, the café was clearing out a bit, until the four friends found themselves alone in the dining area. Titania and Evelyn were busily working and chatting behind the counter.

Titania had a batch of coffee roasting in the back roasting room, and the rich, slightly-charred aroma of the beans combined with their chocolatey, berry undertones filled not only the café, but the entire city block around it.

"No, nothing like that," said Cohen. "Just disturbed and a little shaken, as you might imagine. I mean, what, you're gonna draw a demonic sigil on someone's house? What is that?"

Father Woodrow waved Titania over and handed her a credit card. "Lunch is on me today, friends."

They protested, but he paid for them all. The four men spent a few minutes walking around the café and looking at the artwork on the walls, as well as the distinctive, unique décor of the place. They made small talk with Titania for a few moments.

As Woodrow opened the door for the other three and they exited, he promised to Cohen, "We'll get to the bottom of this."

Chapter 6

Walk the Fire for Me

Apadebata Bahiragata looked down at her bare, brown feet as she focused on what she was about to do: walk over the bed of hot coals. The burning coal beds that street performers in Kolkata made for the Western tourists were one thing: she knew that the walkers had tricks, like soaking their feet in water, patting down the coals to form a protective layer of ash, and other such techniques. But Apadebata's wizened, learned guru, Swami Maitra, knew just how to rake the coals so that they burned, actually *burned*, the feet—not hot enough to cause permanent damage, but enough to really hurt if the walker were not meditating and concentrating on the spiritual rather than the physical.

"Apada!" called Swami Maitra, using Apadebata's nickname as a term of affection between master and student. "Pay attention, girl! Do you think Agni hesitates when he bestows the fire of creation and blessing or the fire of devouring and sacrifice? No, but he fulfills his divine duty without thinking of it. So must you do, girl! You have so much to learn! Come, now, and walk across the fire toward me."

She sighed in resignation. Swami was always the strictest on Saturday afternoons. He allowed Apada one day off per week: Rabibara, or Sunday in the Western tradition. Thus, he became sterner on Saturdays so that she would ponder her lessons on the day of rest.

"Come! Apada!"

She could not put it off any longer. The walk of fire was always the last of her lessons on Saturday, and as the sweltering Bengali sun dipped its toes into the horizon, she looked down at her mini-sun—the bed of coals that she had to walk across. She steeled herself and began.

She allowed each step to last no longer than one second, which was twice the duration of the touristic street performers. At the first step, she felt the unbearable searing of her sole, and she squealed in pain, but she remembered her lessons. *Trust the spirit, not the body*, Swami would tell her over and over again, and so she entered the spirit. She envisioned Vishnu on the other side of the fire walk, in place of Swami. First, she saw the god's pastel blue skin, his four arms reaching out to her to comfort her and lead her on, the glorious halo around his beautiful face and head. Then, before realizing it, she was on the other side of the fire pit.

Swami, characteristically gruff and devoid of frivolity or spontaneous expressions of joy during the lessons, allowed a small smile to betray his lips.

"Very well, Apada. Not perfect, but very well. Remember the lesson tomorrow on your day of rest. The fire burns always, and the difference between burning in it, or lasting through it, is to be in the spirit and not in the body. The lesson is thus ended, and the lesson is thus learned. Be early Monday, Apada, as we have much to prepare for. You must know something, something that I have been waiting to tell you, and I will teach it to you on Monday."

She silently knelt before him, took his right hand in hers, and bowed down to it, touching his hand against her forehead. Then, he lifted her up, and she placed her palms together and under her chin, then said, "Namaste, Swami." He returned the gesture, and finally, she was free, at least for a day!

Apadebata slipped on her sandals and walked to the local street market. She found some tomatoes, onions, and cauliflower to make a curry for the school with the spices and rice she already had at the residence.

Were it not for Swami Maitra, she would be another Kolkata statistic, a teenage girl struggling to live in abject poverty on the streets, maybe kidnapped and forced into prostitution, perhaps a thief, maybe starving to death.

Swami, however, had found her one day when she was about eight years old and begging on the side of the street. He, already an old man by then, had looked at her, squinted his eyes, and said, "You are the one. What is your name, girl? Come with me. I will teach you."

Living in an impoverished, existential hell already at eight years old, she had simply stood up and followed the Brahmin to his school. It was a small building beside an even smaller local temple of Durga, a temple almost forgotten by everyone except the few devotees who lived in the immediate neighborhood.

Like so many of the small, nameless neighborhoods of the vast metropolis of Kolkata, Swami and Apadebata's neighborhood consisted of narrow, dirty alleys bordered by small mud and brick buildings, alleys connected in an unfathomable maze guaranteed to confound anyone but a resident.

Swami Maitra was the primary keeper of Durga's idol and temple. He was also one of the few Brahmins who deigned to live in the mostly Dom caste neighborhood of basket-makers, general laborers, corpse burners, and midwives, most of whom were poor. Swami thought nothing of interacting with the low, unclean caste, as he held a very charitable view of humanity, not considering his caste status as making him better than anyone else. On the contrary, he was quite content serving Durga, keeping up her temple, and running his little school. Old family money meant that he did not have to charge his poorest students; in fact, he gave them a stipend in addition to room and board. As a result, life at Swami's school was a big step up for most of his students.

For Apada, the task of cooking the school meals was a small price to pay to escape the life of a starving street urchin. Moreover, she had faith in Swami Maitra and his insistence that she had a special purpose in life that would be revealed over time and for which he was preparing her. After all, at eighteen years old, the world was open to her, and her future was a mystery.

Before going to the kitchen to start dinner for the other students and Swami, she put her groceries down at the entrance to the shrine of Durga, removed her sandals, and stepped inside. She rang the temple bell, then knelt in front of Durga.

She looked up at the idol of the goddess.

Despite the shrine itself being small and forgotten, the idol was magnificent. She stood thirty feet tall, her ten arms reaching out to protect her children and fight demons. Each of her ten hands held an object representing an aspect of the goddess. She rode a ferocious lion, representing her power and control over the strength and determination of the world.

Her full, healthy face shone with the radiance of confidence and power. Each of her three eyes showed an aspect of her: her left eye, the moon of desire; her right eye, the sun of action; the third eye in the middle of her forehead, the fire of knowledge.

Her white sari, the edges lined in bright red, emphasized the bright and brilliant colors of her multi-jeweled crown, which sat stop her luxuriant, raven hair. She smiled down at Apada with a knowing yet concealed smile, as if the goddess already knew Apada's future and blessed it but knew it was not yet quite the right time to reveal it.

Swami had left a jug of milk and an earthen jar of honey for Apada, so she poured each into a ceremonial bowl, then slid each bowl toward the feet of the goddess. She then placed her palms together under her chin, tilted them forward, and recited the prayer to Durga:

Om Jayanti, Mangala, Kali, Bhadrakali, Kapalini.
Durga, Shiva, Kshama, Dhatri, Svaha, Svadha, Namostu Te.
Esha Sachandana Gandha Pushpa Bilva Patranjali Om Hreem
Durgayai Namah.

Apada contemplated the goddess for several minutes. Durga, the protector of her children, the fighter of demons, the fortress of the pious—the goddess would reveal Apada's purpose at the right time. First, she thought about her future, and then she thought about her past.

Apada's parents had not been impoverished. Part of the Dom caste, they had never been rich, but her father had worked construction jobs, so they had always enjoyed a place to live and food on the table. An only child, Apada had been devastated when her beloved daddy had suffered a construction accident and had died soon thereafter. Her mother had died of heartache, as the doctors had told her, and having no immediate family in Kolkata, Apada had seen no option but to beg on the street.

From five years of age to eight, she had barely gotten by through begging, wit, and a bit of theft when she had gone without food for days. Constantly feeling bad about it, she had nipped a fruit here, a vegetable there, from the markets, but never anything expensive, and never meat; rather, she would take only just enough to avoid death by starvation.

While she had made a few friends of fellow child beggars, she had always forced herself to keep a certain distance. After all, she had known what happened to street kids who were too open and friendly: they were kidnapped and forced into prostitution or slavery. More than once, Apada had outrun kidnappers, zigzagging through the labyrinth of streets and alleys that she knew so well until the attempted abductors were thoroughly lost and confused.

These thoughts led to mentally envisioning one particularly close escape when she had been only thirteen. As she reconstructed the scene in her head, she almost felt like she was there in the present.

Apada is sitting on the sidewalk on a main street of Kolkota, but not main enough for the police to harass her for making the city look bad. Her pockets contain only a few rupees, enough though to find food for the day. No one has yet discovered her sleeping spot—a hole in a wall that she has lined with cardboard, good enough to escape the Kolkata rain.

She is not the only begging orphan on the street that afternoon, and as it is a government holiday, hordes of people jam the sidewalks and streets. Generosity seems to have remained at home, however. She watches other begging children and sees that they are also not receiving many alms.

She sees the five men the moment they turn the corner. Their quick movements, their hats hiding their faces, their eyes not looking at anyone else they passed—these men mean trouble. Without anyone noticing, or perhaps even caring, they surround a street waif, pick him up, and whisk him away and around a corner.

Apada winces, knowing that the poor kid will be pressed into servitude, or worse. Thankful for her own intuition and quick sense of danger, she remains alert. This alertness is rewarded when she spots the same group of men returning to her street and walking fast toward her.

Without time to think or analyze the situation, she bolts upright and begins a sprint off the main street and onto smaller lanes. She knows the neighborhood intimately, and simply prays to Vishnu that the kidnappers do not. They are almost at her heels already.

She feigns right then turns left to duck into a narrow alley. She hears the men's shoes grinding on the gravel as they fall for her feign and have to stop. This gives her a few seconds more of time. She uses it to weave through and among the little lanes, weaving herself like the thread in a tapestry, running for her freedom and life.

A dark shape speeds into her peripheral vision to the right, and she feels someone slam her to the ground. Somehow, one of the men must have become lost in the alleys, yet stumbled upon a path that led to her—a pure coincidence and misfortune.

He cries out to his immoral colleagues, and they find him quickly enough. They grab her arms tightly and manhandle her along the alley, following the sound of traffic on the main street until they are almost there. They reach a van.

Apada knows one thing: if she enters that van, all hope is gone. It will be all over for her. There will be no escape. She cannot allow herself to be pushed into that van.

Doing all she knows to do, she knees one of the men in his groin, and he squeals and hunches over. Before the other men can even calculate what is happening, she knees a second man, who immediately releases her arm to hold his own groin. One free arm is enough.

She begins to punch the remaining men in the face as hard as she can, and it works. They release her and step back, and that is all the time she needs. She sprints away again, this time not stopping until she is completely out of the neighborhood and safe again.

Yes, hers had been a miserable early childhood, and as might be imagined, she placed Swami Maitra on a pedestal just below the gods. Sure, he was strict, sometimes even severe, but he also had a kind heart, and she knew he always did everything in her best interest. The bottom line was that she had a soft, comfortable bed, a decent shelter from the elements, and an abundance of delicious food, not to mention the friends she had made of fellow students.

There were currently five students plus Apada, thus a total of six. The two girls, Abheer and Gayana, were just slightly younger than Apada. The three boys, Iraj, Jagravi, and Kaling, were just slightly older, so the boys had taken it upon themselves to be the protectors of the three girls, even if that protection involved some crushes here and there.

In her ten years as the cook and a student at Swami Maitra's school, she had never questioned him or her tenure there. Life was, overall, just too good to complain. Of course, she missed her parents dearly, but given her circumstances, she could hardly imagine better luck. It also did not hurt that Iraj, who was nineteen years old to her eighteen, was especially cute and funny.

Apada snapped out of her daydreaming reveries, bowed to Durga, then retrieved her groceries and sandals and walked to the school's kitchen, where she began cutting vegetables for the curry.

Swami Maitra watched Apada walk away from the fire pit toward the school and temple. He sighed. The girl was doing well but had so much to learn and grow into. He wondered if she would be ready in time. If not, then what would he do? It would be a disaster.

He thought of his own youthful days when he himself had sat at the feet of Swami Ganguly and learned the secrets of the mysteries of the universe, the gods, and the goddesses. The wonder! The fascination! The innocence and joy! When he waxed nostalgic, as he often did at his advanced age, he wondered what his life would have been like if Swami Ganguly had never lifted the veil for him into the world of the demonic.

Growing up Brahmin in West Bengal, India, Maitra had always believed in the gods and goddesses. After all, most people believe what they are raised with, especially in a culture like that of India, where religion is woven inexorably into the fabric of daily life. So, he had never really questioned the spiritual realm, even its negative aspects, but worshiping an idol in a temple was a different matter than personally encountering a demon.

Swami Ganguly had told the young Maitra the same thing that he himself had told Apada many times: that he had been chosen for a special, spiritual purpose. One day, that purpose had revealed itself. Maitra thought back on his first exposure to the demonic, and it seemed to him as real as if it were happening right there in the present.

"Just a moment," says Swami Ganguly to Maitra in the middle of their lesson, as a courier knocks at the door to the school. Ganguly takes the letter, scans it, then tells the courier, "Tell him that I will be there shortly."

"Come, boy. It is time, finally," says Ganguly. "I've been asked for help. We must go immediately."

Not daring to question his master, Maitra simply stands up, puts his sandals on, and follows the old guru through the neighborhood's winding, impossible tangle of streets and alleys. It is midday, so the streets are overcrowded with throngs of people, as in all Indian cities.

Swami Ganguly bobs, weaves, and twirls through the living sea of people as if it is nothing, and Maitra struggles to run and catch up, sometimes losing sight of his master.

Though he is a native of Kolkata, the assault of the city never ceases to tantalize and enchant Maitra. The bright, varied blues, greens, yellows, reds, oranges, purples, and browns of the buildings and the clothing and the spices in the markets; the loud calling of the merchants and the loud gossip of the women and the disapproving chatter of the old men and the cheerful cries of the children; the lowing of the holy cows as they wander about freely; the sharp, spicy, sweet, and savory aromas and smoke from the various food stalls, roast lamb, roti, naan, tandoori, vindaloo—all of the glorious Indian street senses still charm him.

From up ahead, he hears a commotion even louder than the everyday neighborhood hubbub. Women are howling in mourning around the door of a house, and men are trying to peer in while other men stand guard and keep everyone out. Then, as they see Swami Ganguly and his boy apprentice approaching, the guards push the crowd back and let the two inside the shady hovel. They remove their sandals, and Maitra follows his master within.

Maitra's eyes adjust to the interior, lit only by a couple of oil lamps, and he sees that a young boy is lying on a mat in the center of the room, surrounded by who appeared to be his parents, and a brother and sister—just the immediate family.

The father bends down almost prostrate and touches his hands to Swami's feet, then to his own eyes. The mother and the two siblings follow suit, but the boy on the pallet remains still and quiet, his eyes closed. Like Maitra later, Swami Ganguly does not follow the traditions of avoiding lower castes and their touches. Rather, he sees all souls as equals in the eyes of Brahma. A revolutionary view for his time, he is quiet about it and must still follow the traditions when in mixed castes. He considers the Doms of his neighborhood his friends and views his residing there as a form of charity. This will leave a deep and eternal impression on Maitra, who will go on to conduct the same egalitarian practices.

"How long has he been like this?" asks Swami Ganguly.

"Guru, he has been limp and lifeless for three days now," answers the father.

"Then today is the day that the demon must reveal itself," replies Ganguly. He turns to Maitra, expecting in advance the question to come.

"Swami Ganguly," asks Maitra, "I apologize to ask, but the demon? What does that mean?"

"Today, son, you will learn," is the master's cryptic reply. Then, he looks back at the father and asks, "Have you obtained what I have asked for?"

The man nods and points to the corner of the room with his chin. Ganguly gathers the supplies.

"We must begin immediately," states the guru. He says to the boy's parents, "I ask you two to please restrain him if necessary, to prevent him from harming himself or anyone else." He then turns to the boy's siblings and says, "You must not be afraid, children. Your brother has been inhabited by a demon, an evil spirit. It desires to cause him to harm himself and others. Today, I will drive that demon out of him."

Ganguly looks at young Maitra and explains, "This is your purpose of which I spoke. You, like me, are chosen by the goddess Durga and Lord Narasimha to drive out demons in the people. Watch how it is done, Maitra, so you can learn."

Swami Ganguly places a small piece of coconut husk into his right palm, sets incense into the husk, and lights it. The yellow flame erupts from his hand and fills the room with warm light and the aroma of spices and herbs. The possessed boy immediately opens his eyes and flares his nostrils. Ganguly slowly waves his hand around the boy so that the smoke of the incense surrounds him. He moans, then sits up slowly and looks around as if in a daze.

"Where am I? Mommy? Daddy?"

"Son!" says the mother, reaching for him, but Ganguly holds her arm back.

"You must not talk to him right now. It is not your son yet. It is the demon trying to deceive you."

Ganguly takes a bowl of water and says a prayer over it. The boy eyes the water angrily.

"Mother and father, hold one of his arms each."

They comply.

Ganguly sprinkles the holy water onto the boy's head, face, and body. He shrieks an inhuman howl and begins to thrash his head up and down, almost hitting his forehead on the ground with each dip.

"Hold him tightly while I recite the prayer!" demands Ganguly. He places his palms together and mutters a quick prayer to Durga and Lord Narasimha, then begins to recite the prayer from the Atharva Veda:

Nissâlâ, the bold, the greedy demon, and the female demon with a
long-drawn howl, the bloodthirsty; all the daughters of Kanda, the
Sadânvâs do we destroy!
The boy screams and thrashes even harder.
We drive you out of the stable, out of the axle and the body of the
wagon; we chase you, daughters of Magundî, from the house. In
yonder house below, there the grudging arâyî shall be found; there
ruin shall prevail, and all the witches!

He shrieks and lashes out at his parents, knocking them both onto the ground. Ganguly continues, speaking louder and with great concentration and conviction.

May Rudra, the lord of beings, and Indra, drive forth from here the
Sadânvâs; those that are seated on the foundation of the house.

The boy leaps onto Swami Ganguly and tackles him. Maitra struggles to pull him off as he growls, roars, and bites his arm. Still, the wise, old master does not stop reciting the prayer.

Indra shall overcome with his thunderbolt!

At the mention of Indra, the boy begins to convulse violently, falling onto his back. Still, Ganguly finishes the prayer.

Whether you belong to the demons of inherited disease, whether you
have been dispatched by men, or whether you have originated from
the Dasyus, vanish from here, Sadânvâs! About their dwelling places
I did swiftly course, as if on a race course. I have won all contests
with you: vanish from here, Sadânvâs!

The boy stops shaking. He is exhausted. He looks at the ceiling, arches his back up, coughs three times, and then breathes out a thick, stinking, black cloud, which rises up and through the ceiling and is gone.

Maitra awoke from his daydream and noticed that the shadows were becoming long on the street. He began the walk to Durga's temple, thinking of how he would spend the next day, which was not only Apadebata's day off, but the same for all students and the master himself. He had selected Apada as the school cook because she made large, delicious meals with dozens of dishes. The night before the day off, she always made an incredibly delicious and spicy curry, and he knew that that night would be no different. He involuntarily salivated.

He had almost reached the shrine's entrance when a warm Zephyrus passed over him, and with the west wind came a message from the gods. He heard Durga speak as truly as if the idol in front of him had come to life.

In her sweet, silken, yet powerful voice came the message, "Maitra, it is time for Apadebata's purpose to bear fruit! A great evil has arisen in the West, an evil that Apadebata must help defeat. You will soon receive the words both of you need to know, so look for the messenger!"

As soon as the voice had spoken, it was gone, and Maitra felt like himself again. He knew it was time to fight the demons again, and this time, he would need to trust the ability and skill of Apada. He could waste no time teaching her the rites and the prayers and confirming her mastery of them. He would begin in the morning. There would be no Sunday off this week.

Chapter 7

Eldritch Horrors

"This bar looks more and more shitty each time we try to re-open it," complained Paul to Mary, Matt, Uri, Lâmié, 'Tit Boudreaux, Titania, Isabella, and Varco.

"Oy, he's not wrong," added Uri.

The others surveyed the damage as Paul walked behind the bar to grab a warm can of beer. The goblins had utterly destroyed the interior and some of the exterior of The Gutter Bar, and the giant wall of speakers had fallen into a pile of electronic rubble.

"Yeah, well, I want us to try to open up again in a couple of weeks, on a Saturday night," said Lâmié. "We can all help in the cleaning, and I'll hire a professional crew to make some structural repairs. So what do y'all think?"

"Sounds good to me," said 'Tit Boudreaux. "Y'all gonna play a show, Gravediggers?"

"I think we can," agreed Mary. "I'll try to find some other bands, too."

"What band would be foolish enough to agree to a gig here?" asked Matt. "Every time a band tries, there's some horrible mass slaughter."

Mary smiled grimly and said, "I'll find some. Don't worry."

They all were looking around at the disaster that was The Gutter

Bar. Piles of junk had replaced the booths and chairs, and the bar was a bar in name only, being broken in the middle. A colony of rats seemed to be rather enjoying themselves in a corner, frolicking about as if the destroyed bar were a luxury resort.

Without knocking and without much ado, Barillo walked in the door.

"I have the lab results for that writing on the priest's office wall," he began without much of a greeting.

"Tell us!" said an excited 'Tit Boudreaux.

"Well, it's weird," explained the detective as he boosted himself up and sat on the remaining part of the bar. "It combines human blood, semen, and several other unidentifiable organic elements."

"What the..." said Paul. "The priest wanked one out on the wall?"

"Paul!" said Mary.

Barillo coughed and continued, "It's the unidentified organic matter that creeps me out. So see, I did a little research on hauntings just to humor myself. It turns out this sort of mixed organic liquid is very common in Poltergeist cases. It's so common that it has a name."

"*Ectoplasm*," said Lâmié.

"I've heard that name before, I think," said Uri. "Ghost slime, right?"

Barillo nodded.

Uri tugged at his payot and said, "Ghost slime. Just what we need. Oh, wait, I forgot to tell you all! The night of my audition, after dinner at my family's house, I was in my bedroom practicing my bass, and I heard someone outside my window. So my dad and I went to look, and someone had scribbled this weird symbol on our house."

He reached into the inner pocket of his black overcoat, pulled out a sketch he had made of the symbol, and passed it around to everyone.

"This looks like some demonic shit," said Paul.

"I wonder if it's related to Father Woodrow's office or just random vandalism?" asked Matt.

"Oh, let me see it!" said Titania. She took the sketch and studied it for a few moments. "Yes, I'm pretty sure I know what this is, based on my fair...my past studies," she said, glancing at Uri. "It's almost certainly a demonic sigil."

"Sig—what?" asked Paul.

"For once, I'm with Paul," said Mary. "Sig—what?"

Titania giggled and replied, "*Sigil*. It's supposedly a demon's signature in the demon language. Like, when you sign a document, you write your name in a signature script, right? Well, this is the same, but for a demon."

"Demon? Of all the things on the side of my house, a demon's signature?" said Uri. "Graffiti, I could handle. Gang markers, alright. But a demon? Oy vey!"

A knock came on the bar's door. Uri, who was closest, opened it. Two guys, barely past boyhood, stood in black slacks and crisp, white, button-down shirts with short sleeves and little name tags on their left shoulders. They looked almost identical to each other, with their pale, smooth faces and dirty blond hair combed neatly with a distinct part.

They looked up at Uri's hat, down at his outfit, back up at his payot, and then at his beard. Finally, their mouths dropped, and they remained silent.

"May I help you?" said Uri.

"Uh…" said one.

"Um…" said the other.

"We're…I'm…I'm Elder Brigham, and this is my twin brother, Elder Brigham. I'm Aaron, and he's Amos."

"Nice to meet you!" said Uri cheerfully. "I'm Uri Horowitz. You're Mormon missionaries, I take it?"

They nodded in unison, and Aaron said, "Um, what are you?"

Uri laughed and said, "I'm a guy, but if you mean why am I dressed like this? I'm a Hasidic Jew. The outfit? It's kind of our thing. Come in! Come in! Come meet the gang!"

Before they stepped through the door, Amos asked, "Is this a bar? Like, an alcoholic bar?"

"Indeed it is," confirmed Uri. "I guess you two are from Salt Lake City, Utah, and not used to the weirdness of New Orleans."

They both nodded, then walked into the bar. They stared at Paul's, Mary's, and Matt's Mohawks and leather punk clothing, at Matt's black skin and 'Tit Boudreaux's brown skin, and at Titania's icy blond hair and blue eyes in silent wonder.

Paul snapped his fingers in front of their eyes and said, "Hey, Mormon boys. Snap out of it. Want a fucking drink?"

The Mormons gasped in shock.

"Pardon Paul," said Mary. "He was born without a mouth filter. Y'all are new to New Orleans, I take it. Little more diversity than home? It's alright. Everyone here is cool."

She briefly introduced the missionaries to everyone there.

"Though if you came to convert us," said Matt, "you might not have the success you were hoping for."

"I…we…um, may we…" stammered Aaron.

"…talk to you," continued Amos, "about the gospel of Jesus Christ and the prophet Joseph Smith?"

"Pardon me," interjected Varco in his thick, Romanian accent. "Forgive my ignorance, but your name tags say you are elders. You seem to be about my age. May I ask why you are called elders?"

The two poor, confused boys looked at each other and simply shrugged.

Titania said, "Don't terrorize the poor guys. Come on, friends. Have a seat."

They followed her gesture and sat at a table, placing their Books of Mormon on the tabletop.

"Um, so like, what do you guys do here?" asked a timid Aaron.

Lâmié had a look of pity on his face and said, "Well, this is our bar. It's a punk rock bar. Unfortunately, it's had a few, um, *accidents*, and we're trying to refurbish it so we can open it again. But, in all seriousness, I know y'all don't drink alcohol, so how about a Coke or something?"

"Oh, we're not allowed to drink caffeine," explained Amos.

"Oh, that's right. I forgot," said Lâmié. "Well, here, at least have some water. We can't be rude hosts." He grabbed two bottles of water from behind the bar and placed them in front of the two missionaries, who seemed thirsty and thankful.

"Say, mates," said Paul, who was already beginning to slur his words a bit, "we're having a show here in two weeks, Saturday night. So, you should come and learn something about the punk culture and New Orleans."

Aaron and Amos looked uncomfortable as they rubbed their necks, looked around, and squirmed.

"Um, thanks. Yeah, alright. I…I guess we can come," said Aaron.

"Aaron?" said Amos sharply.

"It's an opportunity to preach the gospel and the good news of Joseph Smith!" hissed Aaron back.

"Tell you what," said Paul. "You come to our show, and I promise we'll sit down and listen to your shtick. Not promising we'll convert, but we'll listen."

"See?" said Aaron. "It's a deal!"

"Now," continued Paul, "you can stay and help us clean up."

The two boys looked at each other but were too polite to refuse.

As they all began to pick up piles of trash, scrub bloodstains, and pull up mangled boards, as well as sweep and mop, another knock came on the door.

"Central fucking station," muttered Paul as he opened the door. "Oh God!" he yelled.

Mary ran to the door and saw what had startled Paul. A man in a black suit and black fedora stood outside. He looked older than written history; his wrinkled skin was so weathered that it could have been a leather purse. His skin was not only wrinkled, but also pallid like an overcooked piece of boiled, gray broccoli. The skin of his head and face, however, was so thin that his head might as well have been a bare skull. He extended a thin, frail arm, on the end of which was a skeletal hand, its pale, oily skin covered in brown spots, to Paul.

"The Reverend Methuselah Skink at your service, brother." Skink smiled, revealing a set of dentures so old that they, too, had yellowed like natural teeth. A fog of sour breath pelted Paul's nostrils, and he winced.

"Um…Mary…help?" croaked Paul.

Mary shoved Paul out of the way and said, "Sorry for my friend here, Reverend. Um, nice to meet you? I'm Mary, and this is Paul. Are you sure you have the right address? This is a punk bar."

Skink stepped inside the bar uninvited and replied, "Yes, I am aware. *The sour grapes of the fathers shall set their sons' teeth on edge!*"

Paul and Mary stared at him, dumbfounded and silent.

The reverend looked around the bar and at the others, who were also eyeing him in amazement. Skink removed his hat, revealing a wrinkled, white, bald pate with little puffy clouds of thin, white hair around the rim here and there.

"Good brothers and sisters," began Skink in a creaky old voice with an accent right out of the Old South, "I am out and about today on behalf of my little flock, the People's Family of the Divine Blessing, spreading the good news of the gospel of Jesus. Yes, even you, good friends, can escape this den of iniquity and come into the glorious light of the Lord!"

Everyone looked at one another uncomfortably.

"We are having a gospel tent revival meeting in two weeks,

beginning on Saturday evening! We are setting up our tent right at the edge of your bar's parking lot, and I would like to cordially invite you, my brethren, to attend! For, as hath said the Lord, *Yet she increased her prostitution, remembering the days of her youth when she engaged in prostitution in the land of Egypt. She lusted after their genitals, as large as those of donkeys, and their seminal emission was as strong as that of stallions!*"

The others just stared at him in utter silence, mouths open in shock.

"Mate," said Paul, "not sure I follow you. Donkey dicks and stallion cum? What?"

"I will leave these fliers here with you!" declared Skink triumphantly as he laid a thick stack of fliers on a table. "Please see that each of your customers receives one so that we may have a full tent for the glory of God!"

"Um..." whispered Mary.

"And one more thing!" said Reverend Skink. "You!" he shrieked, pointing at Paul. "The Lord has a prophecy for you! He hath spoken to me, and he hath said, *You! The one called Paul! You shall endure the suffering and the purging of the flame, and you shall burn or be purified!*"

Skink turned and walked out of the door.

"What. The. Fuck." said Paul.

"Oy, that guy looked like a living skeleton!" declared Uri.

"Was...was that Satan?" asked Aaron with a shaking voice.

"Christ, that was terrifying!" said Mary.

"I've seen better-looking alligators!" said 'Tit Boudreaux.

"I need a drink," added Lâmié.

"Way ahead of you," said Paul from behind the bar.

In fact, everyone except Aaron and Amos took a beer, and they all sat at a large table.

"Um, y'all?" said Mary. "I don't think a gospel revival tent meeting is going to be good for our grand re-opening. It starts the same night, and that weirdo said it's right at the edge of our parking lot. So that can't be a good mix."

Lâmié got on his phone and searched for something.

"He said his church is called the People's Family of the Divine Blessing, right?"

Mary nodded and said, "Yeah. Sounds like a damn cult. *People's Temple* was Jim Jones, and the *Family* was Charles Manson."

Lâmié squinted his eyes at his phone, then said, "There's only one Google result, some amateur-looking religious page. It says, *The People's Family of the Divine Blessing is a weird cult outside the pale of orthodoxy*. That's all it says."

"Fucking great. You know what we need *more* of in our lives? Weird supernatural shit," said Paul. Each time that he cursed, Aaron and Amos winced.

Lâmié stood back up, finished his beer, and then tossed it into a large trashcan.

"Well, y'all," he said, "let's keep cleaning up here. We have a show to put on in two weeks."

CHAPTER 8

Break the Circle

"Palm reading, young man?"

The thick, Romanian accent was directed at Paul. He paused on his way to his favorite music store, Jimmy's Jazz House, for some guitar strings. The store was on the border of the French Quarter and the Faubourg Marigny, in a partly-residential neighborhood of classic, well-kept shotgun houses painted in an array of bright, Caribbean colors.

He looked down at the old lady's setup. She wore a light pink, silky blouse, over which was a royal blue apron of sorts. Her hair was an impossibly wild and chaotic puff of wiry gray strands that formed a nebulous imitation of a very full storm cloud.

Her bright, red lipstick was smeared on, covering not only her lips properly but also a circular swath around them. Her cheeks carried so much badly-applied blush that she looked like a circus clown who was infected with some horrid, tropical disease. She smelled strongly of a combination of mothballs, lemonade, alcohol, and bitter sweat.

"Uh...probably not," he replied.

"Oh, I think you need it, dearie! Sit! Sit!"

Paul looked around awkwardly, rubbed his neck, and said, "For fuck's sake," before sitting down.

"Relax, my child! Madame Who the Roma fortune teller will

read your palm and tell you the secrets of the mysteries of your own soul!"

"Roman? What? Aren't you a Gypsy?"

Madame Who frowned and said, "*Gypsy* is an offensive term, my son! We call ourselves *Roma*."

"Oh, uh, sorry."

"Think nothing of it, my child!" she said in her tinny, old-lady voice while putting on a pair of comically-thick and oversized eyeglasses that made her eyes look absurdly enormous.

She took his right hand into hers and scrutinized it for a couple of uncomfortable minutes while Paul tried to look elsewhere.

"Paul, Paul," she said.

"Wait, how do you know my name, lady?"

She looked up, smiled, and said, "I have the Sight, Paul. I am Madame Who, and your palm tells me many things, many mysterious things. You have had a rough life, son. You were always ostracized and outcast as a boy. Your parents were not supportive, and it hurt you. You fear being left alone, being isolated, being rejected."

Paul smirked and said, "Yeah, that's all true, but you could say that to anyone, and they'd probably feel like it was true."

She frowned and continued, "Such trouble believing, Paul, after all you have seen? Vampires? Werewolves? Goodness, I can see that you've fought evil more than once."

"How'd you know all that?"

"Why don't you listen? I will say again: Madame Who has the Sight! I see all! Let me see your other hand."

He felt his face blushing a little because he was embarrassed by what was happening. In fact, the sight of a punk with a Mohawk sitting with a colorful, Roma fortune teller was gathering a little crowd. Some tourists began taking pictures, and Paul muttered something unpleasant.

He slid his left hand in front of her, palm up, trying to avoid the weird hand-holding session he had endured with his right hand. But, to his chagrin, Madame Who picked up his left hand in hers and studied it intensely.

She gasped, and her eyes rolled back into her head, so only the whites showed. Then, she began to shake and convulse.

"Um, lady? Hello? Shit. Why does this shit always happen to me? Fuck. Should I call an ambulance?"

Just as soon as she had entered into the seizure-like state, she snapped back into her usual self. This seemed to be enough to drive away the overly curious tourists and pedestrians.

"Paul! Oh, Paul!" she wailed. "The spirits have given me a prophecy to tell you! I do not know its meaning; that is for you to discover. But listen closely, child. The spirits say to you, Paul Roy: *You must become a baby again, or you will be burned in the everlasting fire!*"

Paul stared blankly at Madame Who for a few moments, then replied, "What the hell is that supposed to mean?"

"I told you, it is for you to discover! The spirits have not revealed the meaning of the prophecy to me!"

Paul sighed and said, "Um, alright. That was the weirdest palm reading I've ever had, lady. Shit, how much do I owe you?"

"Nothing, Paul! How could I charge such a man as you who are so important to the fight against evil?"

Some city pigeons shat on the sidewalk right next to Paul, and he jumped a little. They cooed in mockery and triumph.

Paul pushed his eyebrows together and said, "A fortune teller giving me a reading for free? Alright, that convinces me that you're for real. That would never happen otherwise."

"I will ignore that offensive comment for now," she said. "The spirits also tell me that you and your friends are being troubled by a noisy ghost, a Poltergeist. Is it so?"

Across the street, some sort of commotion involving a hot dog vendor broke out, but Paul and Madame Who ignored it.

"Um, yeah. Weird shit's been happening around the house. Stuff moving, noises, scratching sounds, that sort of stuff."

"Oh, that is not good! Not at all! You require the services of Madame Who! We shall hold a séance at your house tonight!"

Paul held up his palms again, this time not for a reading but in protest. "Now wait a minute, I didn't agree to that!"

Behind them, a crowd of children angrily chased the hot dog vendor down the street. It did not look promising for him.

She ignored Paul and the vendor and said, "The spirits shall guide me to your house! I will arrive tonight! Be ready, and don't forget that Madame Who likes red wine and snacks! Lots of snacks! Lots and lots of red wine! Now, you must go and let Madame Who make a living!"

"Oh, for fuck's sake," said Paul as he stood up and continued to the Jimmy's Jazz House. He picked up his new strings, begrudgingly paid for them, then caught a streetcar back to the Garden District and hopped off in front of the corner liquor store. He entered just as Uri had finished checking out a customer.

"Paul! You came! Good timing. What's new?"

"I'm pretty sure a crazy fortune teller lady just invited herself to Lâmié's mansion tonight, and she's forcing me to prepare red wine and snacks."

Uri laughed and said, "You must be referring to Madame Who? I've been running into her everywhere! Nice, she is. Mentally stable, not so much. Here, buy a few bottles of this Cabernet along with your beer. A gay couple told me it's delicious, and they know their wine."

Paul sighed. "Alright, fine. I'll get some beer too. You should come over tonight for the séance."

"Séance, even? Oy! I'll go, but I can't tell my family. My parents would kill me! I'll make a bunch of kosher latkes for snacks."

The store's door, equipped with a bell above it to announce entrants, dinged. The entire store emanated the hoppy, sour aroma of beer coolers. Uri had some klezmer music softly playing in the background.

A wraith-thin young woman walked into the store. Her skin bore the telltale pockmarks, divots, and scars of a crack or meth addict but her missing teeth narrowed it down to meth. Her frail, brittle, blond hair was missing in plugs, and her filthy clothes had not seen a washing machine in months. Her sour odor preceded her.

"The Bubonic Plague's treatable these days, you know," said Paul.

"Paul! Be nice!" whispered Uri. "She might have addiction problems!"

"Might?"

The woman walked up and down the aisles, presumably browsing. Uri, not wanting to prejudge people, tried not to keep too careful an eye on her. Paul had no qualms about watching her suspiciously. He paid his bill but waited with Uri until the woman's drama played out. After an uncomfortably long silence, and after the woman had jittered up and down each aisle too many times to actually be browsing, Uri decided to talk to her.

"Is there anything I can help you with, Ma'am? Any recommendations? Help you find anything?"

The woman twitched and jerked, then made her way to the front counter as Paul and Uri stared nervously.

"Oy, miss, what are you on about? Did you come to buy

something?" asked Paul.

The woman stopped, raised a thin, shaking arm, and pointed a sharp, elongated finger at Paul. "You!" she screeched. "You are the one! You are Paul! They speak of you! They know your name! You're going to die and burn in hell! They're going to eat your soul!"

She fell to the floor and began to writhe and slither like a snake. Finally, she crawled across the store and climbed up a shelf of gin. Then, incredibly, she reached the ceiling, climbed onto it, and began to crawl across the ceiling upside down.

"Um, Paul? I think I'm on lunch break now!"

"Yeah, me too! Let's get the hell out of here!"

They sprinted out of the store and ran all the way down the avenue to Lâmié's mansion.

"I'm going to call the owner," said Uri. "Not sure I want to go back today."

"Fuck, that was some top-level *Exorcist* shit there," agreed Paul.

As the two bounded into the house and then into the grand parlor, all of the housemates looked up.

"Um, everything alright?" asked Lâmié.

While Uri called the liquor store owner, Paul explained to the others what had happened.

"This meth tweaker woman came in, told me that I'm going to burn in hell, then—I'm not fucking lying—climbed across the ceiling like in a horror movie. We left quickly. Oh, the woman knew my name, and so did a fortune teller named Madame Who, and she's going to show up here later uninvited for a séance about our Poltergeist."

"Christ, Paul!" said Mary. "How do you attract so much trouble?"

"I guess it's a natural talent," he said with a shrug. "Now, who wants a beer?"

After Uri had gone home and returned to Lâmié's house with fresh latkes, he and the housemates were sitting in the grand parlor and talking about the Poltergeist weirdness. Mary and Paul sat together, their relationship long since revealed to the others, and Isabella and Varco were the same. Baozi and Pidan, the heroic feline goblin slayers, sat in Judy Felix's lap and purred merrily. Then, a knock came at the door.

"Fuck, that's gotta be the Gypsy woman," complained Paul.

"*Roma*, Paul. *Roma*," said Mary.

Paul sighed, forced himself up, and answered the door. As expected, a disheveled Madame Who stood on the porch.

A sprinkling rain—light for New Orleans but torrential for the rest of the world—had begun to smear the streets with its warm, polluted water from the heavens. Poor Madame Who's hair had deflated into a soggy pile. Her overdone makeup had begun to form rivulets on her cheeks that flowed down into the sea of her chin. From there, the liquid makeup created a stunning waterfall onto Lâmié's front porch.

"God..." muttered Paul.

"It is I, the mysterious Madame Who, fortune teller and conduit for the spirits!" she said with a resplendent bow. But then, she lost her balance and almost fell on her face.

Paul caught her, sighed dejectedly, and said, "Yeah, I know. Um, come in, I guess."

He led the dripping mystic down the main hall, then to the right into the grand parlor. The housemates' buzzing conversation stopped the instant that Madame Who entered the room.

"I can feel strong spiritual energy in this house!" she proclaimed in an exaggerated voice. "Yes, the spirits are active here, both good and bad!"

Lâmié stood up, rubbed the back of his neck awkwardly, then said, "Um, Madame Who, I presume? Er, yeah, please come in and have a seat. Let me get you a towel to dry off a bit."

"Yes, yes!" she replied. "A towel, thank you! Madame Who works best when dry and when offered red wine and snacks! Lots of snacks! Lots and lots of red wine!" She looked at Paul. As Lâmié went to the half bathroom in the hall to grab a towel, Paul resigned himself to the weird experience and went into the kitchen to get the wine, and Uri followed him to get the latkes. When the three returned, Lâmié helped dry off the old lady, and she began setting out candles on the coffee table.

"We shall hold the séance here, where the energy is strong!" she wailed.

Paul rolled his eyes.

"Now," continued the Roma woman, "tell Madame Who about this Poltergeist who has been disturbing you!"

'Tit Boudreaux volunteered. "Well, um, Madame Who, we've

had a few things happen. First, things move around all the time when we're not looking. Like, just yesterday, I placed my car keys down right here on this side table, then looked away to talk to someone for just a couple of minutes. When I looked back, my keys were across the room on that other table over there."

Madame Who, who had already gotten into the wine and latkes, pursed her lips and nodded.

"Second, there's been this weird scratching in the walls. Everyone's heard it here in the parlor and our individual bedrooms. We thought it could be mice or something, but we had an exterminator take a look, and he saw no signs of mice or pests."

"Scratching in the walls! A classic sign of a Poltergeist infestation!" she declared, spraying latke crumbs and red wine droplets all over the parlor.

'Tit Boudreaux stifled a laugh and said, "Then, the other day, Paul had put some wine bottles in the kitchen. He stepped out for a moment, and while no one was in the kitchen, one of the bottles was smashed on the floor. The remaining two were stacked, one on top of the other."

Madame Who said something in a loud voice but with a mouthful of latke, so her words came out as unintelligible, muffled whoops. Everyone sat and watched her awkwardly and silently as she took her time chewing that bite, then finally swallowing it and chasing it with a rather self-indulgent amount of red wine.

Finally, she continued. "The classic signs of a Poltergeist. Yes, there is a trapped, troubled spirit here! But, do not worry; Madame Who will set them free. Spirits that remain on earth often have unfinished business. Some do not even know they are dead. It is left to seers like me to send them into the spiritual realm. Let us begin immediately!"

"Oh, for fuck's sake," muttered Paul.

"The lights! They must be turned off!"

Lâmié frowned, but complied. Madame Who lit the candles so that a yellow glow embraced the room.

"Now, everyone, gather around in a circle! We must close our eyes and join hands, and never, ever break the circle, or bad spirits may enter!"

Everyone halfheartedly joined hands in a circle. Madame Who closed her eyes; the yellow candlelight flickered across her wrinkled face, causing it to look like the face of a dead person.

"Spirits, spirits!" she began. "We can sense your strong presence here! I know that you are trapped in this house, in these walls! Speak now to Madame Who, and tell us of your troubles!"

They all waited for over a minute in total silence. Paul coughed. The odor of the spilled red wine from the last time had still not departed the house, filling it with the sticky smell of tannins and musty old grapes.

"They are shy," she whispered to the group. "I'll try again. Spirits! Oh, spirits present here! Speak to Madame Who! Tell us your sorrows, your history, your desires! Madame Who can help you!"

They waited in silence. A cool wind blew through the room, causing their skin pores to pucker and the hairs on their arms to rise up. A sense of dread, of the inevitable approach of something very wicked, filled their fluttering stomachs and minds. They sat for a few seconds more when a slight scratching came from inside one of the parlor walls. Everyone opened their eyes and looked over at it.

"Do not break the circle!" hissed Madame Who. She spoke loudly, "Yes, yes, spirit! Who are you? We can hear you scratching! Tell us your name!"

The scratching continued but died down into silence after a little while, which continued for several moments. Then, a deafening pounding suddenly came from inside the same wall. Everyone jumped and screamed.

Madame Who regained her composure first and said, "Spirit, do not be angry! I am here to help you! Tell Madame Who your problems! Bare your soul to me!"

A ferocious, animalistic growl from the kitchen shocked the fortune-teller into silence. Her hands began to shake. A frigid burst of air blew across them all, and then the entire house began to shake.

The room became dark like midnight in the country, so the only glow was an unnaturally tiny dot of light at the tip of each candle's lit wick. But, as their rods and cones adjusted to the dark, they could see that, even in the pitch shadows in the corners of the room, something else, something *even darker than the night*, hid.

Long, sinewy forms crouched over in the room's corners, creeping *things* with several arms and legs, with horns protruding from heads, undulated back and forth, watching the people around the table.

"What...the...fuck...are...those?" whispered Mary in a shaking voice.

"Spirits..." said Madame Who in a voice not quite as loud and confident as before, "wh...what do you want?"

A baritone, deriding laughter came from one of the corners of the parlor.

"Who is this? What is your name, spirit?"

"NEMO," came a growl from hell itself.

"What...what do you want, spirit?"

"PAUL'S SOUL."

"What the fuck?" yelled Paul, who had evidently had enough bullshit. He stood up angrily.

"No! Do not break the circle!" warned Madame Who.

"Fuck the circle! I've had enough of this supernatural shit! And there's just enough beer in me to not take it anymore! Fuck you, spirit! I'm gonna kick your ass!"

"Paul, no! Be careful!" shouted Mary, but it was too late.

Paul ran toward one of the horrid shapes in one corner of the parlor with his fists raised aggressively. He crashed into the thing and started swinging, but it was no contest: the *thing* hurled Paul across the room. He slammed into the sofa and passed out.

"Enough!" said Uri in a determined tone, and even the things in the corners remained silent in surprise. He then stood up, his tall frame towering over the table. He took the phylactery on his chest into his hand and began to chant Hebrew in a loud and authoritative voice:

Bezeh ha sha'ar lo yavo tza'ar!
Bezot haddirah lo tavo tzarah!
Bezot haddelet lo tavo bahalah!
Bezot hammahlaqah lo tavo mahloqet!
Bezeh hammaqom tehi b'rakhah v'shalom!

The creature in the corner hissed and shrieked. It shouted something in some ancient, demonic, forgotten language—it sounded guttural and *nasty*. It then shrank back into the shadows and disappeared. The atmosphere suddenly felt light and free.

"Fuck! Did you just exorcise that shit, Uri?" asked a stunned Paul, who had come to again.

"No, I suspect not," answered the exhausted Hasid. "I just said a common Jewish prayer meant to ask for peace and keep evil spirits out of homes. I guess it kind of worked, but I don't think I, like, killed it or anything."

Madame Who was staring at the corner, eyes and mouth frozen open, her entire body shaking.

"Um, Madame Who?" asked Mary. "You, uh, alright there?"

She said with chattering teeth, "It…that…not…not a spirit…"

"What?" prodded Mary. "What do you mean? That wasn't a spirit?"

"Not…not a ghost of a dead human," Madame Who managed to spit out.

Everyone looked at one another with puzzled faces.

"Not a dead human spirit? Then what the hell was it?" asked Paul.

She replied with one, simple word, "Demon."

Chapter 9

Suffer the Little Children to Come Unto Me

The *Beth Tzedeq Synagogue* in the Touro neighborhood, a pleasant walk from Lâmié's mansion, displayed some of the former glory of old Jewish New Orleans. Yes, modern New Orleans had a thriving Jewish community, many of whom were pillars of the community. Still, perhaps, a bit of the old-style charm had been buffed out of the shine by assimilation.

In the city's early days, distinct Jewish enclaves were thick with men wearing *kippot*, or even Hasidim wearing their hoiche hats and payot, and women in lovely and modest formal dresses, or among the poorer members, simple black and white attire.

Each early-New-Orleans Jewish neighborhood had welcomed several synagogues, only a few of which remained in the modern city. The Beth Tzedeq gloried in its gargantuan, monolithic styling, with its corner spires towering up into the heavens, like somewhat modest and self-aware Towers of Babel. The gray, granite walls, which in any other application would have spoken to grim Soviet Brutalist architecture, radiated, in the case of the synagogue, a defiant symbol of the resilience of the Jewish people throughout the millennia.

Rabbi Shlomo Cohen, the selfsame head of NOIF, was the *rebbe* at the Hasidic synagogue. A man very well-liked by his friends of other faiths, he was positively adored by the flock of his own synagogue as

HELL'S BELLS: A PUNK ROCK DEMON STORY

a loving old grandfather who always looked out for the good of his charges.

The interior of the Beth Tzedeq Synagogue was full of singing, laughter, tears, joy, and pain on the Sabbath and again during the week at the various group, prayer, and study meetings. Rabbi Cohen worked hard to make it a place of joy as much as possible and a place of reflection and mourning when necessary and appropriate. It was, quite simply, a *happy place*.

For that reason, the atmosphere was decidedly *unnatural* on this particular weeknight at midnight, for an interloper had broken into the holy structure. In the front of the house of worship, in the generous space between the seating and the *bimah*, a dark figure was busy drawing something on the wooden floor with white chalk—it was a magic circle. At the head of the circle was the same sigil that the figure had hurriedly drawn on Uri's house, right outside his bedroom.

The first thing he had done was to turn off the electric *ner tamid*, the eternal flame that must never be extinguished. He had taken great pleasure in doing so.

At each point of the inverted pentagram that the man had drawn concurrent to the circle, he placed and lit a black candle. The cold, pale glow of the candlelight sent waves of dim light across the curtain in front of the *aron hakodesh*. Like a movie screen, the man could see the faint, shadowy form of the *Torah* scrolls behind the curtain. He cackled aloud.

Behind the man, lying on the aisle between the men's and the women's seating areas, a boy of about eight years struggled against the ropes tightly binding his wrists and ankles. He tried to shout through the balled-up sock gagging his mouth but only produced pitiful little puffs of sound.

"Be quiet!" hissed the man, "or I'll make it even worse for you!"

The boy seemed to give up and resign himself to his fate. He became still, and silent tears covered his face.

The man, satisfied that his magic circle was complete and correct, walked to where he had set down his materials and took hold of a small, metal basin with low walls, a sort of trough just large enough to hold a young boy.

The man placed the trough just in front of the aron hakodesh. He took a handheld bottle of lighter fluid from his bag and sprayed a thin layer across the bottom of the trough. Then, he walked back to the boy, picked him up, and, despite the child's squirming and muffled pleading, laid him down in the trough.

The man took the bottle again and emptied the flammable, liquid contents all over the boy. The boy screamed and winced as the stinging lighter fluid flowed into his eyes, mouth, and nose. The man ignored it.

The man took a thick, fragile, ancient book from his bag, then stepped inside the magic circle, carefully looking at his feet to ensure he was entirely within the circle's bounds. He opened the book, flipped carefully to his chosen page, and read aloud. His spoke the invocation in a bizarre combination of the Hebrew from millennia ago and a lost Canaanite language.

Rir, rir, mother of snakes,
Come here unto your servant,
Come here before your masters,
The seven demons of the land!

O Moloch, god of the field,
God of the forest,
God of the harvest,
God of fertility and of children,
God of fire and flame,
Hearken unto this, your servant!

O Moloch, god of the field,
Your servant calls upon you,
Come to the high places
Come to the low places in the valley,
Come to this, your shrine!

O Moloch, god of the children,
You who have kept this, your servant, young,
You, who have given this, your servant,
The gift of eternal life!

O, Moloch, accept my sacrifice,
And eat freely and deeply of it,
And preserve me in eternal life!
Make me like unto you!

The atmosphere in the synagogue changed into a sad, dreadful heaviness. The black candles flickered as an icy breeze tussled the man's hair, and a freezing touch of fear traveled down his spine. The poor boy in the trough thrashed against his bindings, for he also sensed the approach of something wicked and horrible.

From the dark recesses of the back of the synagogue, the distant bellow of a bull trumpeted across the open space.

The man knelt, careful to remain entirely inside the magic circle, and held a Zippo lighter in his hand. The boy, now thoroughly soaked in lighter fluid, saw the Zippo and panicked. He tried to scream frantically, but his gag prevented it.

Insensitive to the boy's terror, the man flicked the lighter and produced a flame, casually tossing the lit Zippo into the trough. A flaming inferno instantly engulfed the boy and began to consume his flesh as he thrashed violently and shrieked in agony.

The man watched in fascination as the boy's skin turned bright red, then bubbled, then charred black. His limbs became rigid as his bones began to brown, and his blood began to heat. He wheezed, vainly trying to suck in oxygen through the viscous, oily smoke coming from his fatty tissue. He gave one last burst of energy to try to save his life: he tossed back and forth and strained, but then the heat and pain were too great. Finally, the boy lay back in the trough and accepted death. The synagogue was replete with the odor of carbonized flesh.

The man shook as he waited for something to happen, but he did not have to wait long. The bull's bellowing became louder until it sounded like a great, bovine beast was in the room with him. The *clip-clop* of bulls' hooves clicked on the tile floor, louder and louder, closer and closer.

The man only looked in front of himself, terrified to see more, but he sensed the presence of something awful and powerful, and then, finally, the demon-god appeared in front of him.

The great Moloch towered up to the ceiling of the synagogue. His torso was that of a muscular man, and at the end of each of his arms was a giant, open hand, palm up. His thick, furry trunk legs were those of a bull, the knee joints backward like those of the animal. He had no feet, but hooves, each the size of the man's waist.

The man forced himself to look up and saw Moloch's head, which was that of an angry bull. Long like those of a Texas steer, two horns protruded from the top of his head and curved inward, almost meeting in the middle, forming almost a perfect full moon.

Moloch bellowed, and black smoke blasted out of his nostrils.

The man quivered as the colossal, hulking beast bent down, sniffed the boy's burned corpse, then ate it. With each crunch of bone and slurp of charred flesh and fat, the man struggled to keep from dry heaving.

After his sacrificial meal, Moloch stood up again to his full mountainous height, and a profound, baritone growl proceeded from his mouth and nose, shaking even the foundations of the synagogue and the man's ribcage.

Moloch looked down into the man's petrified eyes, nodded, and lowed, sending out a flood of black smoke over the man, who instantly felt rejuvenated. Moloch clopped across the synagogue, back into the shadowy corners, and then disappeared. The atmosphere felt lighter, and the man sighed.

He obviously did not have a problem with the sacrifices, although he did not take great pleasure in them. They were to him a means to an end, that end being his eternal youth and evasion of death. The irony was that the man was prolonging a death through actions that would, when he eventually would die, certainly guarantee his infernal destination.

The man cleaned up the mess before daybreak, then tossed and turned in bed while he suffered vivid and horrifying nightmare visions of hell.

CHAPTER 10

The Circus Tent

Two weeks passed quickly for the Gravediggers and friends, and they found themselves marveling at how relatively good The Gutter Bar looked on the day of the show. Through their efforts and that of the professionals whom Lâmié had hired at not a low price, the bar looked remarkably similar to how it had looked before the last massacre.

The walls had been re-covered in punk band stickers and lacked only the years of customer graffiti that would undoubtedly make a quick comeback. The bar itself enjoyed a refurbished look, and the wooden top shone in a layer of new varnish, a varnish whose prognosis for a long life was not good, given the drinking habits of punks, goths, and emos. Wooden booths had been re-installed here and there, and a new set of lights glowed red, casting a bloody pall over the entire bar. Most importantly, the stains and smears of human and goblin blood and gore had been removed—mostly. The remaining splotches made interesting conversation-starters.

The whole gang had gathered to show support, and Lâmié had a place and a role for everyone.

Varco, Barillo, and 'Tit Boudreaux would work the door and act as security and bouncers. Titania would hang out in the back, near the stage, in case any extra magical support would be needed.

The bartending staff consisted of Isabella, Zoë, Evelyn, and Siofra, who were all in their most stylish punk attire, ready to sling beers and drinks.

The Gravediggers—Paul, Mary, Matt, and Uri—would be playing the show, of course, along with another band Mary had managed to convince to take the gig. The band was called Wicked Perverts (insisting that the article *the* should absolutely *not* precede the name), and their style of music was a genre that they called *hardcore evil death punk*, a genre that they insisted they had invented.

Mary had hired them without hearing their music, simply because it was becoming harder and harder to find bands willing to play in a venue with a reasonable chance of being slaughtered.

Lâmié himself, as usual, would keep track of profits and the books in the back office, with occasional walks around the bar to ensure everything was running smoothly.

The rest of the friends and housemates would sit behind the bar safely and observe without interacting, each for their own reason. Yarielis felt a bit too old to be punk. Judy had made significant improvement by even being willing to leave the house, and to be in a crowded bar was her exposure therapy. Still, she was nowhere near ready to interact with customers. Her two furry sons, Baozi and Pidan, sat with her behind the bar, lazily flopping their tails back and forth and purring contentedly.

Erin had made the probably-horrible decision to bring little Grimbil along in his baby carrier with tiny earplugs in his ears. She was near the end of the bar closest to the back storage room, just in case she and Grimbil needed some relative peace and quiet during the night.

Everything seemed promising, except for the fact that the creepy Reverend Methuselah Skink had set up his gospel revival tent directly across the bar's parking lot, and a looming monstrosity it was indeed.

To mistake the tent for the Barnum and Bailey big top would be forgivable, so gauche and tactless did it tower into the sky. Visible through the vast, gaping entrance flaps were countless rows of folding chairs facing a six-foot-tall dais that extended the length of the tent. On this platform stood a single, black preaching lectern, pointing up erect like a giant, black phallus (unintentional, of course, would the good Reverend Skink argue).

As Father Sun began his downward stoop into his horizon-bed, the shadows of New Orleans began to take their rightful place. But, before the customers started to arrive, the Gravediggers and friends stood outside of the front door of The Gutter and watched Reverend Skink's tent fill up.

"God, this is ridiculous," said Paul, a beer already in his hand.

"Yeah, it's so absurd it's comical," agreed Matt. "I mean, that weird Skink dude picked the parking lot of a punk bar to set up his tent?"

"Maybe," reasoned Uri, "he thought that people who come to this bar need salvation the most."

"Not saying he's wrong," said Mary. "We're a pretty sorry bunch."

The people walking into Skink's tent looked out of place for the city. First, they were primarily white, even in a city as diverse as New Orleans. Second, the men wore conservative suits and ties, mostly dark navy or black pants and jackets, white shirts, and muted ties, while the women wore frumpy, floral dresses. All of the clothing looked like it had come from Walmart.

"Christ! They look like they just accidentally stumbled out of the Nineteen-Fifties," whispered Mary. "You sure we killed all the zombies?"

At that moment, Reverend Methuselah Skink stepped outside his huge tent and walked toward the Gravediggers with a disquieting smile, a smile that stretched almost too wide for his wrinkled face to reveal his stained dentures.

"Oh fuck, here he comes," hissed Paul.

"*Thou shalt not boil a kid in its mother's milk!*" declared Skink loudly as he approached them, causing them to look at one another in confusion.

"Uh...you what, mate?" asked Paul.

"The People's Family of the Divine Blessing greets you, my children!" said Skink. "The Reverend Methuselah Skink at your service!"

"Yeah, we know your name," muttered Paul.

"Uh, Reverend?" asked Mary. "May I ask respectfully why you chose a punk bar's parking lot for your tent revival?"

"Indeed you can, young Miss! Indeed you can!" Skink said with a smile. He just looked at Mary in silence.

"Um, alrighty then. Why did you choose a punk bar's parking lot for your tent revival?" asked Paul.

Skink removed his ludicrous top hat, bowed, replaced it, and answered, "A germane question, Sir. Indeed. I will answer you by quoting the word of the good Lord: '*See, I assign to you cow's dung instead of human dung, on which you may prepare your bread.*' Thus sayeth the Lord!"

Mary just stared at Skink in utter confusion.

"Do not undervalue the word, Miss. Also, do not undervalue giving oneself in sacrifice to the Lord! Our lives must be living sacrifices, giving of ourselves in all that we do!"

"Mate," said Paul, "just let us have our show and don't come to preach against us, and we'll be cool, yeah?"

Reverend Skink again removed his stove pipe hat, bowed stiffly, grinned hideously, and said, "Sacrifice. Sacrifice." After that, he walked back to his tent to greet the congregants.

"Well, that's one weird fucker," said Paul.

Uri pulled on his payot and rubbed his neck uncomfortably. "What did he mean about sacrifice?"

"Yeah, that was weird," agreed Mary.

"I mean," continued Uri, "the idea of sacrifice is found throughout the Law, the Writings, the Prophets, and even the New Testament, but when Skink says it, it seems ominous."

Mary shook her head, grimaced, and said, "This whole scene is weird. A punk show sharing a parking lot with a gospel tent revival? Lord have mercy!"

Two guys and two girls were walking toward the bar. They wore black clothes and vampire makeup. They stared in confusion at Skink's tent as they approached The Gutter.

"Well, that's the band," said Mary. "That's Wicked Perverts."

"Hi, Mary. Um, what's that?" asked one of the guys.

"Hey, y'all. Don't worry; you're at the right place. That's some weird preacher dude called Reverend Skink who's holding some sort of tent revival. It's not on our property, so we can't do shit about it except play all the louder."

The band watched the squares crowding into the tent. Skink had set up a system of floodlights, but they all pointed toward the tent, which, in contrast, sort of cloaked The Gutter Bar in relative darkness.

The oak trees in and around the parking lot seemed droopy and sad at the spectacle, and even the usual squirrels who chirped and sprinted up and down the branches were all sitting still, staring in disbelief at Skink and his bizarre cult.

The members of Wicked Perverts laughed.

Mary said, "Y'all can set up on stage. We thought we'd do a song or two to open for you, then the night's yours. All the free beer you can drink, and don't worry, we always pay what we agreed on."

The band walked in, but one of the girls dallied behind a bit, seeming nervous.

"Um, Mary?" asked the delicate waif in white monster makeup and black punk attire. "There were, like, some *murders* here, right?"

Mary eyed Paul and said, "Well, there were, um, a couple of *incidents*, but we've taken care of that. We even have a friend who's an NOPD detective. He's keeping an eye on the place. You don't need to worry."

"Alright, if you say so. Thanks," said the obviously unconvinced girl as she slowly walked inside, looking around carefully as if she were entering a haunted house.

As the members of the People's Family of the Divine Blessing, their guests, and some stragglers filled up the tent, Skink took one last look around, smiled, winked at the Gravediggers, and pulled the tent flap closed. It did not close fully, so it left a gap through which they could easily see right into the interior space.

A few customers were starting to arrive at The Gutter Bar, so everyone went inside to be ready for the night. Aaron and Amos Brigham crept into the bar like shy cats, looking around in terror at all the punks and cringing at the loud Mourning Noise music blaring from the jukebox.

"You came, you marvelous Mormons!" shouted an already-buzzed Paul.

"Oh, um, hello, Paul," stuttered Aaron. "This is…wow. This is nothing like anything we knew in Utah."

"Good! How about a beer, mates?"

They looked at the ground uncomfortably, then Amos said, "That is very kind, but we are not allowed to consume alcohol. The Book of Mormon says that—"

"Your choice, mate. Let me know if you want something else," said Paul as he walked off. Amos coughed.

Around nine o'clock, the bar was pretty full. Beer was selling, and people were happy. Mary turned off the jukebox and climbed onstage, then took the microphone in her hand.

"Thanks for coming out to The Gutter Bar, freaks!"

The crowd cheered loudly. No one seemed too nervous or upset to be where so many massacres had occurred.

"Let's cut the bullshit and start the music!"

Roaring applause shook the bar.

"The Gravediggers, that's us, we're gonna do a song, then after us comes the main act, Wicked Perverts! Grab a drink and get ready for some shitty punk music from us, then some good stuff from the main show!"

Paul, Matt, and Uri climbed onto the stage. The applause became silent for a moment as everyone saw Uri in his full Hasidic clothing, hoiche hat, payot, and phylactery. However, when Paul counted in the first song, they doubted him no more.

As the Gravediggers began blasting a fast-paced, thunderous song, Uri began to jump up and down, whirling around in the air like a dreidel, becoming a blurred whirlwind of black clothes and flopping side curls, yet still playing his bass perfectly as Paul sang (shouted?) the lyrics:

That old black magic,
It's coming for you!
You think it's a joke?
Well man, it's true!

Curses, hexes, Voodoo spells,
All the demons're coming out of hell!
It's their turn to rule the land,
So hurry, take the path of the left hand!

Sinatra had it wrong;
Black magic's not about love;
It's not just a song;
It's hellfire from above!

Curses, hexes, Voodoo spells,
All the demons're coming out of hell!
It's their turn to rule the land,
So hurry, take the path of the left hand!

So eat the rich or kill the poor,
Save the earth or burn it down,

*Choices don't matter anymore,
'Cuz hellfire's raining down!*

*Curses, hexes, Voodoo spells,
All the demons're coming out of hell!
It's their turn to rule the land,
So hurry, take the path of the left hand!*

They ended the song, and Uri stumbled around in a dizzy fugue, then fell onto the stage. The crowd laughed and cheered.

"Alright, that's our new single, y'all. It's a little dark, I guess," said Mary over the mic. "When you've been through hell, you start to see hell everywhere. Yeah, but now it's time for some actual good music. So ladies, gentlemen, punks, goths, emos, and everyone in between or not, please welcome a local band from the mean and weird streets of New Orleans…Wicked Perverts!"

As the customers yelled and clapped, the four band members took the stage and picked up their instruments. Without hesitation, the singer, painted to look like a corpse, counted in their first song, and the others jammed right in with fast, frantic chords. Next, the corpse-singer opened his mouth to sing, but just as he did, another loud voice resonated into the bar.

It was the voice of the Reverend Methuselah Skink, who had cranked up his tent speakers so loud that his voice competed with the punk music!

The Wicked Perverts singer did not care. In fact, he narrowed his eyes angrily at the obnoxious preacher and began to sing even louder. The timing of the singer and the preacher was such that, after each line of the song, a line from the sermon answered it, causing a sort of demented call-and-response fiasco:

Open up the doors of your brain;

The tent doors are open!

Open up your mind before it shrivels up and dies!

Brothers and sisters, tonight, I want to talk about faith.

The zombies are just outside the gates,

HELL'S BELLS: A PUNK ROCK DEMON STORY

I hope you all will join me tonight as we pray together.

They don't think, just search for a brain, no thought, no try!

Choose faith over facts, brethren! Faith will never fail you!

What's it all matter, anyway, if you starve the poor?

The essence of our faith, in fact, is prayer, piety, and submission!

Flagellate yourself, but close your heart to the sick and dying?

Faith is inside us, and it must be about obedience and the loss of self, brethren!

Lost stranger comes a'knocking? Close that fucking door!

For the Apostle Paul said that he beat his own body to bring it under subjection!

Laugh at the homeless? Come on; you're not even trying!

You see, brethren, we are all responsible for our own obedience and our own condition! As the good book says, if a man will not work, then neither shall he eat!

Junkies and addicts sell their soul for a hit,

Faith, my children, is about purity and refraining from sin!

But you scorn and frown, and spit on their shoes,

We, the saved, are God's children! We are better! We have been lifted up!

See, you've never been addicted to shit,

We do not lie down with the dogs and rise up with fleas.

Never had to feed a kid, never had to choose!

No, we are blessed, materially and spiritually!

They tell you to obey someone else, man or God,

And I, brethren, the Reverend Methuselah Skink, was chosen by God to reveal to you his holy will!

To deny your own voice, to submit to your fate;

When you obey me, brethren, you are really obeying God, for I am but his vessel!

But don't you think it's a little odd,

The time may come, brethren, when God, through me, asks you to do something difficult, something that you do not want to do. You must obey in that hour!

That they never forget the collection plate?

And now, brothers and sisters, for the continued work of the Lord, let us pass the collection plate! Give generously, for you give to God!"

The sermon and the song both stopped simultaneously, and as the bar customers cheered for Wicked Perverts, the congregants across the parking lot howled out a chorus of *Amens!* and *Hallelujahs!* It was as if each group was trying to out-yell the other.

And then, the tent revival let out.

As Wicked Perverts huddled to decide their next song quickly, the members of the People's Family of the Divine Blessing and their guests flooded the parking lot and began to investigate The Gutter Bar curiously. Varco, Barillo, and 'Tit Boudreaux eyed them worriedly.

"Um, what do we do?" asked Varco. "What if they want to come in?"

'Tit Boudreaux laughed and answered, "Hell, if they wanna pay cover, then we let them in! Lâmié would agree, I'm sure."

Barillo shook his head and said, "Why do we always get into these weird-ass situations?"

Sure enough, a line of congregants formed at the door, began to pay cover, and entered the bar, dressed in their Sunday best. The punks, goths, and emos looked at them quizzically.

"Um, what the hell?" said Mary to Paul.

"Fuck, can't we ever have a normal night?"

"Well, they *are* paying cover, after all. But why the hell would they come in here? What do they want?"

Wicked Perverts started their next song, and many of the church members covered their ears and looked terrified. Paul laughed. However, he stopped laughing when the Reverend Methuselah Skink himself paid the cover charge and stepped into the bar.

"Mary? What the fuck?"

"Christ," she answered. "This can't be good."

Skink walked up to Mary and Paul and said, "*Let beer be for those who are perishing, and wine for those who are in anguish!*"

"Mate, we're all in anguish here. Want a drink?" said Paul.

"*It is not for kings, Lemuel, it is not for kings to drink wine, not for rulers to crave beer!*" declared Skink.

"Then forgive the hell out of me, *King Skink*!" huffed Paul. "Now, what are you and your lizard kingdom doing here?"

"Why, brother Paul, we, I, we are here to preach the good news of the People's Family of the Divine Blessing!"

"Oh, the hell you are!" said Paul. "Don't come in here bothering our customers, mate. They're here for punk music and drunken fun."

Skink smiled, his greying, chapped lips sliding over his saliva-smeared, yellow teeth, but said nothing. Instead, as Wicked Perverts finished their song, he unceremoniously stepped onto the stage as the band watched, unsure what to do. The singer looked over at Mary, who was on her way to the stage, but not before Skink took the mic and began to speak in his Southern lilt.

"Friends, brothers, sisters, do not waste away your lives in this den of iniquity! Look at the writhing masses of sinners! How sad! How tragic! Such drug and alcohol abuse! As the Bible sayeth, '*The king desires no bride-price except a hundred foreskins of the Philistines!*'"

At first, the bar crowd frowned and began to boo the preacher, but at his recitation of the odd Bible passage, they just looked at one another in confusion. Still, Skink continued.

"God has sent me, his prophet, the Reverend Methuselah Skink, through the body of the People's Family of the Divine Blessing. He has sent me to reap the souls of this wicked place, to save you through blood and fire! Therefore, turn unto me, and unto God, children, or face the everlasting hellfire!"

The members of Skink's church in the bar began to chant: *Repent! Repent! Repent!* Mary stood, her hand on her hips, frowning at Skink, while Paul hurried up onto the stage. Aaron and Amos looked around awkwardly.

Skink started up again, but Paul snatched the mic from him and then spoke into it, "Sorry about this prick, punks! Skink, take your cult members and get out of our bar!"

At their prophet's outrageous insult, the People's Family of the Divine Blessing members began to shout more loudly and shove the punks, goths, and emos around them. Well, anyone who has been to a punk show knows that shoving and pushing are not good ideas. Just as people realized what was happening, one punk shouted, "Mosh pit!" and the fine line between civilization and chaos disappeared.

"Hell's bells!" shouted Paul as he hopped off the stage, ran to the jukebox, and played Knuckle Puck's *Pretense* as loudly as the machine could. A massive brawl erupted between the punks, goths, and emos, and the church members, who, of course, stood no chance. As his congregants were knocked to the ground and fell unconscious, Reverend Skink stared with a gaping mouth, not believing what he was seeing.

"Oh, shit," said Barillo. "Come on, Varco, Marcus, let's bounce these religious nuts out of here. They started it."

Barillo, a grizzled career detective; Varco, a young man filled with vigor; and 'Tit Boudreaux, a swamp-dwelling alligator wrestler had no problems throwing the conscious church members out and dragging the unconscious ones out to the parking lot, much to the cheers of the regular bar customers, who all calmed down immediately once the irritants were removed.

The Reverend Methuselah Skink remained alone on the stage, so Barillo approached him and waved his badge. "Come on; you're leaving too."

"*For no hunchback or dwarf shall draw near to offer the bread of his God!*" insisted Skink.

"I...what?" said Barillo. "Look, Reverend, don't make me drag you out. You look brittle."

Skink shouted, "A talking donkey! A talking donkey!"

Barillo, confused, nevertheless grabbed his arm and pulled. Skink purposefully fell onto the ground and shouted, "The centurion abuses me! Begone, Satan! *He that pisseth against the wall!*" as Barillo dragged him along the ground and out of the bar.

Mary got back up on the stage and took the mic. "Well, that was fucking something!" she said to cheers from the crowd. "Um, yeah, so, let's get Wicked Perverts back up here to continue their show!"

The band played on, and by the end of the night, Lâmié was pleased with the profits. Mary paid the band, and by four o'clock in the morning, the bar was empty, and everyone was ready to go home.

"Well, I'll be damned!" exclaimed 'Tit Boudreaux. "A whole night without a mass slaughter? Can't say it was a normal night, but I'll take a brawl with a weird religious cult over a bloody massacre any night!"

No one could disagree.

CHAPTER 11

Mourning Exorcise

Swami Maitra shook a sleeping Apadebata at six o'clock in the morning. She yawned, opened her eyes, and frowned.

"Guru Maitra, it is Sunday. Why are you waking me up? It's the day off!"

"Hush, girl," said Maitra. "I know what day it is. There is no day off for now. We must train you immediately. The goddess Durga has told me that our...*your* service will be needed very soon in the West. I do not know what that means, only that we must obey the goddess. This means it is time for you to learn your purpose and how to carry it out."

His words seemed to grab Apada's attention. She yawned only once more, then stood up to put on her clothes. She no longer even cared if Swami Maitra saw her in her underwear or even nude. He was like her grandfather and viewed her as a granddaughter, like family.

"I will make breakfast for everyone, Swami," she said factually and did not wait for a reply. Instead, she walked into the kitchen and saw that the two other girls, Abheer and Gayana, and the three boys, Iraj, Jagravi, and Kaling, were already sitting on the floor around the low table. Iraj smiled at her, and she blushed and looked down.

"Everyone up this early?" asked Apada. "Did the world end, and I didn't hear about it?"

Iraj chuckled and said, "Swami told us that you must have

training today, so we've decided to do the cooking for you today. It's not fair for you to have no time off ever."

"I...that's so nice," she said with a smile.

"Yes, yes, now you sit down, Apada," insisted Abheer. "We made some *panta bhaat* since we know that's your favorite breakfast."

"Oh, how lucky am I?" Apada said as the other students set out the bowls filled with the fermented rice delicacy with onions and chili peppers. The pungent sour-sweet aroma filled the room quickly, and Apada salivated. Finally, Maitra sat, and they began to eat.

While the students chatted and bantered—and Iraj subtly flirted with Apada—Maitra chewed silently, contemplating. Then, after a few minutes, he spoke, and the students became silent to listen.

"Today, students, I must reveal Apada's purpose to her and to you as well. The goddess Durga has declared it so. However, in order to do so, we must take a walk to the other end of the neighborhood, where it is said a young woman has been taken by a demon."

The students looked at one another quietly, clearly afraid of the word *demon*.

"Do not be afraid, children," assured Maitra, "for the goddess is with us and will never leave us powerless against the demons."

They finished breakfast under an anxious pall, then returned to their bedrooms to bathe and prepare for the day.

―――――― ++++ ――――――

Sunday in the neighborhood meant more people off work than usual, so in the fresh light of the morning, all of the streets' sounds, colors, and smells were featured in bas relief.

They reached a modest stone dwelling at the end of a small alley. There was no fanfare, no crowd—very unusual for India—outside the door: only a sad-looking man.

"Swami, you have come." The man bent down and touched Maitra's feet, then touched his hands to his own face. "Please, come in."

Maitra, Apada, and the other students crowded into the small, one-room house with a dirt floor. Similar to Maitra's first encounter with a demon, the possessed young girl sat on the floor, and her siblings and mother sat around her. The father sat down behind his daughter.

As soon as Apada entered the room, the girl's eyes flew open, revealing only her whites, and she sucked in a wheezy gulp of air. Then,

HELL'S BELLS: A PUNK ROCK DEMON STORY

she spoke in a gravelly, profound voice.

"The chosen one! She has come to torment us before the appointed time! Leave us alone!"

Apada just stood silently, marveling at the scene before her. She felt a warm tingling in her stomach, arms, and hands, but she did not understand what was happening.

The possessed girl lay down supine, then arched her back upwards, reaching an unnatural angle so that only her fingers and toes touched the ground. Apada flinched, feeling uncanny fright and knowing that, whatever her role in the exorcism might be, she was absolutely not ready for it.

"Kneel before her, Apada," instructed Maitra, and she obeyed externally, but inside of her was a war of emotions. She was shaking, almost paralyzed with fear, but she also wanted desperately to please Maitra.

The possessed girl spewed out of her mouth a thick, black wad of spittle, and some of it landed on Apada's hand. It burned, so she quickly rubbed it off on the dirt floor. The room was silent, but not for long.

The possessed girl crab-walked across the little hut and, like a small and light spider, skittered up the mud-brick wall and onto the ceiling. She looked down to reveal a face transformed from that of an Indian girl to some sort of wrinkled, sharply-angular beast. She growled and barked like an animal, then dropped down directly on top of Apada!

Apada screamed, and the girl began to try to bite her face. Her jaws snapped like those of a hyena right above Apada's nose. She tried to push the girl off her, but the girl's strength was greater than it should have been.

Iraj grabbed the girl by the arms, then drew them behind her back so that he had control of her. Apada's heart raced; she was stricken by mortal dread, and felt like, had the girl been able to bite her face, she would have taken Apada's soul.

"Hold her just like that," said Maitra calmly to Iraj. Jagravi and Kaling joined him in restraining the thrashing girl, who was growling and drooling a thick foam.

Maitra handed Apada a scroll of the Atharva Veda and pointed to the exact same prayer that his own Guru Ganguly had spoken so long ago.

Apada, shaking, began to read the prayer, at first in a weak and trembling voice, but as she continued, she could feel the goddess Durga swelling inside her, emboldening her with great courage:

Nissâlâ, the bold, the greedy demon, and the female demon with a long-drawn howl, the bloodthirsty; all the daughters of Kanda, the Sadânvâs do we destroy!

We drive you out of the stable, out of the axle and the body of the wagon; we chase you, daughters of Magundî, from the house. In yonder house below, there the grudging arâyî shall dwell; there ruin shall prevail, and all the witches!

May Rudra, the lord of beings, and Indra, drive forth from here the Sadânvâs; those that are seated on the foundation of the house.

She did not even have to finish the entire text. The possessed girl started to undulate and writhe like a snake, shrieking at a pitch and in a voice so grating and high that everyone but Apada covered their ears and winced.

"Hold her down!" commanded Maitra, but the boys struggled to keep her in place, so strong was the demon.

"Leave us alone!" screamed the girl to Apada in the deep, gravelly voice of several demons.

"Ask the demon its name!" instructed Maitra.

"Demon!" demanded Apada in a tone of voice foreign to her thus far, an authority that welled up inside of her for the first time at that very moment. It was certainly the influence of Durga. "I command you: tell me your name!"

"Noooooo!" squealed the demon.

"Tell me your name, now! By the power of the goddess Durga!"

At the mention of Durga's name, the demon cried out in a booming, deep voice, "Kabandha! I am Kabandha!"

Even Swami Maitra looked shocked. He began to advise Apada, but she did not need it. Instead, she straightened her back and raised her chin defiantly, which was rare for Apada, as she had always been a taciturn and humble girl.

Then, she spoke with great authority. "Kabandha, demon-eater of flesh, ugly beast, the goddess Durga commands you to leave this girl! Leave her body now!"

The sound of a flute playing harsh and discordant music filled the air, and as the girl thrashed about on the floor, she gave one final cry, and then a cloud of black smoke shot out of her mouth and out the house. She sat up exhausted.

"Mommy? Daddy? Where am I? What happened?"

The hut was filled with the sweet smell of incense from above, and a clear and pure peace filled the hearts of everyone present. Apada, still panting, smiled.

"Bless you and your family, father," said Maitra. "We leave you in peace. Your daughter is free of the demon."

"Wait, Guru! Let me pay you something!" insisted the man, but Maitra refused.

"No, no, it is the gift of Durga. If you want to thank her, make an offering at her shrine. Bless you!"

The man smiled while the mother and the siblings hugged the girl and cried tears of joy. Apada felt like she wanted to stay and celebrate with the family, but Maitra seemed eager to leave. He led his students outside, and as they reached a small plaza, he paused to speak to them.

"Now, you have seen the gift of Durga to Apada. This is Apada's purpose in life, to fight the demons who possess the innocent. What do you think of this, Apa?"

"It felt natural, Swami. I even knew what to say, as if Durga herself were inside of me!"

The other students watched Apada with admiring wonder. Iraj's eyes were wide and sparkling as they gazed upon the object of his love.

"What do we do now, Swami?" he asked.

"Now, grandson, we await the messenger of Durga, who will instruct us further. The goddess has told me that Apa's ability will be needed very soon."

As Swami led them through the now-packed streets back toward the school and temple, they saw a filthy, sickly, aged, blind beggar sitting on the side of the road. As they passed by, the beggar reached out and touched Gayana's calf.

"Do not touch me, you filthy old man!" she protested.

Swami Maitra whacked her behind with his walking staff. "Gayana! Have I taught you nothing? The gods do not look upon a person's outward form, but his inward soul! Now give alms to this beggar, or I will whack you again!"

Gayana grumbled a little, but she reached into her pocket, took out a 100-rupee note, and tossed it into the blind man's basket. The man nodded and thanked her, then looked toward Swami Maitra with unseeing eyes and said something in a language that none of the students understood.

Maitra looked shocked for a few seconds but composed himself and replied in the same language. The two men spoke for several moments, then Maitra gave the man 10,000 rupees, bowed to him, and led the students back to the school. They sat in the main lounge room.

"Swami," asked Kaling, "what was the language that that beggar spoke?"

Maitra sighed, then replied, "It was such a shock to me. That man spoke Sanskrit, and not the modern language. He spoke fluently the classic Sanskrit of our most ancient ancestors and gods. No one speaks that language today but for a handful of the most educated Brahmin in India, and the majority can only read it."

"But you speak it, Swami?"

"I do. How that beggar learned it? There is only one way. No such man could be so educated. The only way is that the goddess has spoken to him. He is a prophet."

The students looked at one another in amazement.

"And Swami," asked Apada, "what did the prophet say?"

Maitra looked at her and nodded gently for a moment before answering, "He said that we are needed in the USA, in the city of New Orleans. We are to travel there, and there we will meet a man of strange hair and clothing who will show us what must be done. He said the goddess Durga will lead the strange man to us."

The students looked excited, and Abheer asked, "We are going to America, Swami?"

"Ah, granddaughter, we cannot all go. It would be much too expensive, and also, someone must be here to tend to the temple and the school!"

The students sighed and complained in disappointment.

"Don't complain!" said Maitra loudly, silencing them. "Do you think this is a fun tourist trip? Do you think we will see all the landmarks and sights? Do you think that we will taste all of the delicacies of the land? No, this is a hazardous, deadly trip. We are going to fight demons! You should recoil from such a trip! Now, I will go, and Apada will go, as this is her purpose. We will need another student to attend to us and assist Apa in her mission. Who will go?"

After his description of the trip, they were hesitant to volunteer. They all looked at the ground and avoided raising their hands, but at last, Iraj looked up and saw Apada looking at him already.

He could not contain a smile and raised his hand. "Swami, I will go."

CHAPTER 12

Slick Oil Lamp

"A priest, a pastor, a rabbi, and an imam walk into a bar..." said Rabbi Shlomo Cohen, and the other three religious leaders laughed. Early on a Saturday morning, Cohen, Father Barry Woodrow, Reverend Don Malbrook, and Imam Mohamed Riyad were standing among the tented booths that had been erected on Jackson Square, in the space between the St. Louis Cathedral and the inner park that housed the statue of Andrew Jackson on his horse.

With permission from the New Orleans Police Department, each religion had set up its main booth, and several other tables and displays peppered the space. The New Orleans Interfaith Council (NOIF) had invited various religions from around the city to participate in what they had decided to name the Religions of New Orleans First Annual Street Fair.

Jackson Square was speckled with groups of tents and tables in a massive, overall festival of faith. The city leaders and the mayor were delighted to approve the idea, as it would offset the city's reputation as only being a place of drunkenness and debauchery and give a more human side to the ancient town. Well, the invitation had raced through the city like wildfire, and twenty-three different religious groups had signed up.

Notable groups with displays were the Church of Christ, the

Mormon Church, the Jehovah's Witnesses, the Methodists, and the Seventh Day Adventists. Even the Scientologists had a small booth in a corner, to the dismay of many.

Cohen walked around, chatting with the other displays and ensuring everything was in place and according to the city's guidelines. He was, after all, the head of NOIF and thus responsible for the festival running smoothly.

Even in the lecherous town of New Orleans and even in the morning after a Friday night, people were beginning to walk through the booths curiously. A few had started conversations, and thus far, none had slid into an argument.

Cohen looked at the Mormon booth and paused in surprise. Two Mormon missionaries who looked like brothers were behind the table, talking to Uri Horowitz, one of Cohen's congregants, and two young men and a girl who were clearly punk rockers. Mohawks, black leather jackets, plaid pants, piercings, metal spikes and studs, combat boots—these did not make it difficult to identify the three. The group was, to say the least, incongruent.

"Uri! Shalom!" said Cohen to the young Hasidic man.

"Rebbe Cohen, shalom! I was about to say hi to you. Sorry I couldn't volunteer for the synagogue's booth, but I had already promised my friends that I would help them out since I owed them a favor," he said in a sheepish tone. Then, he took a deep breath and squared his shoulders before continuing. "Rebbe, these Mormon elders are Aaron and Amos Brigham, and this is Paul Junk Roy, Mucky Matt Moulin, and Scary Mary Gambino. I'm in their band. We're called the Gravediggers. As you can see, we play punk rock."

Cohen shook his head with a smile and said, "Full of surprises are you, Uri! Always full of surprises! Nice to meet you all. Shalom. And you two," he said, nodding to Aaron and Amos, "thanks for signing up for the fair. The more, the merrier, you know!"

The two innocent boys nodded and smiled, unsure what to say to a rabbi. They were still getting over the clothing and hair of the Hasidim, much less able to hold a conversation with people so different than they were accustomed to.

"'Sup, mate," said Paul. "Your Uri here's one hell of a bass player."

"Oh, hush, you," protested Uri.

"The things you learn!" proclaimed Cohen. "Oy! Well, I will have to hear you play soon."

Paul and Mary looked at each other, and Mary said, "Well, since you mentioned it, we're going to play a show this coming Saturday night. Our last one, well, had a little glitch, but this one should go smoothly. But Rabbi, you sure you want to be seen in a punk bar with people like us?"

Cohen made a brushing-away gesture with his hands and said, "Like you? Feh. Don't badmouth yourself like that, young lady. We're all just people trying to make our way through this strange and dark world, right? You may not know this about Hasidism, but we are big believers in song, dance, and joy. It's kind of our thing. You might be surprised!"

Matt said, "Well, damn straight then! It's called The Gutter Bar. Uri knows where it is. Saturday night. The Sabbath's over by then, right?"

"Sundown Friday to Sundown Saturday," explained Cohen," is the Sabbath. I assume your show starts after sundown, so it's no problem. Me? I'm open to new experiences."

"Um, Mister Paul?" asked Amos.

"Jesus, it's just Paul, man."

"Oh, um, Paul? I need to go to the bathroom, and so does Aaron. Could you, like, tend the display booth while we go?"

"Yeah. Go have a nice piss."

The boys winced and left the Hasid and the punks to preach Mormonism. The missionaries walked into Henry's Diner on the corner and relieved themselves. On the way back, they decided to look around at the other booths, purposefully skipping the Jehovah's Witnesses, their mortal spiritual enemies. Finally, they reached Imam Mohamed Riyad's Islamic display.

"Hello, boys!" said the imam. "Take a look! Do you know much about Islam?"

"Um, no, Sir," said Aaron.

"We're sort of not allowed to study other religions," added Amos.

"It's alright, boys. I understand. But Islam's not what you think. It's probably not what you've been taught. You might be surprised! Why not just take some pamphlets? Here."

The Mormon brothers looked a bit uncomfortable, but they

accepted the pamphlets out of politeness.

"And go check out the merchandise table. There are some cool items from Egypt and other Middle Eastern countries!"

"Oh, that actually sounds cool," said Aaron. "I like interesting items like that."

They walked over to the sales table and looked at the many items there: scarab beetle pendants and sculptures, hookahs (which they carefully pretended not to see), bottles filled with intricate sand-sculpted scenes, brass vases, and finally, an antique oil lamp. It was long with a tapering tip and a handle, looking like something from an Alladin movie. It was made of brass that was oxidized into a brilliant turquoise hue.

"Aaron, check out this lamp!" said an excited Amos.

"Now that's cool," agreed Aaron.

The beautiful young lady manning the merchandise booth, whose olive, Arab skin contrasted with her straight, flowing black hair and delicately-carved facial features, noted their interest.

"Isn't it beautiful and interesting?" she asked.

"Yes, it's really nice," answered Amos. "It looks just like Alladin's lamp."

The lady smiled and said, "Who knows, boys? Maybe you will rub it, and a Djinn will come out and grant you wishes!"

The boys looked at each other, a little worried about the magical talk, which would be frowned upon by the Mormon church.

She picked up instantly on their concern and laughed. "Just a little joke, my friends." She did not say anything more in order raise the anticipation in the mercantile seduction. She was a real pro.

"Oh? What's the story?" asked an excited Amos.

"You want to hear? Alright, I guess I can tell you. The lamp is an antique, created by artisans in an ancient culture that is now lost beneath the shifting sands of the desert."

The boys listened in wide-eyed wonder.

"Well, my grandfather, a famous archaeologist in Egypt, was doing a dig in the Kings Valley when he came across this lamp. Buried along with it was an inscription saying that this very lamp belonged to a very important and ancient king named Ozymandias.

"So powerful and renowned was this great king that all of the neighboring kingdoms feared and respected him, and they would pay him tribute every month! This lamp was the first artifact ever discovered that proved the existence of Ozymandias and his great kingdom!"

"Wow..." whispered Aaron.

"Oh man..." whispered Amos.

"You two boys look like just the ones to own this important piece of Arab history."

"How...how much does it cost?" asked an awed Amos.

"Well, as you can imagine, such an important and rare artifact would be very expensive. Priceless, in fact! But, you seem like such nice young men that I would offer it to you at a great price, say, three hundred dollars only!"

The brothers looked disappointed.

"We...we don't have that much money," opined Aaron.

"Oh? How sad," lamented the woman. "How much do you have?"

Amos, the rube, pulled out his wallet and opened it. He counted the bills. "We only have seventy-five dollars."

"Hmm. What a great, great discount you are asking me to accept! I hope you know that, if I were to sell it to you at that low, low price, you would have to absolutely *promise* me that you would take the best care of it, that you would polish that tarnish away to a bright shine, and that you would give it the greatest place of honor in your home, you know, to honor the memory of my dear grandfather."

The boys nodded eagerly.

"We would! We promise! Oh, please sell it to us!" said Aaron.

The woman rubbed her chin for several moments, building up the anticipation. Finally, she sighed and then shook her head.

"Sorry, boys. That price is just too low. I can't accept it."

"Oh, please! Please, ma'am! We'll take the best care of it!" pleaded Aaron.

After several more quiet moments of thought, she said, "Alright. Fine. You've convinced me. I will sell it to you for seventy-five dollars, not a penny less! You drive a hard bargain, boys! You are quite the negotiators!"

"Oh, thank you!" said Aaron. "We're so lucky!"

She turned around to wrap it in paper with a sly grin on her face that the boys could not see. "Here. Be *very* careful with it, please. It is very ancient, very rare, and very valuable!"

"We will! Thank you again!" they said after having the lamp in their hands; they then strolled back to the Mormon display with enormous grins on their faces.

"What the hell are you so happy about?" asked Paul. "Did you meet a girl or something?"

"No! Nothing like that," said Amos. "We just found this really cool antique lamp at the Islam merchandise table."

"May I see?" asked Uri.

Amos looked uncomfortable but agreed. "Please just be very careful with it. It's an ancient relic of a lost kingdom."

Uri unwrapped the paper and looked at the lamp. He looked at the bottom, squinted, and frowned. "Um, how much did you pay for this?" he asked.

"The price was three-hundred dollars, but we worked her all the way down to seventy-five!"

"Oy vey!" declared Uri, trying to stifle a laugh. "Um, good job, guys. I hope you enjoy it."

Then, a towering, wraith-like, naked man who looked like he had not bathed since the American Revolution walked into the clearing in the middle of all the display booths. The crowd parted like the Red Sea. Women screamed and men bellowed at the sight of the man.

The Gravediggers heard the commotion and cries of shock, so they ran over to see what was happening.

Usually, a naked man would be nothing out of the ordinary for New Orleans, and no one would even have batted an eye. But something was very different about this particular crazy person: he was on fire! Even stranger, the Reverend Methuselah Skink—whose church had opted not to set up a booth at the fair—was walking calmly behind the flaming man as if it were perfectly normal.

"What the fuck?" yelled Paul, pointing to the burning man, who, although entirely ablaze, was not being consumed by the fire.

Father Woodrow turned and stared at the man, then snapped out of his daze. "Someone call nine-one-one!" he yelled at no one in particular.

Reverend Malbrook ran out from behind his Baptist booth toward the fiery figure and shouted, "It's a miracle! It's like Moses and the burning bush! *There the angel of the Lord appeared to him in flames of fire from within a bush. Moses saw that, though the bush was on fire, it did not burn up!* This is a sign from God, brethren!"

Rabbi Cohen shook his head and looked again to make sure he

was seeing reality.

He said, "That man needs help! He's dying!"

"This man is not dying, as you might think, my brothers and sisters!" shouted Reverend Skink. "No, but hearken unto me, the prophet of God! Behold and wonder! This man is on fire, but he does not burn up! It is indeed like Moses and the burning bush! This is a miracle, a sign for you all to know and believe that I, the Reverend Methuselah Skink, am truly his prophet. The one true church is the People's Family of the Divine Blessing!"

"That fucker is everywhere!" said Paul.

"No shit," said Mary. "Something's really fishy here."

As the Gravediggers and the Mormon brothers watched in disbelief, people began to surround Skink, fall to their knees, and shout *Amen!*

"He's a prophet!"

"It's a miracle!"

"God is speaking to us!"

"Is he the second coming of Jesus?"

Skink merely smiled, nodded, and extended his arms as if to embrace the entire crowd metaphorically.

"Oh, for fuck's sake," said Paul. "What a fucking charlatan."

"Come, my children! Come! Follow us to the People's Family of the Divine Blessing, where we shall worship God and thank him for his miracle. You shall see even greater miracles, signs, and wonders than this!"

Many visitors to the street fair dropped what they were doing and began to walk behind Skink, following his path, like a throng of disciples following Jesus through the desert.

Even Reverend Malbrook was in the crowd, walking behind Skink and lifting his hands in praise. Rabbi Cohen, Father Woodrow, and Imam Mohamed Riyad called to Malbrook, begging him not to be led astray, but he would not hear it.

"Oh, come on! Oy vey!" cried Uri. "This is absurd!"

"Or is it?" asked Abe, who had appeared almost out of nowhere and had sidled up to Uri. "Surely you believe in miracles, Uri? God has done many miracles in the history of our people."

Uri placed his hand on his forehead and said, "Yes, yes, Abe, but the miracles were to our people, not to some weird cult hack, and not for the glorification of man, but of God!"

"Hmm," said Abe in contemplation. "Perhaps, but can a man be on fire and not burn?"

"Yes, he can, and sorry for interrupting," said Matt, who had stepped into the conversation. "They do it in movies and circuses all the time. You rub some fire-resistant jelly all over yourself, then use a fuel with a low burn point that's not that hot to begin with. Hollywood does it all the time."

Abe nodded and rubbed his chin, then pulled on his payot. "Alright, that's true," he admitted. "But what if I said I have seen real, incontrovertible miracles lately, right here in New Orleans and in our synagogue?"

"Are you serious?" asked Uri. "Now this, I have to see. Alright, Abe. You're an observant Jew. That I know. So, show me these miracles, and I will believe you."

"Perhaps I can soon. Perhaps."

"Oh, for fuck's sake. What fresh hell is this?" Interrupted Paul. Aaron and Amos covered their ears.

Mary, Matt, Uri, Abe, Aaron, and Amos turned to see what Paul was looking at.

Walking across Jackson Square from the direction of the Pontalba building was an old Indian man in white *angarkha*. Next to him was an Indian girl who looked to be in her teens, wearing a bright blue and pink *sari* with a red dot in the middle of her forehead. Finally, on the other side of the older Indian man was another Indian boy about the girl's age, who was dressed in a white and tan *dhoti*. All three were barefoot, and the girl wore anklets and rings on her toes.

"What the ever-loving hell?" muttered Paul. "And yeah, of course, they're coming toward us. Does this shit never end?"

Just as Paul had predicted, the three Indians approached the Mormon table. The old man thrust his chin toward Paul and whispered something to the girl, who nodded.

"And...of course, it's me," muttered Paul.

The two young people stopped, and the old man walked directly in front of Paul. He placed his palms together, put his fingertips under his chin, and nodded.

"Namaste!"

Paul awkwardly put his hand out, then retracted it, then bowed, then tried to make the Indian greeting but ended up poking himself in the nose. "Um, yeah. That," he said.

"Pardon us for bothering you, Sir!" said the man. "I am the Guru Maitra, and these are two of my students, Iraj and Apadebata." The two teens bowed and offered their hands in the *namaste* greeting. "Good Sir, the goddess Durga has told us, through her blind prophet, that we are to seek you to defeat a great demon threatening the world."

Paul looked at Mary, then at Matt, then at Uri, then shook his head and said, "Yeah, why the hell not?"

CHAPTER 13

A Drink of Djinn

'Tit Boudreaux had never made a single Indian dish before, so he began with a simple curry with rice. Nervously, he brought it out into the grand parlor of Lâmié's mansion and presented it to the usual gang, now including Swami Maitra, Apadebata, and Iraj. The three Indians smiled.

"Oh, this is very kind, Mister Boudreaux!" exclaimed Maitra. "This curry looks and smells lovely! How kind of you!"

'Tit Boudreaux blushed and placed a large banana leaf in front of everyone.

"Um, what the hell am I supposed to do with this leaf?" asked Paul.

"Oh, allow me to demonstrate, Mister Paul!" said Maitra.

The guru picked up a small ball of rice with his right hand, dipped it in the curry, held it over the banana leaf, then placed it in his mouth. Apada and Iraj followed suit.

"We Indians enjoy eating with our hands!" explained Iraj. "It adds a new sense, a new dimension, to the enjoyment of food. Not only smell, sight, and taste, but also touch! You know the food's texture."

Paul shrugged and imitated Maitra, but with his left hand. The Indians snickered.

"What? What? I did what you did!" complained Paul.

"Oh," said Apada with a giggle, "you did not know, Mister Paul. You see, in India, we, um, well, we use our left hands for *something else*, so we eat only with our right hands."

Paul raised his eyebrows and said, "You use your left hand for *what* exactly?"

The three Indians blushed and looked down.

"They use it for wiping their asses, you idiot!" said Matt.

"As Mister Matt has so delicately phrased it, yes," said Maitra with a wide smile.

Paul coughed and said, "Oh."

"Um, Swami?" began Lâmié. "I'm happy to have you for dinner, but I think we should discuss what you said earlier, that you came to get our help to fight demons. That sounds…disturbing."

Maitra smiled and said, "Ah yes, I forgot how Americans always want to get right down to business. Very well." He took another bite of curry, and after finishing, he spoke, "I am a servant of the goddess Durga. I upkeep her shrine, which is next to my school. Apadebata and Iraj are two of my students.

"When I was young, like these two, my own Guru taught me my purpose on this earth: to fight demons and cast them out of the poor, suffering souls they inhabit. Well, just as the seasons turn, I have grown old, so I must pass down that great responsibility and duty to another. Durga has made it clear to me many times over the years that Apada is the one who shall take my place."

Apada rubbed her neck uncomfortably and looked down at her banana leaf.

"She performed her first exorcism recently, and indeed, she drove out the demon with a force and confidence rarely seen. Truly, Durga is within her."

Paul finished his curry, tore off a piece of the banana leaf, and started to put it into his mouth. Mary yanked it out of his mouth and shook her head.

"On the way from that exorcism back to the school and temple, a blind prophet spoke to me and told me to come here, to New Orleans, and to seek out the man with strange hair and clothing. Your city is full of such men, so I had to consult Durga again, and she led me directly to you, Mister Paul, and your friends."

Paul began to ask a question, but Mary interrupted him and said, "Alright, Swami, so, let's say this is true. You know, the stuff about Durga and the prophet and Apada's divine purpose in life and all that crap. No offense intended. And *believe me*, we've seen enough of the supernatural to absolutely believe that demons are real. But what do *we* have to do with it? What could we possibly do? How could we ever do anything to stop demons?"

The smile fell from Maitra's lips, and he shook his head from side to side. "Not demons, Miss Mary. *Demon*. There is only one. Yes, there are many evil spirits that we call demons, but they are avatars. Behind them is one great evil, the source of all evil, the original evil."

"And what is that evil?" asked Mary.

"We do not know, to be honest," admitted Maitra. "But there is one, manifested as many."

A timid knocking came from the front door.

"God...nothing good ever happens when people knock on that damn door," said Lâmié with a sigh. "I'll get it." He stood up, walked from the grand parlor into the main hall, turned left, passed the grand staircase, then opened the door, expecting anything.

He saw Aaron and Amos Brigham. They were looking down at their open Books of Mormon and did not see that it was Lâmié.

"Hello, we're Elders Brigham and Brigham from the Church of Jesus Christ of Latter-day Saints. Do you have just a moment for us to talk to you about the good news of the gospel?"

"Guys, it's me," said Lâmié.

"The prophet Joseph Smith was—" Aaron began but stopped himself and raised his head to look at who was standing at the door. "Oh, Lâmié! Hi! Wow, is this your house?"

"Yep. Come on in. There's food if you're hungry."

The brothers looked at each other, unsure what to do, but Amos finally agreed, and they entered. Lâmié led them to the grand parlor. Their eyes and mouths widened when they saw the packed room and the Indians.

"Most of you know Aaron and Amos, our local friendly Mormons," said Lâmié. Then he introduced them to the three Indians.

"Boy, they never told us back in Utah just how diverse New Orleans is!" exclaimed Amos.

"We're talking about demons, lads," warned Paul. "Run now if you can!"

"Um, demons, you say?" asked Aaron.

"Got 'em in Mormonism?"

"Yes, even possession and all that!"

Apada and Iraj were eyeing the Mormons sidelong with a bit of suspicion, never having seen Mormon missionaries before.

"Curry, guys?" offered 'Tit Boudreaux.

"Um, wow, thanks, that's very kind…" stuttered Amos, "but I guess we're more meat-and-potatoes kind of guys, and we just ate."

'Tit Boudreaux shrugged.

Mary continued prodding Maitra. "So, um, Guru, if there's some great evil threatening the world, what in the world can we do about it? We're just a punk band, and our music's not even that good."

"Oy," interjected Uri.

Maitra smiled, nodded his head from side to side, then answered, "The goddess Durga has spoken to me, and she has told me that you must come back to India with us and battle with the demon Kali!"

"Wait," said Lâmié, "isn't Kali a goddess?"

"Not *that* Kali!" said Maitra. "Kali Maa, Mother Kali, is a goddess, yes, but there is another Kali who is a male demon. He is great and powerful, and according to Durga, he is somehow involved in this great demonic threat."

"Yeah, I dunno," said Matt. "I mean, we have a Poltergeist here, or maybe a demon, or whatever. But we're gonna need more convincing that there is a global demonic threat that we can do something about before we just shoot off to India. Why would Durga send you here, just to then send us all right back to India?"

Maitra beamed a smile and said, "There is no sin in asking for a sign from the gods! Durga will give you a sign soon enough. As for the logistics, well, who can know the mind of the gods? But, if I had to conjecture, I would say this. If I had simply telephoned you and told you the same, what would you have done?"

'Tit Boudreaux was scooting around the parlor, making sure that everyone's plates were full, darting back and forth between the parlor and the kitchen to retrieve more curry. The entire mansion inhaled and exhaled the spicy, pungent curry aromas.

"I suppose we would have hung up and laughed," replied an honest Lâmié.

"Yes," explained Maitra, "so, the goddess Durga knew that only in person could we convince you. Now, as to why we must be both in India, specifically Kolkata, and in New Orleans, the answer is simple. Both are ancient, spiritual cities, and as such, the demon has chosen them to appear in. Moreover, someone must be conjuring these demons, and they happen to be in Kolkata and here. How else could we possibly have achieved our task?"

"Well, Guru," said Lâmié, "it seems awfully complicated, but to be fair, all of the things we have had to face have also been absurdly complex. In the meantime, you, Iraj, and Apada are welcome to stay here in my house. No need to rent a hotel room when we have all this space."

"Oh, very kind! Very kind!"

Aaron and Amos excused themselves after half an hour; they had a quota of houses to visit to try to spread the word of Mormonism. They did their missionary work (with no positive results) until late afternoon, then returned to the small Uptown apartment that the Church had rented for them during their two-year tenure in New Orleans. They lived on the top floor of a three-story, old, wooden house—utterly foreign to anything they knew as an *apartment* in Utah. Even so, they found it agreeable and comfortable.

"No luck today," said Aaron as each boy sat on the sofa with a bottle of water in his hands.

"It's not luck, Aaron. It's God's work. He calls people to himself, and we're just the servants," said Amos.

"I know, I know," said an exhausted Aaron.

He pulled a can of Coca-Cola out of his backpack and opened it, the crisp crack of the carbonation filling the apartment.

"Aaron! What are you doing?" yelled Amos. "Caffeine's a sin! It's a drug!"

"Man, I'm not so sure anymore," admitted Aaron. "Look, I tried a Coke the other day, and nothing happened. It tastes good. I didn't get high or addicted or anything."

Amos frowned and said, "It's what the Church teaches, Aaron. Are you being influenced by New Orleans? We're supposed to be *in* the world, but not *of* the world."

"It's not like I'm getting drunk. Chill, man."

Amos was not happy, but he decided to try to change the subject and approach it again later. "Anyway, remember we talked about polishing the lamp from the street fair?"

Aaron looked at the coffee table on which they had placed their prized lamp. Neither of them could help to look at the piece of art every time they passed through the living room. Even through its tarnished patina, it held some sort of beautiful sway on them; it made them feel like they were truly *home*.

"Yeah, maybe we should polish it now," agreed Aaron. "I got some Brasso from the hardware store the other day, forgot to tell you. The guy said it's like magic for old brass."

He went to his bedroom and returned a few seconds later with a large, new bottle of brass polish and a clean kitchen cloth.

"The guy said to put some on the cloth, rub it all over the lamp, let it dry, then polish it off with a new, clean cloth."

"Seems easy enough," said Amos. "You wanna do it?"

Aaron nodded and began the process. Soon, the entire lamp was coated in a layer of brown polish and drying. The two brothers did not say much while waiting, as the soda scandal was still fresh in their minds and emotions. Aaron, however, did not refrain from enjoying the rest of his Coke.

"Alright, now I'm supposed to polish it."

He used a clean, new cloth and began to quickly rub the Brasso off in little circles. As he burnished the paste off, a brilliant, golden shine sparkled from the newly-exposed surface of the lamp. The New Orleans afternoon sun, waving its tentacled rays of heat and fire, reflected off each new inch of fresh brass, spraying dazzling little stars of flame all over the living room's walls as if they had installed a disco ball.

While Aaron continued to rub the lamp, the two brothers gazed at the walls and ceiling in awe, stupefied by the glory of the diffused and reflected light. Then, before either could speak, a black cloud poured forth from the lamp's opening at the end of its long neck. The smoky mass swirled around the living room until it gradually began to take shape.

As if actually from the Hollywood concept of a genie, the mass became solid. A fat torso with a long tail instead of legs trailed down into the lamp's opening. The face was that of a jolly, chubby, Arab man who wore a red fez hat with a tassel. Its skin was olive, and it wore a *thawb* extending to its torso's bottom.

"Ah, thank you! You've released me from the prison of the bottle! I've been in there for, let's see…" It counted on its puffy fingers, squinted at the ceiling, then said, "Five-hundred and thirty-two years!"

Aaron and Amos were stunned into silence.

"Boys? Don't forget to breathe! No need to be scared. Alright, so let's see, what am I supposed to say again? Oh, yes, alright. I'm a djinn. I think you call me a genie in your language, yes?"

Their eyes opened as wide as physically possible, and they just nodded without a word.

"Yes, so I'm a djinn. The whole genie in a bottle thing? Yeah, it's real. So, let's see if I remember how this works again. Half a millennium is a long time, as you can imagine. Oh, yes! I remember. Because you've liberated me from the bottle by rubbing it to a shine, I owe you, and the repayment is that I will grant you three wishes, whatever they may be. But, before you wish for anything, be careful because your words will be taken literally. There are always consequences when magic is used, even ancient, Arab magic like mine. Also, you don't have to decide now."

The boys looked at each other and then back at the djinn.

"Finally, do not ask my name because I will not tell you. And you don't have to decide your wishes now. I'm in your debt, and I'll be going around with you everywhere you go." The djinn smiled, crossed its arms, and nodded.

"I...I can't believe this," stammered Aaron. "We can wish for *anything*?"

"Aaron!" chided Amos. "We shouldn't do this. It just doesn't *feel* right. I don't think the Church would approve of this."

"*Anything*, Amos. Anything! Just think of what we could do with that kind of power!"

"I...I mean, could we maybe use it for good? To help people?" asked Amos.

"Yes! That's what I meant."

The genie had removed its tail from the bottle and was floating around the house, looking into every room curiously.

"So this is how people live five-hundred and thirty-two years later. Where am I, by the way? What kingdom is this?"

Aaron looked at Amos and replied, "It's...well, it's America. It's more of a republic than a kingdom."

"Oh, like Rome," the djinn said. "Well, I can't wait to see what sort of things man has invented in this time." It looked out of the kitchen window onto the street below and then whistled. "What are those things? Those...those chariots without horses?"

"Those are cars," explained Amos. "Wow, there's so much to show you. You can go out with us tomorrow. But, for now, it's almost time for dinner."

The genie nodded pensively, then said, "I'll tell you what, boys. I'll give you one, just one, on the house. You still get your three wishes, but I'm so grateful that you released me that I'm going to make dinner for you tonight."

As they watched in amazement, the djinn crossed its arms, said something in some ancient, long-forgotten language, and nodded purposefully.

Out of nowhere, a large table appeared in the living room, a table topped with innumerable dishes, each an absolute masterpiece of sight, smell, and presumably, flavor. The dishes came from all around the world, from all sorts of different periods of human history, from Ancient Greece to Medieval China to modern Persia, and everything in between.

As saliva dripped from their mouths, Aaron and Amos Brigham, the two Mormon missionaries, forgot about their mission and sat down at the table: they had accepted the gift of the djinn, and there was no turning back.

CHAPTER 14

Always Room for One More

Near the charred ruins of Ushaville, West Virginia, Beast Stalker the Cherokee was working on the small house he had built with his own hands. Having lived on his savings from his years running the former Wild Legends Bookstore, savings that were rapidly disappearing, he had decided that a house was real estate that would hold value, and he would have a place to live while he thought of how he would make a living.

Chief Cloud Mountain, still alive and thriving, would one day die, and at that time, Beast Stalker would become chief and be paid by the Cherokee tribe, both local and national. Until then, however, he had to find work just like any other poor slob, and on an Indian reservation near a small town that no longer existed, the prospects were not exactly numerous.

Beast Stalker sat on the porch of the almost-completed house and sipped tea. He looked out across the fields and piney woods while contemplating his future life as Chief. *Chief Beast Stalker*: he had to admit the title sounded great.

At that moment, the phone rang, so Beast Stalker stood from the porch and went to look for his phone, which he had placed on the kitchen counter. It was Chief Cloud Mountain.

"*Beast Stalker? Can you come by my house when you have time, maybe this evening? It's important,"* the chief said, speaking Cherokee.

"I'll be there, Chief," replied Beast Stalker in the ancient language.

He arrived at Chief's modest house around six that evening. Chief's wife answered the door and ushered him in. They always spoke Cherokee exclusively when no outsiders were around.

"Chief's coming, dear. Have a seat on the sofa, and I'll get some tea. You'll have dinner with us after Chief talks to you."

Beast Stalker nodded and sat in the living room. A couple of minutes later, Chief walked in with his cane. Physically, he was aging, but mentally, he was as sharp as a knife. Chief sat in his favorite chair across the coffee table from the sofa. He thought for a few moments. Then, as per Cherokee custom, Beast Stalker let Chief speak first.

"Beast Stalker, the ancestor spirits spoke to me last night."

Beast Stalker knew it was a serious matter if Chief had called him to talk the day after a vision.

"It's about our friends in New Orleans, the punk rockers."

Beast Stalker had kept in touch with the Gravediggers and their friends for the most part, but being so far away, he was not up to date with their lives. Still, he had endured so much with them that every time they talked, it was as if no time at all had passed.

"What is it, Chief?"

"In my vision, I was in a terrible, fiery place. I think it was like hell. Then, a very ancient ancestor came to me and pulled me out of the terrible place into a separate place that was like a beautiful, lush forest. It was like heaven."

Beast Stalker's eyes widened a bit.

"The ancestor then spoke to me in an older form of Cherokee, a form that very few people in the world would still understand. He told me that a great demon has been summoned by a wicked man who performs child sacrifice as offerings."

Beast Stalker frowned and shook his head at the mention of child sacrifice.

"This demon is a great threat to the world. It is insidiously weaving its way into many people's lives and awakening many other demons as well. For a reason unknown even to the ancestor, the demon believes that our friends, in particular the one called Paul, are a threat and must be killed and their souls damned."

Beast Stalker wrinkled his forehead and asked, *"But why Paul, Chief?"*

Chief thought for a moment, then replied, "*I do not know. I have always sensed something special about Paul, but I do not know. Every person comes into this world with a purpose. Perhaps his purpose is to fight this demon.*"

The two old friends sat for a few minutes in silence, each trying to grasp the meaning of the ancestor spirit's message. Then, finally, the chief's wife brought them tea.

"*What should I do, Chief?*"

Chief nodded and replied, "*Beast Stalker, you and I must go to New Orleans to help them fight the demon. The ancestors will tell us what to do once we are there. Can you call Lâmié and ask if we can stay with him? Didn't you say he has a large house?*"

⋅+ + +⋅

Three days later, Chief Cloud Mountain and Beast Stalker were knocking on Lâmié's front door. He opened it.

"Chief! Beast Stalker! Come in! Great to see you!"

He gave both men a big hug.

The two usually-reserved Cherokees smiled widely and nodded, then followed Lâmié to the grand parlor, where they found Isabella, Varco, Zoë, Barillo, Lâmié, Judy, Evelyn, Erin with little Grimbil, Paul, Mary, Matt, Titania, 'Tit Boudreaux, Siofra, Yarielis, Uri, Maitra, Apada, Iraj and of course the two cats, Baozi and Pidan. Lâmié had also asked Madame Who to be there in order to discuss the demon with the others. The Indians and the other new friends were introduced to the newcomers.

"Wow," said Beast Stalker. "That's…a lot of people. Are you sure there is room here, Lâmié?"

"Come on, Beast Stalker," said Lâmié. "This place is huge. Plenty of empty bedrooms still. You and Chief can be on the third floor, which has nice, large rooms and soft, comfortable beds. Paul, make yourself useful and carry their bags up for them."

Paul grumbled and took a swig of beer, but then he hefted the four suitcases up the stairs and selected two rooms. He climbed back downstairs and sat wedged up against Mary.

"Yeah," explained Lâmié, "and everyone here helps out with cleaning and taking care of the house in place of rent. In fact, 'Tit Boudreaux is really enjoying the cooking, and is becoming quite a great chef!"

Beast Stalker tried not to stare at Uri, as the Cherokee had never before seen a Hasidic Jew, nor did he notice Evelyn staring at his large, shapely, ochre biceps and his long, black, Indian hair. Evelyn's pale, Yankee face turned a deep crimson, and she tried to look away but could not.

"Wow, don'tcha know," she whispered.

The three subcontinental Indians were looking at the two American Indians with wonder.

'Tit Boudreaux said, "Chief, Beast Stalker, I cooked dinner for everyone tonight. I hope all y'all are hungry. I made a Louisiana Creole feast!"

"That sounds great," said Chief. "After dinner, I hope we can all sit down and discuss what has brought Beast Stalker and me here. We know it's a demon, but we need to discuss exactly what we are dealing with and what we can do about it."

Another knock came on the door. Lâmié, resigned to his fate, answered it and saw another Hasidic man.

"Oh, hello."

"Hi! I'm Abe. I'm a friend of Uri Horowitz. He told me he might be here? His father wanted me to pass a message along to him."

"Sure! Come on in. I'm Lâmié, and it's nice to meet you."

He led Abe down the main hall, past the grand staircase, then to the right into the grand parlor.

"Oh, wow. Full house!" exclaimed Abe.

"Abe!" said Uri happily. "You found me! Everyone, this is Abe. Obviously, he's Hasidic like me. He's from New York originally, but he studied recently in Israel."

"How exciting!" said Titania.

"What's your take on Palestine and Hamas, mate?" asked Paul.

Mary slapped him, and Uri and Abe pretended not to hear him.

"Abe, please stay for dinner," offered 'Tit Boudreaux. "I made a Creole feast, so you can get a taste of New Orleans, and don't worry; it's all kosher. I cooked with Uri in mind."

Abe looked a little embarrassed at the gracious offer. He grimaced and looked at Uri for help.

"Stay, Abe! Stay!" said Uri. "Always room for one more at Lâmié's house."

"Alright, alright, you've convinced me. Not exactly a hard sell!"

Abe sat by Uri, and as the conversation in the room picked up again, they seemed engaged in a rather lively discussion, complete with hands and arms in motion.

"Excuse us," said Uri. "We're going to step into a side room to talk about something. Don't worry; it's about the synagogue, nothing to concern you."

The two Hasidim walked across the main hall and into a side study. The reading room, or perhaps the boudoir of one of Lâmié's long-deceased female ancestors, was furnished with Victorian-Era furniture, including a desk and some chairs. The wallpaper was a deep crimson with a gold floral pattern, and one wall was completely bedecked with bookshelves overflowing with leatherbound classics. Uri sat in a leather chair, but Abe just leaned against the large, oaken desk.

"Alright, let's start again with some quiet and some privacy. Who found what where?" asked Uri.

"Your father. He went to help clean the synagogue for Sabbath services, and it looked like someone had broken in, messed things up, and tried to clean up. The *ner tamid* had even been broken and turned off."

"Oy vey!"

"The worst is that your father found some bloodstains around, again, like someone had tried to clean up but was in a hurry."

Uri pulled at his payot.

"That's not all, Uri. This symbol was scribbled in chalk right in front of the bimah. Your father sketched it and asked me to show you. He said you would understand?" He unfolded a piece of paper and handed it to Uri.

On the paper was Uri's father's sketch of the very same symbol that had been painted on the wall of his house.

"Oy. This can't be good."

"What is it?"

Uri handed the paper back to Abe. "That symbol was painted on my house the other night. I showed it to my friends here, and one of them recognized it as a demonic sigil, which is supposed to be the signature of a demon."

"Oy!"

"Come, come," said Uri while standing up. "We need to tell this to the others. But, don't worry; they know what they're talking about and believe in the supernatural. Maybe they can help?"

They returned to the grand parlor and Uri explained to the others.

"Not good, guys. Abe tells me that my dad went to help out in the synagogue, and found it ransacked with blood stains. This symbol, the same one I found painted onto my house, was drawn in chalk in the front."

He showed them the sketch of the symbol. Everyone was silent, hoping against hope that it was just a coincidence, but knowing full well that they were already in too deep.

"Well, can't avoid it anymore," said Paul. "Demons. Fucking demons. What a clusterfuck of a life we lead."

"Dinner first, before it gets cold!" insisted 'Tit Boudreaux, perhaps using food to try to change the subject that no one really wanted to dwell on, though they knew that they would have to address it. "And there are too many dishes to eat in the parlor. So, we're going to use the actual dining room this time."

"Fucking posh," muttered Paul.

They quickly made the place settings in the formal dining room, a long room with delicate, blue, fleur-de-lis wallpaper and elaborate gold-foil sconces and flourishes everywhere. The elongated table, crafted centuries before in Europe in rich, walnut wood, was now decorated with silken placemats and simple but elegant china.

"Geez," said Paul. "A little fucking above any pay scale here."

"Oh, how delightful!" exclaimed Swami Maitra. "A true Western table!"

Apada and Iraj, used to their humble school life in Kolkata, simply stared quietly at the spectacle.

Soon, an exuberant, proud 'Tit Boudreaux began making trips into the dining room with armfuls of dishes: gumbo, crawfish étouffée, chicken sauce piquant, shrimp Creole, jambalaya, red beans and rice, chicken fricassée, smothered pork chops, *truite à la meunière*, oxtail soup, dirty rice, smothered green beans, collard greens, and for dessert, bread pudding with a flaming rum sauce. For Uri, he had made a kosher version of each non-kosher dish. In addition, he had chosen several bottles of Château Margaux, and he had even found a bottle of 2000 vintage. He had done this with the help of some others, of course, but he was the chef, and the grand designer and cook of the fabulous feast.

"Christ, Marcus!" said Mary. "This is, like, way over the top."

'Tit Boudreaux shrugged and blushed a little.

They dined and dined, the rich, saucy, pungent flavors slathering the room in a bath of gusto, friendship, and warmth, a warmth enhanced by the wine.

The chandelier flickered.

"Damn," said Matt. "Bad wiring? I hope?"

The dozens of tiny light bulbs became three times as bright as they normally were, and an electric buzz filled the room. Next, the lights dimmed, then lit up bright again, then the bulbs exploded with a loud *zap*!

Everyone screamed, and Maitra dove under the table. Madame Who shrieked and crawled under a chair.

A bellowing growl came from a dark corner of the dining room, and as they all watched, too scared to move, a thick, black figure rose slowly from the floor all the way to the ceiling. The thing was more of a cloudy shape than a solid being, but they could make out two long, inwardly-curved horns on its head.

It laughed, a baritone, mocking cackle.

"Oy! This again!" said Uri. He stood up and began to pray in Hebrew. This time, however, the prayers did not seem to affect the demon but rather angered it. Its shady, indistinct form swelled even more until it hovered all around them and above them.

Maitra began to chant from under the table in Sanskrit, and Apada, shaking and stuttering, joined him. Their prayers seemed to cause the monster to shrink a little and recoil. Then, finally, it roared, a roar so loud and bass that the chandelier shattered, and then it changed form into an amorphous black cloud.

Madame Who, with a shivering voice, screamed something in Romani.

The dark cloud swept across the room toward Paul, who screamed, "Fuck!"

As his mouth opened, the cloud poured into the orifice and then disappeared. The room became lighter again, and the afternoon sun filtered through the windows.

"Paul!" said Mary, rushing to his side. "What happened? Are you okay? How do you feel?"

"Fucking scared as shit, but otherwise normal," he replied.

"But…it went inside of you!"

"That's what she said," answered Paul.

"Shit. I guess you *are* okay," said Matt.

"Whatever that shadow that went in my mouth was, it's nothing a good beer can't exorcise."

Maitra slowly climbed out from under the table and brushed himself off.

"Well, at least the food was good," said Matt.

Chief Cloud Mountain had observed the entire scene calmly and rationally, his decades of experience and wisdom setting the example for everyone else. Beast Stalker found Evelyn clinging to his arm tightly.

"Oh, er, sorry, Beast Stalker, don'tcha know!"

"It's, um, no problem."

Chief pushed himself up with his cane and began walking back to the grand parlor.

"Everyone, follow me," he said gently. "We need to discuss this."

With many of them still shaking, they all took a seat in the parlor. Paul passed around beers to everyone, and no one refused. Baozi and Pidan, who had fled the dining room during the demonic visit, crawled out from under the sofa and jumped on Judy's lap.

"It was indeed a demon!" proclaimed Madame Who with false bravado. "Madame Who needs more wine to properly assess the situation!"

"Alright," said Lâmié, "what do we know?"

"Let me begin," said Chief, and no one disagreed with the honored elder. "An ancient ancestor spirit spoke to me the other night. He told me that there was an ancient, mighty demon that had entered the world. Someone conjured him. I do not know which demon it is. That demon, for whatever reason, wants to kill Paul and the rest of you and take your souls."

"Oh, fuck me!" said Paul. "Why? Why me? Why always me?"

"We do not know," answered Beast Stalker. "Perhaps it is your…history…of fighting the darkness. The spirit world sees and knows these things. Everything we do here in the physical world causes a ripple effect in the spiritual world."

Swami Maitra took the liberty of producing a pipe, packing it with tobacco, tamping it, and lighting it. No one really seemed to mind after what they had just experienced. Curling tendrils of purple smoke wafted through the air up to the ceiling in a most curious yet satisfying manner.

"Yes, yes," began Maitra, "the blind prophet of the goddess Durga told me much the same thing. These friends, but especially Paul, are marked by the demon for a reason that is not specifically clear. However, we know that the key is that Paul himself must strive against the demon Kali near his temple in Kolkata. That is very important to defeat the demon. In defeating Kali, Paul must learn a great lesson that will aid him in his fight here."

The swami's pipe smoke filled the entire room with a purple haze. Baozi and Pidan purred loudly. Paul took a long swig of beer and shook his head in frustration, and Mary put her arm around him.

"May I add something?" asked Uri. "It seems clear to Abe and me that this demon problem involves us too. The sigil? The mess and the traces of blood in the synagogue?"

Matt yawned and said, "And don't forget the freaky Reverend Methuselah Skink and his crazy cult. They've just *gotta* be involved with this shit somehow."

"Oh, oh!" said Mary like an excited schoolgirl who had just come up with the answer to a math problem. "Don't forget Father Woodrow and the message on the wall of his office!"

"Oh, damn," said Lâmié. "I'd almost forgotten to tell you. I had asked Woodrow if he could stop by tonight and discuss this stuff with us. Unfortunately, he couldn't make it to dinner, but he said he'd come by at some point. I think he's sufficiently open to the paranormal, and at least he knows demons are real. He said he's busy, but he'd try to stop by if he—"

A knock came at the door.

"Good timing," said Lâmié. "Probably him."

It was indeed the priest. Lâmié led him into the grand parlor and introduced everyone.

"Sorry you're late, Father," said 'Tit Boudreaux. "You could've had dinner with us, but then again, you'd have missed the demon attack. I still have leftovers, though."

"Um, demon attack? Boy, after the fiasco at the religious street fair, we really don't need more, do we?"

'Tit Boudreaux made Father Woodrow a plate while the others explained what had happened.

"My goodness," said the priest with a mouthful of chicken and sausage gumbo. "This is serious. According to the literature and the theological tradition, it's very rare for a demon to manifest itself physically. It's only documented to have happened a small handful of times, usually in the absolute worst cases of possession or in cases of intense demon worship. Gumbo's amazing, by the way."

'Tit Boudreaux smiled while the others continued to listen intently to the knowledge of the learned priest.

"By the way, Uri and Abe, Rabbi Cohen showed me the sigil that's appeared on your house and now at the synagogue. So yeah, he told me about the synagogue break-in. I'm still unsure which demon's sigil it is, but I'm working on it."

"Padre," interrupted Paul with a mouthful of beer, some of which dribbled down his chin, causing Mary to sigh, "how're you gonna find whose sigil it is?"

"Well," explained Woodrow, "you basically go through every ancient and Medieval manuscript that describes them, and you try to match it to one of those. So don't worry—if it's real and in the manuscripts, I'll find it."

They all sat quietly (minus Woodrow's gumbo slurping) for a few moments, thinking about all of the crap that they had been forced to deal with.

Lâmié broke the silence. "Alright, so who's going to India? Unfortunately, we can't all go. Obviously, Paul, Mary, Matt, and Uri. I'll finance the trip, but international travel's not cheap, so maybe just a couple more?"

"Chief and I must go," said Beast Stalker. "The ancestor spoke to Chief for a reason and told us we needed to help you."

"Two kinds of Indians in India," said Paul, causing Mary to slap his arm.

"Racist, Paul!" she whispered.

"It's alright, Mary," said Beast Stalker. "We actually don't mind being called Indians, and we even use the term ourselves."

Paul stuck out his tongue at Mary.

"I'm not sure I'm up for international travel," said Chief. "I'm not the young man I once was. So, Beast Stalker, you should go, but I will stay here and try to contact the ancestors for more insight."

Lâmié said, "Alright, the Gravediggers and Beast Stalker will return to India with Swami Maitra, Apada, and Iraj. Whatever ends up happening there, if you three from Kolkata need to come back here for whatever reason, I'll pay for your travels."

Swami nodded his head from side to side with a wide grin and said, "Oh, thank you! So nice! So nice!"

Father Woodrow finished his gumbo, took a sip of beer (he was a Louisiana Catholic priest, after all), then looked very serious.

"Listen, everyone," he said. "Something you need to know about demons is that they are always extremely deceptive. In fact, Jesus called Satan *the father of lies*. So, any time you interact with a demon, it will lie to you and deceive you. Always. Every time. That's why, in the Catholic exorcism tradition, the exorcist is taught to never interact

HELL'S BELLS: A PUNK ROCK DEMON STORY

with the demon except for asking its name and when it will leave and commanding it to leave."

'Tit Boudreaux, with the assistance of Lâmié, served strong coffee with chicory to everyone as they listened.

"If you interact and converse with the demon, it will manipulate you, lie to you, attack your emotions and mentality. Demons know things about us, even secret things, and they will use those against us. They will try to shake us, so to speak, by what they say. In fact, that's the demons' main weapon. Physical attacks are extremely rare."

Paul shrugged sarcastically.

"Father, just a thought: want to go to India with the group? Your knowledge might be a big help," asked Mary.

"Hmm…I'll have to miss some Masses…I could get a fill-in for sure. I *have* always wanted to see India…"

"It's decided then!" exclaimed Lâmié. "You can join them, and it's on me."

Swami reloaded and relit his pipe, then said, "You will all stay with me at the school, of course! It's the least I can do to repay you all for your hospitality!"

"Er…oh boy," said Paul.

"Mister Paul," said Iraj, "I cannot wait to show you India and let you try our delicious food!"

"What about delicious beer?"

"Oh, we have that too!"

"All I need to know."

They all sat and talked until the evening, at which time Abe excused himself, as well as Father Woodrow. That night, everyone slept a fitful sleep full of terrible, vivid nightmares.

CHAPTER 15

Fly Me to the Tomb

On a certain weeknight, at midnight, in a large, crumbling, forgotten family crypt in the middle of Lafayette Cemetery No. 1, a brooding gathering of pale, lithe figures stood. The crowd faced a single girl who looked about fourteen or fifteen years of age. Her almond, partially-Asian eyes were painted across her delicate cheekbones, and her luscious, tempting lips were blood-red, offsetting her raven waterfall of hair. Young and delicate as she appeared, she was clearly in charge.

"My children," she spoke in an almost-liquid voice, "I have good tidings for you and a treat for later."

She nodded toward three burlap sacks behind her. Every once in a while, a sack would move, and a plaintiff but stifled cry would emanate from it.

"Since the goblins were driven from New Orleans and back into their dark and hollow halls underground, our kind has multiplied greatly. We have turned many promising humans into vampires, and now our numbers are like the grains of sand on a beach or the stars in the sky."

Cries of approval filled the old vault.

"There is more!"

The other vampires fell gravely silent.

"The amulet!" she said with a giddy waver in her voice. "I have located the amulet from Ushaville. The amulet with which I, *we*, my children, we will hold the greatest power, the power to mold the world into our image!"

The audience of vampires burst into roaring applause.

"With the amulet, we shall easily defeat the Gravediggers and their friends and take every city in the name of the blood drinkers. We will rule the world!"

Cheers and loud shouts of approval shook the dilapidated tomb.

"What I tell you now, you, my inner circle, must not repeat to anyone. Not yet. Do not spoil my plans, or…well, I know you would not dare. Now listen, my children: the amulet is in hiding with Chief Cloud Mountain, the chief of the Cherokee Indians in Ushaville, or should I say, where Ushaville used to be, before the Gravediggers burned it to the ground, along with countless numbers of our brethren."

Hisses and growls came from the other vampires.

"I do not know the specific location of the amulet, but I do know that a little time with the frail, old Chief, and a little *persuasion*, will reveal it."

"Lady Ophelia?" asked a male vampire from the middle of the group. "Didn't the Cherokee man Beast Stalker endure torture and refuse to give up the location of the amulet?"

Ophelia growled at the young vampire and screamed, "Do not challenge my abilities or persuasion! I will make the old man talk!"

The vampire lowered his head and remained silent.

"Does anyone else care to challenge my authority or my abilities?"

The tomb was utterly quiet.

"Good. Now, my faithful spies have told me that Chief and Beast Stalker are in New Orleans at this very moment, staying with the Gravediggers. We are going to get the location of the amulet from the chief. I suspect that ancient Cherokee magic is involved, so we will need the chief himself to clear that magic and lead us to the amulet. If that Beast Stalker gets in the way, we will kill him without hesitation. No more negotiation; no more bargaining; no more secretive machinations. This time, we kill when necessary, and we take the amulet by force!"

The vampires erupted into an excited roar.

"I will choose tonight which of you will accompany me to Ushaville, but first, I have a little treat for you, three of them, in fact."

She nodded at a female vampire in the front who walked to the burlap sacks and opened them one by one. From each sack, she pulled a young, Catholic altar boy, still in the ceremonial robes but bound and gagged. The three boys, maybe eight or nine years old, looked around terrified. They squirmed and struggled against the ropes that bound them, but to no avail. The crosses had been ripped from their garments.

"Such innocent, holy young boys, aren't they, my children? Such tender flesh and such strong, pure blood. Enjoy!"

At once, the crowd of vampires, fangs extended, flew upon the boys and began to tear into their flesh to get to their precious blood, which they guzzled with great gusto until the three altar boys were only dried husks of skin.

One of the benefits of aging, thought Chief Cloud Mountain as he lay in the soft, comfortable bed of Lâmié's luxurious guest room, *is becoming wiser; one of the downsides is that you become tired much earlier.*

These days, he could barely stay up past seven o'clock in the evening. He didn't mind, though, since he still woke up with the sun. His chiefly duties to the tribe still occupied most of his time, and he loved it that way.

He could honestly say that he had devoted his life to the People, and he knew that, when his day came, the ancestors would welcome him to the spiritual world and that he would be there with his wife. Then he would be among the spirits to advise the Cherokees still in the physical world.

Chief believed that he was ready for death whenever it would come. Like many Indian brethren, he viewed death as just as natural a part of life as birth, waking and sleeping, eating and defecating. Therefore, death was not to be feared, but welcomed, as it was only a transition to the next world.

These thoughts filled Chief's mind as he began to drift into that semi-somnolent state right between waking and complete sleep—right when one is aware of the waking world around him but is also beginning to see the dreams play out behind closed eyelids. At this stage, the mind is relaxed and open.

So, when Chief heard his wife calling to him, he readily accepted it.

HELL'S BELLS: A PUNK ROCK DEMON STORY

"Chief...Chief, it's me. I need to come in!"

Chief mumbled something unintelligible. In his proto-dream, he was in his living room, and his wife was outside the front door.

"Let me in...Chief, invite me in. Just ask me to come in..."

"Honey...is that you? Why are you outside?"

"Let me in...honey, invite me in..."

Something in Chief's reptilian brain tried to warn him that all was not right, but he could not resist his wife's call.

"Come in," he mumbled.

Only, it was not his wife.

In the uncommonly misty and foggy New Orleans night, outside the third-floor window of Lâmié's mansion, right outside Chief's bedroom, a pale wraith hovered.

The thin girl wore a black cape and hood, her moon-pale skin casting a faint, reflected glow in the obscure night. It was Ophelia.

She heard Chief's invitation, and that was all she needed. She quietly worked her delicate, elegant fingers to open the unlocked window, then floated into the bedroom as Chief fell further into the sleep cycle.

She softly alighted beside his bed and looked down at the old man. The human girl she had been thousands of years ago probably would have looked at him with pity. His frail frame, his bald pate, his seeming innocence—the ancient, human Ophelia would have felt something toward him, something akin to mercy.

The vampiress Ophelia, though, felt no such thing.

To her, he was only a piece of meat, a meal, a meaningless human beast, and, in this particular case, the key to finding the amulet.

Despite her anger at the vampire who had spoken out of turn the other night, she knew that Beast Stalker was indeed strong. He had endured physical torture, and her millennia of experience had taught her that almost no humans were capable of that. All of their lofty principles and altruistic beliefs always disappeared the moment that physical pain was applied. Humans were quickly broken, even the strongest of them, but not Beast Stalker.

She knew that if she tried again to torture him to give up the amulet's location, he would only be stronger. Men like that did not weaken and cower with adversity but only became greater and harder.

Chief? She suspected that his age would make him physically weaker, unable to bear the stresses of torture, and oh, what hell she had planned for him! She felt giddy at the thought.

Ophelia closed her eyes for a moment and tried to reach out and feel the house, just to see who was there. She felt a strong, spiritual presence somewhere below. Not good. Someone there was going to be a worthy enemy at another time. In any case, she had but one goal this night.

Tempted by the hunger-lust of her kind to bite into Chief's carotid artery and drink his ancient, wise blood, she had to force herself to resist. She could suck him dry later. She needed that information about the amulet.

In one, swooping motion, she threw her black cape over Chief, picked him up as if he were a sack of feathers, then flew out the window with him.

Chief woke up in the air, flying over the city of New Orleans. He thought that he was still dreaming. Someone was carrying him, holding him tight with cold, pale arms. As they descended into Lafayette Cemetery No. 1, Chief began to realize that it was no dream, but a living nightmare. They landed, and he saw Ophelia.

Stunned and a bit dazed, Chief managed to ask, "Ophelia. What do you want with me?"

"It's simple, Chief. I want the amulet, and you're going to tell me where it is."

She pulled him into a large crypt and slammed the stone door shut.

CHAPTER 16

Sweet Kolkata Rain

As the Gravediggers party walked through the Kolkata airport, the stares, pointing, and whispering were not subtle. Paul, Mary, and Matt were adorned in their traditional black leather, metal studs and spikes and piercings, Mohawk and spiked hair, combat boots, Doc Martens, and plaid trousers.

Uri, of course, sported his black overcoat, black hoiche hat, phylactery, beard, and payot. On the other hand, Beast Stalker wore fairly standard Western clothes: a Polo shirt and some black jeans. Still, over the shirt, he wore a tan, leather vest with some beads on a leather string hanging from it. Even in such a cosmopolitan city as Kolkata, a group of oddball foreigners like these was rare.

"God, everyone's staring," whispered Mary.

A family passed them and the little boy pointed at Paul and burst into tears.

"Good," said Paul. "That's punk!"

A group of college students walked past, looked at Uri, and began praying on their prayer beads.

"Oh, for fuck's sake," muttered Matt.

A businesswoman was drinking coffee, and when they passed, she spat it out of her mouth and yelped.

"Oy! This is awkward!" added Uri.

"Don't worry!" said Apada. "We just don't see many foreigners, and, well, not so many punks and Hasidic Jews. They don't mean any harm. It just means they're interested in you. Take it as a compliment."

"They must be hella interested, then," said Paul as he winked at an Indian girl, who gasped and looked down at the ground. Mary slapped his arm.

Father Woodrow, even in his priestly collar, went unnoticed. India had plenty of Catholics and people of every other religion imaginable.

Lâmié had pre-arranged a car and driver, and although he wanted to pay for a nice hotel, he knew it would be considered offensive to reject Swami's offer of everyone staying at his school.

As their driver slowly pushed through the overcrowded streets from the airport toward the school, the Gravediggers, Beast Stalker, and Father Woodrow were glued to the windows, staring in disbelief at the seething mass of humanity. This ocean encompassed from the starving and begging sea floor to the showy wealth of the tips of the waves.

The first thing that came to mind was *color*. Every building, house, shop, curb, and market was drenched in every hue and tone of blues and greens and reds and yellows and pinks and every other slight gradient of the rainbow.

Next, they were overwhelmed with the sheer number and variety of transports. Their own car, a simple, nondescript black sedan, was but one star in the infinite universe of vans, buses, handcarts, horsecarts, rickshaws, the ubiquitous and intrepid autorickshaws, the Rolls Royces of the very wealthy, and the bare feet of the very poor.

Shocking to all of them except the Indians were the sacred cows walking freely in and among the markets, the stores, the streets (blocking traffic), and the mysterious alleyways.

"This is just amazing," said Mary. "I've never experienced anything like this."

"Welcome to India!" said a grinning Swami Maitra.

They reached the school's very modest stone buildings, and Swami showed them to their rooms: each of them would have a small sleeping chamber with a soft cot on the ground.

"Er…" said Paul to Mary, but she just frowned at him.

"Don't be rude, Paul. It could be lots worse."

"If we were in federal prison, I guess…"

"Hush!"

Apada walked from room to room to check on everyone and tell them that dinner would be ready in an hour. Then, exhausted from the twenty-four-hour trip, they napped.

"Holy hell!" said Paul as he walked into the humble dining room and kitchen.

Any sub-standard ideas about the sleeping quarters were quickly quelled when everyone saw the dinner that Apada had prepared. The low table was overcrowded with innumerable dishes; the aromas, colors, textures, and visual presentations made love to their senses.

Apada explained the dishes to the Westerners. There was *masher jhol*, a spicy fish curry; *kosha mangsho*, luscious stewed lamb; *alur torkari*, potatoes in a rich tomato gravy; *cholas dal*, a spicy lentil stew; and at that point, they couldn't remember all of the other dishes, so many and varied as they were. These were, as always, accompanied by aged Indian rice, all flavors of naan bread, and at least five or six dessert dishes.

"My God..." said Uri. "I've never seen anything as wonderful as this..."

"I made sure there's plenty of kosher dishes, Mister Uri," said Apada. "And Mister Paul, there are many, many beers for you."

Paul grinned.

As they sat on the provided pillows on the ground and ate from their banana leaves, they experienced a culinary orgasm. Hours later, stuffed beyond what was reasonable, they retired to the common room to talk.

"Tonight," said Maitra, "I shall go and make offerings to the goddess Durga in her temple next to the school. Tomorrow, we must all go and offer prayers. Mister Uri, it is alright if you feel uncomfortable in the temple. I understand that you are very observant of your own religion."

"It's alright," said Uri. "All of these experiences are opening my mind to things. I will join you and the others in whatever you do."

"Same," said Father Woodrow.

After a surprisingly sound sleep on the humble floor-cots, they all woke up to a savory breakfast of *radha ballabhi*, a delicious flatbread stuffed with lentils and fried in mustard oil.

The Westerners had to acclimate to bathing from buckets of water and using toilets that were essentially holes in the floor, or even chamberpots. Still, no one complained because they were so well fed.

After breakfast and toiletries, Swami walked them all around the neighborhood as a sort of welcome tour and then wasted no time taking them to the temple of Durga next to the school. He insisted that they all remove their shoes.

Even Paul was impressed by the imposing radiance of the looming idol.

"Gotta ask, Swami mate," he said. "Why so many arms? Is she supposed to be an octopus or something?"

"Oh, the arms, yes," replied Maitra. "Many of our deities have multiple arms. The many arms represent the many aspects and functions of the goddess, and if you look, each hand holds an object. Each object has a significance to Durga's personality."

Deep in thought, Beast Stalker said quietly, "This is a very holy place. I can feel it strongly."

"Indeed, indeed!" agreed Swami. "Now, please kneel and meditate on the goddess as I utter the prayers.

Om Jayanti, Mangala, Kali, Bhadrakali, Kapalini.
Durga, Shiva, Kshama, Dhatri, Svaha, Svadha, Namostu Te.
Esha Sachandana Gandha Pushpa Bilva Patranjali Om Hreem
Durgayai Namah.

As Swami repeated the prayer several times, the Westerners could not help but fall into a state of meditation; they lost focus on their environment and became hypersensitive to their inner thoughts.

Paul's *inner thoughts* started as thoughts of beer, making out with Mary, and cute Indian girls. However, as the repetitive words droned on and on in his mind, he began to experience a sort of waking dream or a hallucination.

He found himself on the muddy shore of the Ganges River, somewhere near Kolkata. Looking down, he saw that he only wore a loincloth—he was shirtless and barefoot, and he could feel that his head was shorn. His entire body was smeared with a thin layer of gray clay and dirt. He held a human skull in his hand, but it did not seem to bother him. Three other men, also dressed like him and holding human bones, stood with him in a semi-circle.

Paul and the others surrounded a funeral pyre, on which were two people: a dead man and his living widow, who was bound by ropes to his corpse. She did not seem terribly distressed but rather had a look of serenity and satisfaction.

Several yards away, a large crowd of Indians stood and watched, expressions of disgust on some of their faces. Others were looking into the heavens and mumbling prayers. Some of the women were wailing and crying.

One of the men dressed like Paul walked to the edge of the pyre with a burning torch. Paul felt dread in the pit of his stomach as he realized what was about to happen, yet somehow, he was not able to move to intervene.

As Paul suspected, the man lowered the torch to the pyre, and the entire structure quickly set aflame. Then, as the inevitable licking tongues of fire tickled the corpse, and the smell of roasting flesh began to drift across the shore, the dead man's living widow, still bound on top of him, began to scream.

Smoke from the fire formed an opaque wall around the scene. Still, it did not hide enough, for Paul saw the widow catch fire, thrash around in panic, and begin to turn black as her skin actually melted off of her. Finally, her head caught fire, and the flames entered her gaping mouth, nostrils, ears, and eyes; her eyeballs burst, and the thick, vitreous fluid ran down her cheeks. Then, mercifully, she slumped over and died after a few moments of agony.

The wails from the crowd of onlookers filled the air, and Paul was shocked at what had transpired. The pyre continued to burn until it was merely a pile of black ashes.

The onlookers slowly began to walk away, some staying to pray and others to bathe in the holy Ganges. Paul's associates used sticks to pull bones from the pyre. One of them held an unburned arm of the corpse, an arm that he had apparently severed before the burning.

The three others gathered with Paul and the arm, which was pallid and beginning to show a few open spots of rot.

The man holding the arm brought it to his mouth, bit into it, and tore out a chunk of flesh, which he immediately chewed and swallowed. Paul wanted to dry heave and cry out, but he was unable to do it; something restrained him.

The man passed the arm to the next man, who also took a large bite, and eventually, it got to Paul. The thought of eating corpse flesh revulsed every part of his being, but again, being controlled by something or someone, he could not resist. He watched as he brought the stinking flesh to his mouth and tore into it with his teeth.

The texture was almost gelatinous as the decaying flesh sloughed off into his mouth: a piece of rancid meat and its slippery skin. The skin separated from the flesh in his mouth, and he swallowed it. He felt the slimy tissue in his throat. He chewed the flesh, and it surrendered itself to his teeth in decomposing acquiescence.

The taste was something out of hell, a combination of sour, acrid, sulfuric egginess that penetrated his oral and nasal cavities. He swallowed the rest of it and felt it posoning his stomach.

The three other men used some of the ashes from the corpse and his widow to smear their torsos with, and Paul followed suit, rubbing the chalky substance all over his bare skin. Disgusted, he had no choice.

The scene faded, and Paul found himself back in Durga's temple, but somehow in another reality.

He looked up at the idol of the goddess and felt warmth and love. The idol herself looked down at him and smiled, then spoke to him.

"Paul, the Aghora defile themselves with the things that society says are unclean and offensive because there really is no difference between clean and unclean: Brahma is in all, and is all."

Paul looked into the resplendent eyes of Durga and tried to grasp her meaning, but he could not.

"I don't understand," he said in his mind.

Waving her many arms, Durga replied, "All is Brahma. All is god. Has he not made the clean and the unclean? That is the purpose of the Aghora. They are outcasts, outsiders. Are you not also an outsider, Paul? Were you not left an orphan early in life? Are you not different in dress, speech, and mannerisms from society? Is what you call punk *really any different from what I call* Aghora*?"*

Paul began to understand some of her meaning, and he nodded.

"Yes, you, too, Paul, are outside of the rest, outside of society, outside of the lower understanding of what is good and bad, what is clean and unclean, for all is Brahma, all is god."

Paul understood, or so he thought.

He asked, "Then what is the point, goddess? I'm an outcast. It's been painful for me all my life."

"Pain is pleasure, Paul. There is no difference. It is all Brahma. You are different because you have a purpose. Have you not known that

evil has always been at your side like a thorn in the flesh? Has evil not always tried to stop you? Vampires, werewolves, zombies, goblins, demons—they are all the same, Paul. And your purpose in this life is to fight against them. That is also my purpose, and that is why I am with you."

He felt the spirit of Durga swell and soar inside of him, and for a brief moment, he understood. He understood everything. He understood the secrets of the universe and the meaning of existence. He understood Brahma, and he understood that he was a part of that everything.

Then, he snapped back into the present reality.

He was lying on the temple floor, and the others were kneeling around him, looking down at him.

"Paul!" said Mary. "Are you alright?"

"What the hell happened?" he asked.

"Christ, you scared me!" she said as she brushed his unspiked hair back from his face. "You fainted, then you started shaking around like you were having a seizure."

"I think…I think I had some kind of vision or something," he said.

"The goddess spoke to you, didn't she?" asked Swami Maitra. "Yes, I can see the glow in your face and your being. You are fortunate, Paul. The goddess chooses carefully whom she speaks to."

"Oy!" said Uri. "What did she say?"

"I…I'm not sure. I have to think about it. Are we finished here for now? I sure could use a damn beer."

CHAPTER 17

Best Wishes

"But we're going to evangelize," protested Amos. "I'm not sure it's a good idea to—"

"Oh, please take me with you!" begged the djinn. "I'll be good and stay in the lamp for now. I promise. Now that I'm free to come and go out of the lamp, it's not a problem to use it as a mode of transport. I'll be quiet!"

The spirit was flitting around the apartment like an anxious dog about to go on a walk.

"I don't know…" said Amos. "It's just that if someone sees you—"

"They won't!" assured the djinn. He flew over to Aaron and made a begging gesture with his smoky hands.

"It's probably alright," said Aaron with a Coke in his hand. "No one would believe us anyway if we said there's a genie in the lamp."

Amos thought for a moment, internally torn, then said, "Oh, alright. Just please don't make yourself known, alright?"

The djinn smiled, nodded, and dove back into the brass lamp.

Aaron and Amos stopped at the first house on their map and

knocked on the door. Amos had already made Aaron throw away his Coke can so as not to give the wrong impression of Mormonism.

A woman with her hair in rollers answered the door. She looked busy, stressed, and irritated.

"Hello, Ma'am!" said a perky Amos. "We're Elders Brigham and Brigham of the Church of Jesus Christ of Latter Day—"

"Mormons? No thanks," said the woman as she closed the door in their faces.

"That didn't go too well," said Amos. "This city is so full of sinners!"

"It's alright," said Aaron. "It's our duty to spread the word. Unfortunately, we can't control people's reactions."

They continued along their path. Despite their stress, the chirping birds and chittering squirrels in the beautiful oaken canopy made them feel happy.

At the next house, however, they did not fare much better.

"Hello, Sir! We're Elders Brigham and Brigham of the Church of Jesus Christ of Latter Day Saints! We're wondering if we might have just a moment of your time to talk about the gospel of Jesus Christ."

"Oh, um..." stammered the disheveled man. "Look, I don't mean to be rude, but I'm a happy Catholic, and I'm afraid you're wasting your efforts here."

"Oh, I see," said Amos. "Well, Sir, maybe—"

"Sorry," said the man. He gently closed the door.

Sighing in despair, the brothers moved on to the next prospect. The house they arrived at looked...*strange,* to say the least. It was built of wood, and from its looks, that wood was very old, as it was warped, and the paint had peeled off much of it. Moreover, the paint itself was black, and where the paint had peeled off, the wood underneath was gray-black with mold.

The oddest aspect of the house was its towering height. It was not that a five-story house was all that unusual in Uptown New Orleans, but the manner of the height of this house was simply screwy. As the house proceeded upwards, it became narrower, tapering almost like a tower but without the same aspect ratio.

At about the third floor, the house began to bend so that the single narrow room on the fifth floor was practically curved to the side. The entire house was like a bent finger.

"This house is kind of weird," noted Amos.

"Yeah, how's it even staying up? It looks like it's gonna fall down at any second," agreed Aaron as he knocked on the door.

The warped, black, wooden door slowly creaked open to reveal none other than the bizarre, crooked figure of the Reverend Methuselah Skink!

Both boys gasped.

"Er, oh, hello, Sir. It's you," declared Amos.

Skink pulled back his fish lips from his skeletal teeth in the semblance of a human smile and replied, "Indeed! Indeed, boys! What great pleasure brings you to my door this fine day?"

"Oh, um…Reverend Skink, we'd like to ask just a moment of your time to talk to you about the gospel of Jesus Christ!"

"You shall not muzzle an ox while he treads out the grain!" said Skink, causing the boys to look at each other curiously. "Well, come in, boys!" continued Skink as his long, sinewy arms waved around.

They stepped inside and beheld a most curious living room. The inside of the house, like the exterior, was painted black, immediately giving the impression of a small, dark grave. Even oxygen seemed to be rare in the house.

The furniture—also all black—seemed out of the Gothic age. The chairs, the sofa, and the tables were all thin, spindly, and curvy, adorned with elaborate flourishes and twirls, little carved gargoyles and horrific faces poking out in bas relief on the ebony wood.

"Please sit, boys," he said in a chilling tone that did not really allow for anything but obedience. They sat.

"One moment," he said as he left the room and returned a couple of minutes later with tea.

"Now, what brings you, boys, my way? Do you want to convert me to Mormonism, boys?" asked the creepy old man in a slithery voice.

"I…well, Sir, I suppose that's our ultimate goal, but you know, the Book of Mormon is such good news and brings us such happiness that…" began Amos, but Skink interrupted him.

"Beware of false prophets, who come to you in sheep's clothing, but inwardly they are ravenous wolves!"

"I…oh, Sir, I assure you, we're not false prophets. On the contrary, we believe in Jesus Christ, dead, buried, and resurrected."

Skink took a slurp of his tea and replied, "Now that's interesting, isn't it, boys? Jesus himself died, but he came back from the dead. Yes, everything in nature, in the universe, is reborn, isn't it? The death of winter becomes the rebirth of spring. So we, boys, shall also rise again from death!"

Amos coughed and tried to remain rational in the bizarre conversation. The silence of Skink's house was uncanny, like a thick blanket stifling all unnecessary noise. It was the silence of relatives sitting with the embalmed body of their loved one, each person scared to be the first one to say something.

"Yes, Sir. In Third Nephi, Chapter Eleven talks about the resurrection of all mankind."

Skink squinted at them with his wrinkled, snaky eyes. "Jesus gave himself up voluntarily unto death, did he not, boys?"

Aaron said, "Yes, Sir. The Bible and the Book of Mormon say that he willingly died for our sins."

"And we are to use Jesus as our model and pattern in all that we do, yes?"

"Yes, Sir."

Skink finished his cup of tea with a chilling sucking noise, then said, "Then we, boys, must also willingly give ourselves unto death. Only then shall we enjoy the resurrection!"

"I...um, I'm not sure..." said Amos.

"Think about it, boys! Only by offering ourselves to death can we live again! It is the great mystery and paradox of life!"

Amos rubbed his neck and grimaced.

"Um, I think we should leave. Thanks for the, um, tea."

As the boys stood up and walked toward the front door, Skink shouted, *"But Zipporah took a flint knife, cut off her son's foreskin, and touched Moses' feet with it!"*

Amos grabbed Aaron's arm and yanked him outside.

"Let's get out of here!" he said as the two ran down the street.

Once they were a safe distance from Skink's creepy house, they stopped and sat on the curb for a brief rest.

"Man, it's so hard to convert anyone, and that Skink is a real creep," said a frustrated Amos.

"It's hard enough in Salt Lake City!" said Aaron. "It's going to be impossible here. People here aren't very Christian, you know? They drink and fornicate and do drugs and all sorts of sins."

The two disheartened boys sat on the curb for several minutes with their chins on their hands.

Finally, Amos said, "I *wish* I could convert everyone!"

The djinn burst out of the lamp and out of Amos' backpack.

"As you wish, Master! You can now convert everyone!"

Amos gasped and said, "Wait, I...I didn't mean...hold on. So you're saying I can convert *anyone*?"

"As you wished, so it is, Master!" confirmed the djinn. "Now, I'd better get back in the lamp before someone sees me!"

It flew back into Amos' backpack.

"Dude, is this for real?" asked Aaron.

"I mean, there's only one way to find out," answered Amos.

A young lady was walking toward them on the sidewalk. As she approached, Amos said, "Ma'am, would you please become baptized as a Christian and join the Church of Jesus Christ of Latter Day Saints?"

The woman stopped for a moment and twisted her lips. She seemed to be struggling with something internally, but then she said, "Yes. Yes! I see the truth now! Joseph Smith is truly the prophet of God, and Jesus is the son of God! I'm going to find the closest Mormon church!" She sprang off joyfully.

"Oh, man," said Amos. "This really works! Aaron, think of all the good we can do! All the souls we can save! Watch this!"

He looked around and saw a group of friends standing down the street outside of a bistro.

"Hey, all of you, do you have a second? Could you come here just for a moment?"

The friends looked at the boys, then walked toward them, a little wary.

"Would you all please convert to Christianity and become members of the Church of Jesus Christ of Latter Day Saints?"

They all began to nod.

"Yes!"

"Absolutely!"

"I believe!"

They walked away with big smiles on their faces.

"Amazing!" said Amos. "It's all I'm going to do from now on! I'm going to save the whole city of New Orleans!"

They saw a middle-aged woman standing directly across the avenue from them.

"Don't yell at her, Amos," said Aaron. "I know you want to, but it's obnoxious. You must go to people, not make them come to you."

"I know, I know," said Amos. "I just want that woman to cross the street and come to us, but—"

The woman looked directly at Amos and began to cross the street toward him.

"Whoa! I can even do that?"

The woman stared at Amos, not looking anywhere else. Then, as she crossed one half of the divided boulevard, a car honked its horn and swerved to miss her. Before Amos and Aaron could understand what was happening, the woman stepped onto the streetcar tracks just as one of the lumbering trolleys approached.

With no intention to stop, the driver began ringing his bell furiously. Finally, the woman stopped, slowly turned toward the source of the bell, and just stood there as the streetcar smashed into her, rolled over her, and dissected her body into slivers of organs, blood, and gore.

Aaron and Amos stared at the horror, unable to speak or move.

Finally, Amos said, "Oh my God! Oh my God! Did I do that? What have I done?"

They saw that the streetcar had not even stopped.

"Stop, driver! You have to stop!"

The streetcar obeyed and stopped in place, but the momentum had to go somewhere; the trolley careened off the tracks and rolled over several pedestrians, instantly crushing them to death, before it smashed into some cars.

Tears began to silently drip down Amos' cheeks.

"What's happening?"

The djinn expanded out of the lamp and backpack. Everyone on the street was running toward the wreck or staring at it, so no one noticed the black cloud of genie.

"Your wish is being fulfilled, Master! You wished to convert everyone. Now, everyone is beholden to your will. As you wish, they must do."

"But...but..." stammered Amos, "I meant convert them to Mormonism!"

"Ah, but that is not how you phrased your wish, Master. Enjoy!" The djinn zipped back into the lamp.

"Amos, you screwed up!"

"Language, Aaron. Look, this is terrible...I have to learn to control it and only use it to save souls."

Aaron turned and glared at Amos incredulously. The screams of the survivors of the accident and the onlookers filled the air.

"No! You have to wish it away! You just killed people!"

Amos thought for a few moments, weighing the possibilities. "I mean, *I* didn't kill them. It was an accident. It could have happened without my wishes. You don't know my wishes had anything to do with it."

Aaron frowned and said, "Come on, man! You know it did! That couldn't have been a coincidence!"

"Aaron, shut up! Listen! I have the power to save souls! *All* souls! I can't give that up, man!"

"Are you crazy?"

Each boy folded his arms and huffed. They did not speak or look at each other for a few minutes. Then, they watched the police and the ambulance arrive at the accident scene and begin working.

"Amos, I'm not repeating this. You *have* to wish that power away. No good will come of it!"

"*Only* good will come of it! Souls will be saved!"

Aaron looked around at nothing in particular, shaking his head angrily from side to side.

"Fine! You want to do this wish stuff? Fine! You know what? I'm tired of everything being a sin! I'm tired of you telling me I'm going to hell for drinking a simple Coke! I *wish* I could enjoy life more!"

Aaron put his hand over his mouth, realizing his rash words, but it was too late. The djinn popped out of the backpack and said, "As you wish, Master!" It folded its arms, nodded its head, then whooshed back into the lamp.

"Aaron! What have you done?" yelled Amos.

"I don't know! Look, let's get back to the apartment for now, alright? It's safer there. We can be rational and figure out what to do there. On the way home, whatever you do, don't wish for anything to happen, for God's sake. Don't say a word, alright?"

They both nodded their agreement quietly and walked briskly and silently back to their apartment.

Aaron fumbled with the apartment keys out of nervousness but managed to slide the key into the hole and open the door. They both felt a little relieved to be out of the chaos of the city and back into the relative solitude and safety of their apartment. Neither had uttered a single word on the walk back.

Aaron walked into the living room first, followed by Amos. Aaron stopped abruptly, causing his brother to run into his back.

"Dude, why'd you stop?"

"Am…Amos…I…look…what…"

Amos looked to the sofa where Aaron was pointing. There lay the beautiful Arab woman who had sold them the lamp at the booth at the religious street fair. If her presence were not surprising enough, she was completely nude, her legs spread open to reveal her thick, hairy mound and engorged womanhood.

"Aaron, I thought you'd never arrive," she said. "Come into me, my love! Come and make love to me!"

Aaron just stared, frozen.

From Amos' backpack came a now-familiar voice: "Enjoy, Master! As you wished!"

CHAPTER 18

Goth Chicks Rock

"Izzy," said Varco, "there's that new girl. We should sit by her. She's all alone, and I already heard the Mean Girls teasing her."

The *Mean Girls* group included three fellow freshmen at Tulane University: Anna Barrois, Lucy Teeser, and Rose Liu, all three stunningly beautiful, athletically-gifted, and with super-wealthy parents, of course.

Isabella and Varco had graduated high school and had both been thrilled to have been accepted at Tulane as incoming freshmen.

The new girl was currently sitting alone at a table in the far corner of the cafeteria, pushing her food around with a fork.

"Yep, let's do it," agreed Isabella.

They walked to the poor girl's table, and Isabella said, "Um, hi! Can we sit with you?"

The girl looked up at Isabella and winced, probably expecting more bullying. Her face was noticeably pale, and she had painted dark, black eye shadow in an Egyptian pattern around her eyes. She wore a thin, leather bracelet on her left wrist with little silver skulls studding it. Doc Martens boots adorned her feet. Varco could not help but find her delicate face and proportioned body attractive.

"Um, yeah, sure," said the girl once she saw that they meant no harm, and then she looked back down at her food.

Isabella and Varco each took a seat and set their cafeteria trays on the table.

"So, I'm Isabella, and this is Varco."

The girl looked up again, still without a smile, and said, "I'm Veronica, Veronica Rizzo."

"Nice to meet you!" said Varco as cheerfully as he could muster.

"Um, you too," said the girl grimly.

Isabella and Varco took a bite of food, looked at each other, then tried again.

Isabella said, "So, where are you from? You just transferred in, right?"

The girl nodded and said, "Yeah. I'm from Boston; my dad moved us here for work. I never imagined myself studying in a place like this. It's...weird. No offense."

Varco laughed and said, "No offense taken. It *is* weird, and I mean New Orleans. If you think that's weird, well, we went to a high school called Our Lady of Perpetual Sorrows!"

For a brief flash of a moment, Veronica smiled. "I actually like that name," she said. "As you can tell, I'm goth."

"That's cool!" said Isabella. "By the way, I saw Anna, Lucy, and Rose messing with you earlier. We call them the *Mean Girls* for a reason. Don't let them get to you. Please tell me if they keep bullying you, and I'll take care of them. I *hate* bullies."

Veronica shrugged and nodded.

"Say," said Isabella. "What kind of music do you like?"

"Goth."

"Punk?"

"That too," said Veronica, seeming to be a little more cheerful.

"Cool!" said Isabella. "So, our friends own this punk bar, and we help out all the time there. You should, like, hang out with us sometime. Also, our friend Lâmié Chasseur has this big house on Saint Charles Avenue, and we usually hang out there after school. He's really cool. He has a local ghost hunting show!"

Veronica smiled and said, "What? Badass!"

"Give me your number," said Isabella. "We're going there to hang out this afternoon. You gotta come! Unfortunately, our friends from the bar are traveling right now, but as soon as they arrive and plan a show, we'll let you know! It's called The Gutter Bar. You'll love it. You can come help us bartend or something."

"Dude, that sounds amazing. Count me in."

The girl who had been sullen and withdrawn just moments before was now smiling and excited.

Siofra, who was now doing some adjunct, part-time teaching history at Tulane University for extra money in addition to the high school teaching, stopped at the table.

"Hey guys! What's going on?"

"Siofra…er…Miss Fay, this is Veronica. She's new here. She's going to come hang at Lâmié's and then help out at The Gutter when the guys are back! Veronica, Miss Fay's totally cool. You can trust her."

Siofra smiled at Veronica, who looked slightly shy but smiled back.

"You have next period free, you two?" asked Siofra. "Good. Come to my office. I wanted to ask you a couple of things."

The end of lunch arrived, so Veronica went off to her classes, and Isabella and Varco walked together, hand in hand, to Siofra's empty classroom. They came across the Mean Girls in the hall.

"Oh, look," said Anna. "It's the Romanian vampire and the bride of Dracula."

Lucy giggled and said, "I saw them talking to that goth chick. Maybe she's a vampire too. They can all suck each other."

The Mean Girls brayed, and Rose added, "They all suck anyway. Weirdos."

"We have a saying in Romania," said Varco, while Isabella tried to hide a smirk. "The only thing in the world that sucks harder and more often than a vampire is a cheerleader in the football team's locker room."

Isabella did a spit take, and the Mean Girls stood with their mouths agape, unsure about what to say.

"Think about that, girls," said Varco as he pulled Isabella along the hall past them.

They stepped into Siofra's classroom and closed the door behind them.

"Hey Siofra. 'Sup," Varco said.

"Hey guys. That Veronica girl seems cool."

"Yeah," said Isabella as she hopped up and sat on the edge of Siofra's desk. "The Mean Girls were picking on her earlier."

Siofra frowned and said, "God, I hate those three. So mean and spoiled. If I weren't a teacher, I'd slap them. I can't believe that even in college, they continue with that juvenile behavior."

Varco and Isabella laughed.

"Ok, a serious topic now," began Siofra. "With this demon stuff, you know."

The two students nodded.

"Well, some weird stuff's been happening on campus, too."

Isabella asked, "What kind of stuff?"

Siofra sat in the chair behind her desk and said, "It started in the teachers' lounge last week. Ms. Annabelle, one of the science professors, came in a little before lunchtime, and she was looking, well, a little unhygienic. If you know her at all, then you know how unusual that is."

Varco was playing with a pencil, twirling it in between his fingers. "What do you mean? She was dirty?" he asked.

"Well, sort of, yeah," explained Siofra. "She looked like she hadn't slept in days and hadn't changed clothes in just as long. She was walking around in a daze, and her eyes were totally bloodshot. She even—I hate to say this about her given she's normally so lovely—she even had a sour odor about her."

Isabella grabbed the pencil from Varco and began to twirl it herself as she thought about what Siofra was saying. "That's *really* unlike her," she said.

"Yeah, I know," agreed Siofra. "Well, she stumbled to the table and sat across from me. That's when I smelled the sulfur, like rotten eggs."

"Maybe she just farted?" said Varco, earning him a slap on the arm from Isabella.

"If only it were that!" said Siofra. "See, the thing is that she was staring at me blankly, *through* me, like I wasn't even there. Then she said something, and this is the creepy part. It was in another language I'd never heard, and I've studied many languages. So I can almost always identify a modern language when I hear it. But this one…it sounded ancient. It was guttural and throaty."

Varco snatched the pencil back from Isabella with a sneaky grin and said, "Yeah, that's a bad sign, I think."

"Well," said Siofra, "even worse is that her voice clearly wasn't hers. Miss Annabelle has a lovely, high, feminine voice with a slight Southern drawl. However, the voice she spoke in was a growl like a wolf or a bear. I hate to say it, but it was demonic."

Isabella grabbed the pencil and snapped it in half. "Oops. Sorry about your pencil. So, like, are demons just infesting all of New Orleans?"

"Seems like it," said Varco. "Nothing new for us, right?"

"God, it never ends," said Siofra. "I'm worried this time for sure. Demons are nothing to mess with."

"Say, Siofra," asked Isabella, "I know your specialty is UK folklore, which definitely helped us against the goblins. But, like, what do you know about demons?"

Siofra nodded and walked to her bookshelf. She pulled down a thick tome entitled *The Complete Demonology Reference*. She laid it on her desk. The book must have been four inches thick, and as she opened it, a puff of musty dust shot out.

"I'm no expert, but I have studied it a lot. So I've been leafing through this reference guide here. But it has been complicated to find out the origin of that sigil on Uri's house and in the synagogue and get some general demon-fighting tips."

Varco slid the book toward himself and scanned several pages.

"Wow. That's detailed. So, how do you kill a demon?"

He involuntarily reached for another pencil and began twirling it.

"You pretty much can't truly kill a demon, at least, I don't think so. You have to banish it, drive it back to hell, or something like that. I'm not completely sure, though. Maybe there *is* a way to kill them. We might end up having to do trial and error."

"Gee, doesn't that sound fun!" said Isabella as she plucked the ill-fated pencil out of Varco's hand and slid it back into Siofra's pencil holder on the desk. Varco grinned sheepishly.

"What do you think we should do about Miss Annabelle?" asked Siofra. "It really seems like she's possessed or obsessed. Obsession is sort of like the first step into full possession. So it goes obsession, oppression, and possession."

"I'm not sure we can do anything, can we? I mean, not yet. We don't even know how to fight them. Let's just hope she doesn't freak out and attack someone," replied Isabella.

"I have an idea," said Siofra. "I think we should pay her a visit at her house and do some investigating. Can't hurt."

Isabella and Varco thought for a second, then they both nodded before Varco said, "We can talk about it at Lâmié's this afternoon. Veronica'll be there, so we might not be able to talk openly, but we'll see."

"Alright," said Siofra. "Demon talk later. You two want to chill here until your next class?"

They agreed, and as Varco thumbed through the book on demonology, Siofra and Isabella chatted about nothing important.

Right outside of Siofra's office door, Anna Barrois, who had been eavesdropping, said, "What the hell? I've gotta tell Lucy and Rose about this!"

That afternoon, Isabella called Veronica from Lâmić's mansion and told her she could go over whenever. Ten minutes later, Veronica was at the door.

"You got here quick!" said Isabella.

"Yeah, I live pretty close. I've passed this house before. My parents are renting a place for now on Peniston Street. But, like, why's it named that? I always think it should be pronounced *penis ton*."

Isabella giggled and led Veronica into the grand parlor, where she introduced her to everyone still on American soil.

"Wow. All of you live here?" asked Veronica.

"It's a big house," said Varco. "Everyone's been through some, well, some shit together, and it's kind of like a big family now. Like a punk loft, but clean."

Another knock came at the door, and Siofra let herself in.

"Miss Fay?" asked a surprised Veronica.

"You can call me Siofra outside of campus. And yeah, I hang out with this lot too. So I hope that doesn't make you uncomfortable."

"No, I think it's cool!"

Veronica sat on the sofa, and Isabella handed her a cold beer. "There. It's hot outside, and you walked."

Veronica looked at Siofra, down at the beer, and said, "Er, I'm only seventeen. I know I'm already in college, but I graduated earlier than my class."

Isabella laughed and said, "And from Boston. Things are different down here in the Big Easy. No one cares down here."

"Well, hell yeah then!" said Veronica with a healthy sip. "Cheers to that!"

Isabella, Varco, and Siofra looked at one another for a moment, all thinking the same thing, but it was Isabella who decided to broach the subject.

Just then, the lights flickered and buzzed like last time. A cold,m oppressive atmosphere descended upon the parlor. A vase on a corner table flew across the room and smashed against the opposite wall. Unlike last time, thankfully, nothing else happened. No demon manifested itself. The house's atmosphere returned to normal.

Veronica stared at the wall with wide eyes, but she did not seem as terrified as would be expected for someone witnessing paranormal activity.

"Um yeah, so, Veronica," said Isabella, "what's your opinion on ghosts and stuff? Like, the paranormal? You know, like Lâmié here has a ghost hunting TV show."

"Well," corrected Lâmié, "*had* one. I keep trying to start it back up, but stuff happens. It'll eventually come to pass, though."

Veronica, now acting as though it had never happened and thoroughly enjoying the fuzzy rules of New Orleans, took another sip of her beer and replied, "Oh, ghosts are totally real. I grew up in a haunted house in Boston."

The others looked surprised.

"Like, what kind of stuff happened?" asked Isabella.

"Lights flickering, footsteps when no one was there, voices at night from empty rooms, you know, the usual haunting stuff. I saw the ghost once or twice, a full-body apparition in white. It was a young woman. The house I grew up in was a couple hundred years old."

"Wow," said Isabella, opening another two beers and handing one to Veronica. "What about other…stuff?"

"I believe all of it," answered Veronica. "I mean, I know there's another realm out there because of the ghost. So why not? Vampires, werewolves, everything. Maybe even fairies. Sure."

They all smiled and thought of Titania, who was at work in her café

Siofra nodded and said, "Well, that makes this easier. We've all experienced that stuff too."

Veronica gave a thumbs-up as she drank her beer and said, "Honestly, if this giant, old house were *not* haunted, I would be more surprised."

"In fact," said Isabella, "we think something's wrong with Miss Annabelle, one of the science professors."

"Oh?" Veronica perked up and looked interested and maybe even a bit mischievous.

"Yeah," said Isabella. "Like, she's in a daze or something. We were thinking—"

"Demonic obsession," said Veronica, finishing Isabella's thought. She, Varco, and Siofra looked astonished. "That's real too," explained Veronica. "I've seen it with my aunt back in Boston, in one of those weird tongue-speaking, snake-handling churches. It's total bullshit, but the possession is real. I saw her preacher once exorcise a demon from this dude…he was *messed up*. He did, like, superhuman things, even crawled up a wall."

Isabella sat down next to Veronica and said, "Damn. Well, I think you'll definitely fit in with us!"

"We're going to visit Miss Annabelle at her house this evening," said Siofra. "Want to come along?"

"Um, hell yeah!" said Veronica. "Right up my alley."

CHAPTER 19

Siesta Fiesta

Cardinal Caroselli stood outside of the Pope's day office quietly, hands folded behind his back. He had been standing there for several minutes, watching the Pope typing something on his laptop, oblivious to the cardinal. Caroselli coughed.

"Hmm? Oh, Cardinal. Come in. I hope you've not been waiting there long."

"Not at all, Your Holiness."

The Pope offered his hand as Caroselli knelt in front of him and kissed his ring. "Have a seat, Cardinal."

The two men sat on opposite sides of the Pope's massive desk, which was scattered with papers, photographs, handwritten notes, and a few theological magazines and books.

"You've received intelligence?" asked the Pope.

"Yes, Your Holiness. The task force returned yesterday with their findings."

"I see. What did they find?"

"Well, Your Holiness, it is as you believed. Demonic activity, including infestations, obsessions, oppressions, and possessions, have increased exponentially. They're being reported in parishes worldwide and by leaders of other faiths."

"I see."

His Holiness sat back, sighed, placed his hand under his smooth-shaven chin, and thought for several moments. The cardinal remained silent and looked down at the desk.

Then, finally, the Pope spoke. "Very well. We have to do something. I hate to say it, but we need Pierre Lascif. Where is he these days?"

"No idea, Your Holiness."

"Can we find him?"

"I am positive we can. I'll send a search team out this afternoon."

"Good, good," said the Pope. "Find him, and convince him to help us. Then, we can pay him, say, up to a million dollars."

"Whom should I send to find him, Your Holiness?"

"Let's see. Send Father Pitman. If Lascif refuses, tell Pitman to become a bit more, well, *insistent* in his persuasions."

"Consider it done, Your Holiness."

++++

Pierre Lascif, flat on his back on his dingy, sheetless mattress, watched the roach on his ceiling with half-closed eyes. His olfactory receptors were assaulted with the stench of three-day-old tacos, farts, and a general manly lack of hygiene.

"*Merde, mais comme ça pue!*" he muttered.

He tried to lift his head and was rewarded with a hammering headache that shot agony through his entire skull with every mocking heartbeat. He strained to look to his left based on a sliver of a hunch that had managed to survive through the blackout.

Yep. There lay a thin, brown-skinned, local girl, cute as hell. The usual crippling depression hit, and he sighed.

"*Señorita. Hey, señorita! Despierta!*"

Damn, my Spanish accent still sucks, he thought. *Good thing some locals speak passable English too.*

He gently pushed the girl, and she woke up. She seemed just as lost as he was. She looked around, baffled, then a lightbulb seemed to switch on.

"*Oh...oh mierda...*"

"Yeah, I know," agreed Pierre. "Pretty wild night. It's *Lupe*, right?"

"*Sí, Lupe. Te llamas Pierre, no?*"

"Yeah, Pierre. Surprised you remembered. We got pretty

hammered."

And then I hammered you, he thought with a sly grin.

Lupe was one of the local girls who liked to hang out at the expat bar, Joe's Trading Post, hoping to meet a white foreign man. Pierre had somewhat of a *reputation* at the bar and in the village, so he was surprised that Lupe had gone home with him. Surely she knew that he was no white knight, ready to whisk her away to a wealthy, happy life in Europe.

"Got to go," Lupe said. "Sorry."

"No need to be sorry, babe. Had fun. See you around."

"*Que idiota*," she mumbled as she got dressed and walked out the door of Pierre's tiny, disheveled house.

He became suddenly nauseated and dry heaved, too dehydrated to even vomit. Thankful that he still had a few bottles of water around (the village water was unsafe to drink unboiled), he guzzled them dry and felt a little better, but still pretty bad.

"Nothing helps but the hair of the dog that bit you," he cursed, digging through a smelly pile of old clothes to find a half-drunk bottle of rancid red wine.

He pinched his nose to cut off the sense of taste and sucked down the last half of the stale wine. Then, after a few minutes, the first fingertips of a buzz began to poke at his brain.

"Better. Better. I think." He burped, and a spritz of wine and bile shot across the room. "Oh, Christ."

Pierre stumbled to the dirty shower he shared with a broad fauna of insects and turned it on. Unfortunately, there was no hot water in the village pumping system, so unless he wanted to boil his own, he had to just grit his teeth and endure cold showers. Usually, though, it was so damn hot outside under the homicidal Mexican sun that he really didn't mind too much.

What should I do today? he asked himself in his mind. It was a rhetorical question. The day would turn out like every other day in the Mexican existential hell he subsisted in.

First, given it was already noon, he would walk down to the little local café on the corner and eat some tacos. Beer would accompany the tacos. He would then return home and work on the novel he had been unsuccessfully working on for the past several years.

About four in the afternoon, after a little siesta, Joe's Trading Post would start picking at his mind, and he would walk through the town toward the bar, stopping along the way to talk to various townspeople. Despite his apparent laziness and worthlessness, people had proven more than welcoming and hospitable to the drunken gringo (his Frenchness did not matter; every foreigner with white skin was a gringo). He was not a *bad person*, after all.

The occasional Mexican grandmother or mother, concerned about his health out of motherly tenderness, would pull him into her little abode and force-feed him soup. He was also grateful, of course, and had made friends with several families. But unfortunately, one of them, shockingly poor, kept trying to push their teenage daughter on him, jokingly—but not really joking—asking him to marry her and take the entire family to Europe. Of course, he would always treat it as a joke, playing dumb with a laugh and a smile, a little tempted, but knowing what his fellow French citizens would say to a *citoyen* who returned from Mexico with a teenage girl.

Whenever he visited a local house or family, he would find an excuse to give them a little money. Their culture of humility did not allow them to outright take it, so he would invent little reasons. But, Lord knew Pierre didn't need the money. After his lawsuit settlement with the Catholic Church back in Paris, he was a multi-millionaire, and the life of a peso was so short and cheap in the little Mexican town of San Miguel.

Most of that money was in a bank account in Switzerland accruing obnoxious amounts of interest, and every few months, Pierre would have a little wired to him down in Mexico, just enough money to get by, to eat enough tacos to survive, to buy all the alcohol he wanted, and to help the locals when he could.

He had long ago lost his sense of purpose in life. *The incident*, as he called it, had taken all of that from him. Like a moonbeam falling to the earth, he had fallen from a lofty position within the Church to a bottom-dwelling, faithless, ex-pat bum. He was quite content to remain such until the day of his death.

For that reason, he grimaced when, the moment he reached Joe's Trading Post, Corin, the bartender from Ireland, said, "Oi, mate, you got a phone call and a message earlier."

"Shit," said Pierre. "How did anyone know where to find me?"

Corin looked at Pierre with a deadpan face and said, "Mate. Really? Everyone in Mexico knows to find you down the pub."

"Yeah, good point," conceded Pierre. "How about a red wine?"

Corin already had the drink poured and waiting, so timely and regular was Pierre's daily appearance.

"Tab?" asked Pierre.

"Yeah, but you gotta pay that soon, mate. It's getting up in the thousands."

"*Merde*. Alright, I'll get some money sent this week."

Corin nodded, satisfied. The Frenchman had never neglected to pay his debts. That was one positive thing you could say about him. Also, he was a nice guy overall, just a hopeless alcoholic and slacker. However, he had never completely opened up to his ex-pat friends about the origin of his troubles, about the *incident*.

Corin handed Pierre a scribbled note with the phone message: *Bishop Prince called around noon and asked you to please call him back, urgent, services required.*

Corin eyed Pierre as he read it and said, "Don't mean to but in, mate, but a bishop? Your services? What kind of shit're you dealing in?"

Pierre laughed and said, "It's not so sinister as that. I was in the seminary once, a long time ago. I dropped out, but I kept in touch with some of the people. That's all. Occasionally, they call me for a reference or a translation or something."

"Alright, that's better than you being some sort of International Vatican assassin."

The two men laughed, and Pierre took a long drink of wine. Then, as the regular ex-pat crowd and the local hangers-on slowly shuffled into the bar, Pierre could not help but think back on the *incident*. The call from the bishop had triggered him.

Despite what he had told Corin to get him off his case, the Church most decidedly did *not* contact him occasionally. In fact, they never did. Never. Pierre knew that the Bishop's call was bad news of the worst kind. The bishop had tracked him down in San Miguel, a town he had chosen precisely because it was tiny and untraceable in the middle of nowhere. Yet, Bishop Prince had gone to the trouble of doing just that.

He had no plan to call the bishop back, of course. As far as he was concerned, the Church could go fuck itself and everyone in it. But, as he drank his wine and nodded at his fellow lushes, his mind slipped back to ten years in the past, when he was just a young, hopeful seminary student in Rome.

His interest in demonology has attracted the attention of Bishop Prince, himself an exorcist for the Church. So the bishop calls Pierre into his office.

"Pierre, have a seat," the bishop says, and the timid boy sits. "I'll get to the point. I've noticed you are interested in demonology. You excel in ancient languages, memorizing the rites and Church history, and spend lots of time reading the ancient manuscripts."

Pierre blushes and looks down, not sure how to handle the comments.

"Pierre, you've got the makings of an exorcist. Unfortunately, the office of Exorcist is dwindling in the modern Church, and I think that's a shame. Demons are real, you know. I've exorcised many myself."

Pierre looks up, surprised that the bishop speaks so openly of possession and exorcism.

"I'd like to have you accompany me on an exorcism to see what it's really like. What would you say to that?" asks the bishop.

Pierre's stomach leaps in a combination of excitement and fear.

"Your Excellency," replies Pierre, "I'm...I'm not sure what to say. Of course, I'd love to go, but are you sure I'd be any help? I'm just a seminary student."

The bishop smiles and says, "I know what I'm doing, Pierre. Don't worry. You'll be a great help."

Pierre goes to sleep that night, dreaming of demons and heroic acts of exorcism.

Real exorcism, as he had soon learned, was anything but heroic. On the contrary, it was a horrible, disgusting, soul-searing experience that had opened his mind to the knowledge of real evil in the world, and it had scared the hell out of him.

Even so, Pierre had taken to the task like a prodigy, and before long, Bishop Prince had been bending Church rules by allowing Pierre to take a very active part in the rituals. Together, Pierre and Bishop Prince had dealt with several cases of extreme possession, each nastier and more shocking than the next.

At every exorcism, Pierre had not only helped but quite naturally taken charge. He would speak the rites perfectly in English and Latin. He had possessed the ability to completely ignore the demons' lies as it had tried to outsmart or shake him. He had been able to force the demons to reveal their names almost effortlessly.

So powerful an exorcist had the young Pierre became, that when he would enter the room of a possessed person, the demons would cry out his name in fear.

Then, he had encountered the demon Asmodeus, Father of Lust.

When Pierre and Bishop Prince had entered the young girl's bedroom, they could each sense that something was just *off*; something was different this time. The feeling of wicked dread was stronger than ever before, exponentially stronger. The room had reeked of sour death and ripe sulfur, and the poor possessed girl had looked like a gaunt corpse.

They had begun the Rite of Exorcism immediately. Still, this time, as Pierre and the bishop had alternately and forcefully read the lines of the ritual, the demon had only laughed.

Still unshaken, Pierre had continued, even as the demon had called him by name and insulted him, his family, the Church, and said filthy and vulgar things about Christ himself.

"A boy? You're just a stupid, unqualified boy!" hisses the demon through the mouth of the possessed girl in a voice that a young girl could never physically achieve. "Oh, Bishop! You send a boy against me? Don't you know that I am a prince among demons?"

"In the name of Christ, tell me your name!"

The demon laughs heartily and says, "You don't have to compel me, boy! I'll gladly tell you my name. I am Asmodeus!"

Hearing that name, Pierre and Bishop Prince look at each other. They know very well that Asmodeus is a demonic prince, extremely powerful, and the demon of lust.

"My name and reputation precede me, I see!" says the demon gleefully.

Pierre forces himself to ignore the demon's taunts and continues with the rite.

Hold Lord, almighty Father, everlasting God and Father of our Lord Jesus Christ, who once and for all consigned that fallen and apostate tyrant to the flames of hell, who sent your only begotten Son into the world to crush that roaring lion; hasten to our call for help and snatch from ruination and from the clutches of the noonday devil this human being made in your image and likeness. Strike terror, Lord, into the beast now laying waste your vineyard! Fill your servants...

The demon giggles like a schoolgirl, utterly unaffected by the prayer. "It won't work on me!" sings the demon in a child-like melody. "I know something you don't know! Want to hear it? The bishop loves dicks! Little boy dicks! Limp little tiny boy dicks! He likes to suck them, lick them, and beat them until they get hard like little sausages!"

Pierre is used to such demonic taunts, but something about this one was different.

"Shut up!" yells the bishop.

Pierre looks at him in surprise. Never before has the bishop reacted to a demon. He is a consummate professional who can always resist interacting with the demons' wiles. This time, however, Bishop Prince is becoming quite discomposed.

The demon giggles and snorts. "It's true! The bishop loves little boy dicks! Ask him how many he's sucked! Dozens? More? Tiny little boy dicks! The bishop fucks little boys!"

"Shut up! Shut your mouth, demon!" yells Prince.

The demon howls in laughter. Then, without warning, the possessed girl rises out of bed and leaps on Pierre. With the strength of three large men, she knocks him to the ground, straddles him, mimics riding him sexually, then leans over so that her face is right against his, her eyes looking directly into his.

Her eyes haze over and become all black. Her breath is like an open grave. Her tongue, longer than should be physically possible, slides into his mouth and slithers around like a snake. She removes it and grins.

"You're going to die in your work, Pierre, and you will burn in hell forever." She stands up casually, walks back to the bed, and lies down. The girl falls into a deep sleep.

Pierre and Bishop Prince had been unable to drive the demon out of that girl. Another exorcist had tried with modest success, although the girl had later died in a car accident. Pierre had always suspected that the demon had somehow been involved in the death.

Deeply shaken by his failure to exorcise the girl and by the physical attack, he had fallen into a deep depression. The final revelation that Bishop Prince had been arrested for, in fact, molesting young boys, had driven Pierre away from his faith, from the Church, from his exorcism, and out of the seminary.

The Church, from her highest ranks, had offered him an ungodly amount of money to keep his mouth shut, both about the exorcism and Bishop Prince. In addition, the Church had managed to pay off the right people, and the bishop had suffered no consequences and had since been promoted in the ranks of the Vatican.

Pierre, having no qualms about accepting dirty cash, had found himself with more money than he could ever use, and so, on an angry, depressed whim, he had moved down to San Miguel, Mexico, and had never looked back.

It was therefore understandable why Pierre Lascif, long hidden from society and the Church, would feel concerned about a phone call from the bishop.

"Another wine, Corin?"

"Just buy a bottle, mate. It's cheaper, and it's not like you're gonna stop."

"*Merde*. You're right. A bottle *alors*."

Corin opened the bottle and poured a glass.

A couple of other ex-pats walked in and waved to Pierre; he greeted them, and a local girl sat next to him. He tried to ignore her obvious flirtation.

"You gonna call him back, that bishop?" asked Corin.

"Hell no! I hate that bastard."

"Wow. Strong reaction there," said Corin.

Pierre chuckled sarcastically and lit a cigarette. "If you only knew, *mon ami*."

―――――― ·+++· ――――――

The following day, predictably, Pierre woke up with a pounding headache and a cute, local girl in bed next to him. He went through the usual morning routine: the girl called him names and left; he showered; he had lunch at a local family's house; he made a pretense to give them some money; he took his usual spot at Joe's Trading Post.

Sartre's brand of Existentialism argued that if we repeat something enough times, then that becomes how others see us, and we eventually become that thing, immutable, unchangeable unless something shocking happens to cause metaphorical death and rebirth.

Pierre had indeed become lush—not *a lush*, but simply the essence of *lush*—yet he was quite happy in his existential hell. *Hell is others*, Sartre had suggested, and if those *others* consisted of a friendly Irish bartender, lots of good wine, good tacos, and cute young women, he would accept his fate.

He certainly did not expect something shocking to cause death and rebirth.

Thus, he was horrified when a black Mercedes with tinted windows and a Mexico City plate pulled up outside Joe's. His intuition told him that it would not be good and that he would be somehow involved.

That intuition was confirmed when the driver, a Mexican man in a suit, stepped out of the car, opened the back door, and a collared priest exited the vehicle.

"Oh, fuck this," said Pierre, standing up and walking to the back of the pub.

He planned to sit at a table in the back of the pub, facing away from the door, and simply hide. The plan worked for about thirty seconds, at which time the priest sat down at his table facing Pierre.

"For fuck's sake…" muttered Pierre.

"Ah, Pierre Lascif, it really is you," said the man. "I'm Father Pitman on a mission directly from the Vatican, with orders from high up, *very* high up, if you understand my meaning."

Pierre sighed, his glass of wine still in his hand, and said, "I don't care if your orders come from God himself. You can just fuck right off."

Unfazed by the hostility, the priest just looked at Pierre for a moment, then turned around, got Corin's attention, and called out, "Cold beer, please."

Turning his attention back to Pierre, the priest said, "Now, back to what I was saying."

Corin brought the beer. The priest took a long sip and sighed in satisfaction; the Mexican sun was especially belligerent that day.

"You've fallen a long way since your seminary days."

"I've moved up in the world. By the way, you're the one harassing me here. Insulting me doesn't exactly add to your charm."

The priest considered the remark as he took another cold, satisfying sip of beer. The mirror in the back of the pub reflected the priest's driver in the front of the pub, just standing there with his arms crossed in the front like some sort of low-level Mafia enforcer.

"The Vatican sent a goon with you."

"He's just a driver."

"Yeah, sure."

The priest looked around the dingy pub and sighed. "This place is pretty depressing."

Pierre shrugged, sipped his wine, and said, "Just get to it. What do you want?"

The priest collected his thoughts for a moment and replied, "You know, Pierre, you were the most talented exorcist the modern Church had ever seen, even when you were just in seminary."

"So what?"

"Pierre, listen carefully, please. There's been a massive demon infestation in various places around the world. Something big and evil is happening. Obsessions, oppressions, possessions are being reported in parishes all over the earth."

"What a shame," said Pierre. "Sounds like something for the Church to deal with."

The priest tilted his head and looked at Pierre. "Your talents and abilities are needed, Pierre."

Pierre drained his glass of wine and replied, "Maybe the Church should have thought about that before pairing me with a kiddy diddler, then getting him off the hook. The demon's attack wasn't all that pleasant either."

The priest said, "The Church is well aware of her *issue* with pedophiles. The current Pope..."

"Don't care," interrupted Pierre. "Consider this a strong and unequivocal *no*. Add to that an official *go fuck yourself*, and that's my reply to the Vatican."

The priest let a puff of air out of his nose. "Pierre, the Pope personally asked for you."

"Oh, really? Is that the same Pope who hid Bishop Prince's child molestation? Or the one who paid me off to not talk about it like a damn mobster?"

"The demonic world is coming into our own, Pierre. It's going to affect you just like it's going to affect everyone."

"Great!" said Pierre. "Then the end of the world will come sooner. So it's a win-win situation in my book."

The priest swallowed the last sip of his beer. "Will you think about it?"

Pierre laughed and said, "Think about it? Sure. I'll think about how the last thing on earth I will ever do is to assist an organization as corrupt and criminal as the Vatican. So please tell His Holiness that he can kiss my ass."

"There's money involved," suggested the priest.

"Don't care. I have more than I could ever use."

The priest sighed heavily and stood up, scraping the wooden chair against the tile floor. He laid his card on the table. "If you change your mind, call me. To be blunt, the fate of the world depends on it."

Pierre gave the priest a classic French *bof*.

+++

"What the bloody hell was that about?" asked Corin after the priest's car had left. "I've got a reputation to protect in the pub here, man. You're gonna scare off all the drunks."

Pierre chuckled. "Just more bullshit from a bullshit Church. Another bottle of wine, how about it?"

That night was one of the occasional nights when Pierre did not take a girl home from the pub with him. Instead, still quite drunk, of course, he lay on his grimy mattress and looked up at his cockroach friends as they crawled all over the ceiling.

His brain was itching. He always called it an *itching*, at least. It meant that something deep inside of him was worrying him, troubling him, and it would not let him go until he resolved it. It was an itch that could only be scratched through the identification and resolution of the conflict.

Demonic oppression? Shit. Could it really be as bad as Father Pitman had said, or was it just a lie to get Pierre back into the service of the Vatican?

He fell asleep and immediately into a vivid, realistic dream.

In the dream, he stood on a small island in the middle of a vast sea of fire. The heat from the sea tormented his skin as if he were really feeling the burning in the waking world.

In the sea, terrible creatures writhed, horrible, foul-shaped demons with limbs, horns, fangs, mouths, tails, insectile thoraces, and all manner of disgusting forms and deformities.

Among the demons swam the souls of the damned, those poor people who had lived a life that had led them to hell in the afterlife. Their flesh burned and melted and crackled eternally as they moaned and howled in agony, regret, and hopelessness. Wasn't that the real horror of hell, after all? The loss of any hope, of any redemption, of any love...forever.

For the briefest moment, a quantum slice of one millisecond, whatever forces control dreams and destinies allowed Pierre to feel that hopelessness, the hopelessness of hell, to really and truly feel it.

So utterly empty and unloved and without a future did he feel that it shocked him awake with his own screaming terror.

"*Merde alors,*" he cursed, knowing he had no choice; he would have to respond to the call for help.

CHAPTER 20

Past the Expiration Date

Something was rotten on Prytania Street, or at least, so it smelled. Sure, most of New Orleans constantly smelled like sour beer, piss, and vomit, but the Garden District, with all of its flowers, trees, and general upscale housing, tended to be a little easier on the nose.

However, that evening, Miss Annabelle's house exuded the specific smell of rotten eggs and slightly-sweet cabbage. If possible, the house also had a peculiar atmosphere, a distinct feeling of fear and dread, so pedestrians would cross the street without even thinking about it as if their reptilian brain were warning them: *Danger! Avoid!*

Siofra, Varco, Isabella, and Veronica stood in front of Miss Annabelle's house, looking up at the tall, two-storied Queen Anne structure. Unfortunately, what would normally have been a lovely testament to the Neo-Gothic style of architecture, with its charming and quirky asymmetry, its cantilevered gables, columns, and spindly, elegant detail—all painted in various pastel, Caribbean hues—had taken on a gray pall, not of the paint itself, but rather a mysterious ether that almost eluded the eyes, but not the emotions.

Even the garden and its plants had fallen prey to the gloomy and ghastly caul. Flowers hung their heads in despair, and trees sagged to the ground as if trying to hide from the forces within the house.

"Well, shit," said Varco.

"Um, goth's one thing," said Veronica, "but this is ridiculous."

"It just *feels* wrong, like the house shouldn't even exist in this world," added Isabella.

Siofra just looked at the house quietly. Then, instinctively, they all joined hands and forced themselves to slowly walk up the path through the garden and then up the three wooden stairs to the porch. Siofra took the lead and rapped on the door. It slowly opened by itself.

Veronica said, "Um, this is the part in horror movies where the white people are most definitely not supposed to go inside, but we do anyway."

"I'd normally laugh, but you are spot on," said Siofra. "Um, shall we?"

All four, still holding hands, were led by Siofra into the foyer. The stench of rotting milk and sulfur ambushed them, and Isabella dry-heaved.

"Damn...this can't be healthy," noted Varco. "How is she still managing to live her life and go to work?"

A burst of rumbling laughter came from upstairs.

"Oh, God. That's her," said Veronica. "Not her voice, but it's her. That's a terrible sign."

Miss Annabelle spoke again; this time, her voice sounded like the regular old, sweet science professor.

"Who's that downstairs? It sounds like Miss Fay and some students. Sorry dears, I'm feeling sick. Could someone please bring me a glass of water? I have a fever, and I can't really get out of bed. I'm so sorry I can't be more hospitable!"

The four looked at one another, trying to decide what to do.

"Alright, we all go together," whispered Siofra. "I'll run and get a glass of water in case it's, well, in case it's still *her*."

After just a couple of minutes, with a glass of ice water in her hand, Siofra led the way up the stairs. With each creek of the vintage wood, they felt a twang of fear in their stomachs. Reaching the upper landing, they looked down the dusty hall, a hall that looked like it had not been cleaned in weeks or even months. A couple of large cockroaches scurried across the wooden floor, drawing an *eek!* from Isabella.

"My bedroom's the third door on the left," said Miss Annabelle in her usual voice.

With more than a little trepidation, the four, hand-in-hand still, reached her bedroom, whose door was open, and stepped inside. Siofra gasped.

The entire room was beyond squalid—it was nauseating. Roaches scampered about freely like squirrels on a nature reserve while two large rats were fighting over something in the far corner. Enormous, spindly spiders had set up shop in thick spiderwebs draped over and across every piece of furniture. A few old Popeye's chicken boxes littered the floor, the remains of the fried meat seething with maggots.

Miss Annabelle lay on the soiled, unmade bed, herself a monster of filth. Her corpse-gray skin was marked with pocks, and her teeth had become a feverish hue of jaundice-yellow. Her normally carefully-styled brunette hair was thick with body grease and stuck out at all angles, like the hair of a cartoon character after a cigar explodes in its face.

"Miss...Miss Annabelle...are you alright?" asked Varco tenderly.

"I think so," she replied. "I'm just a bit under the weather."

"Shouldn't you see a doctor?" asked Siofra.

"I...I'm not sure," answered Miss Annabelle, her tone sounding increasingly confused. "I...how long have I been sick?"

"Well, you haven't been to campus in several days. Look, I really think you need to see a doctor. We were concerned about you, but I must tell you, dear, that you look really sick. Like, shockingly so," explained Siofra.

Siofra handed Miss Annabelle the glass of ice water, and she gulped it down in two swallows.

"Oh, now, I feel a little better. The water...so good, so refreshing..."

Siofra looked for a place to sit, but not a single piece of furniture was fit for a human to touch.

"Look, Miss Annabelle," began Siofra, "I'll be honest with you here. The last time I saw you in the faculty lounge, you looked rather ill. I was concerned. I expressed my concern with Isabella, Varco, and Veronica here, and they agreed to come with me to check on you. Now that we're here, well, I'm much more concerned."

Miss Annabelle looked directly at Siofra and grinned, an uncanny grin matched with eyes that looked just one shade too dark to be natural. The eyes immediately changed back to normal.

Veronica moved slightly forward and said, "Miss Annabelle, I'll get you another glass of water. That seemed to make you feel better."

Miss Annabelle nodded and smiled, her lips seeming just a bit too wide to be natural. A couple of minutes later, Veronica returned with another glass of ice water. She handed it to Miss Annabelle.

As Siofra kept trying to encourage the sick teacher to see a doctor, Miss Annabelle took a sip of the water, spat it out, howled in pain and anger, and lobbed the glass across the room. It shattered on the wall.

"What the—" yelled a startled Siofra.

"It's holy water," said Veronica. "I brought it to test her. She's possessed. Her reaction proves it."

Siofra, Isabella, and Varco stepped back cautiously from the bed, and Miss Annabelle began to laugh in a deep, demonic voice.

"So clever...so clever, this new girl. She knows what she's doing," growled the Annabelle-thing.

Veronica ignored the demon and said to Siofra, Isabella, and Varco, "I thought I'd bring it just to see. It's a pretty standard test since the demon can't know it's holy water without actually touching it."

Varco was pale white, staring at Miss Annabelle, but he had bravely pushed Isabella behind himself to protect her. Miss Annabelle, growling in the inhuman, animalistic tone of the demon, began to levitate about three feet above her mattress.

"Oh, shit," said Isabella. "That can't be good."

Miss Annabelle levitated all the way to the ceiling, which she then sprang upon upside down, causing the ceiling roaches to scatter in fear. Then, finally, she crawled on the ceiling toward the four friends.

"What do we do?" yelled Siofra.

"We get the hell out of here!" replied Veronica. "Go! You three go first! Don't argue!"

They did not argue. Siofra, Isabella, and Varco, in that order, rushed out of the bedroom and back into the hall. Miss Annabelle had almost reached the ceiling area directly above Veronica when the young girl reached into her pocket, pulled out a Catholic Host, crumbled it, and spread it in a line across the room's threshold. She scooted back into the hall, shut the door, and locked it.

They heard Miss Annabelle roar from inside the accursed bedroom.

"It's a consecrated Host. Don't tell the campus priest I stole it. It'll keep her in there until we remove it, so we have some time to figure out what to do," explained Veronica.

"Damn, you're good!" exclaimed Varco. Isabella eyed him with a frown but said nothing.

"I told you, I've experienced some things," answered Veronica.

"Let's get the hell out of this house!" said Siofra. "We can talk about what to do back at Lâmié's place."

CHAPTER 21

In the Houses of the Unholy

"I could really get used to Indian breakfast," said Mary between mouthfuls of *luchi* and *cholas dal.*

"Me too!" mumbled Beast Stalker, crumbs falling out of his mouth.

Paul had already opened his first beer of the day.

"Mister Paul," said Apada, "is it the custom in New Orleans to drink beer this early in the morning?"

"Only among the cool people," he said with a grin.

"More like only among the hopeless alcoholics," said Mary.

"Mister Paul, you must be blessed with a very holy liver!" said Iraj, causing Mary to burst out laughing.

"More like a miraculous liver," she added.

Some birds had begun to chirp in the little school's courtyard, and a pleasant breeze caressed their faces. It would have been a lovely vacation but for the reason they were there.

"I have a more serious question," said Uri, "if it doesn't spoil the brilliant, intellectual conversation so far."

Paul smirked.

"We came here because, for Lord knows whatever reason, we've been chosen to fight the demon Kali. Well, how do we do that? How do we start? How do we even find Kali?"

Swami nodded his understanding of the question. Then, after several moments of chewing his dal, he spoke, "I suppose that the best place to start surely is the temple of Kali."

"Wait," said Father Woodrow, who had just finished his breakfast. "You mean there are temples to demons?"

"Oh, Father!" said Maitra. "Our Hindu religion has many, many gods, countless gods. Some people worship these, others worship those, and yes, some worship demons. They believe the demons give them favors and prosperity in this life."

"Sounds much like Western Luciferians," said Woodrow. "Alright, I can understand that."

As Apada began to clear the metal bowls and plates from the table, and Iraj made the rounds and poured tea for everyone, Maitra continued, "The problem with worshiping demons is that they can be very, very tricky. They can twist your words, manipulate you psychologically and emotionally, and do all sorts of things. So only the very daring, or perhaps the very stupid, choose to worship a demon."

Father Woodrow took a sip of his *chai* and said, "Delicious! Alright, so this demon Kali. What is he like?"

Iraj brought Paul another beer and refilled everyone's tea as Apada finished washing the dishes. Mary looked at Paul's beer, then glared at him. He just shrugged and took a sip.

Maitra leaned back against his pillow, lit his pipe, took a few puffs, then answered.

"Kali. Yes, well, Kali was originally a Gandharva, a nature spirit, not too dissimilar to your fairies or sprites."

"Or fucking goblins," muttered Paul.

Maitra continued, "He went to Princess Damayanti's wedding and became angry that she had not considered him as a husband. So, Kali decided to harm Damayanti's husband, Nala. He waited years for the right moment. Then, one day, Nala forgot to wash his feet before his prayers, which is a sin. That sin, that weakness, allowed Kali to possess Nala's body."

The sounds of the rousing city began to waft in from the neighborhood—people chatting, carts rolling, cows lowing.

"He then arranged a dice game between Nala and his brother, Pushkara. Kali's friend, Dvapara, was able to actually possess one of the dice in the game. As Dvapara ensured that Nala lost every round, Nala, who was actually being possessed and controlled by Kali, gambled and lost his entire kingdom, causing Nala and Damayanti to be banished and homeless."

"Geez, it's getting a little hard to follow there," said Paul between swigs of beer and momentarily distracted by a colorful Indian squirrel that scooted up a tree in the courtyard. At the same time, the palm leaves danced in the breeze.

"Then," continued Maitra, "one thing led to another. That drama was solved, and Kali was exorcised from Nala and cursed into a beastly form. Kali became a wandering spirit. He runs across King Parikshit and asks if he can make a home in his kingdom. The king says no, but says that Kali is allowed to inhabit any place with gambling, alcohol, prostitution, the killing of animals, and gold. To the ancient Hindu mind, these were considered five great vices."

Paul put his hand to his forehead, trying to keep up with the complex history of the gods.

"There is more to the story, but it is far too complicated for a breakfast discussion. Now, in the modern age, Kali is no longer a nature spirit, but a full demon who reigns over those five vices."

"Hey, Swami dude," said Paul while gesturing to Iraj for another beer, "are all the Hindu god stories that damn complicated?"

"Oh, I gave you the simplified version! And yes, they are."

Mary asked, "How do you keep track?"

"Careful study," said Maitra.

Father Woodrow, who was sipping his chai luxuriously, said, "And I thought the Catholic saint stories were complicated!"

Swami, having finished his pipe, lit another and said, "There is a temple to the demon Kali here in Kolkata, but I must warn you. It is in a very dark and dangerous part of the city. The temple is in a slum, but the bad part is that the entire neighborhood is inhabited by people who worship all sorts of demons. There are several temples to many different demons, but Kali is the worst. The Aghora sect also inhabits the area."

"The who?" asked Mary.

Paul quickly swallowed his current sip of beer, raised his hand like a schoolboy, and said, "I know! I know!"

Everyone looked at him in surprise.

"Mister Paul, how do you know about the Aghora?" asked an incredulous Maitra.

"The vision. Durga. She showed me. They're this sect that handles corpses, eats human flesh, and keeps human bones as souvenirs. Durga said they do that to blur the line between what is good and bad, to show that everything is Brahma and is ultimately the same thing," Paul explained.

Maitra blew out a startling puff of purple smoke and said, "Yes! Yes! Quite right! Oh, but how blessed you are that Durga gave you this vision!"

Paul just shrugged and said, "They seem pretty nasty to me."

Uri agreed with a nod. "All of that is very, very taboo in Judaism."

Iraj, Apada, and the other students nodded affirmatively.

"So what do we do when we get to Kali's temple?" asked Mary.

"Oh, Durga shall guide us at that point. Just trust the goddess," assured Maitra.

They did their toiletries and met again in front of the school for Swami to take them to the demon-temple neighborhood.

Walking through the enormous metropolis of Kolkata, their senses were overwhelmed by all of the chaos and color. Everywhere they went, people stared at them, from the wealthy peering out of the backseat of their driven cars, to homeless beggars on the curbs.

They passed through a business district, the home of tall and shiny buildings, people in business suits, and espresso bars. That changed into a more residential area with narrow streets, street food stalls everywhere, little local groceries, spice markets, food markets, laundries, and everything else people needed to live in their neighborhood daily.

That area bled into a poorer zone, the multi-storied apartment buildings gradually morphing into one-story houses, shacks, and huts along skinny dirt lanes, forming an ants' nest of humanity. Here, the shops were smaller and dirtier but still sold everything imaginable. Vendors also lined the alleys, those unfortunate souls who could not afford to rent a storefront but rather had to survive by hoping and praying that they would be able to procure something to sell and that someone would buy it, or else they would starve.

Swami stopped at a *phuchka* stall and bought the snacks for everyone. They bit into the hot flatbread, shaped into hollow balls and filled with all manner of potatoes and spices. The flavors burst to their tongues, causing moans of delicious satisfaction.

"How do you make food so good?" asked Uri.

"Thousands of years of practice!" said a cheerful Maitra.

Paul spotted a small corner store, dashed in, and reappeared with several bottles of beer, which he stuck in his backpack, save one for the road.

"Mister Paul, you can drink so much beer!" marveled Iraj with wide eyes.

"It's his one and only talent," said Mary. "But he's definitely the best at it."

As they walked farther, the environment decidedly changed. What was simply a poor neighborhood with regular people just living their lives quickly turned into a dark and depressing series of skinny alleyways, ominous in their introversion.

Filthy little abodes lined the dirt lane where dingy, hanging fabrics covered the doors and windows. Dark, suspicious faces would peek out from underneath the fabric, then pull away just as quickly.

Notably lacking were the busy little street stalls: the only vendors were the thin, sad-looking figures behind the counters of minuscule shops whose shelves seemed half empty. It was not hard to spot human waste lining the alley.

The first demon temple they passed was a pitiful, crumbling stone structure that emitted a putrid, sour stench. As they walked past it, they glanced inside and saw the idol.

The statue towered over the temple's interior. The demoness was represented as a hideous, frightful hag with sneering, gnashing fangs and two swollen, sickly breasts. In her lap were statues of the corpses of several babies and children, whose dismembered body parts hung from her ravenous mouth.

"Putana, the child killer," explained Maitra.

"Christ!" exclaimed Mary. "Who the hell worships her?"

"Very dark people," replied Maitra. "Very dark indeed. She is thought to take revenge on others for her worshipers, but for a terrible price."

"I don't want to know," said Uri.

They passed another temple, relatively larger than Putana's temple. This one was in slightly better repair. Inside were several men on their knees, offering prayers to the monstrous idol.

The statue itself was a tall, chubby man with a sneering, terrible face that seemed to take great pleasure in the pile of mutilated human bodies beneath him. Under the statue, several actual human corpses had been laid out.

"What the fuck?" whispered Paul.

"That's Narakasura. He enjoys torturing people to death," clarified Maitra.

"Sorry, but I gotta know," said Paul. "Who would worship that, and for fucks sake, why?"

Maitra answered, "Most who worship demons want strong boons and favors and are willing to pay a severe price for it. Revenge, money, fame, power—all of these things can the demons grant, but there is always a catch. Others worship them simply because they love evil."

"Yikes," said Matt, very much awake that day.

They continued down the dark path, and Mary cuddled up to Paul's side. They passed the third temple. This one seemed broken and unused, but inside sat a blind priest, facing the idol and praying. The giant statue was of the rear half of a buffalo, but the torso and head of a fierce man. His many arms held spears and swords, and the sculpture of a dead woman with a sword in her chest lay at the demon's feet.

"Mahishasura," said Maitra. "The hater and killer of women and a shapeshifter."

Block by block, temple by temple, they beheld idols of all sorts of wicked creatures from the Hindu pantheon. The entire neighborhood seemed to be turning darker and darker until even the trees on the street were dead and gnarled. No birds or squirrels flitted and chittered about, but rather only the sounds of the city were audible: tuk-tuks, negotiations, chants, scuffles. Not a single holy cow walked any street, lane, or alley. No children played in the streets.

Then, Maitra pointed down the lane.

They looked to where he indicated and saw what must have been the temple of the demon Kali. It was different than the others. First, it rested in a shallow, sunken pit of earth, so it stood below most of the neighborhood as if it were beginning the descent to hell.

Second, unlike the general box shape of the other temples, this one was a rotunda with columns, a mossy, grimy mockery of a Greek temple. Surrounding the temple, sitting just on the outer edge all around, were a dozen Aghora men, their naked flesh smeared in gray clay, each holding some human bone from this or that part of a human body.

Third, and perhaps the most disturbing thing within the temple, was some sort of burnt offering smoldering before the idol, an offering that looked suspiciously less like an animal and more like a human.

The idol itself rose fifty feet in the air, a monstrous mountain of carved stone. Its body was that of a rotund yet muscular man, a fierce wrestler's body, atop which sat a beastly head, some vile chimera of wild boar, lion, crocodile, and something else less identifiable yet no less savage. Kali's hair was an enormous, wild, curly black mess that hung down to his waist. In the idol's hand was a long and sharp sword of metal, and its eyes glared down in hatred at whoever dared gaze up into its eyes.

"Behold, the demon Kali!" said Maitra with a bit of awe and even reverence. "They are Aghora, those men."

"They are naked, those men," said Uri.

"They are disgusting, those men," added Matt.

"They take some getting used to, for sure," agreed Swami.

They stopped close to the temple and looked at it quietly.

"That's some messed up shit," said Paul. "So we're here. What now?"

Swami put his hand to his chin and thought for a moment.

"Well, Mister Paul, you see, those Aghora men are not the temple priests. They are worshipers of the demon. We should find the temple priest and simply tell him why we are here. I do not know him, but I am Brahmin, and he will see that by how I am dressed today. Thus, he will not harm me or any of you, no matter how frightening he may seem. Or, he may be a friendly person. I just don't know, so we will have to see. Come."

Maitra led them all to the temple of Kali. The Aghora, deep in their prayers and meditation, simply ignored them. Then, along with Apada and Iraj, Maitra took off his sandals and indicated for the others to take off their shoes.

Following Swami's example, they entered the temple and sat cross-legged on the stone floor in front of the idol. They sat silently, most of the Westerners looking up at the idol with great apprehension. Because of its size and appearance, their eyes tricked them into wondering if it was making little movements here and there.

After a few minutes, the temple priest came out from a rear chamber. The man stood over six feet tall and rail-thin. His ancient, wrinkled face was mostly covered by a tufty gray beard. His worn, almond eyes were topped by eyebrows and a forehead that naturally curved downward in the middle, giving him a perpetually angry effect. His red and yellow priestly robes offset the brown tone of the idol's skin.

The priest stared at the group for several moments, then sat down with them, crossing his legs.

"I am Subhash Bagchi, priest of the temple of Kali. Welcome."

Maitra said, "I am Maitra, priest of the temple of Durga."

HELL'S BELLS: A PUNK ROCK DEMON STORY

At the name of the goddess, Bagchi squinted his eyes and breathed in. "Why do you come here, priest of Durga? Is there nowhere else in Kolkata more suited to your faith?"

Swami Maitra, remaining calm and impassive with a still face, replied, "I come, not for myself, but for these, my students and friends. The goddess has called them here from across the ocean, and their fate is entwined with that of Kali."

Bagchi did not act surprised but said, "Then they are true, the visions that Kali has given me. These are those from the West, the ones with strange hair, who have come to challenge Kali."

A lone crow cawed loudly from just outside of the temple.

"And will you strive against them, Subhash?" asked Maitra.

"And strive against Durga? How can I strive against a goddess? I am here to serve Kali and to keep his idol. So I can only do what Kali gives me to do."

"Then you are wise," said Maitra. "And so, what has Kali told you about the battle?"

"The one of you named Paul," explained Subhash as he gestured with his hands, "must wander in the Taki Golpata wilderness, where he will face various temptations and struggles. If he survives, then he will face Kali himself in battle."

"Oh, for fuck sake," said Paul. "This shit again?"

Mary put her hand on Paul's shoulder for comfort.

"And what if I refuse?" asked Paul.

"Then," answered Bagchi, "you will have surrendered to Kali, and the great demon uprising will proceed."

"Um, wait," said Uri. "This great demon uprising you mention. That sounds like it needs a little explanation. It doesn't sound like something we should rush past."

Bagchi looked at Uri with a little surprise, then frowned.

"Have you come all this way, across the world, into the temple of Kali, and still you are unaware of what is happening? Surely you have seen the signs. Possessions, hauntings, infestations, demonic forces—they are increasing all over the world. I cannot say why the gods have chosen you, especially this Paul with his strange hair and garments, but who can understand the mind of Lord Shiva? Or who can penetrate the heart of Brahma?"

Uri facepalmed himself. "Oy vey. So let me get this straight," he said while pulling on his payot as a nervous habit. "Demons are rising worldwide, and they want, what, to take over the world? And humanity's one last hope is, no offense, but Paul? That's *meshuggeneh*!"

"I mean," said Matt, "it's crazy, yeah, but it's just as crazy as any of us fighting vampires or werewolves or goblins or zombies or whatever. Life's pretty fucking crazy already."

Paul acquiesced. "Alright, to hell with it. I'll do it. Whatever. Plus, it's totally punk to fight a demon."

"Damn right it is!" said Matt.

"Christ, Paul, wait a minute. Just think about it," pleaded Mary. "How could anything be more dangerous? I can't lose you now after all we've been through!"

Paul took Mary's hand in his, much to the disapproval of Bagchi, whose preference would have been for no women to even be allowed in the temple. He was making an allowance for the foreigners and their lack of knowledge of Indian culture and religion.

"Mary," said Paul, "look, babe. If I do it, we have a chance to stop this demon shit. If I don't do it, there *is* no chance, and we're all dead anyway. I've been pretty damn lucky so far, I'd say. I'll make it through this too. Now, let's get the hell out of this creepy neighborhood. I need a drink."

CHAPTER 22

Ten Little Indians

"Ophelia, I'm not going to tell you where the amulet is. It's too powerful. If you get your hands on it, then you're practically unstoppable," said Chief Cloud Mountain, lying flat on top of a sepulcher. He was bound with ropes inside a large vault in the middle of Lafayette Cemetery No. 1.

"A man will give all he has for his own life," said Ophelia. "It's easy to say that now, Chief, before the fun begins. I'm going to enjoy this so!"

"Beast Stalker will return to New Orleans, find me, and stop you."

Ophelia cackled mockingly.

"Oh, but he won't. Vampire magic is strong, and any spiritual activity he might engage in to find you is likely not powerful enough to pass through the walls of this vault."

"Then the ancestor spirits will protect me. You can't win here, Ophelia. Evil never wins in the long term."

Smiling, she said, "Oh? How many thousands of years do you consider to be long-term? Do you know how long I've been alive? How many civilizations and nations I've seen rise and fall? How many wars I've lived through? How many great enemies I've conquered? And yet, this one still survives!"

Chief steadied his face, clenched his jaws, looked straight ahead, and remained silent.

"So that's your game then, old man? Playing tough? You know, I came very close to breaking Beast Stalker. His pestering friends came too soon. He would have cracked. He would have told me how to use the amulet. He was on the verge. Here, I have the advantage. No one knows where you are. No one's coming to rescue you. I'm going to break you, old man, break you until you beg me to kill you to end the pain."

Still, Chief remained resolute. His expressionless face looked forward, and he said nothing. In his mind, he was already steeling himself, preparing himself by thinking about the history of his people, the Cherokees.

How many brave warriors had fought to protect the people's magic and honor? How many had fallen under more tremendous pain and duress than this? How many countless hours of torture and torment had innumerable Cherokee warriors endured yet not given in to the enemy? Yes, Chief Cloud Mountain came from this firm and proud tradition. He would bear the pain of torture. He would withstand it, and if it meant his death, he would join the ancestors in paradise, and Beast Stalker would take over his duties as Chief of the people. If that were his fate, he would happily accept it and be a spirit guide to Beast Stalker.

Ophelia frowned and growled a deep, guttural growl unbefitting what seemed like a cute, thin, teenage girl. She opened her mouth, extended her vampire fangs, and then licked them sensually.

"I think I'll begin with just a little snack. You understand, don't you, Chief? I skipped lunch today."

Chief was immobile on the marble slab, so he could not move his arm as she stroked it softly with her fingernails, licked it, and plunged her fangs deep into his flesh. He winced and grunted but did not utter a single word.

Ophelia drank for a few seconds, then pulled back. She licked the dribble of blood off her lips. "Some vampires are turned off by drinking the blood of old people. They prefer the young and the beautiful. Not me. I learned long ago that old blood contains deep wisdom and experience, complex and earthy flavors. So, I'm drinking your long life, Chief, and everything you know. It's delicious. But, alas, I can't drain you too much yet. We still have so much fun to do. Let's see, where shall I begin?"

She opened her right hand, a delicate, spindly, pale little hand with sharp, black nails that were more like claws. She traced a fingernail against the palm of Chief's hand, then thrust it right through his hand down to the marble below. He hissed in pain but did not complain.

She giggled like a delighted child, then reached down to the floor and opened a toolbox. She pulled a simple hammer out along with a few nails.

"Now I know these nails won't penetrate the marble, but it will be fun to pretend you're a little Jesus that I'm crucifying. Not your religion, I know, but humor me. It has meaning to me. I was there, you know, when he was crucified."

She placed the tip of a nail against the wound she had already made in his hand and hammered it down to the stone. She repeated it with the other hand, smiling as Chief flinched and whimpered from the sharp agony, the nail splitting a tendon.

"Always wanted to do that," she said. "I should have made a cross, but I digress. Too late now. Wasn't that fun?"

Chief remained stonewalled and just looked up at the ceiling, resigned to his destiny.

"*One little two little three little Indians,*" sang Ophelia to the melody of the old children's song, taking one of Chief's fingers in her hand for each *Indian*. "*Four little five little six little Indians, seven little eight little nine little Indians, ten little Indian boys!*" She giggled. "What do we do with the little Indians, Chief? We set them free, of course!"

Chief kept his face looking up but turned his eyes to the side to watch as Ophelia reached down into her bag and retrieved a smallish but very nasty-looking pair of branch cutters, their stout blades sharpened to perfection.

"Chief, it doesn't have to be this way, you know. Look, you know what's coming, and you know I have no trouble doing it. In fact, I love this sort of thing, torture. I'm *still* willing to stop right now and let you walk out of this tomb and go back home. *All* you have to do is tell me where the amulet is. That's all. So simple, so easy, so pain-free."

Chief did not turn his head to look at her, but he replied, "No. You'll never get your hands on that amulet, Ophelia. Never."

She made her face into an exaggerated caricature of pouting, then shrugged. "As you wish, Chief. You might want to take a deep breath right now."

She picked up the pinkie finger on his left hand and positioned the branch cutter blade around it.

"Last chance, Chief."

He remained silent and steeled his jaw.

She squeezed the handles, and the blades efficiently sliced the finger off, crunching through the bone in the middle. Chief sucked in air and hyperventilated. His body uncontrollably shook at the searing, burning pain.

"Hurts, doesn't it? *One little Indian*. Tell me, Chief. Where's the amulet? This can stop right now. You have my word, and vampires do *not* break our word."

"Honor among thieves?" hissed Chief from between clenched teeth.

"Oh, good one!" said Ophelia. "Really. That was good. I can admit that. *Two little...*"

She sliced off his left ring finger. It thudded as it hit the old, stone floor. Chief hissed in agony.

"Come on, Chief. You can't *possibly* be enjoying this. It has to hurt, frankly. Tell me where the amulet is, and I'll stop immediately and let you walk right out that door. I give you my word."

"Never!" grunted Chief through his tight jaw.

"You are one stubborn old man! Oh well, I tried. *Three little Indians...*"

She slivered off the third finger. Finally, Chief could not keep his cool anymore; he screamed and thrashed.

"Ouch," mocked Ophelia. "I'm getting to you. Good. *Four little...*"

The bone of Chief's index finger audibly crunched as she sheared it off. He could not contain the pain. He shrieked for several seconds.

"Oh, this is getting good!" she boasted. "Might as well finish off that hand; I hate to break up a set. *Five little Indian boys*!"

Crunch went Chief's thumb as it fell to the ground. Blood spurted from the thumb's former location, so Ophelia placed her mouth below it and allowed the blood to fall down her throat.

"Delicious!"

Chief wailed in pain.

"Chief, Chief, Chief. I am truly impressed with your resolve and determination. I mean that. I almost wish I could turn you into a vampire. You'd make a good one. But I need the amulet too much for that; plus, what would a vampire without fingers be?"

Chief growled at Ophelia, his pain preventing him from speaking, but his intent nevertheless clear.

"I know you're angry with me. I would be too, honestly. I'll let you rest for a moment, clear your mind."

She walked around the vault, casually inspecting each coffin and humming the *Ten Little Indians* tune. After a couple of minutes, she returned to Chief's supine form.

"Chief, merciful as I am, I'm still offering you the chance to stop all this. It's so simple. All you need to do is tell me where the amulet is. That's all. A couple of words from you, and I'll immediately stop the torture, unbind you, and let you go. I'll even hold the door for you. Vampire's word."

Chief took a deep breath, turned his head, and looked directly into Ophelia's eyes.

"I'll die before telling you," he said in a resolved tone of voice.

Ophelia frowned and said, "Dammit, Chief. Very well, then. Your choice. We continue."

CHAPTER 23

Who Needs Some Exorcise?

Lâmié, sitting in the grand parlor of his mansion, ended the call and told the others, "Well, Mary said they've made some discoveries in India. Something about Paul going on a quest in the jungle."

"Oh, God," said Titania. "That sounds…not good. I can't imagine Paul in a jungle. Maybe a lightly wooded park, but not a jungle."

Barillo, who had the day off, added, "The fate of the world depends on Paul again? Is this some sort of cosmic joke?"

Lâmié laughed and said, "Yeah, but he *has* pulled it off before. Have faith, Pace."

Barillo shrugged and nodded.

As the tropical sun began its lazy descent to its bed on the horizon, delicious smells drifted from the kitchen into the grand parlor. 'Tit Boudreaux, inspired by Madame Who, had learned a few Romani recipes; he emerged from the kitchen carrying a few different dishes.

The first plate held a dozen stuffed bell peppers, the green flesh filled with a mix of meat, vegetables, and spices, especially paprika. Another dish was *ciganypecsenye*, a giant platter covered in grilled slices of beef, pork, duck liver, and veal, surrounded by mounds of fried potatoes. Yet another platter was covered with cabbage rolls stuffed with rabbit meat. A vast casserole dish of *kugel* accompanied the rest, and the cornmeal porridge called *mămăligă* as a side.

Finally, he returned to the kitchen and brought out mugs of cold ale.

"Confession time, everyone," said 'Tit Boudreaux. "I've been learning how to brew my own beer out back. I have a little setup in the backyard, and I've been doing lots of research and practice. Let me know what you think!"

"Well damn, Marcus!" said Lâmié. "This is nothing short of amazing!"

'Tit Boudreaux blushed. Madame Who saw the meal, and her crazy eyes lit up.

"Oh, my God! This is wonderful! It's like my food!" she proclaimed. "And hand me a beer!"

Before long, the grand parlor was quiet except for a symphony of chewing noises, slurping, swallowing, and sighs of satisfaction.

"You outdid yourself," said Barillo through a mouthful of meat. "God, I think we must eat better than most of the human population in the world."

They heard the front door open and footsteps. Soon, Siofra, Varco, Isabella, and Veronica stepped into the grand parlor.

"Just in time for dinner!" said 'Tit Boudreaux. "Tonight's Romani food. Whoah…what's wrong?"

Everyone looked up from their food to see that the four newcomers were pale and scared. They looked down at the floor as if they were in another world, and the veil of fear and dread affected everyone in the room. Even the aromas of the food seemed to dim in their grim presence.

"Come sit down," said 'Tit Boudreaux. "Y'all look like you just saw a ghost!"

"More like a demon," said Veronica. "And we did."

They explained what had just happened at Miss Annabelle's house, and as they replayed the incident aloud, it seemed to help them deal with it and calm down. Before long, the four were eating and drinking like the others.

"It leaves us with a little problem, doesn't it?" asked Lâmié between bites of the roasted liver. Barillo seemed to be avoiding the liver, so Lâmié felt no shame in taking Barillo's portion.

"Yeah," replied Veronica. "One of our professors is possessed, and we have her locked in a room behind a protective layer of Host powder."

Isabella giggled, and Varco raised one eyebrow at her.

"What?" she said. "*Protective Host powder* sounds funny! And all these situations we get into...it's so ridiculous it's comical, like black humor!"

"Who you callin' black?" asked 'Tit Boudreaux.

"I...I...wait...I didn't mean—" stammered Isabella.

'Tit Boudreaux broke out laughing and said, "I'm just teasing you. Relax. But yeah, it is pretty comical, despite it being so serious. I mean, I can only think of one thing that can help your professor...Miss Annabelle's her name, right? And that's an exorcism."

Everyone looked around to see the others' reactions, but they were all the same: defeated resignation. No one wanted to be involved in an exorcism, but duty demanded it of them.

"Who's gonna do it?" asked Lâmié. "Father Woodrow's in India. Who else can perform an exorcism?"

"What about Woodrow's friends, that imam, and that Baptist preacher guy?" asked Isabella.

"I mean, I guess they can perform exorcisms," said Lâmié.

"Don't forget, the Baptist dude ran off with Reverend Skink and his cult," said Varco.

The food and beer had seemed to work their magic in lifting the feeling of dread from the room overall.

"Shit," said Lâmié, remembering the incident. "Yeah, true. Well, I guess we can ask the imam. Does anyone know his name?"

"I got his card at the street fair," said Varco. "It's Imam Mohamed Riyad. Let's give him a visit tomorrow at his mosque, yes?"

Everyone agreed, except Madame Who.

"No, no, no!" she said surprisingly loudly. "The poor professor is possessed? We cannot wait. We must go *now* and exorcise her, and I will do it! Well, I mean, right after dinner. Madame Who will commune with the spirits and command the demon out of her by the power of God and the spirits!"

"Oh, Lord," muttered 'Tit Boudreaux. "This can't end well."

After everyone finished dinner, Madame Who began walking toward the main hall and toward the front door, calling out, "Everyone, fall in line and follow Madame Who! It's time for an exorcism!" She

HELL'S BELLS: A PUNK ROCK DEMON STORY

had made sure to pack several more beers with her in her enormous purse that, like the Tardis of Dr. Who, seemed larger on the inside than the outside.

The ones who ended up following her, for her own protection mostly, were Lâmié, 'Tit Boudreaux, Siofra, Varco, Isabella, and Veronica, who brought along her own mysterious bag.

Marching through the Garden District toward Miss Annabelle's house, the troop looked comical, so diverse were their appearances. But then again, it was New Orleans, so no one really paid them any attention.

Soon enough, they stood on the sidewalk in front of Miss Annabelle's house.

"Oh, this house is accursed. Accursed, I say!" yelled Madame Who. "I can smell the evil coming out of it!"

"The evil...and the fact that she hasn't bathed in weeks," added Veronica. "Oh shit, Isabella, look who it is."

Anna Barrois, Lucy Teeser, and Rose Liu—the Mean Girls—were strolling down Prytania Street that evening.

"Oh, dammit," whispered Isabella.

The Mean Girls stopped, and Anna said, "Oh my God!"

Lucy said, "Look who it is!"

Rose added, "Those must be their *friends*."

The three broke out into mocking laughter.

"Oh my God," said Anna. "Like, they hang out with old people, weirdos, and fortune-tellers!"

"Oh my God!" repeated Lucy.

The three approached Isabella's group and stood with their hands on their hips, looking everyone up and down. Then they looked at Miss Annabelle's house.

"Ew! They're hanging out in front of a smelly dump! What's *wrong* with them?" asked Anna.

"Weirdos!" mocked Rose.

"Anna, Lucy, Rose, hey, I heard a good joke!" said Varco, catching the Mean Girls off guard.

"Um, whatever," said Anna.

Varco continued, undaunted, "Why are cheerleaders always quiet in the football players' locker room?"

The Mean Girls looked confused.

"Um, like, why?" asked Lucy.

Varco answered, "Because their parents taught them it's impolite to talk with your mouth full."

Isabella and Veronica snorted, and even Lâmié and 'Tit Boudreaux had to look the other way to hide their laughter.

"Oh my God!" said Anna. "Like, whatever!"

The three girls stormed off past Miss Annabelle's house and down the street, grumbling among themselves.

"Damn, Varco! Good one!" said Veronica, shyly putting her hand on his arm for a second. Isabella noticed and did not look happy. Varco just blushed.

"Enough!" shouted Madame Who. "We have an exorcism to perform! Let's go!"

She stormed right up the steps onto the porch without hesitation, knocked on the door thrice, then entered. When they were all inside, she pulled a brush of sage out of her purse, sprinkled some sort of scented oil on it, and began to shake it all over the house, spraying droplets of the oil all around.

As Madame Who performed her preliminary cleansing, they heard a growling from upstairs. The demon knew that they were there.

"No time to waste!" declared Madame Who. "Madame Who will speak to the spirits and the gods and drive the demon out! The demon will not be able to resist the spirits and the power of Madame Who! Just, er, let Madame Who grab a quick beer first."

She pulled a beer from her purse, opened it with her hand, and guzzled it in quick order.

"Wow," said Veronica. "That's some talent. Paul has some new competition."

"Madame Who needs courage for the exorcism!" the Roma explained. "Now, follow me upstairs!"

They plodded up the stairs, almost more worried about Madame Who than the demon. They reached the door to Miss Annabelle's bedroom.

"How is she contained in the room?" asked Madame Who.

"I crushed a Catholic Host and made a line across the threshold," explained Veronica.

"Very good, young lady!" said Madame Who. "Madame Who shall now break the seal!" She opened the door, held her nose because of the unbearable stench, and stepped inside the bedroom. The others followed.

The room was frigid.

Miss Annabelle, or at least the human formerly known as Miss

Annabelle, lay on the rotting mattress, her flesh the same color as a corpse of four or five days. With every breath she inhaled, she rasped in a sub-baritone growl, and with every exhale, a black smoke spewed out of her oral cavity and dissipated in the room.

"Oh, wow," said Veronica. "This is very not good."

Madame Who wailed uncontrollably then opened and guzzled another beer.

"What is the poor girl's name?" asked the fortune teller.

"She's Miss Annabelle, one of the science professors at our campus," said Siofra. "My colleague, as I said before."

Madame Who nodded, pulled up a foul chair to the bed, then sat in it. She used a handkerchief to wipe the gritty sweat from Miss Annabelle's forehead and face.

"The poor dear is completely possessed by the demon. Do not fear, however! Madame Who shall drive the filthy beast from her body!"

Miss Annabelle's eyes opened. She turned her head toward Madame Who, then began to laugh in the guttural demon's voice.

"Who comes to bother me? A fortune-teller?"

"I am Madame Who!" she said and stood up. She produced a bottle of yellow oil from her purse and a large, golden pendant in the shape of a star inside a circle. She rubbed the oil onto Miss Annabelle's forehead, then placed the pendant on Miss Annabelle's chest.

"Now, demon, you must tell Madame Who your name!" she commanded loudly.

"I will not!" roared the demon, causing the others to jump back.

She sprinkled more oil onto Miss Annabelle and said again, "Demon! You must tell Madame Who your name!"

"Fine! My name is…Ned."

Madame Who squinted her eyes and said, "A demon named Ned?"

The demon laughed and said, "No, you fool! I will not tell you my name! Who are you? What authority over me do you have?"

"I am…" she stumbled over her words, losing a bit of confidence. "I am Madame Who, the great Romani fortune teller, the communicator with the spirits, the channeler of the gods!"

"Is that supposed to impress me? You're just a crazy old lady!" The demon laughed so loudly and deeply that the entire house's frame shook.

"I say to you, demon, tell me your name!" she continued.

Taking the pendant in her hand, she raised it to Miss Annabelle's forehead and pressed it down against the skin. The skin sizzled, and the demon yelped in surprise and fear.

"What is that? What have you done to me?"

"It's a very powerful Romani charm, demon! Now, tell me your name!"

"No!"

Madame Who and the demon bantered back and forth for several minutes, but the demon would not reveal its name.

"Oh, you're so frustrating!" yelled Madame Who. She took more oil, leaned over Miss Annabelle's face and eyes—now wholly black—and sprinkled oil all over her visage. "Come out of her! Come out now, demon! The spirits command you! The gods command you!"

Miss Annabelle began to thrash, and in the demon's voice, she cried out as if in pain. "Leave me alone!" bellowed the demon.

Madame Who leaned right in against Miss Annabelle's face and called out, "Come out of this girl now!"

Miss Annabelle stopped thrashing, and the demon laughed. "Is that all you can do? Yell at me to come out? Very well. I will come out, old woman!"

Miss Annabelle's mouth opened, and she coughed. A thick, black, opaque cloud erupted from the mouth, and before she could stop, it entered Madame Who's mouth, making her involuntarily gasp and breathe it in. Then, she fell to the floor.

"What...where...where am I?" asked Miss Annabelle in her regular, lady-like voice. "What...oh God, my room! It's disgusting! Miss Fay? Isabella? Varco? Who are the rest of you, and what's going on?"

Veronica eyed Madame Who, who had begun to shiver on the floor.

"No time to explain, Miss Annabelle!" said Veronica. "You need to come with us now!"

"I...I need some rest and—"

Veronica grabbed Miss Annabelle's arm and forcefully pulled her out of bed. "Sorry!" she said. "You'll thank me later!"

Madame Who began to make sickening, squishy noises in her stomach.

"Um, Veronica?" asked Isabella. "What the hell is happening?"

"Transfer!" said Veronica. "The demon transferred into Madame Who! Everyone, get out of the room now!"

"But..."

"I said *now!*" yelled Veronica with such an authoritative and confident tone that no one argued.

They all pushed out of the bedroom door and watched Veronica, who pulled a water gun from her bag. She shot what was obviously holy water at Madame Who, and when the water hit her skin, it hissed and smoked, causing Madame Who to yell out in the deep voice of the demon. She began to rise and levitate off of the floor.

Veronica worked quickly. She reached in her bag again and pulled out several Hosts. Crumbling them like last time, she made a thick line across the room's threshold, then closed and locked the door.

"Well, hell's bells!" said Lâmié. "The demon just jumped from one person to another?"

"It can happen," said Veronica, "especially with someone like Madame Who, who, well, no offense, doesn't know what she's doing and was taunting the demon."

"So, what the hell do we do now?" asked 'Tit Boudreaux.

"We keep her in there," answered Veronica, "and find someone who is actually qualified to perform an exorcism."

"Oh, for God's sake," said Lâmié.

They did not talk much on the way back to Lâmié's house, but when they reached the parlor and took their seats, Isabella asked, "Veronica, I gotta know. How do you know so much about demons, exorcism, and the paranormal?"

Veronica leaned back in her overstuffed leather chair and replied, "Well, I think I mentioned to you guys that I grew up in a haunted house. Well, when I was in that house, when I was, I don't know, maybe twelve years old, some friends and I decided to try to communicate with the ghost or ghosts with a spirit board. Well, things kind of got out of hand..."

While she recounted the tale to her new friends, she relived it and felt like she was there again in her mind.

Her two best friends, Becky and Melissa, sit with her in the living room of the haunted house of her childhood. They are sharing a large pizza and watching Buffy the Vampire Slayer *on the television. Like any other sleepover night, they are chatting and gossiping about the boys in their class at school and making prank phone calls here and there.*

Without warning, the television screen flickers then becomes blazingly bright, then a loud zap and a puff of smoke comes from the back of the set. The three girls shriek. Before their terrified and disbelieving eyes, a small vase holding a single rose falls off the table and hits the floor.

Veronica, Becky, and Melissa huddle together on the sofa, knowing they must have surely just seen the work of a ghost. Veronica's friends know that her house is supposedly haunted, but this is the first time they have experienced it personally.

Nothing else happens for ten minutes, so they relax a bit.

"Hey, we should try the Ouija board! Maybe the ghost wants to tell us something!" suggests Veronica, and the other two unenthusiastically acquiesce.

They set up the board and the planchette, and Veronica begins by asking, "Hello! Is there a spirit here with us? If you are here, please communicate with us! Who pushed the vase onto the floor? Who burned out the TV? Reveal yourself to us!"

Becky and Melissa look nervous—their hands are subtly shaking. The three girls wait several minutes without any reply. Then, they hear a scratching in the wall right behind Melissa. The poor girl, terrified, whips around to face the wall, removing her hand from the planchette.

The girls jump and gasp when three loud, hard poundings, seemingly from the inside, hit the wall. They gather on the other side of the room, grabbing one another in a bundle.

From the other wall, as if passing through it, a misty, full-bodied figure steps into the room. They are frozen but can make out a basic human form with a featureless face. It reaches out its arm toward them, and they shudder.

As they watch, the figure turns from a misty white to a cloudy, foul black. Horns appear on the thing's head, and two bright, white eyes stare at them with hatred. Veronica, scared but the bravest of the three by far, composes herself and steps in front of her two friends.

"Leave, ghost!" she commands in her high-pitched girl's voice. "You may not stay here! I command you to leave my house!"

The thing cocks its head slowly to the side as if trying to comprehend Veronica's words and boldness. A low, rumbling growl comes from the thing, and then it lunges. It lunges at the girls, floating quickly through the air right at them.

They wince, but it passes directly through them, and as it does, they feel great waves of rage, fear, confusion, loneliness, maleficence, harm, violence, and destruction. Never have the three young girls felt such negative emotions, and certainly not to that degree. The thing *passes through the wall behind them and disappears.*

Overcome with the maudlin and rageful feelings, the girls fall to the carpeted floor, hold one another, and sob for several minutes.

"Wow!" exclaimed Isabella. "That's...both amazing and horrifying."

"Yeah, it was bad!" agreed Veronica. "Anyway, after that, I began to study, research, and learn everything I could about ghosts and demons and the paranormal. I think I must have read every book ever written on the subject. I learned all about possession, exorcism, and preventing harm from demons. So I guess I'm self-taught but based on a real-life experience."

Lâmié stood up, went to the kitchen, then returned with beers for everyone. After that story, they needed a drink.

CHAPTER 24

Sex Pistol

"What...what are you doing here?" said Aaron to the nude Arab girl on his sofa.

She smiled, not making any effort to hide her breast with their brown, erect nipples or her thick, kinky bush of pubic hair. Instead, she opened her legs directly at Aaron, showing him her already-engorged and moist womanhood.

"I saw the way you looked at me at the street fair. Come on, don't be coy."

She licked her lips. Aaron's mouth fell open. He had never seen a woman's thigh, much less her everything. Even Amos had fallen silent behind his stunned brother.

"Oh, boys, don't worry about my father, the imam. What he doesn't know won't hurt him. Come over here and sit next to me. There's nothing to be afraid of, Aaron."

"I...you...he...I mean...what...I...ma'am...I...I think that might be a sin!" stammered Aaron.

She stood up, revealing every part of her glorious body, and the two boys remained frozen in place. Finally, she swayed over to Aaron and stood so close to him that her nipples poked his white Oxford shirt. He looked down at them with enormous open eyes.

"Kiss me, you silly boy!" she taunted.

Aaron drew back and bumped into Amos behind him. "I'd better not, ma'am. I'm a Mormon, and I want to live a pure life, and it's a sin to—"

She interrupted him with a deep, wet kiss on his mouth. At first, shock prevented him from pulling back, but then he began to enjoy the lush, sensual experience he had never before enjoyed. She rolled her tongue around in his mouth, and he reciprocated, and within just a few seconds, his hands were on her breasts.

He rubbed her nipples and began to moan, but Amos from behind said, "Aaron! Stop! Stop sinning now! I order you to stop sinning!"

Aaron simply ignored his brother as the girl pulled him across the room to the sofa. Then, as if he were in a trance, he stood still as she removed all of his clothing, making him entirely nude, his erection pointing up at the ceiling.

"Oh, goodness!" yelled a horrified Amos from across the room.

"I...I can't help it!" protested Aaron, quite unable to stop the sexual process any more than a starving person might resist a thick, juicy cheeseburger, or a person with a full, bulging bladder might resist urinating.

Amos watched in jealous disgust as the girl took Aaron's penis in her hand and began to slide her hand back and forth gently.

"Are all Mormons circumcised?" she asked, and as a reply, Aaron simply moaned.

She knelt down, slid his hardness into her mouth, and bobbed up and down on it. Aaron grabbed the arm of the sofa to keep himself from shuddering to the ground. As the girl felt him approaching climax, she stopped and pushed him down on the sofa.

She straddled him and slid him inside herself, then rode him until he burst forth inside her, his copious semen sliding down her inner thighs.

The room was silent and still as both Aaron and Amos tried to grasp the gravity of what had just occurred. Finally, the girl stood up and went to the bathroom, where she cleaned herself up and got dressed.

"Bye-bye, boys! Anytime you need relief and release, just come to the mosque and ask for me! Oh, I took the liberty of stocking your refrigerator with beer. A nice, cold one is always good after sex."

After she was out the door, Aaron became embarrassed and quickly put his clothes back on. Amos sat across from him in an overstuffed chair.

"What did you do, Aaron? You've sinned greatly! You need to repent and pray for forgiveness!"

Aaron sighed and said, "You know what, bro? I'm kind of tired of always feeling guilty about everything, and I'm tired of you always bossing me around and criticizing me. You know what? I'm going to have a beer, and you can't do anything about it!"

"Bro, no! No! Coke is one thing, but beer is very sinful! Joseph Smith said—"

"To hell with Joseph Smith!" screamed Aaron, causing Amos to throw his hand over his own mouth.

"Repent, Aaron! Repent!"

"Repent this!" countered Aaron as he opened a beer bottle and took a large gulp. "Oh, yeah. That is *good*."

"Aaron! Why won't you listen to me? This is a great sin! You never listen to me; no one ever listens to me. I *wish* people would respect me!"

The djinn flowed out of the lamp, crossed his arms, nodded his head, and said, "As you wish, Master! This concludes your three wishes!"

"No, wait...I didn't mean...wait!" protested Amos, but the Djinn ignored him.

"I have granted you three wishes, just as I promised. The wishes will be fulfilled exactly as you phrased them. Now, I am free from the curse of the lamp and my obligation to grant your wishes! Goodbye, boys! I am free!"

In a thick cloud of black smoke, the djinn whisked itself away through the window and was seen no more.

Aaron had already finished the first beer of his life and was smiling with mellow eyes. He opened another and sat down at the kitchen table to enjoy it.

"I could get used to this life," he said softly. "I think I might go out to a bar tonight."

Amos simply glared at Aaron and frowned. "Well, I'm going outside to preach the gospel, Aaron. You can stay inside and sin, but I want to save souls, including yours."

So, Amos left the apartment alone with nothing but his Book of Mormon. Huffing, he marched right up to the first house he saw and knocked on the door. A girl about his age opened it.

"Hello, ma'am. I'm Elder Amos Brigham of the Church of Jesus Christ of Latter Day Saints. I was wondering if I might have a moment of your time to tell you about the gospel."

The girl knelt and said, "Oh, Elder Brigham! You're so wonderful and great! I will always worship you, my Lord!"

"What? Wait, no! No, no! I'm just a servant of the Lord. It's blasphemy to—"

"Mom, Dad! Come see! Hurry!" shouted the girl, and in a few seconds, her parents appeared behind her.

"It's Elder Brigham! Bow down and respect and worship him!"

"Wait, no!" he protested but to no avail.

Now, the girl and her parents were kowtowing to him.

"We respect and honor you, Elder Brigham! Respect him! Respect him!"

"Oh, no. The wish," he lamented. "This is going to be ridiculous."

A small crowd had gathered around Amos, and as everyone fell to their knees and bowed down to him, he felt both terribly guilty and embarrassed. Still, there was a slight twinge of pride deep within his soul. What was that?

CHAPTER 25

Dry Run

"Wait, what the hell?" said Lâmié to 'Tit Boudreaux as he pulled his SUV into the parking lot of The Gutter Bar. "Um…"

The two friends stared at their bar, not because it was still in disrepair from the latest crisis, but because it was full of people dressed in their Sunday finest.

"Oh, God. Oh no. Look, Marcus."

Lâmié pointed, and 'Tit Boudreaux followed his finger to see the odious, weeping-willow figure of the Reverend Methuselah Skink standing at the bar's front door, shaking hands and welcoming people in.

"What…the…fuck…" said 'Tit Boudreaux.

Lâmié parked in one of the last available spaces, and they jogged to the door.

"Skink!" accused Lâmié. "What the hell are you doing at my bar?"

"*And the priest answered David, 'I have no ordinary bread at hand, only holy bread—provided that the young men have kept themselves from women!'*"

"What the hell is that supposed to mean?"

"Language, Sir! Language!" admonished Skink. "David's

hunger took precedence over the rule about not touching the holy bread. Well, I required a place to preach the word of God as revealed to the People's Family of the Divine Blessing and me, the prophet, the Right Reverend Methuselah Skink. The will of God is much more important than the minor laws of man, such as private property and trespassing."

Lâmié facepalmed himself and said, "Look, *Reverend*, your weird religion is none of my business, but you absolutely cannot break into my bar, and you most certainly do *not* have permission to use it for your, your, your revival meeting or whatever you call it. Get out, or I'm calling the cops."

Skink smiled his damp, slimy grin.

"Why, my child, your anger is an obstacle between you and God! You must come and hear the good word! In fact..." He looked at his watch. "...it's time to begin!"

Skink stepped inside as two muscular ushers shoved Lâmié and 'Tit Boudreaux into the bar, which Skink had converted and decorated to look like the inside of a Protestant church, complete with an altar and a giant crucifix hanging on the wall.

"Oh, good grief," said 'Tit Boudreaux as he pushed the ushers off them. "Where did Skink go?"

The slithering reverend had weaved and slinked through the crowd so quickly that they had lost sight of him. After only a few seconds, though, the reverend climbed the stage and stood behind the altar. 'Tit Boudreaux and Lâmié looked at each other and shook their heads in disbelief and frustration.

"Brothers and sisters!" began Skink through a microphone that magnified his reedy, crackling voice much too loudly. People grabbed their ears.

"For fuck's sake," muttered Lâmié.

"Now you all know that God has spoken to me, his prophet, and through People's Family of the Divine Blessing, to send you the message of salvation and rebirth!"

The crowd applauded enthusiastically, and several people shouted *amen*!

"Do we not follow the pattern and example of our Lord Jesus, brethren? I declare that, yes, we do!"

Most of the congregation raised their hands in religious ecstasy and waved them around.

"And so has the Apostle Paul written, *But if it is preached that Christ has been raised from the dead, how can some of you say that there is no resurrection of the dead?* And again, brethren, Paul says, *For the trumpet will sound, the dead will be raised imperishable, and we will be changed.*"

The audience whooped and hollered.

"Yes, brethren, the resurrection is our goal, our aim, our entire reason for existence! If our Lord willingly gave himself up to death, was buried, and rose from the dead, then so shall we! That is the apostle's meaning."

"Hallelujah!"

"Amen!"

"Preach it, Reverend!"

"Amen!"

"Then, we would be right, would we not, brethren, to hasten the death of this poor, mortal body so that we might hasten the resurrection in our new bodies. Nay, I say that we would be wrong, we would be *in sin*, to *not* hasten death, brethren! We must hasten death!"

Hasten death! Hasten death! Amen! Hallelujah! Hasten death!

Lâmié and 'Tit Boudreaux looked at each other, unable to believe what they were hearing.

Lâmié said, "Is he suggesting they kill themselves?"

"Sure as hell sounds like it!" replied 'Tit Boudreaux.

The religious fervor vibrated through the air. Even the Reverend Don Malbrook was in the front row with his hands raised and shouting.

"Now, brethren," continued Skink. "Our ushers will be passing around refreshments, some nice, red Kool-Aid. Do not fret, brethren. These are just refreshments. It is not quite time yet for our transformation and resurrection. No, not yet. Let us consider this our dry run, our practice. Drink to resurrection, brothers and sisters!"

Drink to resurrection! Drink to resurrection! Drink to resurrection!

Lâmié and 'Tit Boudreaux looked in horror as ushers passed around little paper cups of red Kool-Aid. Then, they tried to knock the cups out of people's hands as everyone started drinking while also screaming warnings not to drink. As the congregation drank, however, nothing happened, so apparently, it really was a practice run.

"I guess these ones are harmless," said 'Tit Boudreaux.

"Yeah," said Lâmié, "but what about next time when it's for real? We need to tell Barillo about this. I'm calling him now."

Fifteen minutes later, Barillo and two uniformed police arrived and began shuffling everyone out of the bar, leaving only Skink himself inside. Barillo sent the uniformed officers on their way, then sat down with Skink, Lâmié, and 'Tit Boudreaux.

"Reverend Skink," began Barillo, "you can't just invade someone's property and have church. It's illegal. Now, you're lucky that these two guys here don't want to pursue any charges against you, and I'll agree to that because of the, well, the *weirdness* of the situation."

Skink grinned maniacally and said, "As God has said, *you shall not round the corners of your heads!*"

"Um, what?"

"Indeed!" continued Skink. "*Do not wear clothing woven of two kinds of materials!*"

Barillo, Lâmié, and 'Tit Boudreaux looked at one another, frustrated.

"Look, um, Reverend," said Barillo, "I'm not here for a theological discussion. That's your business. But I am concerned about you telling your congregants to *hasten death* by drinking Kool-Aid. That sounds a little too close to the Jim Jones incident. Now, I'd like you to tell me right here and now: are you planning to have your congregants kill themselves?"

Skink's grin grew so wide that he actually began to resemble a toad. His long, brown tongue licked his yellow teeth.

"Why, Detective! There is no death! For the servant of God, death is an illusion. Neither I nor my congregants will die. It is impossible."

Barillo rubbed his forehead and said, "Look, I'm not good at talking in riddles. Just know that I'm professionally obligated to keep an eye on you because of what you preached. I hope, I sincerely hope, that you are not planning to do anything stupid. If so, I'll arrest you immediately. Understood?"

Skink stood up, bowed in an exaggeratedly ceremonious manner, nodded, and exited the bar, his long, thin legs hopping along like those of a grasshopper.

"God, that fucker's weird," said Barillo. "Need to keep an eye on him. Call me if he takes over the bar again, and I'll arrest his ass."

He sat back in his chair and sighed, looking even more worn and ragged than usual. His hair was tussled, and he had buttoned his shirt unevenly.

"Speaking of," said Lâmié, "the brawl with the church people last time did some damage here. We need to get The Gutter back in shape and have our next show when the Gravediggers return from India."

"Yeah," said 'Tit Boudreaux, "if demons don't take over the world by then."

CHAPTER 26

Wager Danger

On a hot Kolkata morning, just outside the city, Paul, Mary, Matt, Uri, Father Woodrow, Beast Stalker, Maitra, Apada, Iraj, and Subhash, the priest of Kali's temple, stood at the edge of the Taki Golpata jungle.

"This is actually really pretty," said Uri. "What, a demon chooses a beautiful forest to fight in? Oy, what kind of a demon is this anyway?"

They gazed at the countless palm trees gently dancing in the warm, tropical breeze. These were mixed with mangroves and several other varieties of trees and plants, a lush forestscape.

The lightest mist was fluffing down from the heavens, and among the countless branches, shrubs, and vines, birds called out in song, and other small animals chattered to one another. The verdant blush of the forest was a welcome breath from the urbanity of Kolkata, a seemingly impossible contradiction of environments.

Mary, who was holding on to Paul's arm and looking around nervously, said, "Wales was beautiful too, you know."

Paul put his arm around her and said, "Don't worry, kitten. I'll be fine. I brought some liquid courage." He opened his bag to reveal several bottles of *Bangla*, a West Bengali drink made of distilled sorghum, and several cans of beer.

"Christ, Paul. What the hell is that?" asked Mary.

"Oh!" said Maitra. "I see you've found our Kolkata fire water! Careful, that stuff packs a real punch!"

"If anyone can handle it..." muttered Mary.

Matt said, "Paul, I have confidence in you. All the shit we've, you've, pulled off? And never forget: fighting a demon's totally punk."

"Damn right it is!" said Uri.

"Yeah," said Matt. "Imagine Glenn Danzig actually fighting a demon instead of just singing about them!"

Somewhere in the distance, the pleasant sound of water gently lapping a shore carried across the breeze. The smell of rain and grass and leaves and wet nature enlivened them all.

Father Woodrow approached Paul and said, "Look, Paul, I know you don't believe in my Catholic faith, and that's your business. But please let me at least bless you before you go. It might give you a little protection when you most need it."

Paul shrugged and said, "Yeah, alright. No harm, I guess. I don't believe that crap, but if it makes you feel better."

Woodrow made the sign of the cross on Paul's forehead and uttered a brief blessing.

"Well, no time like the present," said Paul. "I'm not sure what to expect, so I'll just walk around."

"Oh, Paul!" said Mary, hugging him tightly. "Please be careful. I'm so worried."

He felt a tinge of regret, of sadness. Would this be the last time that he ever saw Mary and his friends? Was this going to be it, the final end of Paul? His stomach flipped.

"I'll be fine, Mary," he said, then kissed her hard on the lips. "I'll pull it off somehow."

Mary nodded as she wiped a tear from her cheek.

With a final wave to everyone, Paul hiked off into the jungle, his Doc Martens laced tight.

Paul meandered along lovely, grassy paths, surrounded by tropical trees and plants. Generally not spending much time in nature, he found it rather pleasant and relaxing. After an hour or so, however, he started to feel lonely.

"Shit," he said aloud to the jungle. "Kind of alone out here. Anyone around?"

A bird tweeted back at him.

He reached a clearing and sat on a large stone to rest. He opened his bag, pulled out a bottle of Bangla, and took a sip; he almost did a spit take.

"Shit!" he said after he managed a swallow. "That's some harsh stuff. Geez."

That did not stop him from continuing, however.

After a few more minutes of drinking, he heard some laughing voices from somewhere in the distance. Curious, Paul decided to follow the noise carefully. It was morning, so he had plenty of light, but he remained cautious nevertheless.

Following a narrow grass path flanked by verdant, leafy shrubs and palm trees taller than he was, Paul could not see to his sides, and the more the path curved, the less he could even see in front of him.

He almost felt like he was in a video game, knowing that his path was linear, determined, and fated, should he choose to continue. Then, again as if in a video game, he came upon a small structure out of nowhere.

The little house was typical of West Bengal: a squat mud structure with a thatched roof of bamboo; a single, doorless entrance in the front; and windows all around, each of which was surrounded by little decorative flourishes in yellow and brown pigment.

The most striking aspect of the little hut, however, was the noise coming from inside. Paul heard various male and female voices, all speaking some local language that he could not understand and sounding absolutely delighted and joyful, as if they were at the party of the year.

Among the voices was the tinkling of glasses, and it was not only the sounds that attracted Paul. The fragrant aroma of delicately spiced and roasted meats wafted out to him, smelling like the most delicious and masterful dishes ever cooked by a human being.

"Oh, fuck yeah!" he said, already buzzed from the strong Bangla.

Stumbling from the effects of the harsh alcohol, he made his way to the front opening of the little building. On the threshold stood perhaps the most beautiful girl he had ever seen. She looked about eighteen years old and wore a golden sari and matching golden tiara. Her shape hinted at firm breasts underneath her clothing.

Her skin, as smooth as a windless sea and brown like New England leaves in the fall, almost glinted with the reflection of the golden sun rays into the sparkling forest. Her eyes, gently sloping like a small hill covered in flowers, smiled along with her supple, moist, brown lips, which revealed little glimpses of her straight, white teeth.

"Oh, hell!" said Paul.

In soft tones of charmingly-accented English, she said, "Greetings. Please come in and join our perfect happiness."

Unable to deny the allure, Paul stepped inside the house. It was indeed filled with young men and women in beautiful clothing of obviously-high quality. No one in the room was less than gorgeous, and they seemed to almost glide across the floor as they flitted about, drinks in hand.

The center table was overfull with dishes of roast game, and as Paul entered, the other guests looked at him with broad smiles and gestured for him to eat. He accepted the invitation.

As he bit into tender, perfectly-roasted morsels of various types of meat, the sublime, ambrosial flavors exploded onto his taste buds. The warm umami of the meat itself and the slight tang of wild gaminess were enhanced by a graceful, exquisite accompaniment of Indian spices—salty, sour, bitter, sweet, spicy, and an entire gamut of exotic palates of multi-colored herbs and other spices. So delicious was the food that Paul's knees crumpled, and he almost fell onto the floor.

Another table on the other side of the room was topped with several decks of cards. Some delighted and boisterous men sat around the table, cross-talking one another and dealing cards. With every hand, shouts of joy and surprise would fill the area, and the dealer would push piles of money—US dollars—toward a winner. Everyone seemed to win one hand or another, and no one was really losing.

One man caught Paul's eye and waved him over. As Paul strode across the room, a beautiful woman handed him a pint of dark beer with a thick, foamy head. He took a sip, and the beverage tasted rich and flavorful; Paul immediately felt warm, loving drunkenness take over his body, mind, and soul.

One of the men pulled a plush chair out for him and all but pushed him into the seat.

"Paul! Let's play some games!"

The world had become pleasantly hazy, and Paul slurred, "How do you know my name?"

The man ignored his question with a smile and said, "Your quest, Paul! All of your quests—wouldn't it be nice to be done with all the responsibility and danger? To finally stop the forces of evil, once and for all?"

"Mate, I don't mind the fight. It gives me something to live for."

"Oh, Paul, but you know that's not true. Inside you, behind the leather and spikes and Mohawk, there's still just a scared little boy, so sad that his parents abandoned him, all alone in the world, isn't there?"

"Well, I—"

The man continued to press him while dealing cards.

"And your friends, Paul. Maybe Mary's seen a glimpse of the real Paul, but what are you to the rest of them? A clown? Comic relief? A useless drunk? What do you offer them anyway, besides a few laughs?"

Paul frowned for a moment, then replied, "Mate, I've saved the world, you know."

"So you are their stunt-man? Disposable? The one to throw at evil when the others are too scared or too smart to fight back?"

"They...no! They like me! They do!"

The man placed a gentle, comforting hand on Paul's shoulder and softly said, "Paul, you know that's not true. They *use* you, Paul. I think you know that in your heart. How could they love you, Paul? They don't even know you."

Paul was feeling a sort of dread clawing inside his belly, as if an Indian tiger was using his claws to grab itself on Paul's stomach muscles. Even if he wanted to be strong and resolute, the stranger was indeed touching the deepest recesses of his insecurities.

"You hide inside that hardened shell and make the world hazy with drink. Why should you owe them your life, Paul? Even your soul? Do you not know that Kali can take your very soul? Are you going to give your soul for people who don't even care about you? Why, Paul?"

Paul had no answer to give. After all, the man wasn't wrong, was he? Had any of his friends really made any effort to know the real Paul? Mary, sure, she'd seen him exposed. She probably liked him a little. But the others? No.

They really did use him.

What a fool he had been! Volunteering to risk his life for them? Sure, let the funny drunk go die, so we don't have to. Well, things were going to change for Paul.

"I guess you're right," he said to the man.

The man patted Paul on the back and said, "Well, Paul, the first step in achieving Nirvana is to pull back the curtains of the illusions of what we call reality, and to see the bare truth, no matter how hard it may be. You have done well. Now, Paul, join our game. I have a wager that you will find interesting."

Paul finished his beer in one sip, and as the beautiful woman appeared instantly to hand him another, he said, "Let's play."

The man grinned widely, and the other men at the table applauded and cheered gleefully.

"The game's blackjack."

"You play blackjack in India?"

The man just winked at him and continued: "Blackjack, I'm dealer. The wager? If you win, Paul, then your fight against Kali is over. You win. You can go right back to New Orleans, the world is saved, and you never again have to risk your life against evil. You spend the rest of your life playing music, drinking beer, eating good food, and chasing beautiful women."

Paul's eyes opened wider. "Hell, mate, that sounds good to me! And what if I lose?"

"Oh, that's simple. If you lose the hand, then Kali gets the soul of one of your friends. You choose which one."

He paused for just a second, but his self-doubt won. "Alright. Fuck them. I'll take the bet. Just one catch: you can't take Mary's soul. She's off-limits completely."

"Fine! I agree," said the man happily. "Let's play!"

He dealt Paul a card face-up: it was a ten. The dealer then dealt himself one face-up card: also a ten. Paul's second card was a nine, giving him nineteen in total. He smiled. The dealer placed his own second card face-down.

"Paul, you have a good hand!" declared the man.

"Mate, I know I bloody well do. I'm standing on that!"

The dealer nodded, never losing his pleasant smile. "Good choice, Paul. Now, let's see what card I have."

In one smooth motion, the man flipped his card over to reveal a...ten.

"Sorry, Paul. You have nineteen, and I have twenty. I win."

Paul stared at the cards with his mouth hung open. "How...how the hell?"

"The luck of the draw, Paul. The luck of the draw."

The man smiled, gathered the cards, then turned to face Paul. The other people at the table were still gaming and laughing, seemingly oblivious to Paul's losing hand.

"Paul, you know the terms of the wager. You lost, fair and square. Now, which of your friends' souls will you choose for Kali to take?"

"Shit, I...I didn't really—"

"You know you cannot renege on a bet—gentleman's code. Now, which friend? Choose carefully, as there is no redemption for them once the demon has their soul."

Paul looked at the man's face, and for a brief moment, the man was too greedy; his eyes flashed red, and his face became gaunt and hollow like a corpse, for an almost imperceptibly short time.

"Wait a minute, mate. What the hell are you?"

The man smiled, and his smile became wider and wider until it split his face from ear to ear. His human face peeled off and fell to the ground, revealing a reptilian horror, a demon.

"I knew I could not hide my true nature from you for too long, Paul! I knew your insidious, damned nature would see through me! It does not matter; you are still bound to the wager! Choose a friend, Paul!"

Paul knew immediately that he had been tricked. He also knew there was no way out of a wager with a demon or a god. What a fool he had been! Of course his friends liked him, loved him. The demon had deceived him and had influenced his mind against them. No, he would not harm his friends!

"I...I choose myself! Take my soul in place of theirs!"

The demon shrieked, knowing that it had been defeated.

"No! No!" it cried. "Selflessness and sacrifice, I cannot abide! You have figured me out, Paul! Curse you! Curse you! The trial is not over yet!"

Everything around Paul—the house, the tables, the food, the beer, the people, and even the demon—disintegrated into a dazzling, sparkling mist and then into nothing, and he found himself in the middle of the forest again as if the house had never existed.

"Well, shit," said Paul to the trees around him.

Chapter 27

Paul's Addiction

"Not a fair fight!" screamed Paul to the jungle around him. "Come fight me to my face! No more illusions!"

The silence mocked him.

"Oh, gonna be one of these stupid test things, oi? Bring it the fuck on." A multicolored Indian squirrel looked at him, then scurried off. "Same to you," Paul muttered.

Looking for a place to rest, he found a tree stump and sat for a bit. He was glad that Mary had packed him some food and water (and, of course, the Bangla and beer that he himself had packed). He found several masala dosas and several water bottles, and he silently thanked Mary. The sandwich-like dosas, filled with some sort of luscious, moist chutney, caused Paul to moan almost erotically.

"Damn, that's good!" he said aloud. "If Kali kills me, at least I'll go out with some fucking delicious food. They can put dough around my body and bury me as a giant samosa."

He heard some giggling laughter from behind a patch of bushes.

"Oh, fuck. What now?"

A teenage girl peeked out from behind the bushes, covered her mouth, and snickered.

"Oi! Come out. Might as well do this now."

The girl stepped out. She had the almost-blue skin of the ancient

Dravidian peoples of the South and wore a very traditional, multi-colored sari. Her feet were bare.

Out stepped another girl who looked about the same, perhaps a sister, just a little older.

"Oh, hello, Sir," said the older girl in passable but heavily-accented English. "Please pardon us! We live near here, and we are collecting berries for our family. We would never be so bold, but we have never before seen a foreigner! Are you American?"

Paul eyed them suspiciously but said, "Yeah, I'm American. You sure this ain't some kind of trick?"

The girls looked hurt.

"Oh, no, Sir!" said the older sister. "We are sorry! We would never bother you!"

"Ah, it's alright. Come on, then. You can have some dosas. I can't eat them all."

The girls, barely fleshed out enough to fill their saris, stared at the Indian sandwiches like wolves who had never seen red meat before.

"Oh, Sir...we...it would be so rude to take your food—"

The younger girl tugged on her sister's sari, but the older sister slapped her hand away. They whispered some things back and forth in their language.

"Don't be shy. Come on, girls. Really, I can't eat them all."

The teenage girl walked toward Paul and pulled her sister along, who was blushing and looking at the ground.

"Look, I'm American, alright? We're not as formal as you. Here, have some water too."

The girls, a little embarrassed, swallowed the dosas down as quickly as possible, trying their best to be polite, but they were obviously undernourished. They each gulped an entire bottle of water down afterward.

"Oh, thank you, Sir. That was delicious! You are so kind. Are all American boys so kind and handsome?" asked the younger sister, causing the older one to turn bright red and chastise her sister in their language.

"Debatable," said Paul with a grin. "So, where am I? Am I near the middle of the forest?"

"Yes, Sir, I suppose so," said the older. "Please forgive us, but we must go to continue picking berries for our mother. However, we will never forget your kindness and this meeting with an American boy! If we see you again in this forest, we will repay you!"

Paul pursed his lips and said, "No need, girls. Seriously, happy to share. Be careful out there, alright? It's dangerous."

The girls simply giggled, bowed, and walked off together until they were no longer visible in the thick of the jungle.

"Well, damn. If I were single…" muttered Paul.

He looked into his bag and eyed the beer. As much as the Bangla performed its work quickly, the flavor was brutal, so he decided that a beer or two would be just the thing. He cracked one open, and it was still cool.

"Oh, fuck yeah," he sighed as he took a gulp.

It was the best damn beer that he had ever tasted. Maybe it was the stress of the situation or the heat of the jungle, but the beer was liquid heroin cascading down his parched throat. He immediately relaxed and felt whole and complete. Before he knew it, he had finished all the beer bottles.

He looked at the Bangla and shuddered. "God, even I'm not sure if I can handle more of that rotgut filth."

He looked inside the bag wistfully, but he noticed another beer bottle.

"Oh, hell yeah! My lucky day!"

He opened the bottle, and, as he drank, he felt ecstatic, as if he were floating up into the heavens. Every worry, every stress, every guilt, every pain, every burden of being human washed down his gullet with every swallow of the golden elixir.

"Gotta remember this brand! Damn!"

He finished the last bottle sadly, but when he looked again in the bag, there was another bottle! A sober Paul might have hesitated at the seemingly magical, endless supply of beer, but so drunk was he that all he felt was happiness and relief at the phenomenon.

After a couple more beers, his entire body was not only free of any sort of stress or pain, but tingling pleasure scintillated all over his arms and legs. His entire being, not only his body but also his mind and emotions and spirit, felt on the verge of the mother of all orgasms.

As the beers kept appearing in the bag, Paul kept drinking them until he might as well have been in the clouds. He had no plans to stop.

Hearing some rustling in the forest, he looked to his left and saw someone in the distance approaching. As the figure drew closer, Paul saw that it was an old hag, her face wrinkled like the crevices of the Himalayas, and her back bent like the ridges of the Purvanchal Mountains.

She leaned on her crooked walking cane as if it were her sole support upon the earth, and the closer she hobbled to Paul, the older and older she looked. Without a word, she slowly bent down to sit on a stump near him, who was feeling so good that he just shrugged.

Eventually, the ancient woman spoke in English. "Hello, child. It is not often that I see foreigners in this area. Are you visiting India as a tourist?"

Paul chuckled and said, "Not so much. I wish I were, though. Great country you got here, lady."

"Very old country. Very old," said the woman. "Many ancient mysteries and legends. Some say there is magic here."

"Oh, I bloody believe it," affirmed Paul.

The woman just nodded.

"Want a beer?" offered Paul. "They keep…wait. What?" Paul looked into his bag and saw that there was no more beer. "Oh, hell no!"

His euphoric state immediately began sinking. He started to feel sad and empty as if his soul were leaving him. A nauseating migraine headache ravaged his mind, and his muscles became sore like with the flu.

"Does it hurt, child?"

Shivering with feverish chills, Paul looked curiously at the woman.

"You need the beer, don't you?" asked the woman. "Here, I have one for you."

She produced one of the beers and reached her hand out. Paul crawled to her, took the beer greedily, barely managed to open it, and voraciously guzzled it. The withdrawal symptoms were immediately replaced with a return of the pleasure.

"Oh, God, yes," he mumbled.

"You should be careful, Paul. You've become dependent on the beer."

"Been dependent on beer for years, lady."

The woman cackled and bore her few remaining teeth in a mocking smile. "Then we only have to wait, don't we?" she said.

Wait they did, and it did not take long for the effects of withdrawal to begin to slam Paul's body and spirit. Soon enough, he was doubled over in pain.

"Please…please…another beer…" he struggled to say.

The woman laughed and handed him one more, which he quickly imbibed, causing the pleasure to return. They repeated this ludicrous cycle a few more times until, in one of Paul's cycles of agony, the woman held out a beer, and as Paul staggered to her to retrieve it, she pulled it back at the last second.

She clucked at Paul and said, "No, no, child. We cannot do this forever. Now, your pain is going to become worse and worse, never abating, an eternity of hell in this jungle."

"Fuck...give me the beer..." Paul croaked, his throat like a desert.

"I can lift your pain, Paul, even without the beer. With but one touch of my crooked old finger, all of your torment will fly away like a bird into the sky, and your addiction to the beer will also be gone."

Paul hacked, coughing up some blood. Every one of his muscles burned, and it was becoming hard to breathe.

"Then do it, you old hag!" he hissed.

"I will do it at a price."

Containing another batch of cough, he said, "For fuck sake...does everything here come at a price?" He was struggling to speak through the pain. "Whatever...happened...to...just...being nice?"

Chortling at Paul, mocking his pain, she explained, "You must choose one of your friends as a sacrifice. Deliver their soul to me, agree to it, and I will end your pain immediately. Just one word, Paul. Just say *yes*."

"No," he managed to say through clenched teeth and with a parched throat.

"The pain will not go away. It will become eternally worse, but you will not die. You will suffer forever here, in this jungle, until you say yes."

Paul, who was shaking involuntarily, replied, "Then...I...will...suffer..."

"No man can endure that much pain, Paul. All men eventually relent."

Now almost thrashing back and forth, trying fruitlessly to shake off the pain, Paul said, "I'm...not...all...men...you bitch!"

"Then I will just sit and wait," she said nonchalantly, crossing her weathered hands and rocking gently back and forth.

After several minutes, Paul began to chatter his teeth and groan involuntarily. His mind could only focus on the pain, and even his vision began to blur.

"One word, Paul. You only need to think of the name of one of your friends. Just think of it and assent, and your suffering is over."

"Fucking...never..."

Within, however, Paul was tempted. Physical torture was forcing every cell of his body to want to spew out the suffering, and the brain to agree to anything to stop the agony.

Would he really continue forever, never dying, the pain increasing all the time? It truly would be intolerable. Death would be a gift.

Death would be a gift.

That was it, Paul thought, with the last tiny part of his mind still capable of rational thought beyond the torment. Death. It was the only way out. If the pain and the old witch would not kill him, then he would kill himself.

There was a small pocketknife in his bag. He had insisted that Maitra find him one for protection in the wilderness, protection against animals or humans who might assault him, outside of his battle against Kali. So, swami had taken Paul to a street vendor, and he had picked out a simple, cheaply-made, folding pocket knife.

The pain had progressed past the point of Paul caring for his own life. The trichotomy was brutal but simple: suffer increasing pain forever, damn the souls of one of his friends, or kill himself. The only real option was the third.

His arm convulsing against his will, he took a minute to reach into the bag and find the knife with his twisted fingers, but he did find it.

Just do it quickly, and without thinking, he told himself.

He fumbled about with the blade but finally opened it and held the tip against his chest, right toward his heart.

"Will...never...betray...friends..." he growled at the hag and prepared to die.

His pain immediately left him. He felt like normal Paul again. He gasped and dropped the knife to the ground.

The old woman began to transform, her wizened frame growing to an impossible height, her wrinkled face ballooning into a mockery of a buffalo, a wolf, or both. Her thin, remaining strands of white hair blossomed into a vast mess of inky, black curls, her weak, stringy muscles expanding into formidable masses. She had become Kali's avatar.

"Self-sacrifice! Self-sacrifice is the one way out of the trap! Curse you, Paul! How did you know?"

He spat on the ground in front of the demon and said, "I didn't. It was just in me."

"It's not over!" cursed Kali as he changed into a whirling black cloud and whizzed off among the jungle trees.

"Well, shit. I'm not drinking that brand of beer again."

CHAPTER 28

Well, That Blows

Worn out physically and emotionally, Paul took a few moments to lie down right on the forest floor, ignoring the leaves, sticks, and even insects.

"Not exactly the demon fight I was expecting," he mumbled.

He closed his eyes for a few moments, but he could not fall asleep at first, the trauma of his day still in his thoughts. Eventually, however, he dozed off, and because his body had suffered so much stress, he slept right through to the next day.

He smelled a lovely, perfumed fragrance and opened his eyes to see a girl about his age standing right above him. He shouted in surprise.

"Oh, pardon me!" she said in a silken, liquid voice that reminded Paul of comfort and home. "I did not mean to startle you, Sir."

He sat up and said, "Um, no, it's cool. Who are you? Maybe I shouldn't ask after the day I'm having."

She smiled gently and sat down on a stump.

She wore the traditional sari with elegance, the pink and blue silken fabric sliding across her flawless, brown skin. Her face represented the Indian ideal: cheekbones slightly wide, eyes sloping gently toward the suggestion of the Asian almond shape, and plump lips in a light pout. Her hair, so raven that it almost melted into a royal or funerary purple and straight as the golden thread of fate, coyly hid behind a dignified, regal veil. A blood-red *bindi* adorned the precise center of her forehead.

"Wow," exclaimed Paul. "You're…you're just beautiful."

The girl hid her face behind a fan and looked down, fanning her face as it blushed.

"I am being much too bold, Sir," she said, "but I saw you lying on the forest floor, and I was worried that you were hurt."

"Oi, I was hurt, but I feel better now that you're here."

The girl smiled and looked down again. "Sir, are you lost?"

Paul scratched his chin and said, "Well, I guess I am, come to think of it. I mean, this forest can't be *that* big, so I'm not really worried."

The girl stood up and offered her delicate hand to Paul, each finger graced with a golden ring, and silver bracelets tinkling on her willow wrist.

With a swell of tingling heat in his stomach, Paul could not help but take her hand in his and stand up.

"Sir, my sisters and I live very close to here. I can see that you've been hurt. Please, come with me, and we will clean your wounds. We have food and water to refresh you."

Paul paused for one brief moment and thought of the earlier illusion of the house. Still, this girl felt so kind and genuine that he was willing to take the chance that she was just a truly lovely soul trying to help.

She led him on a hidden path through the forest to a modest little house, really nothing more than a large mud hut. It was dimly lit inside with a single lamp and a little sunlight through a slit window, but Paul could make out a straw bed and a plush rug covering most of the one room.

Seated casually on the rug were several women, each more beautiful than the next. Like the girl who had led Paul to the house, they were local with mocha skin. Unlike the girl, they were all completely nude.

"Whoa," exclaimed Paul. "What the hell?"

"Please, sit and relax," said the girl.

Feeling uneasy but finding it difficult not to accept the invitation to sit among a harem of beautiful, naked women, Paul sat on the rug. The girl handed him a mug of hot chai.

"Do my sisters make you uncomfortable, Paul?"

"I mean, besides being every man's dream situation? Nah. Wait, how'd you know my name?"

She simply smiled. "You are a very handsome man, Paul. So exotic. My sisters find you to be very attractive."

"Flattered, really, but I have a girl already."

She seemed surprised. "How disappointing. But she is not here now, is she? Come, relax and play with my sisters and me. We will not tell anyone. Your girl will never know."

Paul sighed and forced himself to think of Mary and how she had stuck with him through all of their trials. But then again, he could not help but feel the sexual urge soar through his body.

"Shit. No, I can't do it. Sorry. Thanks for the tea."

He stood up to leave, but the nude girls on the rug tugged at his arms and pulled him back down.

"Whoa, easy girls. Gotta go before this gets out of hand."

They all giggled and pushed him down on his back.

"No, no, no!"

They held him down, pulled his shirt off, and then began unbuttoning his jeans. For one instant, he could make the choice. He still had the physical and mental strength to break free of their grasps, stand up, and run out of the house. He teetered on the edge of the decision, feeling his body's lust and compulsive yearning yet also striving to keep a mental picture of Mary at the forefront.

Alas, all men are mortal, and remarkable is the man who can resist such temptation. Paul feigned struggle, then relaxed and let the girls remove all of his clothing.

They kissed and rubbed his entire body, and his erection throbbed and moved with every accelerated heartbeat. Three of them took him into their mouths in turn, and another sat on his face.

As yet another playfully pushed the three away, she straddled him and prepared to allow him to enter her.

Any man having been in such a position knows the sheer impossibility of turning back at that moment. Beyond belief, however, something deep inside of Paul, some little voice that, though irritating at the moment, nevertheless he knew was right and true, whispered to him.

He remembered the other illusions and trials, and he remembered Mary.

"No!" he cried, and with the strength of his youthful vigor, he threw the girls off, quickly dressed himself, and backed up out of the hut.

"It's another fucking trick!" he said.

The hut faded into the forest, and the girl who had taken him there transformed into a gaunt, pallid corpse.

"You will suffer for every mistake!" it said in a creaking voice.

"I'm not dead yet!" he replied. "I didn't give in all the way!"

The corpse cackled through its hollow torso, then disintegrated into dust, blown away by the forest breeze.

Paul sat on the ground, guilty and ashamed of his mistake. He had not had actual sex with any of them, but in a very real sense, he had been unfaithful to Mary. He knew that it would have to come out, that he would have to tell her. What would this mean for his quest against the demon Kali?

CHAPTER 29

Man's Best Friend

"How long is this shit going to last?" said Paul to the forest. He jumped a little when an answer came from a voice among the thick foliage: "Long enough to take your soul, Paul."

An Indian man in a long, red robe stepped out from behind the trees. His white beard flowed down to his stomach like an icy waterfall. His eyes, equally icy, glared at the punk rocker.

"Let me guess," said a weary Paul. "An avatar of Kali. This is getting old, mate."

"You can end it, then, Paul," said Kali in his human form. "All of this can end, all the illusions, trials, and temptations, not only in this forest but in your life. Behold!"

The man gestured his arms toward a copse of trees, and Paul looked. The forest sparkled and then faded away, revealing a vision of an immeasurable ivory palace. Inside the palace sat Paul on a golden throne. On the polished, tile floor, piles of gold coins rested casually here and there. Two beautiful Indian girls in glowing silk saris stood fanning Paul with palm leaves.

In front of his seat, a sizable table boasted dozens of rich, sumptuous dishes, Indian style, along with a delicately-stacked pyramid of bottles of beer.

"Wealth without limits, Paul. Every luxury, every whim,

instantly fulfilled. No suffering, pain, or even loneliness."

Paul stared at the vision as Mary and the others entered the palace room. Everyone was talking, smiling, and laughing.

"How would you like to live out the rest of your life like that, Paul?" asked the man.

"Looks fucking great, but I've learned by now that there's always a catch."

"Just a small task, almost nothing really," said the man. "Look!"

A little dog, really just a short-haired mutt, barked excitedly and ran to Paul. It jumped on his legs, wagging its tail furiously.

"What? Dimple? What the fuck?"

Paul was transported back to his childhood, during that brief period when his parents had actually been there, and he had lived with them in a house.

He saw himself walking down the dirt lane from school, whistling. He remembered that time as the last time in his life that he was truly, innocently happy. As little Paul walked toward his house, Dimple ran out to greet him, tail wagging and a big dog smile on his face. Young Paul picked Dimple up and carried him back home, laughing as the dog licked his face frantically.

The scene faded, and another one replaced it. This scene was much less happy. Little Paul was walking home from school again, but as he neared home, he just felt that something was wrong. Then, from a distance, he saw a little lump in the road, and his stomach sank because he knew immediately what he would find.

It was Dimple, no longer running to him and wagging his tail, but dead, hit by a car, the dog just a furry pile of blood, intestines, and bones, flies buzzing all over him.

The thick loss and horror of that day had never left him, and seeing the vision brought back the raw emotions as if it were that day.

The scene disappeared, and Paul looked down again at Dimple. Almost instinctively, he picked up the dog, and he was as solid and real as he had ever been. Even the smell of his fur triggered Paul's memories.

"Dimple! Oh my God!"

As Dimple licked his face like in his youth, the tough, punk shell Paul had carefully constructed throughout his life melted away. He began to sob uncontrollably, and Paul the punk rocker was once again just a fragile little boy, unable to cope with the tragedies of life.

Paul fell to his knees and pet Dimple with all of the love in his heart. He knew it was just a trick, an illusion, but it just seemed so damn *real*, that, to his emotions, it was indeed real. When it mattered, the mind and its reality were but a slave to the emotions and their reality.

"You cruel fucker," said Paul to the man between sobs. "You cruel, cruel piece of shit."

The man grinned with satisfaction. "Even this pain can I take away, Paul. All pain, all suffering. You and your friends, living together in utter luxury and joy and communion and wealth. Limitless gold. The most delicious dishes in the world, every day, without limit. All of the best beer. All in a never-ending cycle. You and Mary, always together. Never a tear, disappointment, pain, no loss ever again. All of this, I can make happen for you. My word as a god is inviolate."

Paul looked down at the realistic illusion of Dimple. He was tempted; he was honestly tempted. He would even take Dimple with him to the palace. Paul's greatest, most dreaded fear would be gone forever. Never again would he have to feel alone, lonely, ostracized, or outcast. Instead, he could live out his life with friends, family, Mary, happiness, joy, laughter, and luxury.

"You sure you're not gonna lie and break your word?"

The man smiled. "A god cannot break his word, Paul. So I give you my word, the word of Kali the demon and the god, that, if you complete the task I will ask of you, I will give you all of this and more."

Paul looked at Dimple again and contemplated the situation. What disadvantage could there be? He believed that gods could not lie. He already knew that vampires could not lie, so how much, even more so, with gods? Surely Mary and the others would agree. Who wouldn't want to live such a happy life?

"What's the task?" asked Paul.

"You have a knife in your bag, yes?"

"Yeah. A pocket knife. Why?"

"Take the knife, and kill Dimple, and all I have shown you will immediately be yours."

"What the fuck?" exclaimed Paul. "Kill my dog? Hell no."

The man walked closer to Paul, his bare feet making little imprints on the forest floor. "Paul, you know very well that it is not your dog. It is an illusion that I created. It is nothing, just a trick of the eyes. You know that."

Paul looked down at Dimple. Yes, he knew; he knew that it was not *really* Dimple. It was just as unreal as the illusions of the house, the gambling party, the hut, the naked girls, and the old lady with the beer.

He envisioned himself plunging the knife into Dimple's chest. The dog would squeal and shriek as it felt the pain. It would look up at Paul with hurt eyes of betrayal, not understanding why his beloved human companion would do that to him. The thought broke Paul's heart.

"Just an illusion, Paul. The real Dimple died those many years ago and is nothing but dust in the earth where you buried him. You know that."

Paul pursed his lips and said, "I know that."

The man's eyes opened greedily as he felt he was changing Paul's mind. "Just an illusion, Paul. Just take the knife and kill it. Kill the illusion. Destroy the illusion to enter what is real."

Paul handled the knife, turning it back and forth as he thought. Just an illusion. Just an illusion. What, though, would the real Dimple think? Was Dimple still alive in spirit? Do all dogs really go to heaven? He would be dishonoring the memory of the real Dimple, and he would never be able to live with himself, even in an ivory palace filled with gold. He had an idea.

"Alright, I'll do it," he said. "You have to come to witness it, so there's no damn mistaking it. You can't claim I didn't really do it."

The man, grinning almost maniacally, stood right beside Paul as Paul took Dimple in his left arm and held the knife in his right.

"You sure, you fucking *promise* me that you'll give me everything in the vision?"

"Yes! Yes! Kill the dog now!"

"Alright."

Paul raised the knife in his right hand, paused dramatically, then brought it down with all of his strength. He did not plunge it into Dimple, however. Instead, he swung his arm to the right and plunged the knife's blade into the man's stomach.

Both of them quiet, the man looked down slowly at the knife in his stomach, then back up at Paul. The man's face transformed from eager, giddy excitement to shock and rage.

He stood up, took the knife out of his torso, and began to change into the towering, beastly, wild, true form of Kali the demon.

CHAPTER 30

The Last Temptation of Paul

"Oh, shit."

Paul, the skinny punk rocker, stood across the forest clearing from the enormous demon Kali in his true form, and it was not much of an even match. Kali had a long, silver sword, and Paul had his pocket knife, the knife he had managed to retrieve as Kali's avatar had removed it from his stomach and hurled it across the clearing.

"I guess demons don't believe in fair fights," said Paul.

Kali roared out something that must have been laughter, but that came out as vicious, bass growling. "Prepare to die, Paul," said Kali with a guttural fry. "I will kill your body and take your soul!"

"Fuck," muttered Paul, holding the pocketknife toward his opponent.

As he prepared for the demon's attack, Paul noted the irony within the peaceful forest. Birds chirped, and beautiful, multi-colored squirrels chattered as a delicate, wispy breeze caressed his bare arms. The sky, a blue-green azure beginning to close its sleepy eyes to welcome the evening and then the darkness of the night, looked down on him nonchalantly.

"Peaceful out here," said Paul. "Too bad I couldn't be here for good reasons. Alright, Kali, you son of a bitch, bring it on. If I'm gonna die here, then I'll go down fucking fighting you. I'm not scared of this evil shit anymore; I'm just tired of it. Come on, you prick!"

Kali moved his monolithic mountain of a body, and with each labored step, as each foot planted down onto the forest floor—feet that were each longer than Paul was tall—the forest shook.

Kali neared Paul, and Paul looked up at him like someone sitting in the very first row of a cinema looking up at the big screen. Paul laughed, realizing the blackly comical nature of existence. Having defeated vampires, werewolves, zombies, and goblins, he was about to die in a forest in India, sliced up by an ancient Hindu demon.

Paul took a deep breath, exhaled, decided to go out fighting, and charged Kali with the pocket knife. Because Paul's full height barely reached Kali's calf, all he could do was plunge the knife into the demon's calf muscle.

His ferocious, fearless, and unexpected charge startled the demon, who roared in pain. He kicked at Paul and knocked him across the clearing and into a tree.

"Ugh," said Paul as his body slammed into the stout trunk. He heard a nauseating *crack* and a stabbing pain in his chest, letting him know that he had broken a rib or two. He was dizzy, and blood trickled from his ears and nose.

His legs were shaking, but he pushed himself back up and faced Kali.

With a quivering voice, he called out, "You might as well just kill me already and get it over with. I'm not gonna stop fighting!"

Barely able to run without tripping, he charged Kali's other leg, stabbed the calf muscle, then pulled the knife down with a sawing action. Kali roared, then reached down, grabbed Paul with an enormous fist, and threw him hard against a tree.

Almost knocked unconscious, Paul weakly crawled away from the tree and went toward Kali again.

"You do not give up, Paul!" said the demon, his two legs bleeding a thick, black fluid. "You are a warrior, so I will give you a warrior's death. Lie down on the ground, and I will cut your head off quickly with my silver sword!"

"F...fuck...you!" hissed Paul, but he could not help falling onto his back in the middle of the clearing. He was too weak to charge again, and he was losing lots of blood from the open wound where his arm had hit the tree. He was almost positive that his ribs were broken, and now his right arm was broken, too. He could not even move it.

He struggled to stand up again, but he just could not. He looked up to see the giant demon standing above him, holding the silver sword in the air.

Bending his monstrous head down, Kali said, "Last words?"

"Kiss my ass!"

Time slowed for Paul, and his mind went back to the trials that he had endured in the forest. Something clicked, and he remembered the words of Swami Maitra: *Kali is allowed to inhabit any place with gambling, alcohol, prostitution, the killing of animals, and gold. To the ancient Hindu mind, these were considered five great vices.*

Had he resisted so hard, had he gone so far, only to be decapitated? Would the gods, whoever they may have been, ultimately just watch and let him die after his long journey?

As Kali raised the sword for the final blow, Paul heard a girl's voice call out, "Stop!"

So unexpected yet authoritative was the voice that Kali stopped, lowered the sword, and turned around. Paul looked up and saw the two young sisters who had been foraging for berries and to whom Paul had given the dosas and the bottles of water.

"What...what are you doing here? Get lost! It's dangerous!" said Paul, straining to yell.

Kali laughed. "I will kill you two once I finish with Paul."

The older sister stood tall and screamed back, "You will *not*!"

"What the fuck?" whispered Paul.

The girls began to change. At first, their little frames seemed to shimmer, to become translucent and unreal, but then their shapes transformed. The older sister grew and grew, and as she reached Kali's height, several arms grew from her torso. Paul recognized her immediately as the goddess Durga.

At the same time, the younger sister also grew and changed into a mighty warrior, a man with blue Dravidian skin, seated on a white steed.

"Do not worry, Paul!" said Durga. "I am Durga, and this is Kalki, the avatar of Lord Vishnu! You have resisted the temptations of the demon Kali, and when you saw us hungry and thirsty, you gave us food and water. We have heard your pleas for help, and we will fight with you!"

For the first time since Paul had seen him, Kali looked scared—*really* scared.

Kalki rode his horse around to flank Kali while Durga, a great ruby sword in one of her hands, approached Kali from the front. Like a cornered animal, Kali began to thrust and parry with his silver sword while Durga fought back from the front.

Kali landed his sword on one of Durga's arms and sliced it right off; it hit the forest floor and shook the trees. The goddess' shriek blasted leaves off trees in its shrillness, but she did not relent. With her arm that held the sword, she lunged at Kali and landed the top of the sword in his shoulder. He growled and stepped back out of the range of the stinging blade.

Kali whipped around and located Kalki on his horse. Kali raised his sword and spooked the horse. It reared up and bucked Kalki off its back. He landed on his back and lost his breath for a moment, which Kali took advantage of by leaping upon him.

Paul watched, having trouble believing what he was seeing, as the two ancient Hindu gods wrestled and punched each other on the forest floor, two gargantuan forms fighting for their very existence.

Kali landed several punches on Kalki's face and body, weakening the avatar, but Kalki summoned his divine strength and gained control, sitting atop Kali. Kalki grabbed his sword from the ground and raised it, but Kali threw him off and to the side.

Durga flanked Kali and sliced her sword into his stomach, not deep enough to penetrate the guts – or whatever a god had in his stomach – but enough to cause great pain. Kali doubled over, holding his stomach and yelling.

Kalki, carrying his sword of sapphire, lunged at Kali and struck him in the back, the blade piercing through his chest.

With a shriek that rattled the entire jungle around them, Kali fell to the ground bleeding and begged for his life.

"Lord Kalki! It is not yet time for you to defeat me! It is still the *Kali Yuga*! The time for *Satya Yuga* is not here! Let me live! Let me go!"

Kalki looked down in disgust and pity at the demon. He looked back at Durga, and the two held a brief conversation in an ancient language that no one even understood anymore but the gods. He looked back down at the groveling Kali and just stared at him with hatred for several moments.

"You may go," said Kalki finally, "but you must also leave Paul and his companions alone. So you must retreat to your temple for now. Begone, vile demon!"

Without a word of thanks, Kali struggled to his feet and jogged off into the forest, shaking the trees.

"Um, thanks?" said Paul.

Durga said, "Paul, you have resisted the temptations of the demon, but you also did not completely resist the third temptation, the temptation of the prostitutes. You, therefore, cannot remain untouched by the gods. So stand and come here, Paul."

Paul felt his entire body heal and his pain leave him. He quickly stood up and walked to Durga, looking up at her in wonder. She reached down and gently touched his right shoulder. He felt it dislocate and heard the bone crunch.

"Shit!" he cried in pain.

"That is the price of giving in to a part of the temptation. You will forever have this shoulder wound to remind you of your flaw and your own mortality. Now, go down that path to the left, and you will go out of the Taki Golpata jungle. Your friends will be waiting for you there."

Paul looked toward the leafy path, then back at Durga.

"So, like, is this demon thing over now?"

Durga looked sad and replied, "Oh, no, Paul. Remember my lesson: all is one. Good and evil are illusions, and everything is the Lord Brahma. You have proven yourself a flawed hero by fighting Kali, but now you must return to your home, New Orleans. You must face the original evil there, and once you and your friends have stopped that evil, the demon uprising will be over."

Paul nodded and walked toward the path that Durga had indicated. Pausing, he turned around and asked, "But what about—"

Kalki and Durga were gone, disapparating into the cool evening air. Paul followed the path and, after only about fifteen minutes of walking, he saw Mary and the others standing where he had departed from them initially. Mary ran to him and threw her arms around him.

"Oh, Paul!" she cried. "You're alive! I didn't know—"

"I'll tell you all about it over dinner. I think I need to set my shoulder at the school. For now, I need a beer."

CHAPTER 31

Gag Me

New Orleans had become even weirder than usual, which was not easy to do. The staggering drunks, rebellious punks, striving poets and playwrights, self-styled Lotharios, emos, goths, gourmets and gourmands, and all the other characters who populated the ancient city were still active, of course. But now, another sort of personality had become increasingly common in the previous few months.

On street corners in the greasy French Quarter; on oak-lined boulevards of the Garden District; on cobblestoned, uneven sidewalks of Uptown; under the dilapidated, wooden buildings of the Ninth Ward; outside of the trendy new restaurants and cafés of the Warehouse District; and all over the great and swampy Babylon, people were behaving abnormally.

They were twisting and contorting; they were levitating with glassy eyes; they were speaking and growling in gravelly voices much too deep for humans. All over New Orleans, demons were obsessing, oppressing, and possessing people. Bodies were deteriorating while still alive; souls were being lost to an eternity in torment; people who had once been good and just were killing, stealing, and destroying.

When a demon obsessed a person, it attacked that person from the outside with temptations. The next stage was oppression, wherein it began to use supernatural occurrences, fear, and doubt to plague the victim. Finally, in possession, it harmed the person from the inside. All three stages were on flagrant display in the city where the usual flagrant display was nude dancers.

Barillo had been working overtime arresting people for murder, arson, theft, rape, and other major and violent crimes. The city had even produced several serial killers and cannibals.

"It's bad, y'all. It's *really* bad out there," said Barillo to everyone in the grand parlor of Lâmié's mansion. "You might want to stay inside if possible."

Lâmié had tried his hand at cooking to give 'Tit Boudreaux the night off. Without any culinary talent, Lâmié had started with something simple: baked chicken. He had failed miserably, the poor bird coming out of the oven entirely black, so they had ordered pizza. The least Lâmié could do was to open several bottles of some 2000 Château Latour to accompany the excellent pizza: authentic Napolitan style from a local place called, simply, *The Pizza Maker*, owned by an Italian man named Marco.

"Reminds me that we need to pick Paul, Mary, Matt, Uri, Father Woodrow, and Beast Stalker up from the airport tomorrow. It's safer to take the Microbus," said Lâmié.

Miss Annabelle, who had fully recovered from her possession and looked as jolly and rosy as ever, had agreed to stay at Lâmié's mansion for a while to avoid problems with the citywide infestation.

"I hate to bring it up," she said, "but Madame Who is still possessed in my bedroom. I feel terrible, like it's my fault. How are we going to rescue her?"

Lâmié opened another bottle of the fine Bordeaux and topped off everyone's glasses.

Veronica put a hand on Miss Annabelle's shoulder and said, "It's definitely *not* your fault, Miss Annabelle. It's not like you asked to be possessed."

Miss Annabelle nodded, trying to hold back tears.

"As for rescuing Madame Who," said Lâmié, "I've already talked to Father Woodrow. As soon as he returns from India, he's going to do an exorcism on Madame Who."

A desperate banging came from the front door.

"Oh, God. Nothing good ever comes with that knocking. I guess I'll get it," sighed Lâmié.

He exited the parlor, walked down the long hall past the grand staircase, and to the front door. Taking a deep breath in preparation for whatever fresh hell there would be, he opened the door to see Aaron and Amos standing there with desperate eyes, both of their mouths taped over with duct tape. A crowd of cheering, frenetic people was running down the street toward them.

"What the..." said Lâmié. "You know what? Just come in. Nothing surprises me anymore."

The brothers, still dressed in their Mormon missionary outfit of black slacks, a white Oxford shirt, black ties, and Elder name tags, nodded frantically and rushed in as Lâmié locked the door behind them.

Lâmié sighed and led them down the hall and into the grand parlor on the right. The others looked up puzzled as Aaron and Amos took a seat on one of the sofas. Amos began to speak beneath the duct tape, producing only a series of unintelligible mumbles.

Lâmié sighed again, rubbed his aching forehead, and said, "Guys, I guess I'll be the one to state the obvious. You can't tell us what's happening while your mouths are taped over."

The brothers looked at each other and communicated clearly with a series of grunts and hand gestures. Aaron slowly peeled the duct tape off of his mouth.

Speaking unnaturally slowly, torturously choosing each word as precisely as possible, he said, "We made a mistake. We bought a lamp from the mosque display at the religious street fair. It had a djinn in it. The djinn granted us three wishes. We worded them badly, and they ended up being terrible curses that we don't know how to get rid of."

He quickly covered his mouth again with the duct tape.

Lâmié looked simply defeated. He facepalmed himself, then slumped down in his chair.

"Um, alright," he said. "Before I met the Gravediggers and their, er, *unique* friends, and I know I'm one now, I would have thought you were a crazy person. But after all we've seen? I believe you. Alright, so, what, you rubbed the magic brass lamp, and a genie came out? A djinn, I mean? Same thing."

They both nodded desperately. Even though they were clearly under great duress, they were eyeing the pizza hungrily.

Lâmié just shook his head slowly. He noticed their pizza-lust, so he slid some slices in front of them. They began to eat, but ended up smashing the pieces against the duct tape that they had neglected to remove. They settled on removing the tape for a bite, then replacing it over their mouths as they chewed.

'Tit Boudreaux entered the conversation: "Alright, so after *exorcising Madame Who*, let's add *end the cursed wishes* to the list. Oh, don't forget to *stop the demon uprising*. Damn, I'm gonna need to learn some new recipes to get us through this. No offense, Lâmié, but maybe I'll just continue to do all the cooking from now on."

"Hallelujah!" piped Yarielis from the corner.

Lâmié continued with the boys: "Alright, Aaron, I want you to take off the duct tape again, and please, carefully and slowly, so you don't accidentally activate a wish, tell me what you and Amos wished for."

Isabella, Varco, and Veronica sat together on a loveseat, doing some research for a history class and listening to the conversation. Varco was sitting in the middle, which Isabella did not care for, since his leg was touching Veronica's, and neither seemed to mind much.

Aaron slowly picked the tape from his mouth, then spoke slowly: "Alright. So, the djinn granted us three wishes. All three we made were accidental because we just used the word *wish* in conversation without realizing that it would activate it."

Lâmié nodded. His worn eyes seemed ragged with the constant supply of supernatural crises.

"So," continued Aaron, "Amos made the first wish. He wished he could convert anyone, meaning to Mormonism, but the djinn made it so that he can command anyone to do anything, even from a distance."

"Oh, God," muttered Lâmié as he drained his glass of Bordeaux and poured another. "Go on."

"So, like, I accidentally made the second wish. I wished I could enjoy life more, and I got sucked into some dark Hedonism. Drinking, drugs, sex, stuff like that."

"Holy crap!" said 'Tit Boudreaux.

Everyone looked at the Mormons with raised eyebrows. They tried to imagine either of them doing anything even slightly naughty and failed.

"Yeah, I know," confessed Aaron. "I've repented, but I'm still really, really tempted, and women are constantly throwing themselves at me, and alcoholics and drug addicts have been shoving free product in my face. It's really hard to resist, and I'm afraid I won't be able to keep resisting if I don't stop the wish."

"One man's trash is another man's treasure," whispered Varco, producing giggles from the girls. Isabella jokingly punched Varco's arm.

"Alright," said Lâmié. "As fun as that sounds, I can see where it would be a big problem. So, what was the third wish?"

"This one's the worst," explained Aaron. "Amos was mad at me for my wish, and he wished that everyone would respect him. Well, now everyone worships him as a king. It got to his head, and he now sort of commands a large crowd of people to do his bidding. I think he knows that is wrong now, but still, everyone worships him like a god. The temptation is too much."

Amos nodded hard.

"I have some thoughts," said Lâmié, "but this situation demands more wine. So stay put a minute, and whatever you do, *don't* say anything in case you accidentally activate one of the curses!"

The brothers nodded, and Lâmié trotted to the wine cellar to grab some more bottles, cursing under his breath the whole way. Finally, he returned with a few bottles of 1990 Torgiano, some of the rarer bottles from his collection. He poured everyone more wine, including the high school students. They were past caring about the law.

Lâmié, after a long, full drink of the Italian red, said, "Alright, first thought. Why aren't the girls here in this room throwing themselves at you, and why aren't we worshipping Amos as a god?"

The brothers shrugged.

"I actually have a theory," said Lâmié. "This house is old, and it's ancestral. We've put up lots of supernatural protections around. I've put salt lines, Yarielis has put Voodoo blessings on the house, and Titania has even used *her* magic to put protections on the house. So I believe that this house is a sort of supernatural safe space. Maybe the Gravediggers have something to do with it too, like, all of their, and our, fighting against evil. Maybe there's some good mojo here or something."

Everyone in the parlor nodded in agreement. The pizza was almost gone, but not entirely, so Amos and Aaron finished it off.

"Makes as much sense as anything," said 'Tit Boudreaux, "which is why you two should stay here for now. The second y'all step outside, you're gonna be rushed by the crowds."

Aaron and Amos shrugged and nodded, their eyes showing relief that they had a safe place to stay for now.

"You don't have to keep that tape on your mouth," suggested Lâmié. "Just…and for God's sake, listen carefully…don't start wishing for things or talking about them just in case. Hell, don't even use the word *wish*, alright?"

The brothers nodded and removed the tape from their mouths.

"Now," said Lâmié, "enjoy that pizza, guys. You've been through a lot."

After everyone had finished dinner and had a good buzz on (except Amos and Aaron, who were carefully avoiding any alcohol), Barillo brought up a topic that everyone else had missed: "Y'all, I've been busy at work, but where's Chief?"

"Shit!" said 'Tit Boudreaux. "You know what? I haven't seen him since yesterday morning. I just assumed he'd gone for a walk or was resting or something, but has anyone seen him at all today?"

"Not me," said Lâmié, and everyone else concurred.

"Well, shit," said 'Tit Boudreaux. "Does this mean he's missing? Hold on a sec." He bounded up the stairs to look in Chief's room, then came back momentarily and said, "He's not in his room!"

Barillo looked around at everyone else. Then, finally, he stood up from the red, Victorian Era chaise-longue in which he had been relaxing.

"Well," he said, "sounds like a missing person case to me; plus, it's Chief. I'm worried too, especially with all the demon crap going on out there. Hold on a second; I'm calling in an APB and a BOLO for him, then I'm going out to patrol. Who wants to come with me?"

"Yeah, I'll go," volunteered 'Tit Boudreaux.

"Me too," offered Lâmié. "We can take the van. It's still pretty beaten up from the last time we used it, but it's the safest way."

They began with a drive down St. Charles Avenue all the way to Carrollton Avenue, then turned back around and headed toward the Lee Traffic Circle and then onto Canal Boulevard.

On the sidewalks were all manner of bizarre people, clearly possessed. One woman was levitating a foot off the pavement, peeing onto a man who was writhing on the ground. As they drove, a crowd of homeless men glared at them with red, glowing eyes. One of the men spat at them, and fire came from his mouth.

They turned right onto Decatur and into the French Quarter, traditionally the weirdest part of New Orleans, and it did not disappoint. People were vertically climbing the old, Spanish-style buildings and hanging off the wrought-iron-guarded balconies.

A band of jazz street musicians were violently raping their instruments in a horny pile of brassy lust. Next to them, a Catholic priest was attempting an exorcism on a woman crawling on the filthy

French Quarter sidewalk. They watched as the woman leaped onto the priest and bit his throat.

The three men spent most of the night driving around town looking for Chief without success. However, Beast Stalker would be in town the next day, so they determined to continue the search with him, hoping he would have some insight.

No one slept well that night. On their minds were Madame Who's possession, Aaron and Amos' cursed wishes, Chief's going missing, and, of course, the demonic infestation threatening the world.

CHAPTER 32

The Call of the Ancestors

"Only one person has used this warehouse in over a hundred years," said the man to the Reverend Methuselah Skink in a dilapidated old building in the Warehouse District. "It's perfect, right? Apparently, some guy named Pellerin had leased it to do some kind of black magic, and he was killed or left town or something, but the lease is still active for another year."

Skink smiled; his long tongue slid over his yellow teeth and thin, greenish-gray lips.

"And no one will disturb us?" the withered old freak asked.

"No one. I looked into it. The owner of the warehouse doesn't even live in the city. No security guard, no one ever comes here, just that poor excuse for a lock that we cracked open without an effort. It's big, paid for, and no one wants to come here."

Skink rubbed his oily, sweaty hands together in satisfaction.

"The next thing," he said, "is the idol. What is the progress?"

The man was on the raised platform at one end of the warehouse. The inside was mostly bare, the walls hung with rusted, old tools here and there, and the ceiling rafters were the home to a few pigeons. The floor was covered in sawdust.

"I told you about the Vietnamese guy in New Orleans East, right? He was willing to build it, no questions asked, all-cash transaction. He should be finished any day now."

"Built to specifications?" asked Skink, hissing out each hyper-sibilant *s* in his question.

"Precisely," replied the man. "Just like we used to have it in Geh-Ben-Hinnom, at Tophet, many thousands of years ago."

Skink paced back and forth across the width of the warehouse, his long, narrow little shoes scraping lines in the sawdust. A little line of white, liquid pigeon shit fell onto his hat, but he seemed not to notice or care.

"And your…this demon of yours. Are you *absolutely sure* that he will grant me eternal life?"

The man stood up in his Hasidic trench coat and hoiche hat, under which fell long, curly payot, and joined Skink in his pacing.

"That's is how it works, yes," he assured. "Of course, that depends on the *sacrifice*."

"Yes, yes, I know. I have the congregation poised to do it. They are all willing to drink the Kool-Aid when ordered, just like they did on the practice run. They will offer themselves in sacrifice to Moloch when the time comes, believing they are doing it for Jesus. Fools. And it includes the children."

The man coughed a little; the pacing had stirred up the dust in the warehouse, causing it to shade the beams of sunlight that were shining in through various little holes in the old, corrugated iron roof and sending the particles into his lungs.

"And what about these, they call themselves, what, the Gravediggers? That stupid band that Uri is a part of? The demon has told me to watch out for them. So what's their deal?"

Skink jerked his head toward the man at the mention of the Gravediggers.

"They are trouble, yesssss. They will need to be dealt with. I will think of something."

"Alright," said the man, "then that just leaves the matter of payment. You don't access the demon without something in it for me."

Skink hissed at the man.

"I told you I have it. We've had good collection plates lately."

Their conversation was hidden from the world outside of the warehouse by the electric hum of the fan they had set up to try to ward off the New Orleans heat vainly. Skink handed the man a suitcase filled with money.

HELL'S BELLS: A PUNK ROCK DEMON STORY

38,000 feet over the Atlantic Ocean, the rushing hum of the Airbus A350 Ultra Long Range's Rolls Royce jet engines filled the enormous cabin with nine-abreast seating. Paul, after having endured the trials of the demon Kali, had experienced no remorse about using Lâmié's credit card to buy first-class seats for Mary, Matt, Uri, Father Woodrow, Beast Stalker, and himself. But unfortunately, he had to sit on his left side because his right shoulder was in a cast; it would heal, but it would never be fully functional again, a constant reminder of his weakness.

He was also experiencing no qualms about ordering alarming amounts of drinks from the increasingly worried flight attendants.

Mary, the next seat over, was sipping on some Champagne while Matt and Uri played cards. Father Woodrow was engrossed in a book on demonology; he had spoken to Lâmié on the phone about Madame Who's exorcism, and he was preparing himself. Meanwhile, Beast Stalker was fast asleep; the throbbing of the jet engines overpowered even his loud, buzzing snores.

They had decided that Maitra, Apada, and Iraj should return with them to New Orleans for their help in defeating the demons from a Hindu point of view. The three Indians, never having flown on an airplane, much less in first class on a large, commercial jetliner, were amazed at the trip and the technology. Their first trip to New Orleans had been on a ship.

After Paul's emergence from the forest, they had all returned to the school, where he had debriefed them about his trials and temptations. He had intentionally left out the part about partially giving in to the naked girls; however, he planned to confess to Mary later in private.

Following a night of conversation and a great Indian feast prepared by Apada, they had wasted no time booking tickets and leaving for New Orleans as soon as possible.

As Beast Stalker dozed, he first enjoyed a deep and dreamless sleep, but soon enough, the dreams came.

He found himself standing amid a cemetery. It must not have been in New Orleans, for the graves were all below-ground burials. The pungent smell of burnt wood and charred flesh filled the graveyard, smoldering piles of bodies and buildings surrounded the area, and he could tell he was up on a mountain.

From a distance, the sound of beating drums and chanting songs in Cherokee floated toward him. The spirits of his ancestors—hundreds of men and women of the People—appeared in a ring around him. They all pointed to a grave at his feet.

He looked down and was surprised to see Chief Cloud Mountain lying on top of the grave in the pose of a corpse, his arms folded across his chest. Then, from the other side of the tomb that Chief was on, he saw Ophelia. She stood straight up, her fists clenched and her arms straight and rigid at her sides, in a stance of defiance. He looked down again at Chief and saw that the magical amulet of the People was now on his chest, protected by his large, tan, wrinkled hands.

Beast Stalker, startled by a passing member of the flight crew, woke up with a jump. The dream had been too heavy and vivid for just a dream. He was certain that it had been a vision given by the ancestors.

He left his seat and squatted in the aisle in a position that was among his friends so they could all hear him. "Guys? I think I just had a vision," he said in a low voice to discourage eavesdropping.

They all looked up at him and listened. The only other passengers in first class were asleep at the moment.

"I think I know the meaning already. It was in a cemetery in a place that had been burned down, both buildings and people. That represented Ushaville, or what used to be Ushaville. It's burned down now, of course."

"Oh, God, that name brings back *interesting* memories," said Matt.

"Same," said Beast Stalker. "Remember that I lived there long before I met you guys. So, in my vision, a crowd of my ancestors appeared. They pointed to a grave, and Chief was lying on it like a corpse. Ophelia was there too, glaring at me. The amulet, yes *that* amulet, was on Chief's chest."

Mary said, "Weird, but what's it mean?"

Beast Stalker stood up to let a flight attendant pass with a smile, then squatted back down and explained: "Here is my interpretation. Ophelia wants the amulet, but Chief is protecting it. So she's harming Chief, maybe even torturing him, and she's willing to kill him to get to the amulet. And since it's Ophelia, she has him somewhere in a cemetery."

"She's got Chief kidnapped?" asked Mary.

"I would bet on it. The moment we land, I want to call Lâmié and ask about Chief. I have a horrible feeling that he's in big trouble."

HELL'S BELLS: A PUNK ROCK DEMON STORY

Half a day later, the Airbus touched down on the tarmac at New York's JFK Airport in a smooth, professional landing. The Gravediggers and friends walked out of the jetway into the terminal, and stretching their legs after the long flight felt good.

Several of them found the bathrooms, while Beast Stalker found reception on his iPhone and called Lâmié. They talked for several minutes, and his face looked grim as they spoke.

"Bad news?" asked Matt as they all regathered.

"Chief is missing," explained Beast Stalker. "Over a day now. When we arrive in New Orleans, we must look for him. Barillo has been searching for him, and he put out an APB to the police force, but they've been busy dealing with the…" he looked around to make sure no one could hear him. "…possessed people. I am sure that my vision meant that Ophelia had him in a cemetery. Knowing her, it's in some old, abandoned vault in the middle of one of the big cemeteries."

They were silent for several moments, thinking of the kind old man and the evil vampiress who could be torturing him right then.

"We'll find him, mate," said Paul. "We have a few hours 'til the next flight. So let's go find a restaurant that serves beer."

That late afternoon, they landed in New Orleans, where Lâmié and Barillo picked them up in Mary's van. She took over the driving, as Paul was quite drunk by that time.

"I'll drop off Maitra, Apada, and Iraj at your place, Lâmié. They're guests, and—"

"Nonsense!" said Swami Maitra from the backseat. "We're in this together. Go now and find Chief. We're going with you. We're friends, and friends help one another."

Beginning with Metarie Cemetery on the way from the airport, they drove cemetery by cemetery, canvassing New Orleans, walking among the rows of the dead, searching for a vault with activity within. Finally, around midnight, they reached Lafayette Cemetery No. 1.

"This is the one," said Beast Stalker. "I can sense the ancestors' presence and the old Cherokee magic they bring. Ophelia and Chief are in this cemetery."

CHAPTER 33

Grave Danger

Beast Stalker paused outside of the vault. He motioned for the others to stay back. Gently placing his ear on the stone door, he listened for several moments, then looked back up.

"Yes, they are in there," he softly said to the others. "How should we do this?"

"Quick cram session for the Indians," said Matt. "You've met Chief, of course. The girl in there with him is Ophelia. Don't let her appearance fool you. She looks like a cute, young schoolgirl, but she's really a vampire who's thousands of years old. She's very powerful, and she's trying to make Chief tell her where an amulet is. She'll be almost unstoppable if she gets her hand on the amulet."

"Oh, my goodness!" exclaimed Maitra as he instinctively guided Apada and Iraj behind himself, like a protective father or grandfather.

An owl hooted from somewhere across the dark cemetery, and the full moon reflected her yellow hands as they caressed the old, gray tombs. A warm, southern breeze glazed across everyone's skin as a dark cloud covered a quarter of the moon, darkening the scene somewhat.

While the others stood in thought, Mary trotted off for a few moments to an ash tree, then returned with several crude stakes that were nothing more than broken branches but quite sharp enough to stop a vampiress. She handed them out.

"I can still hardly believe that vampires are real, but if demons are, then I suppose anything is possible," said Maitra.

"I feel the same way," agreed Father Woodrow. He palmed the stake and turned it around in his hand, finding just the right grip for it.

"What's the plan?" Paul asked as he held his stake in a battle position.

"She's probably already sensed that we're here," said Beast Stalker. "I say we just open the door and confront her. No other options, really. Our goal is to rescue Chief, and secondarily, to make sure she does not get to the amulet."

Everyone nodded and stood in a defensive stance, following Mary's lead. Beast Stalker counted down from three, then shoved the crypt's granite door open. It swung open easily and silently, having been recently used.

As expected, Ophelia stood facing the door, her hands on her hips and an arrogant smirk on her face.

"Well, I suppose Cherokee magic is stronger than I thought," she said offhandedly. "So you found me. Congratulations."

Behind her, Chief lay in a pool of blood on the grave top.

"Is he alive?" asked Beast Stalker calmly.

"Quite," she answered. "He's just having a little rest between sessions. Oh, you might notice that he's missing one hand and the fingers from the other hand. Strong old man, that Chief. He still hasn't buckled."

Beast Stalker's nostrils flared, and he clenched his fists, but his demeanor mainly remained calm and stern. "I can tell you, Ophelia, that Chief Cloud Mountain will gladly die before he reveals the amulet's location. The same goes for me, but I think you already knew that."

"Time will tell, Beast Stalker. Every man has his limits. I know how to take a man to the edge of life, then bring him back, again and again. Unfortunately, it usually drives them insane quickly. Chief is strong, but I've broken stronger."

Chief regained consciousness and strained his head and neck to see Beast Stalker and the others outside.

"Beast...Stalker..." Chief croaked in a tortured voice, "go away...don't let her get you too...I will die honorably, will never tell...do not tell her where the amulet..."

He lay his head back again, exhausted from his excessive blood loss but still alive and conscious.

"Ophelia," said Beast Stalker calmly but with an ocean of rage and hatred underneath, "I will give you the chance to leave right now. If not, I'm going to stake you. Mark my words: I will kill you if you do not leave."

Rather than her usual smirk, mocking laughter, or snide comment, Ophelia must have seen something in Beast Stalker's eyes that startled her. She slowly backed up toward Chief, and as Beast Stalker realized too late what was happening, she moved at vampire speed to untie Chief, grab him upright, and extend her fangs to his neck. His head lolled around from weakness.

"Another step and I kill him," said Ophelia, staring directly into Beast Stalker's unblinking eyes. For a moment, it was a standoff.

Beast Stalker growled at her, then said, "Let him go, Ophelia. We all have stakes out here. You hurt him any more, and we'll all make sure you turn to a pile of dust."

"Well, it looks like we're at an impasse here," said Ophelia in an even tone. "I'm not letting him go unless—"

"Unless what, bitch?" asked Paul from behind Beast Stalker.

"Paul, always so uncouth and uncivilized," retorted Ophelia. "Unless Beast Stalker tells me where the amulet is. Tell me that, and I will let Chief go right now."

"Don't…do…it…" wheezed Chief.

"Chief…" said Beast Stalker in a tone of pleading.

Then, a few things happened rapidly.

Ophelia screamed, and several vampires flew out of the night and surrounded the Gravediggers and their friends. This caused everyone except Beast Stalker, who would not ignore Chief, to turn around defensively and raise their stakes in warning. Apada and Iraj, the youngest of the group, were shaking in holy terror but did not back down.

They understood too late that the vampires were not intended to be an actual threat but merely a distraction. Ophelia picked up Chief as if he were a sack of straw, then, at vampire speed, rushed past Beast Stalker. He swang his stake at her heart, but he just could not keep up with her supernatural speed. Ultimately, the top of the stake only grazed her arm and drew a little blood. He heard Chief groan at the physical stress.

Ophelia took flight with a burst of triumphant laughter, then fled into the night. Her vampire minions followed, leaving the Gravediggers and friends standing alone in the stillness of Lafayette Cemetery No. 1.

"Well, shit," said Paul. "That happened fucking quickly."

"Where's she taking him?" asked Mary.

"There is only one possible answer," replied Beast Stalker. "She's taking him back to the reservation where Ushaville used to be. She knows the amulet's hidden there somewhere, which it is. I fear—"

A crow cawed from a tree above them, a malignant omen.

"Fear what, Beast Stalker?" asked Mary.

"I fear she'll go after his wife. Chief is willing to die to keep the amulet from Ophelia, but I'm not sure he's willing to let his wife die."

"Fuck," cursed Paul. "Then we have to go back to Ushaville and stop her."

Lâmié said, "The fastest way to get there is a private helicopter. The soonest I can arrange one is for tomorrow morning. I know a pilot from…from my past. And we can't all go. Some need to stay here to try to exorcise Madame Who."

Quite shaken by the experience with Ophelia, Father Woodrow offered, "I'll stay for the exorcism."

Suddenly, a scream came from somewhere across the city in the soulless night, the sound of a woman in terror.

Paul looked in the direction of the sound for a moment, then turned back and said, "I'm going to Ushaville. Why stop now? Shit. Mary? Matt? Uri? Go with me? Just the Gravediggers?"

The three others agreed.

"And me, of course," said Beast Stalker.

"Of course you," said Paul.

"Alright, let's get back to Lâmié's house for now and get some rest. We need it," said Matt.

Exhausted and sleepy, they all piled into the Microbus, returned to Lâmié's mansion, and quickly fell asleep.

Chapter 34

The Ashes of Ushaville

"Wait, how the hell did you find a private Sikorsky X2 for hire? That's the world's fastest helicopter!" asked Matt to Lâmié early the following day. "You know what? I don't even want to know. The price you must have paid…"

Lâmié remained enigmatically silent.

"Oh yeah, I'd forgotten you're into planes and shit," said Paul.

"It's called *aviation*, Paul," grumbled Matt, "not *planes and shit*."

Paul just shrugged.

Everyone felt well-rested and had made their way down to the grand parlor for coffee and 'Tit Boudreaux's specialty, Creole shrimp and grits with a roux-based gravy. Paul was accompanying the dish with a stiff Bloody Mary, but everyone else was content with coffee or tea.

"What, are we gonna drive to the airport in the Microbus to meet the helicopter?" asked Mary as 'Tit Boudreaux brought out another casserole dish full of shrimp and grits, the rich, warm aroma filling the room.

Lâmié looked down, a little ashamed.

"Oh, God," said Mary. "What did you do, Lâmié?"

"It's…I mean, I didn't really do it. My grandfather did it when he lived here. There's a…well, there's a helipad on the roof."

"No shit!" exclaimed Mary. "Christ. Dude. Just how much money *do* you have exactly anyway?"

"You don't want to know," answered Lâmié. "And I'll never tell."

Still using the mansion as a hidey hole from the throngs of worshipers, Aaron and Amos had just finished their breakfasts. They sighed, then wrapped their mouths back up with duct tape.

"So," continued Lâmié, "Paul, Mary, Matt, Uri, while y'all go to rescue Chief, Father Woodrow and a few of us need to exorcise and rescue Madame Who."

"Typical clusterfuck," muttered Mary.

"Language!" cried Yarielis from the corner of the room.

―――――・✦・―――――

Later that morning, the Gravediggers and Beast Stalker were packed and ready, having packed not only their clothes and necessities, but an enormous duffle bag full of stakes, holy water (supplied liberally by Father Woodrow), and even some fresh garlic pods, just in case.

At about ten o'clock, they heard the unmistakable clopping of a helicopter's rotors and the roar of a powerful engine from up above.

"Well, there's your ride," said Lâmié. "Come on; I'll introduce you to the pilot."

They climbed up to the third floor, then up a set of stairs that were semi-hidden within a closet in the last bedroom on the left down the hall. This led to a locked hatch, which Lâmié unlocked and opened. Finally, they all climbed up onto the roof.

The entire roof area was enormous, an entire city block in area, a tile hat matching its massive mansion head below. In the center of the many peaks and gables of the roof, a flat helipad was built on a raised structure. On it sat the sleek Sikorsky X2, whose pilot had just shut off the engine.

"Holy shit," said Matt with a yawn despite his excitement. "Sikorsky X2, dual coaxial rotors, rear-thrust propellor, LHTEC T800 turboshaft engine. Until recently, there was only one of these in the world. There are still not many. Just fucking amazing."

The aircraft's door popped open, and a thin woman stepped out. She looked quintessentially Italian, and she introduced herself in an Italian accent.

"*Buongiorno*, everyone. Hello, Lâmié. It has been a long time."

Mary raised an eyebrow, wondering what history the two had.

"I'm Eli Cadere. Obviously, I'm the pilot. Is everyone *pronto*?"

Paul looked out across New Orleans from his vantage point. "You and Lâmié know each other, eh? What, juicy romance? Torrid summer fling?" he taunted.

Lâmié answered, "First, Paul, I'm surprised you know what the word *torrid* means, but we became…friends…when I spent some time in France. Not important now, is it? Y'all have a mission. Now look, I've arranged for Eli to fly you to the Cherokee reservation near Ushaville. Because of your mission's sensitive nature, she'll fly out to a remote station and await your call, and then she'll fly you back here. I'm paying her for her services, so, you know, don't dally about."

"I can wait as long as you need," said Eli with a wink. "Now come on, let's load your bags first."

Half an hour later, they were speeding across the countryside, only about 7,000 feet above the ground. Matt was seated in the co-pilot's seat, an enormous grin pasted on his sleepy face as the craft reached over 200 miles per hour. In the cabin, Paul was staring out of the window at the ground below as Mary tightly held on to his arm. Beast Stalker just peered pensively out of the window next to him.

Poor Uri, his hands white from their terrified grip on his seat, was muttering desperate prayers in Hebrew. Seeing the ground so far away in a jet airplane made flying seem surreal, metaphorical. It felt just like being on the ground. But such a fast helicopter so close to the ground made the sensation of flying all too real.

"Not a fan of helicopters, mate?" asked Paul.

Uri, his jaws clenched, just shook his head quickly before returning to his prayers.

Matt spoke over the radio comm system, his voice reaching everyone's ears through their headphones.

"Eli's gonna fly over Ushaville a little when we get there. I wanna see what it looks like now."

Just over three hours later, they were above West Virginia. Unfortunately, since Ushaville had never officially been on any maps, including Google, Eli had to use the Cherokee reservation as an orientation point. Even so, it was not hard for the Gravediggers to see the remains of what had once been Ushaville.

In the piney forest, that vast ocean of pine needles and crisp bark that covered most of West Virginia, a distinct, enormous rectangle marked the old town perimeters. The rubble of the former buildings, defined in square blocks by now-overgrown streets, was still black with the charring of their own destruction and the vampiric flesh that had burned up within them.

Nature, usually so quick to reclaim the parts of her being that mankind had conquered then later abandoned, seemed hesitant and even fearful of creeping back into the accursed, unhallowed ground of the former vampire stronghold. Instead, her encroachment was shy, and testing—a vine, a tendril, a plant, a tree, but none of them were thick or numerous enough to truly retake the town as they would have in any other abandoned town.

"Wow," exclaimed Mary. "Look, that's where the Pallid Horse used to be! Holy crap! And that was Beast Stalker's bookstore to the left, and then Titania's café…"

"My bookstore…" whispered a mournful Beast Stalker.

"And the Summer Linden Hotel!" said Matt. "It's so sad. We had some real, well, some times in that town."

Paul chuckled and said, "That's putting it lightly, mate."

Uri, who had forced himself to look down, said in a shaky voice, "Oy vey! So that's the infamous Ushaville? Wow, you all really did a number on that town. Geez."

Eli slowly circled the helicopter around a few more times as they gazed in wonder at the place where so much death, drama, and destruction had occurred, the area that was now nothing but burnt stones.

"God," said Paul. "So fucking weird. There's just almost nothing there now. I feel kind of torn. I miss it because it was our first adventure together, but I'm also happy that the damned place is gone."

Eli straightened up the flight path and traveled to the Cherokee reservation. Beast Stalker pointed out where Chief's house was, and Eli set down the chopper right in his backyard, in the large clearing between his house and the forest, where the spiritual visions had occurred in what seemed like a lifetime ago.

The helicopter's engine whirled down to a stop, and everyone stepped out into Chief's backyard.

"Before we do anything," said Beast Stalker, "I need to check on Chief's wife!"

He sprinted across the yard at a velocity that would not have seemed possible for his large, muscular frame and burst through the back door. They heard him calling out and stomping around the rooms, and then he came back outside.

"She's not there. This is not good," he said. "She stays home most of the time. Chief's old truck is still here. I suspect Ophelia took his wife, too, to leverage him."

Sparrows twitted and tweeted about in the forest; a crow called, and another answered. To the animals, oblivious to the drama, it was just another day.

"Where would she have taken them?" asked Uri. "This area, I don't know well, obviously, but the town's burned down to the ground. I didn't see any actual buildings left. So where could she possibly take them?"

They all thought about the question for a couple of minutes, the refreshing West Virginia breeze tussling their hair about, except Paul's well-greased Mohawk, which could easily stand up to a New Orleans hurricane.

Mary broke the silence: "The tunnels."

"Oh, shit!" said Paul. "Good call, Mary."

"I'm sorry, but I have to ask...*tunnels*?" added Uri.

Matt rubbed his forehead, sighed, yawned, looked up at the blazing sun, then back down. "Yeah, tunnels," he explained. "There's a maze of tunnels underneath what used to be Ushaville. They're ancient; some of them even predate the Cherokee people. The last time we were here, they were filled with these really ancient, withered-up vampires, so old they could barely move anymore unless they got some blood on them. They hopefully all died in the fire, but the tunnels...it's the perfect place for Ophelia."

Paul nodded and said, "Always dark, no sunlight, easy to hide and get lost in. The perfect torture chamber."

"Well, shit," said Uri, to the surprise of the others.

"Never heard you curse before, Uri!" said Mary.

"I usually don't, but some situations deserve a good curse. Sometimes, a strong *oy vey* just doesn't cut it."

They went inside Chief's house to find supplies for the tunnels. Loading up with food, water, flashlights, and batteries, they rested for a few minutes, then drove Chief's pickup truck toward the ruins of Ushaville while Eli flew the helicopter to a safe location to await their phone call.

CHAPTER 35

Punk Resurrected

"This is fucking surreal," said Matt as they hiked the overgrown former streets of Ushaville.

"Understatement, mate," agreed Paul.

What had been buildings making up city blocks were now just piles of stones and rotten wood, most of it black from the fire. Even still, a gray haze hung over the city, a sort of fog of memory manifested into reality by the ashes of the inferno.

Unlike in the forest behind Chief's house, no birds were heard in Ushaville, and no squirrels were seen darting about. In fact, they did not see any life at all, anywhere, not even insects. Instead, the silence and pall of the grave engulfed the razed town, setting everyone's emotions on uncanny edge.

They determined that they were on the Eastside as they passed the rubble of the Pallid Horse. But, unfortunately, they could only recognize it by the enormous, fallen horse statue that had once sat atop the strange bar where they had played that fateful show. Somehow, the horse had avoided the fire.

"How do we find an entrance to the tunnels?" asked Beast Stalker. It's hard to recognize anything here."

"There was one in the Pallid Horse, behind the stage, remember? That's how we escaped the riot," said Mary.

"Yeah, Nancy helped us..." began Matt, but as he remembered Nancy and how much he still missed her, his voice trailed off.

Mary patted him on the back.

"Well, let's look here then," suggested Beast Stalker. I can kind of make out the original layout of the bar in the rubble."

They climbed over charred wood, stone, and tile across the area that had once been inside the Pallid Horse.

"Alright, I think I can imagine it," said Mary. "I think this was the stage over here."

Paul carefully climbed over to where she stood and looked around. Then, he mimicked singing into a microphone.

"Yeah," he said. "This was the stage for sure."

"I guess your music really brought the house down!" said Uri. The others just looked at him and either rolled their eyes or shook their heads.

"Let's see here..." muttered Matt as he lowered himself to his hands and knees and crawled around, searching for the old tunnel entrance. "Ow, shit!" he cried out, having scraped his elbow on a cement block. "Damn, that hurt. But I think I found the tunnel entrance."

The others helped him pull back burnt beams of wood, crumbled chunks of brick, and cement panels to reveal a person-sized hole that led downward.

"Oh yeah, you found it, mate," agreed Paul. "Fuck, that brings back memories. That's the last place I want to go to right now."

"Yeah," said Mary as she brushed the chalky brick dust off her hand on Paul's leather jacket. "We had some horrible experiences down in the tunnels."

Uri, who was repositioning his voice hat on his head, asked, "Um, yeah, so what's down there exactly? You mentioned ancient vampires. That alone makes me not too anxious to climb down."

"Those things were down there in these crypts," explained Mary. "Then, there were these jail cells with withered old vampires in them, like the old ones, too old and dried out to move. At first, we thought they were dead bodies, but some blood riled them up."

"Jail cells, you say?"

"Yeah, apparently they put vampires down there who broke the vampires' rules or the sacred trust or whatever the hell vampires go by."

"Oy."

Beast Stalker peered down into the dark hole. "Wow. I wonder if the fire made it down there and killed the ancient vampires. If not, wouldn't they be all dried up again by now? The little bit of blood that made them rise has to be gone by now, right?"

"I fucking hope so," said Paul. "We outran those fuckers once already. But, don't feel like pressing my luck, you know?"

They pulled their heads back out of the dark entrance and looked at one another. It was still only a bit past noon, so if they did encounter any active vampires, they could just run back outside, and the sunlight would stop them.

A few beads of sweat erupted on Beast Stalker's smooth, red-brown forehead. "Remember, friends," he said, "we're doing this for Chief and his wife first. Second, we're stopping Ophelia from taking New Orleans and the world."

"Again," added Matt.

"Again," agreed Beast Stalker. "I'll go down first and ensure it's structurally safe at this entrance. Make sure you have easy access to your stakes and holy water, just in case…"

He did not finish his sentence, but there was no need. They all knew what might still be underground.

Paul stepped in front of Beast Stalker and said, "No, I'll go first, mate. I'm the one who said those stupid things into the mic at the show. So it's all kind of my fault."

Paul found the remains of the small, wooden stairs that used to be the means to climb down. There were enough rungs left that he was able to make his way awkwardly down and land on the stone floor.

Using the bright beam of his LED flashlight, he scanned the area and saw that the tunnel looked perfectly intact. The ancient construction had held up over the centuries, possibly the millennia, and even the great fire of Ushaville had not harmed it.

"Damn, those ancients knew how to build," he muttered, then called up to the others, "Come down. It's fine; just be careful. There's still part of the old stairs, so just use the rungs that are whole."

They all climbed down in turn: first Beast Stalker, then Mary, then Uri, and then Matt. They dusted off their clothes and shone their flashlights around.

"Damn," said Mary. "It looks exactly the same. I guess the fire didn't really hurt it."

"Right," said Beast Stalker. "Remember, these tunnels were built long, long ago, some of them even before my ancestors arrived in West Virginia. The ancient peoples understood some sciences and arts much better than we do today."

Matt tapped the stone walls and said, "Yeah, no particle board, drywall, and vinyl siding bullshit here."

"Remember the *really* old ones?" asked Mary. "The ones with dirt floors and the openings were much smaller...I wonder how old those ones are."

"Unimaginably old," said Beast Stalker. "Now, who remembers the layout? We can't just wander around aimlessly. Did you bring the string, Matt?"

Matt pulled an enormous spool of kite string from his backpack. He carefully tied the string to one of the solid rungs of the stairs.

"This way, we can always trace our path back," he clarified.

"Good thinking," said Uri with a shiver. "Jews don't do so well with dank underground mazes."

They walked down the tunnel until the entrance was just a small square of light behind them.

"I remember this one," said Mary. "It branches off in a few places but leads to the Summer Linden Hotel through one branch. But really, we're not traveling around town. All we need to do is find Ophelia. Beast Stalker, I'm sorry to phrase it this way, but we need to *listen* rather than *look*. There's going to be, well..."

"Screams," said Beast Stalker, finishing her sentence. "I know. We can just explore as long as we have the string."

Matt patted his backpack and said, "I have other spools, too, if we need to start a new route or whatever."

"Smart," said Uri.

"Smartass," said Paul.

As they proceeded deeper into the tunnel system, the tunnels sloped downward, delving much deeper into the earth. The atmosphere became silent and oppressive, the thickness of the ground above them dampening sound and spirit. Finally, they reached a sort of roundabout, a clear circle from which stemmed a few tunnels.

"Alright, where to?" asked Paul.

"Too bad Titania's not here to guide us with her green light," said Mary. "But we didn't know we'd be coming into the tunnels. I mean, I guess we should just pick one and try it, right?"

They all agreed, so they warily entered one of the tunnels and explored. Before long, they saw something on the ground ahead of them. Sauntering, stakes in hand, they approached and came upon some piles of dust suspiciously in the shape of human bodies.

"Hmm, maybe some of the fire did get down here," said Beast Stalker.

"There are tons of entrances and air vents and exits all over," said Matt. "Totally possible. I mean, these were obviously vampires."

"Weird," said Mary. "Come on, let's keep going."

They stepped over the piles of ash, and as they proceeded down the tunnel, the stone ceiling gradually became a bit lower, and the regular, neat masonry of the walls became a bit more rough and knobby and uneven. The air smelled stale and unused. Soon, the stone floor turned into packed dirt.

"We're going into one of the oldest sections," noted Beast Stalker.

Soon, they saw a stout, wooden door in the left wall of the tunnel.

"What the hell? What's behind that?" asked Mary.

Paul said, "Only one way to find out."

He tried the metal bar hanging across the door, which gave way quickly, being old and rusted. He opened it all the way, then shone his flashlight inside.

"Holy shit!" he exclaimed. "Get a fucking load of this!"

He stepped inside the large room, carved right into the bedrock that also comprised the tunnels, and everyone else followed him inside. They pointed their flashlights around and began to understand what they were seeing.

In the middle of the room, bolted directly into the stone floor, was a long, adjustable chair, like the kind dentists might use, only much older and constructed of wood and metal gears and crank handles rather than vinyl and electric motors.

A few wooden tables were scattered about the room, and atop a couple of them were metal medical trays holding an array of rusted knives, scalpels, drills, shears, and other instruments of nightmares. The floor was covered in aged, black stains—there was no question about what they were.

"It's a fucking torture chamber," said Paul.

"Thanks, Einstein," said Matt. "But why?"

"Why not?" said Mary as she walked around, poking around in the trays and lifting a particularly nasty-looking rib spreader. "I mean, they *are* vampires, after all. They enjoy blood and gore and torturing humans. Hell, maybe they even tortured one another. Remember how Ushaville had a set of vampire rules? So maybe vamps and humans who violated them were punished down here too."

Beast Stalker frowned and picked up a long, rusty scalpel. "You know what I'm thinking," he said.

"Shit, Beast Stalker, you're right. Chief," said Mary, understanding his meaning.

"Yeah," he said, "if this torture room is here, then there are probably others, and if Ophelia knows about them—and why wouldn't she since she has been here so long?—then she probably has Chief and his wife in one."

Mary shuddered, dropped the rib spreader, and said, "Then what are we waiting for? Let's get the hell out of here and rescue Chief!"

They exited the horrible room, wondering what tragic and dreadful memories its walls held.

Continuing down the ancient tunnel, they came across more wooden doors, behind each of which was another torture room. They must have passed a dozen of them when they heard a shrill woman's scream from the tunnel ahead of them. Beast Stalker looked at the others, then sprinted toward the sound. The others followed and found themselves outside of one of the rooms.

"It has to be them," whispered Beast Stalker. "Everyone, get your stakes in hand and be sure you have easy access to holy water. I'm going in."

He counted to three, then kicked the door in, breaking the frame in half. He leaped into the room, and the others followed. What they saw broke their hearts.

Chief's wife was strapped into the torture chair, and Chief himself was tied up with ropes in another standard chair, facing his wife. Ophelia stood over Chief's wife with a scalpel in her hand. When Beast Stalker broke into the room, she looked up and stared in surprise, then quickly regained her composure.

"Let them go, Ophelia!" roared Beast Stalker in an angry, beastly tone that no one had ever heard him use before. It seemed to even astonish Ophelia and even frighten her a bit.

"I'm rather impressed that you knew where to find me," she said to the group, having regained her icy composure. "Then again, I suppose the tunnels are the most logical place to look, given the state of Ushaville. I have *not* forgotten, by the way, that you burned down my town."

"Let them go now, Ophelia," he repeated.

Chief's head was hanging low, his energy sucked out of him. Beast Stalker winced, noting that Chief's other hand was now severed.

Looking at Chief's wife, he saw that Ophelia had made some incisions on her arms and a cut across her forehead, but her hands and fingers remained. The cuts looked shallow, and Beast Stalker figured that Ophelia was not planning to go heavier yet, but rather wanted to use Chief's wife as a pawn against him, so the longer she lived, the better.

"Don't think of trying to use those stakes or that holy water," warned Ophelia. "One quick movement of your hands, and she gets it."

"More of us than one of you, bitch," said Paul, causing Ophelia to laugh.

"Rephrase that: more humans than one vampire. I'd rip through all of you before you even realized what happened."

"Then why haven't you?" taunted Matt.

Ophelia hissed at him, then edged the scalpel blade close to Chief's wife's throat. "I'm glad you all came to visit, in any case. This way, more human emotion is involved, and thus you're easier to manipulate. Watch how you react to this, for example."

She swiftly drew the blade across Chief's wife's cheek, cutting a deep, bloody gash and causing the poor old woman to cry in pain. Then, beast Stalker lunged at Ophelia, who extended her fangs at a vampire's speed and placed the tips against Chief's wife's neck.

Breast Stalker stopped.

"Told you," she said. "Your loyalty to your own kind is, well, it is charming, I suppose, but it's also a great weakness among you humans."

"You used to be human too, Ophelia," said Mary.

A strange sort of relaxed sadness swept across Ophelia's face, but then it disappeared, and she said in a soft voice, "But that was so long ago…" She retracted her fangs and stood up again. "I have all the advantage here," she said to the humans. "I want the amulet. If I get it, then I have almost unlimited power. If Chief doesn't squeal, then I kill all of you, something I've been wanting to do anyway, for what you did to my town and our kind. But, then, I have all of eternity to find the amulet anyway. It will just take longer."

Beast Stalker took a slow step back to avoid a repeat, saying, "Ophelia, you need to understand that we are not going to tell you where the amulet is and how to access it."

"*We?*"

Beast Stalker realized his mistake and remained silent, frowning at the vampiress.

"So you *do* also know where it is!" said a bubbly Ophelia. "Oh, goody! That makes this even easier!" She looked back into the room's dark corners and said, "Come, children!"

Seven nasty-looking, muscular male vampires appeared from out of the shadows in the back of the enormous room. They had not been visible in the darkness before.

"See, I knew you would probably find me," admitted Ophelia. "I was counting on it, actually. It's an integral part of my plan, so thank you for that. Now, empty your pockets of your stakes and holy water. Place them slowly in a pile on the ground."

She looked back at the vampire thugs and nodded. Then, as the humans did what she had asked, each vampire casually strode across the room and took a position with one human so that every human had his and her own bloodsucking guardian; this included Chief and his wife.

"Here is how this is going to work," stated Ophelia. "First rule: anyone who tries anything funny is killed immediately. No compromise on that, even if that means I don't get the amulet. Second, I'm going to make life really, really bad for Chief's wife, and there's nothing you can do about that."

Beast Stalker glared at her, seething with rage but keeping it under the control of his mind. Mary pushed back against her vampire guard, growling at him to stop touching her. He merely smirked.

"Third," continued Ophelia, "there actually is something you can do about it; the moment any of you agree to tell me where the amulet is, I mean the very *second* you say the word *yes*, I stop the torture. I'm not uncivilized, after all."

Paul made a sarcastic *hmm* sound.

"Fourth, once you actually tell me where it is, we take a little trip there so Chief can undo the Cherokee magic. Finally, I get the amulet, and you can go on about your lives. I'll even give Chief and his wife a tiny sip of my blood. It won't turn them into vampires, but it will immediately heal their wounds. Chief will even regrow his hands. You have my word as a vampire, and we do *not* break our word. Understand?"

Beast Stalker looked back at the Gravediggers. Poor Uri was shaking, entirely unused to this sort of thing. His usually-pale skin might as well have been translucent, so much had the blood drained from his face from sheer terror.

"Relax, mate," whispered Paul to Uri. "We always make it out alive. Most of us, at least."

Beast Stalker looked at Chief, but the old Cherokee was unconscious. However, his bare chest, smeared with blood, raised and regularly lowered, assuring Beast Stalker that he was at least still alive.

He looked at Chief's wife, and the scared look of dread on her face, the pleading in her eyes, touched his heart. He knew that, though he could stand up to the most incredible torture without revealing the amulet's location, he simply could not stand and watch Chief's wife, that sweet old woman who had shown him such kindness over the years, be tortured mercilessly. He could not.

"Fine, Ophelia," said a defeated Beast Stalker. "I'll tell you where the amulet is. I can't let you harm Chief's wife. It's just too much."

"Beast Stalker?" questioned Mary. "What are you doing?"

As he spoke, he turned around to look at Mary: "I will gladly sacrifice myself to stop her from getting the amulet, but I can't sacrifice someone else, and I can't watch Chief's wife be tortured. We *cannot* let that happen. So we will find another way to stop her."

Ophelia's mouth was open, struggling between a laugh of satisfaction and mischief and a sigh of disbelief.

"Is that all it took?" she asked. "Threaten an old woman, and you give up? A part of me is disappointed. I was looking forward to hearing her scream. But, I meant it when I said that a vampire's word is unbroken ."

Ophelia used one of her sharp fingernails to scratch a line in her arm to draw blood. Then, she allowed a couple of drops to fall into Chief's and his wife's mouths.

"That will start their healing process. They will be as good as new in a few hours."

Something sounded from outside the room, from the ancient hall outside. It was a scraping sound accompanied by moans.

"Oh, shit," said Matt, looking at his scraped elbow. "Shit! My elbow…the blood…I think it dripped on the way here and aroused some of the really old ones!"

The scraping drew louder and closer until it reached the torture room door. Without pomp, one of the ancient, skeletal vampires entered. He stumbled creakingly toward Matt, specifically for his bleeding elbow.

Even Ophelia looked surprised. She backed up along with everyone else in the room. A dozen Ancient Ones flooded the room behind the first one, some staggering, some crawling, others barely pulling their old bones and tight, worn skin across the floor. They were all zeroing in on Matt's elbow.

Ophelia rang out in laughter and said, "Well done, Matt! You awakened the Ancient Ones and brought them all to you! It's like a Greek tragedy. I think I'll just stand back and watch them devour you. Do you know how strong vampires that old are? In fact, watch; I'll help them out a little!"

She cut into Chief's wife's arm again. She cried out, and Beast Stalker growled at Ophelia, but there was nothing he could do. Ophelia allowed several ounces of the old woman's blood to pool into her pale hand. She casually walked to the first old one who had entered and held the blood to its bony, creaking jaws. As soon as the blood touched what had been its lips, it began to change.

First, it stood up straight, no longer hunched and staggering like a zombie. Then, its papery remnants of skin laced together with other remnants and plumped into normal skin, its tone olive. Its eye sockets—empty and gaping blindly for centuries—actually grew eyeballs that shone with deep-blue eyes. Next, his nose formed, then his mouth and lips, then his muscles, and once he had finished lapping up the blood with his new tongue, the old clothes that had been but tattered scraps reformed over him and into the form of a European Medieval knight's armor.

Had they not known of his vampirism, he would have struck them as a handsome, noble man, a warrior from ages ago. There was nothing noble about him, however.

He offered his thanks to Ophelia in a long-forgotten language, then turned toward Matt and stared at his bleeding elbow. As he approached Matt slowly, doubtlessly unfamiliar with using legs since he had not walked in hundreds of years, Ophelia went about collecting more handfuls of Chief's and his wife's blood and feeding it to several other Ancient Ones. Matt danced around the torture chair, avoiding the onset of the vampire knight.

After not too long, among the old skeletal vampires who were creaking about, stood five recomposed Ancient Ones. Besides the European Medieval knight, there was a Chinese warrior from an ancient dynasty, possibly the Zhou or Qin; a Middle Eastern warrior with thick, curly, black hair, so likely a Hebrew or Canaanite or Hittite; a black African warrior with a glorious blue waistcloth and multicolored headdress; and a female magician from ancient India, in a sparkling, brightly-colored, green, blue, yellow, and red gown.

"It's almost fucking beautiful!" exclaimed Paul. "Too bad they're a bunch of damn bloodsuckers!"

Being behind the table and chair, Matt had come upon the pile of stakes and holy water that Ophelia had forced them to put down. Paul, Mary, and Uri looked at him and, with an understanding that could only exist among people who have been through much trouble together, Matt nodded and yelled, "Now!"

He tossed the three other Gravediggers and then Beast Stalker a stake and a bottle of holy water each. They caught them, and the battle began.

Paul lurched across the room with a stake and, catching the Medieval knight off guard, plunged the stake into its heart. It crumbled into a pile of gray ash.

"Oh, shit! I did it!" yelled a surprised Paul as all hell broke loose in the torture room.

His luck did not last, for the African vampire grabbed Paul from behind and tossed him across the room as if he were a stick. Paul slammed hard into the stone wall and fell to the ground. He grunted and seemed dazed.

At the same time, Mary and the African warrior vampire wrestled on the ground. She was not much of a match for his ancient strength, so she squirted some holy water onto his face. It hissed and smoked, and he shrieked and rolled off of Mary, holding his face and whimpering.

Uri saw this and said, "Oy vey! Why must I get into these situations? Here goes nothing!"

He jumped across the space between him and the African vampire, his payot flying behind him like a cape. He landed on the vampire's back. Then, taking no time to think about it, he stuck the ashwood stake into the vampire's heart and suddenly found himself kneeling on a pile of ashes. He seemed completely surprised that he had succeeded.

That left the Indian, Chinese, and Middle-Eastern vampires and Ophelia and her seven minions.

"Oh, hell. This shit again?" said Matt. The Indian magician vampiress hissed at him and revealed her long, curved fangs. The tips glistened with her wicked saliva. She said something in an ancient Indian language, but the tone was clear: she was taunting Matt.

She flew through the air, made solid contact with Matt, then the

HELL'S BELLS: A PUNK ROCK DEMON STORY

two flew back into the wall, Matt first. His back slammed the wall and he yelled. He fell, the vampiress on top of him.

Before he could try to roll off, she bit into his neck and barely missed his artery, but the blood still flowed out into her mouth. She drank deeply, guzzling hot, salty blood directly from the human for the first time in millennia.

"Oh no you don't, bitch!" yelled Paul, who had recovered from hitting the wall. He sprinted across the room, took a flying jump, and plunged the stake into the vampiress' heart before she could drink enough of Matt's blood to kill him.

"Shit, I owe you one!" said a weakened Matt.

"You owe me many!" retorted Paul with a grin. He spun around and started spraying holy water all over the room. It sizzled against the skin of the remaining two Ancient Ones, Ophelia, and her seven servants. They hissed and recoiled backward, giving the Gravediggers and Beast Stalker time to regroup. Matt stood up shakily but with steely determination.

"Keep the holy water spraying!" instructed Beast Stalker. The Gravediggers squirted it onto the vampires' burning skin while Beast Stalker ran to Chief and his wife to try to rescue them. Paul, who had been purposefully aiming at Ophelia's face, ran out of holy water, so Ophelia quickly recovered. She hissed and rushed at vampire speed to the space in front of Beast Stalker.

"Don't even think about it!" she growled, stopping his plans. She pushed him hard in the chest, and he flew across the room back to where the Gravediggers were and hit the ground hard.

Mary saw the Chinese vampire curling up in pain from the holy water. She focused her spray on his face, trying to blind him.

"Go, Paul!" she shouted, and he understood.

He ran to the Chinese vampire and staked him good and hard. He poofed into a pile of dust.

The Middle-Eastern vampire turned his back to the water spray, regained his vision, spun around at vampire speed, and rushed to Uri, whom he grabbed from behind. The vampire extended its fangs above Uri's neck.

"Hell no!" shouted Matt. "Circle up, guys!"

He, Paul, and Mary formed a circle around the vampire and Uri, stakes in their hands. The vampire was not sure what to do. He dropped Uri and lunged at Paul, but Matt flanked him quickly and stabbed the ashwood stake into his ancient heart. He fell to the ground, no more than dust.

"The others!" said Paul, who began kicking the skeletal beings.

Then, finally, they retreated into the hall, too powerless without blood. Mary, Matt, and Uri joined in pushing them back outside the room, and Paul slammed the door shut.

Ophelia clapped slowly from the corner.

"Well, I'll be damned," she said sarcastically. "I mean, I am damned, literally, but yes, good show, Gravediggers. You've improved since I first fought you. Even so, there's still me and these seven others. You're all out of holy water, and one of your stakes is over there in a pile of ashes. Also, I have this advantage."

At superhuman speed, she zoomed back to Chief's wife. She dragged a nail across the poor old lady's cheek and licked the blood that trickled out. Unfortunately, Chief's wife was losing too much blood too quickly.

"Now, let me make it simple." She extended her fangs and hovered them millimeters above Chief's wife's throat. "Before the interruption of the Ancient Ones, you were saying that you were ready to show me to the amulet. So go ahead, and I won't rip her throat out."

Beast Stalker held his hands up in resignation and defeat.

"Alright, alright," he said. "I'll lead you to the amulet. Just stop harming them. Leave them alone. They are innocent."

She looked at two of the vampire thugs and said, "Untie Chief and his wife."

They obeyed, and Beast Stalker and Matt put their arms around Chief's shoulders to allow him to stand without falling out of weakness. Ophelia had Chief's wife's arm in hers.

"A little insurance that no one tries to run or trick me," she explained. "I will not hurt her. Now, follow me; I know a close exit from the tunnels. If anyone tries anything funny, my guards will put a quick stop to it and to you."

As the Gravediggers and Beast Stalker glared at Ophelia, she tugged on Chief's wife's arm and led her along past the others and out the door of the torture room. Then, continuing down the tunnel in the direction the Gravediggers had been walking, she led them down a narrow side tunnel that sloped upwards after only about twenty yards. The guards were surrounding the five the entire way.

They could see the last hints of daylight poking down through the opening, so Ophelia stopped and made them wait for about fifteen awkward minutes of silence as the sun finally set.

Finally, they stepped out of the tunnels and into the ruins of Ushaville. They could see that they had somehow circled around and were back near Chief's truck.

"Where are we going, Beast Stalker?" asked Ophelia.

"Chief's house," he grumbled.

"Now, here's what's going to happen," explained Ophelia. "You five and your guards will take the truck back to Chief's house. Chief's wife and I will have a lovely little flight and meet you there. If you try anything on the trip, I'll hurt her. Then, we will reconvene in Chief's living room and have a nice, civilized little chat about the amulet."

Ophelia took Chief's wife in her arms and levitated her into the air and away toward the reservation. The others loaded into the truck, Beast Stalker driving with his guard in the passenger seat, and the rest crammed into the bed. They began the drive to Chief's house.

Half an hour later, the Gravediggers, Ophelia, Chief, and his wife sat in Chief's living room while the vampire thugs stood guard among them. Chief already looked like he was feeling better from Ophelia's blood drop, and his wife, also revived, was still terrified of the entire situation. She would, without a doubt, be traumatized for life.

"When I was human," began Ophelia, "no one would ever dream of having guests without serving them food and drink, but you moderns lack many of our old graces. I digress. Now, Chief, Beast Stalker, or both of you, kindly retrieve the amulet for me. Your guard and I will go with you. The other guards will remain here with the Gravediggers. You know the condition: try anything stupid, and I start slashing."

"I'll go with Chief," offered Beast Stalker. "I don't trust you alone with him."

Ophelia shrugged and stood up. "Come on, then."

As the Gravediggers waited in the living room, sneering at the vampire thugs (except for Uri, who was still quite rattled and had withdrawn into himself, arms folded against his chest), Chief and Beast Stalker led Ophelia and one vampire guard across Chief's backyard and into the forest behind his house.

Using their flashlights to follow a worn footpath about one hundred yards into the pine trees, they came upon a spotted oak tree that rose to heights greater than all of the trees around it and whose trunk was so thick that three men would not have been able to join hands and wrap their arms around it completely. Chief stopped in front of the tree.

Any other time, the forest night would have been peaceful and charming. The full moon lit the area so well that they could turn off their flashlights. The never-ending stars sparkled against the black void of the universe, and each little speck of light seemed to wink at them. Nocturnal animals barked and chirped and scurried about, and the owls called and screeched throughout the branches of the trees around them.

The two Cherokees looked at each other, the tragic sadness in their faces evident.

Chief said to Beast Stalker in Cherokee, *"We can still choose to die rather than betray the power of our people."*

Beast Stalker also replied in Cherokee, *"I would gladly die a thousand deaths to protect the amulet, but I cannot allow your wife to be tortured and die for it. That is not my decision to make. It would be an unjust sacrifice."*

Chief, understanding Beast Stalker's sentiment, simply nodded.

"English!" growled Ophelia. "No secret plans in Cherokee!"

Glaring back at Ophelia, Beast Stalker said, "The amulet is hidden in the heart of this sacred tree. The only way to ask the tree to release it is to perform Cherokee magic, which must be in the Cherokee language; otherwise, it will not work."

Ophelia narrowed her eyes, studied his face for a moment, then told the vampire guard, "Watch them carefully."

Chief and Beast Stalker knelt before the tree in a praying position, and Chief spoke a simple Cherokee magical prayer.

Sgĕ! Ha-nâ'gwa hatû ᵐgani'ga Nû ᵐya Wâtige'ĭ, gahu'stĭ tsûtska'dĭ nige'sûⁿna. Ha-nâ'gwa dû ᵐgihya'lĭ. Agiyahu'sa nv-ya o-sa-ni, haga' tsûⁿ-nû'iyû ᵐta dătsi'waktû'hĭ. Tla-'ke' a'ya a'kwatseli'ga.

As he completed the prayer, they heard crunching and cracking sounds from deep within the tree. Ophelia watched in amazement as a line in the trunk became a deeper line, then a rift, and then the trunk slowly opened itself like a chest opening to reveal a heart.

Inside the trunk, they saw woody tendrils and heartstrings squirming like worms or Chinese noodles, then opening to reveal the brilliant blue of the sapphire amulet in their midst. Even the distant light of the stars joined the reflected light of Sister Moon to sparkle and tinkle brilliantly, ephemerally, casting blue disco-ball specks of light

HELL'S BELLS: A PUNK ROCK DEMON STORY

all over the forest around them. Even Ophelia stared and took a deep breath when she saw it.

"It takes a lot to impress a vampire as old as me," she said in a soft and reverent voice, "but it is beautiful."

She slowly reached her hand and arm into the heart of the sacred tree and grasped the amulet. It glowed, and its azure hue changed to show traces of red. She pulled the amulet out slowly, deliberately, but just as it passed outside the tree, the trunk snapped quickly shut, almost taking her hand off.

"Your tree must not like me so much," she said. "I suppose it matters not; I have the amulet. Now, nothing can stop me!"

She held the amulet up in the air and marveled as the moonlight prismed through the now-red gemstone.

"Very well. I keep my word. I will leave you here to find your way back home. I am going to collect my servants and leave. You and the Gravediggers are free to go. Chief, you will heal soon enough, as will your wife." She and the vampire thug levitated into the air a few feet, then Ophelia said as she looked down at the two Cherokee men, "A pleasure, as always."

She cackled mockingly, and then the two vampires flew back towards Chief's house.

When Chief and Beast Stalker arrived back at the house, they found the Gravediggers in the living room. Ophelia and her thugs had left as promised. Mary had filled a glass of ice water for Chief's wife and was dabbing her head with a cool, damp washcloth.

Chief ran to his wife, and the two embraced. Tears fell from his wife's eyes and rolled down her cheek.

"Oh, Chief..." she said.

"I know, dear. I know."

CHAPTER 36

The Clash and the Crash

"Chief, you and your wife, please sit. I'll find everything I need. You need to rest!" insisted Mary as she scrambled around Chief's kitchen to try to whip up something for them to eat. She found some bread, along with some rabbit that Chief's wife had prepared earlier and had stored in the refrigerator. She heated it up, and everyone ate together while Beast Stalker told them exactly what had happened with Ophelia and the amulet.

"Beast Stalker," said Chief, "did you see the sacred tree's reaction to Ophelia's hand? And did you see how the amulet turned red when she held it?"

Beast Stalker nodded and squinted his eyes, trying to understand Chief's meaning.

"I suspect," explained Chief, "that the sacred tree and the sacred amulet, such important and ancient parts of our people, sensed her evil and her intent. There may be hope yet."

"I hope so, Chiefy mate," said Paul. "Either way, we're gonna get her, don't you worry. No one messes with nice old ladies in front of me and gets away with it. Say, got any fire water for your old pal Paul?"

"Paul!" chided Mary as she slapped his arm.

"Good to see you haven't changed a bit, Paul," said Beast Stalker as he walked to an entertainment cabinet in the living room and produced a bottle of whisky. "Chief?" he asked.

"Help yourselves," the old man said. "I think the missus and I need a stiff drink too, after all that."

Paul took a long swig of the Cherokee-made whisky and sighed.

"Oh, yeah. That's some good shit. So, where's Ophelia going? New Orleans?"

"Gotta be," said Mary. "It's her home now."

After a rest, they called Eli to bring the helicopter back for the ride home. Beast Stalker had called some Cherokee women to go to the house and stay with Chief and his wife, caring for them until they were fully healed.

The unmistakable roar of the high-performance chopper filled Chief's backyard. So, with hugs and goodbyes, the Gravediggers, along with Beast Stalker, who had decided to return to New Orleans until Ophelia was stopped, boarded the aircraft. Then, with a few deft flicks of Eli's wrist, they rose into the air and soared off southward.

A few short hours later, at 7,000 feet, the swamps of Louisiana around New Orleans came into view below. Despite everything they were going through and the distress of the situation, no one could help but stare down at the beauty of the green wetlands. The matte, mossy surface of the endless swamp was broken up by groves of cypress trees, little patches of moss and algae, and tufts of islands here and there.

"This is beautiful," said Uri as he nervously grasped his seat.

Though he was no expert on the various sounds and sensations of flight, he was reasonably certain that he should be terrified when the steady bass drumming of the turboshaft engine began to sputter and misfire erratically.

"That sound? That cannot be good!" he shouted into the mic over the comm system.

"Everyone hang on!" said Eli from the cockpit as she descended rapidly and slowed the craft to a hover. "Matt, take the pitch control, the stick! Hold it as still and steady as you can!"

Somewhere between thrill and horror, Matt obeyed the pilot's order. The helicopter was still about 1,000 feet above the swamp. Eli reached under the control panel on her side and fiddled with a few wires.

"Shit!" she said. "It's gotta be the fuel line. It's cut. Someone sabotaged us while I was taking a nap!"

"Ophelia!" said a panicked Paul. "Gotta be that bitch!"

"Why do we have such bad fucking luck with aircraft?" shouted Matt.

Then they heard the worst sound you ever want to hear on a helicopter: complete silence. Starved of fuel, the engine had cut out. So the helicopter yawed drastically to the left.

"Don't panic!" said Eli through the comm. "I can bring it down with autorotation!"

Uri was fervently muttering Hebrew prayers. Mary grabbed Paul's hand with an iron vice grip. Beast Stalker held onto his seat with a tense face, and in the cockpit, Eli took the control from Matt. She immediately flattened the pitch of the rotor blades, and the helicopter began to fall into the swamp.

Thanks to her experience and expertise as a helicopter pilot, the air from below the craft passed upward through the blades as they fell, causing the blades to rotate, the centrifugal force allowing the craft to descend at a reasonably stable rate like a maple tree seed. Only a little over a minute later, the helicopter landed roughly but safely in a shallow patch of swamp.

"Fuck my life," said Paul. "I need a fucking drink."

"Hey, what's another plane crash?" said Mary.

Uri leaned up into the cockpit and said, "Eli, thank you, thank you, thank you so much. You saved our lives. I never knew a helicopter could do that."

"It's nothing," replied Eli. "Just physics. I think it's more urgent now to find our way out of this swamp, not to mention the massive financial hit I'm going to take with the helicopter. Shit."

They watched as a disturbingly-large alligator swished about, a bit too close for them to relax.

"Let's get to that little island," said Beast Stalker. We're not safe being exposed like this."

He watched the alligator swim off far enough away, then led the others, wading through the waist-high, brown water, making slow progress as the soft mud below the water strove to suck their feet down and stop their progress.

With much straining and struggling, they reached a small island covered in cypress trees, their woody, knobby knees poking up here and there.

The ordeal with Chief had taken until first light, so the sun was beginning to rise above them. But, even that early, it pelted them with burning, ultraviolet rays as if Zeus himself were angrily hurling lightning bolts at them.

"Get in the shade," said Beast Stalker. "Anyone have any water?"

Mary opened her bag and passed out bottles of water, which they all quickly and greedily emptied. Paul pulled a beer out of his bag and chased the water with alcohol.

Looking around, they saw nothing but swamp to the horizon in every direction.

They remained stranded on the island all day long, and as the melting, marshy sun dripped down toward the horizon, the shadows began to lengthen. They were starting to feel a bit nervous.

"Oy," said Uri, "what are the chances that we're never found? Is this like a Cajun version of Gilligan's Island? And, if so, does that make me Gilligan?"

Mary chuckled and said, "Dude, you can be funny sometimes. But I think Paul is definitely Gilligan here."

"What, you think you're the skipper?" said Paul to Mary.

"The skipper's definitely Eli!" said Matt. "Of course, if Lâmié were here, he'd be Mister Howell."

They all broke into laughter, even Beast Stalker, which helped lower their stress and make them feel a little less afraid. However, the laughter ceased when a large alligator climbed up onto the bank of their island.

"Oh, shit," said Uri. "Pardon my language."

Beast Stalker said, "Be still. No sudden movements. Maybe it just wants to sleep on the bank."

It did not want to just sleep on the bank. Instead, the prehistoric behemoth used its squat legs to approach the group slowly; it opened its jaws and bellowed out a profound croak.

"Fuck fuck fuck," whispered Paul. "It wants to fucking eat us."

He very slowly, very carefully moved in front of Mary to protect her. Even in her terror, she smiled at his unthinking bravery.

"Too bad 'Tit Boudreaux's not here," whispered Matt. "He's a reptile expert. And I'm pretty sure this isn't Big Bessie."

The group slowly backed up until they were against a large cypress tree, offering some protection from the back but not between them and the alligator.

"And we left our stakes back in Ushaville, so we don't have any weapons. Anything back on the helicopter that we could use as a weapon?"

"Sure, probably, but it's too far away," said Eli. "Shit, I'm trying to think."

The thinking was barely possible, though, as the ancient, armored beast drew closer to them. Its steely, glassy eyes stared at them as its reptilian brain made the primitive assessment: threat or food?

It seemed to have decided on the *food* option, for it walked even closer, then squatted down as if anticipating a pouncing attack.

A deafening gunshot filled the air, and the alligator zipped around and back into the water faster than it looked like it could have done.

"Get outta here, you! You hear me?" yelled the creaking voice of an old man. "Y'all okay? He didn't got y'all, no?"

The bow of a *pirogue*, hollowed out of a log by hand, appeared from behind a cypress tree, and then the entire canoe-like boat glided into view. Standing on it with a long stick in his hand was a wrinkled old man with a white beard shaped like a cumulus cloud and wild hair to match. He wore a Budweiser baseball cap and jean overalls.

"Dem gators jes always causing' trouble, dem. So how y'all managed to get on dis island anyhow? Oh, sorry, I'm bein' rude not introducing' myself. I'm Horace Hebert, *traiteur*."

"Um, you what, mate?" asked Paul.

Mary slapped his arm and said, "Hello, Mister Hebert. Thank you for driving the alligator away. I think he was planning to have us for lunch."

"Oh, it ain't nothin'. Dem gators is not so smart, you know? Jes make some loud noises and jump up and down, and dey get scared off. Dem damn gators."

Uri asked, "Sir, what's a *traiteur*?"

"Oh," explained Gaston, "we traiteurs, we's kinda like a combination of faith healers and shamans, and some people might even call us witch doctors!" he said with a wink and a grin. "Now, y'all gotta get off dis island. I saw dat helicopter crash, me. Dat was y'all, I'm guessin'?"

Turtles, snakes, alligators, and other swamplife made slithering and splashing sounds around them, reminding Paul, Mary, and Matt of their previous experience in the swamp with Aunt Tilo, a memory that they would have preferred not to re-experience.

"Yep, that was us," said Erin. "I'm the pilot."

"Well, I watched dat fall," said Gaston, "and you must be da best pilot in da world, landin' a chopper like dat with no engine!"

The sun had almost set, casting gorgeous red, orange, and yellow-hued swaths of glossy light all over the swamp. For a moment, it was truly beautiful.

"Alright, y'all, I live pretty close to here, me, so I'm gonna load y'all in dis pirogue and take you to my little cabin. It ain't nothin' fancy, you hear? But you can stay der tonight, and tomorrow, I'll take y'all back to civilization, I will."

Horace divided them into two groups since the simple pirogue could not hold all of them at once. Before long, they were all seated in his one-room cabin. Made of solid cypress logs, the little dwelling was rustic but stout, filled with the necessities of swamp survival without the little touches of grace that a woman might have added. Nevertheless, it was more than comfortable and spacious.

On the walls hung taxidermied deer heads, ducks, and even a whole alligator, trophies of past hunts. There was a wood-burning stove and even a Honda generator right outside the door for when he needed electricity. That night, though, he lit a couple of lanterns and some candles, providing ample light for the little shack in the middle of the inky swamp.

On a small table against a wall stood a statue of the Virgin Mary, behind which was hung a crucifix.

Horace had gone duck hunting early that morning, so he made a large pot of duck and pork sausage gumbo on the wood-fired stove—a true culinary treat to rival even 'Tit Boudreaux's masterpieces.

"Fucking delicious, mate," said Paul. "Say, got any beer?"

"Paul!" muttered Mary.

"Cher," said Gaston, "I'm a Cajun. Dat's like askin' if da swamp gots water." He opened an ice chest and passed out cold cans of Bud Light. "Drink up! Plenty more where dat comes from!"

As the moon replaced the sun in the clear, marshy sky, the gumbo bubbled and the beer flowed, and before too long, they were all talking like old friends—laughing, joking, philosophizing.

Sometime near midnight, Horace regained a more serious visage and became quiet for a few moments.

"You alright, mate?" asked an inebriated Paul.

"Yeah, yeah Paul, I'm good. It's just...Paul, have anyone ever tole you, der's something' special about you?"

"Oh, he's *special,* alright," joked Mary.

Horace chuckled and said, "See, as a traiteur, I talk to dem angels and dem saints, and to dem spirits out der. You know, dey's real, dey is, spirits and such."

"Oh, we know all too well," said Uri under his breath.

"See, right now, cher," explained Horace, "dey tellin' me dat you're special, Paul. A long, long time ago, and I mean before my French ancestors arrived in dees swamps, back in de Old World, your ancestors had some kind of power, some kind of secret, and dey made some kind of prophecy, you see. It gots something' to do with you, Paul. Dat's all I see, but I see it clearly."

They sat silently for a few minutes, listening to the symphony of chirping crickets outside and pondering Horace's words inside.

"It would explain some things," said Mary. "Like, why it's always Paul who seems to save the day."

"Which is a miracle in itself," said Matt, "especially since he's always drunk."

Paul grinned.

Uri said, "This, I can see. There is something special about Paul, despite his, well, his *colorful* personality."

Mary and Matt laughed.

"Colorful. That's a good word!" said Mary.

"I'm gonna tell y'all somethin' dat you need to listen to, you hear?" said Horace with a serious face. "I can sense that y'all facin' somethin' evil, *really* evil. I can tell y'all done faced evil before too, yeah."

They listened quietly as the fire's licking flames cast waving lines of darkness and light upon their faces, giving the cabin a ghostly atmosphere.

"The way to defeat dat evil is to understand Paul's prophesy. *Comprenez*? Until y'all understand Paul's prophecy, dat evil gonna keep comin' and comin' and comin' over and over again. Y'all understand? Dat's what dem spirits tellin' old Horace, dem. So all I know to do is to pass along der words."

A crow called from somewhere close to the cabin, and Horace

smiled.

"Dat's an omen, dat. It means dem spirits are talkin' to y'all, and y'all best listen. Now, if y'all excuse me, dis old man needs some sleep. I'll take y'all back to the city in my bass boat tomorrow. I got no reception here in dis shack either, so sorry, your phones won't work. Goodnight, y'all."

Horace rolled out several very soft sleeping cots for everyone, then climbed into his own little wooden-frame bed. Within five minutes, his half-whistled, old-man snores filled the room, causing Mary to giggle.

The Gravediggers, Uri, and Eli were exhausted; after all, who the hell gets into a helicopter crash and survives? So they all lay down on the cots, finding them more than accommodating and cozy, and soon, they were all asleep as Horace and Paul played dueling snores against each other.

The following day, Horace woke them all at six o'clock, too early for their taste, but that's the hour of the morning when old men seem to feel most awake. He led them to the back of the little island on which his cabin was built, to his green, metal, bass fishing boat, which was large enough to seat them all. After a boat ride of only a couple of hours and many thanks, they found themselves back in New Orleans.

They surprised Lâmié with a knock on the door, then explained to everyone else everything that had happened on the trip to Ushaville. Lâmié, the brilliant host as always, invited Eli to stay there at the mansion. He determined to talk to her soon about the supernatural and convince her of everything he knew was real. Of course, she accepted, and it did not take Mary's woman's intuition to tell that they had once been lovers and that a spark still remained lit in their eyes.

CHAPTER 37

A Deal with the Devil

The slimy Reverend Methuselah Skink sat on a park bench in the middle of Audubon Park at midnight. His black top hat, slacks, and jacket were camouflaged in the darkness, but his pale skin acted like a lighthouse beacon as it reflected the moonbeams. He licked his wet lips with his long, slithering tongue.

A raccoon on the prowl for food sniffed the ground as it approached the reverend. It stopped near the bench and looked up at him. He wiggled his fingers to call it over and made a sickly, wet, slimy, clicking sound with his mouth. The poor creature squealed and ran off in terror.

As if from nowhere, a petite young woman appeared in front of him. She was in full black clothing, including a black balaclava. Had she not purposely stood in front of Skink, he never would have seen her.

"You startled me!" he hissed.

"That's the point," she retorted in a whisper. "I told you I'm a pro. Now keep your voice down, for fuck's sake."

"You will speak to me with respect, young lady! I am your preacher, after all!"

She sighed and said, "Yeah, sorry, Reverend. You have the money?"

Somewhere in the deep recesses of the park, an alligator bellowed. Crickets chirped all around the two figures.

"Of course," he replied indignantly. "I told you I would, didn't I?" He moved a black suitcase toward her, but as she reached for it, he snatched it back. "Not so fast! The deal stands, yes? You have the target under surveillance?"

She put her hands on her hips and replied, "Yes, as I said. And *your* deal still stands, too, right? So I do this job, I get the money, and I'm exempt from drinking the Kool-Aid, yes?"

"Yes," he promised. "Yes. Now go take him out as soon as possible!"

He handed her the briefcase. She placed it on the ground and briefly opened it to reveal stacks of one-hundred-dollar bills.

"Can do!" she said with a smile, then disappeared into the night.

CHAPTER 38

An Alley and a Roofie

Pierre Lascif took a taxi from the New Orleans International Airport to his hotel, the Monteleone in the French Quarter. After all, having lived in a shack for the past years, a touch of luxury would not hurt, would it?

It was still early evening, and though his trip was very serious business, he nevertheless wanted to walk around and see the famous old city. Moreover, his stomach growled, so he also wanted to taste some of the famous New Orleans food.

He spotted a sign down the street that read *New Orleans Bistro*, so he headed that way. Traversing the cobblestoned street and heading toward the restaurant, he took in the atmosphere. However, something seemed a bit off.

Yes, there were the usual glasses and silverware clinking and jingling; the conversations, laughter, and arguments ongoing; the warm, sweaty smell that permeated the entire French Quarter, a smell improved by the savory and spicy aromas of gumbo, shrimp Creole, freshly-shucked oysters, boiled crawfish, boiled shrimp, fried oyster po'boys, and more. The buildings seemed right out of Medieval Spain or France, with their wooden construction and second-story balconies terraced with intricate, wrought-iron art that also served as railing. The old, cobblestoned streets added an Old World charm.

Yet, for every drunk, gourmand, gourmet, or Lothario on the street, there was another contorting his or her body into impossible bends. People were growling, spewing out green saliva, and even vomiting blood. One man even appeared to be levitating above the sidewalk—probably a street magician? It all did not seem quite right. He knew New Orleans' reputation as a wild and unique place, but people were acting, well...*possessed.* And he hated to even think the word.

Before reaching the bistro, he passed a dark, narrow alley on his left and heard his own name.

"Pierre...Pierre...you have come so far..." said a whispering yet gravelly voice.

"What the hell?" he muttered as he stopped and tried to peer into the darkness that pervaded the old alleyway. Now he knew that something was wrong. It was most decidedly supernatural.

He reached into his pocket; he had decided to take along a crucifix and some holy water on his New Orleans trip, just in case. The thought of more exorcism sickened him, but hell, if there really were a demonic uprising, then he supposed he had a duty to humanity.

He took a deep breath, pulled out the crucifix, and stepped into the alley. In the alley itself, no longer under the streetlamps, he could see to its end. The alleyway's sides were lined with old garbage cans and piles of refuse, and he saw a couple of rats scurrying about. There was nothing unusual about the alley until something appeared out of nowhere at the alley's end.

He gulped and stopped in his tracks. A black cloud made of thick smoke swirled into existence. He stared at it as it began to take form. First, it grew taller and wider, and then he could make out limbs and a head. Next, the cloud became more and more solid and material until he saw its final form.

"You! You son of a bitch! Can it be?" he cried out.

The demon was in the form of a giant man but with a bull's head, horns, and hooves. He recognized it immediately as the demon Moloch. However, he knew very well that even he was not prepared to deal with such a powerful prince of demons.

Moloch bellowed like a bull, and black smoke and fire spewed from his bovine nostrils. The trash lining each side of the alley caught fire, creating a sort of burning pathway.

Pierre backed up slowly, but Moloch matched his movement with giant footsteps forward, footsteps that shook the wooden buildings

HELL'S BELLS: A PUNK ROCK DEMON STORY

lining the alley. Finally, Pierre reached the street, but Moloch did not stop. He saw in the bull's eyes and lowered head that it meant to run, and if Pierre knew one thing, it was that he could not outrun a thirty-foot-tall demon.

"*Merde alors!*" he shouted. He turned and ran, not caring that he bumped into people, knocked over some, and even shoved some out of the way. Moloch was after him specifically; he just knew it. Because of his previous career as a talented exorcist, he had made a name for himself in hell.

He quickly turned back to look, and, as predicted, Moloch was loping and bounding after him while ignoring everyone else on the street. That is not to say that Moloch went out of his way to avoid others—he squashed some people to mush with his giant hooves. It was only to say that the demon's target was Pierre.

He sprinted as much as his alcoholic body could take until he found himself in Jackson Square. He meant to run into the center park, but it was closed, so he just slammed against the gate. He turned around, his back against the wrought-iron gate, and watched as Moloch bounded toward him. He believed that it must have been his time to die.

He heard a loud car horn hoking, the kind of aftermarket horn that sounded more like a steamship's foghorn. Then, turning to the left, he saw a speeding van bursting through the traffic barriers and right into Jackson Square. The van was armored and even had a turret on top and guns sticking out of the sides. It looked like it had been beaten up and rolled over by a Mac truck, but it ran nonetheless.

A young guy popped up out of the turret. He had a Mohawk hairdo, facial piercings and wore a black, leather jacket.

The van screeched to a stop right in front of Pierre. Moloch was only a few dozen yards away.

"Get in, mate. Unless you wanna be demon soup!" shouted the punk as the van's side door slid open.

"Don't mind if I do!" shouted Pierre back. He jumped into the van, and it zoomed off before he could even close the door.

"I'm Mary, this is Uri, that's Matt, and that's Paul on the roof! We'll explain everything later!" said the punk girl driving the car. In the passenger seat next to her was a Hasidic Jew, Uri. In the back with him was a black guy, Matt, also in punk attire with a glorious afro hairstyle.

The van drove back onto the street and sped through the French

Quarter. Then, it made a turn, and Pierre saw Moloch on the cross street. The demon spotted them and ran after them. Pierre saw that the van had been initially a Volkswagen Microbus but had been souped up and armored beyond belief.

"Oy vey!" said Uri. "It's gaining on us!"

"Watch this!" shouted Mary, and the van screeched and careened around corners. "Watch what Lâmié installed!" She pressed a button, and a whooshing sound came from outside the back of the van. Pierre looked through the holes in the armor and saw a flood of water spraying out of the van's rear. "It's a holy water canon!"

The water hit Moloch hard right in his stomach, and he began to sizzle, smoke, and burn. He roared so loudly that the van rocked, but he stopped chasing them. Pierre saw him dissolve back into the black smoke and then down into the earth.

"Oy, that was close!" said Uri. "Still, don't slow down!"

Mary drove quickly through New Orleans until they were on a beautiful, oak-canopied boulevard with train tracks in the median. She veered down a side street and slid into a garage. She clicked another button and the garage door swiftly and decidedly closed.

They all sat in silence for a few moments, all of them breathing hard.

"Pardon my French," said Pierre, "but what the hell?"

"Just…just come in," said Mary. "We'll explain."

They entered the opulent mansion. Pierre saw that it was furnished with a mixture of fine Victorian and Napoleon III antique furniture. The walls were decked with old oil paintings of stuffy-looking characters. Beautiful chandeliers hung in every room they passed. They finally turned into a parlor in which several people were sitting. The delicious smell of pizza filled the air and Pierre's nostrils.

The four van passengers took a seat, inviting Pierre to do the same. Then, a handsome man with black hair approached Pierre and said, "Hi. I'm Lâmié Chasseur. Welcome to my home. Any friend of the Gravediggers is a friend of mine."

Pierre shook his hand, thanked him, then asked, "Who are the Gravediggers?"

"Lâmié, mate, how about you open up a bottle of that really good Champagne?" yelled Paul from across the grand parlor in Lâmié's mansion. "We just had a run-in with a fucking demon. A fucking *huge* demon."

"My God," replied Lâmié. "That's 1992 Dom Pérignon. Do you

know what each bottle costs? Never mind. Of course, you don't."

He sighed, walked into the next room, the kitchen, and returned with a Magnum bottle of the fine, sparkling wine. He popped it open and filled everyone's glasses around the room.

Lâmié introduced Pierre to everyone.

"So," said a dark-skinned man as he walked into the grand parlor with homemade pizzas. "How are we gonna go about doing everything we need to do? I mean, first, Madame Who's still…oh, hello. I'm Marcus Boudreaux."

"I am Pierre. Boudreaux is a good French name!"

Pierre was offered some pizza, which he eagerly and thankfully began to eat. Of course, he did not refuse a glass of the fine Champagne either.

"Well, guys," said Mary, "I think we need to fill Pierre in. We were driving back from the St. Louis cathedral. We got a ton more holy water from there, by the way. We saw Pierre being chased by what would only have been a giant demon. We stopped and rescued him, and here we are."

Outside the parlor's windows, the sounds of the city made it seem like any other typical night. There was even jazz music playing loudly from somewhere. Apparently, there were still unpossessed people left in New Orleans, and damn if they were not going to enjoy themselves.

"It was the demon Moloch," said Pierre. The others looked at him curiously, clearly wondering how he knew that. "You see, it's a long story, but I was a Vatican exorcist. I lost my faith, spent years in Mexico, and now I'm called up again from the Vatican. It's great luck that you were there to save me. I was hardly prepared to exorcise a demon's giant, physical manifestation."

Paul burped and giggled. Mary slapped his arm.

"Now, Pierre," said Mary, "we should tell you about ourselves. You obviously know about the supernatural. Well, Paul, Uri, Matt, and me, we're the Gravediggers, a punk band."

"And we suck!" added Paul. Mary ignored him. The air-conditioner audibly kicked on, a relief to the ones who had just come from outside. But, as usual, New Orleans was a cruel oven that night.

"Yeah," continued Mary, "so, we have this annoying habit of running into all sorts of supernatural evil thingies and having to fight them. I guess we're kind of like you in that way."

"Fucking understatement of the year," said Paul.

Mary slapped his arm.

HELL'S BELLS: A PUNK ROCK DEMON STORY

"Language!" yelled Yarielis from the corner.

Paul replied by finishing off his tall glass of Dom Pérignon.

When everyone finally finished every morsel of their pizza and Champagne, Paul brought a case of beer from the kitchen into the grand parlor.

Paul handed out beers to everyone. Many of them were quite buzzed enough from the Champagne, but Paul had no trouble continuing the drinking. Pierre seemed to also have no problem with it. Outside a window, a crow cawed.

'Tit-Boudreaux seemed both delighted and nervous to be serving food to a Frenchman, known as the French were for their gastronomy and culinary excellence. He returned from the kitchen with servings of *crème brûlée*.

"Oh, *Monsieur* Boudreaux, this is wonderful!" declared Pierre, and 'Tit Boudreaux beamed with pride but acted humble.

"So, what sorts of demon problems are you facing right now?" asked Pierre with a mouthful of the sweet custard.

"Where do we begin?" said Matt, who was sitting on a short sofa, along with Isabella, Varco, and Veronica, who had practically moved in. "First, our friend, er, acquaintance, Madame Who, is possessed. At first, Miss Annabelle here," he said as he gestured toward the biology teacher, "was possessed, but the demon jumped or something. Madame Who's locked in Miss Annabelle's bedroom right now."

Pierre sipped his beer in the caring, almost sensual way that only the French could. "Alright, that's one exorcism. What else? *Quoi d'autre?*"

"Second," explained Matt, "a demonic sigil's been painted in a few different places around town. Then, we have this batshit crazy preacher who, we think, is gonna try to get his whole church to commit suicide, Jim Jones style."

"*Merde!*" exclaimed Pierre.

"Gotta ask, mate," said Paul. "Cursing, drinking—aren't you from the Vatican?"

Pierre smiled coyly and said, "Oh, I'm no priest. I hate the fucking Church. But, I have a natural, well, *ability*, and I can't just get drunk and get laid in Mexico while the world literally goes to hell."

Paul raised his eyebrows at the description of Pierre's life in Mexico.

"And I didn't mention," said Matt, "Paul already fought the demon Kali in India."

Almost spitting out his sip of beer, Pierre said, "What? Holy crap, man. I need to hear that story, but let's deal with the present first. This demonic sigil? Do you have it here?"

The sounds of nocturnal New Orleans increased outside the house and in the neighborhood—the sounds of dining, the laughter of friends, the arguments of enemies, the music of live bands and jukeboxes blasting out of bars.

Lâmié stepped into the main study, then re-emerged with the sketch of the sigil. He handed it to Pierre, who only studied it for one second before his eyes grew wide.

"Oh, *merde.*"

"Um, that doesn't sound good, mate," Paul said as he opened another beer.

"This is the sigil of Moloch. King fucking Moloch. It's the demon that was chasing me today when you ran across me. Where did you say it's appeared?"

"Side of my house," piped up Uri, "and in my synagogue."

"Hmm. That figures. You're Hasidic, yes?"

"How did you ever guess?"

Pierre chuckled and said, "Alright, well, this is very serious. Uri, what do you know about Moloch?"

Uri pulled on his payot, then replied, "I know he was a demon or an idol in ancient Israel. God especially didn't like Moloch."

"Precisely," agreed Pierre. "Let me tell you all about this horrible prince of demons. But first, perhaps, it might lubricate my throat for conversation a bit if there were some red wine…"

Lâmié sighed and said, "I think you and Paul will get along just fine. Hold on, I'll get some."

Lâmié returned and opened the bottle, and Pierre whistled.

"*Mon Dieu*! Is that a two thousand vintage *Grand Vin de Château Margaux*?"

"The very same," said Lâmié with a smile.

"Wow. *Un vrai bon vivant.*"

"It's actually wine that I inherited. I didn't buy it myself, but yes, it's lovely. There's more as well, so please drink freely."

"Someone pinch me, please. I think I'm dreaming," jested Pierre.

'Tit Boudreaux brought out a platter of *profiteroles* that he had been learning how to make.

"Oh my God!" said Pierre. "This is too much!"

"The demon, mate?" probed Paul.

"Ah, *oui, oui*," replied Pierre as he stuffed a *petit* profiterole into his mouth and looked like he was having an orgasm. "*Magnifique, Monsieur* Boudreaux. Yes, so the demon Moloch. Demonologists such as *moi* believe he is a very high-ranking demon in hell, at least a prince, and at most, second only to Satan himself. Moreover, he was a god of the Canaanites, a god they worshipped fervently. He offered good harvests, wealth, and pleasure."

Paul, drinking his wine much too fast for the rare delicacy that it was, said, "Alright, so what's the problem then? Do a little prayer, get money and food. Sounds alright to me."

"There is always a catch with demons, Paul," explained Pierre. "Always. For Moloch, it was the very price of the worship that he demanded."

Pierre paused to take a sip of the exquisite wine, which acted as a build-up of suspense for the listeners.

"Well?" prodded Paul. "Moloch's price?"

"Children," answered Pierre. "Moloch demanded the burning alive of children in sacrifice."

"Oh, shit," said Paul, putting his glass down.

"Yes," explained Pierre, "the most horrific, painful death to the most innocent of souls. This is what makes Moloch so highly ranked in hell. He destroys innocence in the worst way."

Some crows cawed from outside the house, and Paul looked out the window, trying to see if he could spot them. A shiver ran down his spine.

"But then why the hell would anyone worship Moloch? Aren't there other gods of fertility or prosperity?" asked Lâmié. "In fact, I know there are countless fertility deities that don't require human sacrifice!"

"Results," said Pierre. "Moloch gives results, immediate and always. Now, I said that his preferred sacrifice is burning children alive. That is true, but Moloch also accepts any human sacrifice, especially mass sacrifices. The more, the better."

"Skink!" blurted Isabella.

"Where?" said Veronica, jumping up in fear.

Isabella giggled and said, "No, relax. Not an actual skink. That weirdo, Reverend Methuselah Skink. Lâmié, didn't you say he gave his followers fake poisoned Kool-Aid and preached to them about killing themselves?"

Lâmié nodded, rubbing his chin. "I wonder," he said. "That old

Skink freak. He showed up in town right when the demonic activity began. He certainly doesn't come across as especially good or holy. I mean, what kind of *Christian* wants to provoke mass suicide? Maybe he's planning the suicide to be a mass sacrifice to Moloch. It's not exactly a huge leap in logic."

"Reverend Skink?" asked Pierre. "He sounds like a real snake. I'll want to meet him and interrogate him. It can't just be coincidental that Moloch's sigil appears around town, and some weirdo is planning a mass sacrifice. But the sigil's appearance: what's the Jewish connection? You said it appeared at Uri's house and the synagogue."

Uri scratched his bearded chin and said, "I wonder…no, I can't be uncharitable and accuse people of things."

"What, Uri? Tell me. Every piece of information is important," said Pierre.

Uri seemed to struggle morally for a few moments, his eyebrows rising and lowering several times in a cartoonish manner, before he answered: "Alright, so, there's this new guy at the synagogue named Abe. He says he's been in Israel studying for the past few years and just got into town. Now, he arrived right when the sigil appeared on my house, and in fact, he was at dinner that very night at my house. Again, probably pure coincidence."

"Probably, but maybe not," said Pierre. "In demonology, I have found that there are, in fact, very few coincidences. Demonic infestations in locations come in waves, and all of the scum of humanity usually tag along. Weird people appearing right when the activity starts? Often means they are involved."

"I should not have said it," said Uri. "Abe's actually a really nice guy."

'Tit Boudreaux cleaned up the plates and glasses from dinner, then served everyone some of his home-brewed beer as an untraditional nightcap.

"This is excellent," said Pierre. He took a long draught, sighed contentedly, then said, "Alright, I suggest that we do the exorcism of your friend Madame Who first thing tomorrow. If we went tonight, the demon would have the advantage. They own the night. Mornings? They are weaker. Then, I'd like to talk to Reverend Skink and Abe."

"How long can Madame Who survive? Doesn't she need food and water?" asked Mary.

Pierre replied, "The demon will keep her alive supernaturally. The thing it fears is her death. That would mean it had to go back to hell."

After eating, Aaron and Amos wrapped duct tape back around their heads and mouths. Pierre raised an eyebrow.

"Oh yeah, I forgot to tell you about them," said Lâmié. "They found an old lamp and conjured a djinn. It gave them three wishes—"

"And let me guess," interrupted Pierre. "They did not word them correctly, and now the results of the wishes are out of control, *oui*? That is how djinns operate. Do not worry, though. We can reverse the wishes, but it will require a very careful rite. I will brush up on it tonight, and we may be able to do that tomorrow."

The two Mormons nodded enthusiastically.

"Pierre," offered Lâmié, "everyone lives here in the house with me, especially for safety during the demon uprising. Why don't you stay here as well? There is plenty of room."

"Oh," said Pierre, "that is very kind, but I have a room at the Hôtel Monteleone. I need some privacy tonight to prepare myself for the exorcism tomorrow. In fact, I should go now."

"Wait," said Lâmié. "The French Quarter's too far for safety, and that's where Moloch was chasing you. Look, there is a hotel almost across the street from us called the Columns. It is excellent, very nice. It also has a famous bar that many locals love. If you insist on some quiet and privacy to prepare for tomorrow, then at least let me put you up at the Columns. You only have to cross the street."

Merci beaucoup for your wonderful hospitality. Do not worry about paying. I am on a very generous Vatican expense account. I will certainly, however, take your advice and stay at the Columns. It sounds lovely; plus, I would normally just return to my original hotel, but the prospect of facing Moloch again…"

Lâmié walked Pierre to the door and, wishing him a safe night, watched him make the short trek to his hotel.

Pierre stepped into the lobby and glanced into the bar. The entire hotel was a large mansion built in the Victorian era, and careful attention to detail had rendered it a beautiful, luxurious example of the era from which it came. The bar, all lined with mahogany panels with red velvet stools, beckoned Pierre inside, and he thought it would be a crime to stay in New Orleans without experiencing one of its famous bars. It did not take much to convince him, for he noticed a stunning young woman sitting alone.

He sat next to her and ordered a mint julep, just for the experience. The girl made eye contact with him, coyly smiled, then demurred, looking back down at the bar top.

"*Bonsoir*," said Pierre.

She giggled and smiled and said, "Hello."

"I'm Pierre. Just visiting New Orleans."

"Oh, hello, Pierre. I'm Aimée, New Orleans born and raised."

The bartender placed the mint julep in front of Pierre; the drink's pale, yellow hue was accented with the mottled mint leaves and the mint garnish. Pierre took a sip and found the sweet, minty combination delightful.

"Why are you here alone, dear?" asked Pierre.

The girl blushed a little, then said, "I live down the street. My roommate's boyfriend is over, and they can be annoying, so I just stepped out for a drink or two."

"Well, how lucky for me!"

Her face turned a deep crimson, and she looked down shyly. "You must be from France?" she asked.

"Is my English that bad?"

She laughed and said, "No! Just the accent. I spent a summer in Paris a few years ago. It was wonderful."

"Paris is my hometown, well, originally. You know, New Orleans is lovely as well. Such a unique city, very much more like a European city than an American one."

The two flirted and chatted for over an hour when Pierre decided to make his move.

"You know, I was thinking," he said, "why don't I order some nice wine, and we can go up to my room and talk about Paris?"

"Why, I thought you'd never ask, Pierre."

"*Ah, bon?*"

He grinned at her, flashing that swarthy, French smile that always drew ladies to him. He waved the bartender over and asked for a few bottles of their finest Bordeaux to be sent to his room. After all, he was on the Vatican's expense account, so why should he care?

Pierre looked at the second half of his mint julep and thought it would be a shame to waste it.

"Just one moment, my dear," he said in a silky tone. "I must run to the restroom, and then we'll go up."

She playfully offered her hand, and he took it in his, and as he backed away, he let their hands touch as long as possible before he turned around and strolled to the restroom.

One empty bladder later, Pierre returned to the bar to find the girl missing.

"Bartender? *Monsieur*? Did you see where the lady I was talking to went? Maybe the restroom?"

"Sorry, my friend, but she got a phone call, then walked right out the door."

Pierre trotted to the front door and onto the sidewalk. He looked left and right, but there was no sign of the girl. He returned to the bar.

"*Merde*," he said. "I guess she got cold feet. Well, there's always time for ladies."

"Sorry, buddy," lamented the bartender.

"It's alright. I'll finish my drink here, and please still have the wine sent to my room. There is no disappointment that good, red wine will not alleviate."

Deciding not to let the girl's sudden departure ruin his evening, he sipped the last half of his mint julep and prepared to go upstairs to his room, but he felt dizzy. Had he drunk that much at Lâmié's? He was a veteran drinker with the tolerance of a bull. It was not possible that he had already become so drunk for the world to spin.

Overcome with sudden nausea, his hands began to shake involuntarily, and his head pounded in unexpected pain.

"Whoa, you alright there, buddy?" asked the bartender.

"I…who are…where am I? This is…why am I not…wait, is this Mexico?"

He vomited and fell to the floor clutching his stomach, and then he entered a full-body seizure before passing out.

Pierre awoke in a hospital room. His eyes fluttered open, first resisting the bright, fluorescent light, then adjusting and allowing him to see that Lâmié, Paul, Mary, Matt, and Uri were there in his room.

"I think he's awake," whispered Mary.

Lâmié stepped into the hall and said, "Nurse? Can you help, please? Mister Lascif is awake!"

A nurse speed-walked into the room, and a doctor followed her. The nurse began to immediately take Pierre's vital signs while the doctor felt the pulse in his wrist, then shone a light into his eyes.

"Mister Lascif? Are you awake? Can you hear me?" asked the doctor.

"*Oui*, yes, yes, I'm awake."

"Can you please tell me your name and where you're from?"

"Pierre Lascif, originally from Paris, France. I'm twenty-five years old, and I'm in New Orleans at the moment."

"Alright," said the doctor, satisfied, "it seems the cognitive impairment is no longer an issue."

"What the hell happened?" asked Pierre, looking around at the Gravediggers. "I was hitting on this girl at the Columns bar, and now I'm in a hospital."

"You were poisoned," said the doctor.

Pierre looked confused, then a look of understanding came upon his face. He said, "The girl—the mint julep. I went to the restroom, so she must have slipped it into my drink. What was the poison, *Monsieur le docteur*?"

"Cyanide," said the doctor grimly. "You are a *very* lucky man, Mister Lascif. I happen to be extremely familiar with poisons and their treatments. Another doctor at another hospital? Might have missed it. I recognized the signs and did a rapid test, and sure enough, cyanide. I administered hydroxocobalamin and sodium thiosulfate intravenously. See, I've done specialized work for the government and the military before becoming a civilian doctor, so I knew the treatment. Like I said, the fates must be smiling on you that you randomly ended up at this hospital under my care."

Pierre coughed, and Mary handed him a bottle of water, which he thankfully gulped down.

"So, I'm alright?" asked Pierre.

"You are," said the doctor. "It looks like the effects of the poison have been eliminated by the treatment. Still, don't do strenuous physical activity for a week or so. Get some bed rest. You'll be fine."

"Vitals normal," said the nurse to the doctor. Lâmié stepped back to give the nurse room to move to the other side of the bed.

"And the girl?" asked Pierre. "The bitch who tried to kill me?"

Barillo stepped into the room, panting from trotting down the hall.

"That's where I come in," he said between gasps of breath. "Damn, I need to start exercising more. Yeah, so I'm on the case. I got statements from the Columns bartender. By the way, his quick call to 911 saved your life. You should buy him a drink sometime. There were other eyewitnesses, too. We're going to find her and put her in jail. Don't worry."

"Get some rest," said the doctor to Pierre. "The rest of you? Go easy on him, alright? You can visit for a while, but he needs a good night's sleep tonight."

The doctor and nurse exited the room.

"Wait," said Pierre with a small stutter, "how did you all find me? How did you know I was here?"

The hospital room was filled with the various flashing lights and beeps of the machinery.

"Luck," answered Barillo. "I happened to get the call from the bartender who saw you faint. When the ambulance came, Lâmié stepped onto his porch across the street to see what all the fuss was about, and he saw you and identified you."

Pierre nodded and said, "I was lucky then. But what about the exorcism. Madame Who. We have to do that. I can't stay in the hospital."

"Isn't it dangerous to leave this soon?" asked Barillo.

"The doctor said I'm perfectly fine, just to take it easy."

"And an exorcism is *taking it easy*?" said Barillo.

"Good point. But this is more important than me now. If we don't start taking some action against the demons, they will be too powerful to stop, and my health, or anyone's health, won't matter anymore."

Around midnight, they arrived back at Lâmié's mansion. It had taken some convincing and some of Barillo's authority, but they had finally persuaded the doctor to discharge Pierre. After all, he was a patient, not a prisoner. Feeling basically normal, Pierre insisted that they do the exorcism the first thing the following day.

Chapter 39

Who's Afraid of the Big Bad Demon?

"Ah, what a beautiful morning for an exorcism!" said Matt sarcastically.

"And for a nice Bloody Mary!" said Paul.

Mary put her hand out to stop his arm from raising the drink to his lips and asked, "Didn't Pierre say you have to be sober and pure for an exorcism?"

"First," reasoned Paul, "he was wasted the night before he had planned to do it, before the poisoning. Second, every time I've fought evil, I've been drunk. Why risk a good thing?"

Mary, sighing, removed her hand. "I guess you have a damn point," she said.

Pierre walked down the grand staircase and then into the grand parlor. He moved a bit slowly and deliberately.

"How you feeling, Frenchy?" asked Paul.

"Oh, pretty normal, I think. I mean, normal for someone a girl tried to kill with cyanide."

"Fancy a drink?"

"Normally *oui*, but I should be sober for the exorcism."

Isabella, Varco, and Veronica were sitting on the loveseat across the room. Isabella had noticed more than once that Veronica was flirting with Varco, or at least trying to flirt in her own nerdy, goth way, and Isabella did not appreciate it. But, on the other hand, she liked Veronica and was not even sure that the girl was aware of her flirting. It was more like a natural, instinctive reaction to a cute boy.

"Pierre," said Veronica, "I need to warn you. Madame Who's been alone in that room for a couple of days. It's going to be nasty and stinky and horrible."

"Merci," he replied, "but I've done many of these, and I've seen what you describe. Sometimes, yes, it can get really bad."

"That's my fault," said Miss Annabelle, who had essentially moved into the mansion. "When I was possessed up there, it got messy."

"Miss Annabelle," asked Veronica, "I hope this isn't too personal of a question, but what did it *feel* like to be possessed?"

Miss Annabelle took a sip of the coffee that 'Tit Boudreaux had brewed and replied, "It's really funny. I don't really remember much. I remember feeling like I wasn't in control of my own body, and then just lots of darkness and loneliness and sadness and hopelessness."

"It's what they feel," whispered Pierre. "The demons. That's what they feel all the time. So sad, so lonely, dreading the final judgment day, permanently cut off from love, hope, faith, and anything good. It must be horrible."

'Tit Boudreaux served everyone his perfectly-folded omelets. They ate quickly, remembering the unpleasant task ahead of them.

"I'll need some assistants," said Pierre. "Uri, you're a person of faith. Will you go?"

He nodded without hesitation.

"Paul, you should come. You have a talent or something, like we talked about."

"If he goes, I go," said Mary.

Pierre nodded.

"Since it's my house, I feel responsible," said Miss Annabelle. "I should go."

"And if she goes, we go," said Varco.

Pierre held a hand up and said, "Okay, okay, *c'est assez*. That's enough. Paul, Mary, Uri, Miss Kate, Isabella, Varco, and Veronica. And, of course, Father Woodrow, who will be performing the actual rite of exorcism. I will be his main assistant. *Bon?*"

"While you're there," offered Lâmié, "I'll track down Reverend Skink and try to get you an audience, Pierre."

"And after the exorcism, I'll invite Abe over," said Uri.

"*Parfait*," said Pierre. "Let me gather my supplies from my room upstairs, and then we go to save Madame Who!"

Forty-five minutes later, the exorcism group found themselves standing on the sidewalk in front of the monstrosity that was once Miss Annabelle's lovely, charming, Garden District home. Deteriorated further by the evil residing within, the house sagged, not physically but spiritually, for each house has its own spirit.

A slimy mold had overtaken every wall, and the roof was teeming with maggots. The sour, bitter smell of rot permeated the entire block. The tiny front garden was overgrown with thick, black weeds, and a dead cat lay decomposing in the middle of it.

The grey Spanish moss that had charmingly draped down from the descending branches of the ancient oaks had turned black and oily, and it stank like sulfur.

"*Merde!*" said Pierre. "Must be a powerful demon possessing her."

"Moloch?" asked Mary.

"I doubt it," said Pierre. "He's not known for mundane possessions. He's more likely to commit genocide than to possess a fortune teller for fun. Still, this is a powerful one to cause all this degradation of physical reality."

The warm, tropical breeze blew across the house, carrying the onerous, nauseating stench of the demon with it. Isabella dry-heaved, and Veronica gagged.

"Oh, God, not again," said Veronica, pointing down the street. There, like rabid dogs, prancing and prissying down the sidewalk, were the Mean Girls: Anna, Lucy, and Rose.

"Look!" said Anna loudly enough to be heard around the entire block. "The losers are at that gross house *again*! It's like flies attracted to poop!"

"More like poop that attracts flies!" said Lucy.

"With their loser friends again!" added Rose.

They approached, and when they saw Pierre, their demeanor changed.

"Hello!" said Anna cheerfully. "I'm Anna Barrois, and you're cute!"

"Girls," said Pierre, "you probably don't want to stay near this house for too long. Bad things can happen here."

"The only bad thing here is Isabella, Varco, and the new Goth girl."

"*Veronica*," said Isabella. "She has a name."

"Whatevs," said Anna flippantly. "Why do you gross people always hang out by this gross house?"

"Why do you always follow us here?" asked Varco.

"As if! Don't flatter yourself, Romani boy!"

"It's *Romanian*, you idiot."

The Mean Girls looked at the house with their noses wrinkled, clearly trying to think of another insult. They were not clever enough. Without a word, they turned and continued down the street.

"Well, that was fucking stupid," said Paul.

"Forget them. Let's go save Madame Who," Pierre insisted.

He led the way into the putrefying house, and the smell intensified the closer they walked to the bedroom. They stood in the hall right outside of the door. From within, strange rumblings, growling, and baritone cracks sounded like the bedroom was a giant stomach with indigestion or a creaking ship upon a roiling sea.

"What the hell?" said Paul.

Pierre replied grimly, "You hear those loud, echoing growls and sounds in the last and worst stage of an exorcism. This will not be easy."

"This is the worst kind of possession," agreed Father Woodrow, who was wearing a white surplice and a purple stole. In his hand, he held a small book simply entitled *Rite of Exorcism*.

"Listen very carefully to my instructions," said Woodrow.

They gathered around the priest and Pierre, everyone already fearing the demon that they would meet inside the room.

"Do not, under any circumstances, engage the demon in conversation. Do not reply to it, and do not react to its taunts or mockery. The demon may reveal personal things about you, things that are embarrassing or humiliating and private. Ignore these. It only mentions these to tempt you to react and to engage it in conversation."

They listened, trying to ignore the increasingly frenetic growling echoing throughout the entire house.

"Jesus called Satan *the father of lies*," explained Woodrow. "Assume everything the demon says to be a lie, even accusations. In the rite of exorcism, Christ compels the demon only to state two truths: its name and the hour of its departure. Assume anything else to be a lie or a trick. It wants you to respond to it because that will sow confusion and disrupt the exorcism process."

A deafening *crash* came from beyond the bedroom door, causing everyone, including the priest, to jump and cringe.

"Fuck!" hissed Paul.

"Quickly! Listen to me and ignore the demon! It's already trying to psych you out. Madame Who will have superhuman strength. When we enter, I first need you to subdue her and hold her down on the bed, all of you except Pierre, who will be my main assistant. Finally, parts of the rite require another to repeat prayers. All of you can do this: the more people who pray, the more powerful the prayer. We do not stop until the demon leaves. Understand?"

Something slammed against the door from the inside.

"Understood"! said Mary as she winced.

Father Woodrow made the sign of the cross, muttered a quick prayer, and then nodded to Pierre, who pushed open the bedroom door. A blast of foul air rushed past them as if they had opened a mine or a tomb that had been sealed for centuries.

Isabella vomited, then stood back up and forced herself to continue.

Madame Who sat cross-legged on the bed, facing the foot of the bed. Her head turned an unnaturally-long way to face them.

"Hello! I have company!" growled the demon in a terrible, guttural voice. It looked at Father Woodrow and laughed. "A weak priest! I can spot them every time! And who are—" It saw Pierre and stopped talking. The room turned freezing cold in one instant. "You. You! Why do you bring him to me? Why do you torment me? That one! He's fallen so far. So far from the seminary! A drunk! A drunken lush! A fornicating loser!"

In anger, Pierre squinted his eyes but remained silent and did not react.

"Subdue her," instructed Father Woodrow, a vial of holy water in his raised hand as if to warn the demon that he would use it if it fought back.

Madame Who cackled amusedly but did not resist as everyone but Woodrow and Pierre gently lay her back onto the bed, then held her arms and legs down.

Madame Who looked at Uri and said, "You like it rough, you filthy Jew? Why did you bring a dirty, filthy Jew to me? They killed the one, you know! You know that, priest? Dirty filthy Jews killed the one you worship! I was there! I whispered in their Jewish ears to crucify him!"

Woodrow ignored the demon, instead making the sign of the cross over Madame Who, over everyone else, and then on himself. He then sprinkled holy water on the others and then on Madame Who. The water splashed onto her bare arms, legs, and face, hissing and smoking as it touched the skin. She howled in pain.

"You son of a bitch!" screamed the demon. "You sadistic son of a bitch! You fucking priest! Keep that fucking water away from me or I'll fucking kill you and everyone you love!"

An almighty *creek* and *crack* issued from the bowels of the house, and Varco looked around in panic.

"Ignore it, Varco!" said Pierre. "It's just smoke and mirrors."

"Fuck you! Fuck you!" shouted the demon. "You're just a fucking drunk and girl fucker!"

Woodrow knelt and said, "Everyone? Repeat the prayers I say. Follow Pierre's lead."

"Fuck you!"

Woodrow began:

"Lord, have mercy."
Lord, have mercy.
"Christ, have mercy."
Christ, have mercy.
"Lord, have mercy."
Lord, have mercy.

"Fuck right off, priest!" shrieked the demon.

"Christ, hear us."
Christ, graciously hear us.
"God, the Father in heaven."
Have mercy on us.
"God, the Son, Redeemer of the world."
Have mercy on us.
"God, the Holy Spirit."
Have mercy on us.
"Holy Trinity, one God."
Have mercy on us.

"Have mercy on my cock!" snarled the demon, causing Paul, despite the seriousness of the situation, to have to strain to hide a laugh.

As Woodrow proceeded through the long rite of exorcism, the demon's taunts revolved around sexual and perverted topics, but when it saw that those were not working, it changed tactics.

"Our Father, who art in heaven, hallowed be thy name..." recited Woodrow faithfully.

"Pierre's a fucking drunk! His father was a drunk! His grandfather was a drunk!"

"...thy kingdom come, thy will be done..."

"Paul's a drunk too! Paul, you'll die of liver failure at thirty-five! Ha ha ha! Paul's going to die at thirty-five unless the demons get you first!"

Paul winced but did not reply. A feeling of inevitable dread and isolation caused his stomach to sink. Was not death, after all, the ultimate loneliness, the ultimate ostracizing?

"Paul is all alone!" taunted the demon with mocking, guttural laughter. "None of your friends really like you, Paul! That's why you're a fucking drunk! Drinking makes you happy because you're really all alone! And you'll die soon, and then you'll *really* be alone, forever and ever!"

"...on earth as it is in heaven..."

"Mary doesn't really love you, Paul! She's just using you like a clown!"

"That's not true!" cried Mary. "I do love you, Paul!"

"Don't engage the demon!" warned Pierre.

"...give us this day our daily bread..."

"She doesn't love you, Paul! She sucks cocks all around New Orleans! She takes them all in her mouth and pussy every night!"

"Fuck you!" shouted Mary. "That's not true!"

"Mary!" hissed Pierre. "Ignore it! It's just trying to disrupt the exorcism!"

"...and forgive us our trespasses..."

"Paul's no angel either!" screamed the demon. It must have seen a slight twitch of panic in Paul's face because it cackled gleefully.

"...as we forgive those..."

The demon sang in the melody of a child's nursery rhyme, "Paul cheated on Mary! Paul cheated on Mary!"

Mary looked up at Paul, but Paul remained focused and tried to ignore the demon.

"Paul went into the forest in India and cheated on Mary with young naked Indian girls! They sucked him off, and he ate their pussies!"

"Paul?" asked Mary in a trembling voice.

"Ignore it, Mary," said Paul. "It's just fucking with us."

Mary looked back down at Madame Who, trying to compartmentalize what the demon had said to deal with later.

"...who trespass against us..."

"Father Woodrow broke his vow of celibacy last year! He fucked a hooker in the French Quarter!"

"...and lead us not into temptation, but deliver us from evil. Amen."

Madame Who's body thrashed and writhed. The poor woman was gaunt and gray with a touch of green. Her clothes, smeared with vomit, bile, and feces, were shredded over most of her body.

Woodrow continued the lengthy rite, and as he progressed, the demon became more desperate and vulgar in its words. Woodrow reached the point in the ritual where he commanded the demon to reveal its name.

"I command you, unclean spirit, whoever you are, along with all your minions now attacking this servant of God, by the mysteries of the incarnation, passion, resurrection, and ascension of our Lord Jesus Christ, by the descent of the Holy Spirit, by the coming of our Lord for judgment, that you tell me by some sign your name, and the day and hour of your departure!"

"No...no name..." growled the demon.

"I command you! Tell me your name and the day and hour of

your departure!"

"Never, priest! Cocksucker! Whorefucker!"

Pierre looked at Father Woodrow and nodded. The priest took two steps backward, and Pierre stepped directly in front of Madame Who's body. The demon hissed and growled, and the entire house rattled and shook.

"Get away from me, you drunken lush! You whoremonger!"

Pierre calmly turned to Uri and said, "Uri, please step back from Madame Who and pray in Hebrew. Do you know any prayers against demons?"

Uri nodded, bowed his head, folded his hands together under his chin, and began to pray and bob his head up and down.

"No!" protested the demon. "The old language! The old language! Not fair! Shut up, you filthy Jew"!

Pierre turned back to Madame Who and said, "Now, you son of a bitch! You won't listen to the priest? Then you *will* listen to me!"

He splashed Madame Who liberally with holy water, and again, it sizzled and hissed and smoked as the demon groaned in pain.

"You!" cried the demon. "You old piece of shit! You left the Church because the bishop sucked little boys' cocks! He loved their tiny little peckers!"

Pierre took the large crucifix from Father Woodrow's hand and held it directly over Madame Who. The demon turned her head as if someone had punched it in the face.

"Get it away! Get it away! The Nazarene!"

Pierre seemed to actually glow with white, heavenly light as he spoke in a booming, thunderous, commanding voice that was much too great for his small, Gallic frame.

"Vile demon, God Himself, Jesus the Son of God, the Church, and all the saints command you! Now, tell me your name and the time of your departure!"

Madame Who's back arched upwards at an impossible angle, then slammed back into the bed. The demon roared and shrieked like a banshee, and Madame Who's body levitated slowly to about a foot above the bed. Then, it slowly lowered back down and landed gently on the mattress.

"Tell me your name and the hour of your departure!"

The room filled with the sound of the squealing of a sounder of swine.

Pierre's heavenly voice exploded: "Tell me your name and the hour of your departure!"

"Gressil! I am Gressil! Leave me be! Stop tormenting me!" wailed the demon.

"Gressil, the demon of filth! Prince of all that is putrid and rotten, I expel you in the name of Christ!" cried Pierre.

Madame Who's body relaxed a bit, and the room turned cold again. Fog filled the bedroom as if they were in a wintery, New England fishing village.

"Paul must die!" rasped Gressil in a labored voice. "Paul is unclean too! We will kill him before the battle! Kali told on Paul, told me right there in hell!"

Pierre gave the crucifix a final thrust toward Madame Who's face and yelled, "In the name of Jesus the son of God, I exorcise you from the body of this servant of God and from this place!"

Madame Who turned over and over violently then fell onto her back and relaxed. She coughed, made a gagging sound, and then a foul, black mist proceeded from her mouth. The dark cloud poured through the cracks in the old frame of the bedroom window and dissipated outside.

"This woman is clean," declared Pierre as he lowered his head, exhausted.

Madame Who opened her eyes and said, "Where is Madame Who? Madame Who is thirsty!"

CHAPTER 40

Ooh, Baby, When You Cry

Paul sat alone on the front porch of Lâmié's mansion, watching the daylight recede and the nightlife ingress into the Garden District in that ancient, haunted Babylon called New Orleans. He sipped a cold can of IPA, several more in a cooler at his feet, his mind stuffed with jumbled streaks of fears, threats, suspicions, surmising, and wonder.

Mary stepped out onto the porch and sat next to Paul on the porch swing. Paul continued looking straight ahead, and neither said anything for five minutes. Finally, Paul handed her a beer, and she opened it. The crickets were beginning to sing, and the restaurants and bars were beginning to fill up.

Paul broke the silence. "That exorcism was fucked up."

"Yeah," Mary agreed. "I'm not sure we've ever seen anything that evil, that intense, even in Ushaville."

"Yeah, at least not that close up."

"So which Paul am I talking to right now? The funny, irreverent Paul who hides behind his masks and feigns a British accent, or the real Paul within?"

Paul chuckled and said, "The real Paul, I reckon."

"Good. That's the Paul I need to talk to right now."

"Yeah, that's never good when a girl says she needs to talk."

Mary chuckled and took a long sip of beer. "You're not wrong," she sighed. "The demon. What it said."

"Demons are liars. That's what Woodrow and Pierre said," replied Paul.

"Yeah, they said that. I just wanted you to know that I'm not going around New Orleans fucking guys. That was a lie. I wouldn't cheat on you. Never."

"I know," he said. "I'd never think you would. You come across as honest above everything else. I feel like you'd tell me if you wanted another dude."

He finished off his beer and opened another. From down the street, a girl laughed loudly outside a pub. A crow cawed from somewhere above them, up in the canopy network of oaken branches.

"The demon said some pretty terrible things," said Mary. "I guess it wanted to get into our minds and throw us off, to stop the exorcism. Turns out Pierre is a real badass against demons."

"Yeah, he totally fucked that demon up."

The silence between them was familiar yet presently uncomfortable. It was broken only by the signs of life down the street. From somewhere, the luscious smell of fried oysters perfumed the air.

"Paul?"

"Yeah?"

"The demon said something else. Something about you."

Paul looked straight ahead. His hair was not in a Mohawk, so it just limply flopped down across his forehead. "Yeah?"

"It said you cheated on me in the forest in India."

"Yeah, it said that."

They sat quietly for several moments, pretending to watch the street life passing by. Although the demon infestation around the city was causing more people to either become possessed or just stay in their houses scared, apparently some people did not care. Several people walked past Lâmié's mansion.

"Paul?"

"Yeah?"

"Just tell me it's not true. Just say it."

There was silence for about a minute. Mary's face looked anxious.

He took a long sip and replied, "I can't tell you that."

She looked at him and said, "Fuck. Are you serious?"

"Just let me explain."

She folded her arms and huffed. "You can fucking explain, but it doesn't make it alright."

"Listen, Mary," stammered Paul. "In the forest. I told you how it went. Kali made me hallucinate. I was in a daze the whole time, like, in this weird world between the two worlds. I didn't know what was real."

Mary clenched her fists and tensed her jaw, trying to control herself. "So, the little house you told us about. The one with all the naked girls. It was them, wasn't it?"

"Yeah, it was." He lowered his head and looked at the wooden porch's floor.

"So you fucked a bunch of girls? You had a fucking orgy? Boy, when you cheat, you really do it right!" she fumed.

The crickets all around them in the night stopped chirping as if they were listening to the conversation.

"Look, Mary, there's no excuse. I mean, I didn't actually have *sex* with them. They sort of...mobbed me and started doing some shit—"

"I don't want to know the fucking details!"

"I know. I know. Just know that I didn't, um, well, *penetrate* them. Also, they technically weren't even real. They were hallucinations of gods."

"Well, that's not really the point, is it, Paul? The point's that they were real to *you*, and you *wanted* them! That's cheating!"

Knowing he had no argument or defense, Paul just sat quietly.

"I'm furious at you, Paul. Fucking angry. I know you like to make sexual jokes and shit, but I always thought that was just a part of the funny Paul mask. Now, I don't know. Maybe that really is who you are."

A streetcar passed by, dinging its infernal bell.

"Mary, it's not. It was a weird situation, a terrible mistake. I'm really, really sorry for what it's worth."

"I'll see if I can forgive you one day, you jerk." Mary stood up and stormed back into the house, leaving Paul alone with his beer and his regrets. He could not believe that she had acted so out of character and violently, but to be cheated on usually invokes primal, purely-emotional reactions in people. It touches something deep inside of humanity, the feeling of being deceived and made a fool of. He could hardly blame her.

Flashes of the forest temptations crossed his mind, but deeper than those was a disturbing darkness that had been nagging him ever since the demon had appeared in the dining room and the black cloud had entered his mouth.

At the time, he had felt perfectly normal, and the two elements might have been unrelated. Still, somewhere deep within his soul, Paul had sensed a nagging annoyance that had evolved into anger and rage until it had finally become a great dread. Perhaps India and Kali had brought it out, or maybe the return to Ushaville, but he felt he was dealing with many issues, and the rising darkness within only exaggerated them all exponentially.

Even his conversation with Mary had irritated him when it should have made him feel only guilt and anguish. He remembered how his experience with the goblins had changed him into a foul creature that had barely remembered his true self, and he hoped with all of his mind and spirit that this would not be the same.

CHAPTER 41

Eat Me

"Don't shoot me," said Lâmié to a grand parlor full of his friends and associates.

"I mean, I wasn't planning to, but now that you mention it..." said Uri with a grin.

"Couple of things," continued Lâmié. "First, Uri, did you convince Abe to come over for dinner tonight, so we can stealthily interrogate him?"

"Yep, even though I felt a bit guilty doing it." He tugged on his payot. "He's still my friend and my brother in the congregation, after all."

"Alright, good," said Lâmié. "I've also, well, *arranged* a talk with Reverend Skink, mostly for you, Pierre. But here's the catch."

"Oh, fuck me," said Matt as he facepalmed himself. "Please tell me you didn't invite the freak to dinner too!"

Lâmié looked at the ground and shrugged.

"Oh, shit. This is going to be one interesting fucking dinner," said Matt with a resigned sigh.

"Yeah," continued Lâmié. "So that's the worst of the bad news. The better bad news is that I think we should open The Gutter up this weekend and have a show. I've been spending lots of money lately, and I don't mind, but it'd be nice to have some sort of positive income. I don't have literally unlimited resources. I'm not a Rockefeller!"

"Sounds good to me," said Paul. "I think we could all use a distraction."

Mary added, "Yeah, and I can find some local bands pretty quickly, I think. I mean, I know New Orleans is in the middle of a damn demonic infestation, but for some people, that makes the show even more desirable. Let's do this."

Paul kept stealing glances at Mary, trying to make eye contact, but she refused to look his way. Even when he spoke to everyone, her face flushed an angry red, and she clenched her fists.

"Good," said Lâmié, "'cuz I already hired a crew to do some cleanup and repair."

"I can neaten up the place my own special way!" said Titania from a chair in the corner. She giggled.

"Forgive me for interfering in your bar business," said Pierre, "but is it a great idea to try to hold a punk show in the middle of a demon infestation?"

Everyone looked at Lâmié, awaiting his reply. It was, after all, a very good question.

"That's the thing," explained Lâmié. "It's on purpose. Think about it. We have all this stuff to fix, to wrap up, right? Well, it's like last time, when we wanted to attract all of the, er, evil creatures in town. So we played a loud show, and sure enough, they came. This'll do the same and draw the demons."

Barillo, who had been working an overnight shift, stumbled exhausted into the parlor. His hair was a wild mess, and he wore two days' worth of stubble. He blurted out, "Shit. The city's gone to shit."

"Yeah, but how do you really feel about it?" said Matt.

"Possessed people are freaking everywhere. I mean, the city's still full of tourists and drunk locals, and it's hard to notice someone's possessed since most people in this damn city are so damn weird already. But I can tell. They're everywhere. The French Quarter's a madhouse: rape, murder…God."

Lâmié filled Barillo in on the conversation, and everyone agreed they would try to hold the show that coming Saturday night. Mary, as usual, would find local bands, and the Gravediggers would also play. The usual friends would tend the bar and work security.

"Well, looks like I gotta make some dinner for y'all, a weirdo death cult preacher, and a suspicious Hasid. Uri, I'll make some kosher dishes as usual. Let's see, what do people who worship demons like to eat?"

"Deviled eggs?" said Varco, causing Isabella to slap his arm and laugh.

Barillo sat across the coffee table from Pierre and got his attention.

"Pierre, we found a suspect in your poisoning. Some girl with a long rap sheet. She's associated with some cult. In the interview, she told me her cult is ushering in a new age of demons on earth and that she tried to kill you because she knew that you were an exorcist agent of the Church. She would not name the cult, though."

Pierre shook his head and sighed.

"Well, that explains it, I suppose. Looks like this demon uprising is much more popular than we knew," he said.

Barillo continued, "Yeah, and we want to infiltrate the cult. She refused to say more, though. She chose jail over telling us the cult's name."

Pierre rubbed his chin and thought for a moment, then looked back up at Barillo with wide eyes. "Wait, a Satanic cult? You don't think she's an agent of Skink, do you?"

"Oh, hell's bells!" replied Barillo.

A knock came at the door at seven o'clock, and Lâmié let in Abe.

"Thank you for the invitation, Lâmié," he said as they walked together into the grand parlor. "And thanks to the chef for making some kosher dishes. I don't want to be trouble."

"Shalom, brother," said Uri.

"Shalom!"

"Shalom, mate," added Paul. "What's happening with the Hasidim?"

"He's an idiot, Abe," said Matt. "Just ignore him." Abe just chuckled.

Another knock came at the door, and Lâmié sighed. "Well, I guess I know who that is," he lamented.

Sure enough, he opened the door to an oily, grinning Reverend Methuselah Skink. The froggy preacher wore his standard-issue night-black, three-piece suit, his black fedora, neatly perfect and uncrushed, and his broad, pale lips that revealed yellow teeth slathered with saliva.

"*But if she bear a maid child, then she shall be unclean two weeks!"* spouted Skink jovially.

"Er, please come in?" said a baffled Lâmié.

Skink removed his hat, bowed ceremoniously, and stepped into the mansion. *"For in my mansion, there are many rooms!"* said Skink as Lâmié led him past the main staircase, down the main hall, and then right, into the grand parlor.

Most of the Gravediggers and friends had encountered Skink before, but Abe and a couple of others gasped at the bizarre sight of the walking skeleton.

Skink bowed again and proclaimed loudly, *"Everyone brings out the choice wine first and then the cheaper wine after the guests have well drunk!"*

This made everyone look down uncomfortably and feign fiddling with their hands or scratching their heads.

"Well, everyone, um, this is the Reverend Methuselah Skink," said Lâmié.

"Of the People's Family of the Divine Blessing!" added Skink. "And how kind of you to invite me to dinner. I see that we have two of God's chosen people with us. Blessings to you! Blessings to you!"

"Um, thanks?" said Uri. "And, er, bless you too."

Abe, the only present who did not seem shocked by Skink's appearance and mannerisms, simply nodded.

"Since there's so many of us here tonight," said Lâmié, "I thought we would dine in the formal dining room across the hall. Beforehand, why don't we have some wine and chat?"

He stepped into the kitchen, where 'Tit Boudreaux was busy making dinner, and returned with a cart, on which were several bottles of various fine Bordeaux, Bourgogne, Chianti, and Torgiano.

"I hope everyone likes red? I do have some white in the cooler if anyone would prefer that."

Everyone seemed fine with the red, especially Madame Who, who was recovering from her possession but seemed to be back to normal in terms of drinking, and especially Paul and Pierre, who were sitting next to each other on a sofa.

Mary was conspicuously sitting across the room alone, and Isabella, Varco, and Veronica sat together on a loveseat, Varco in the middle, much to Isabella's chagrin and jealousy. Varco, contrarily, seemed quite content, perhaps a bit too much.

Everyone who spoke to Skink and Abe stuck to small talk, for the time being, waiting for dinner itself to try to steer the conversation toward demons.

Uri spoke to Abe in Hebrew just to have some practice so he would not lose his skills in the language. As they spoke, though, Lâmié noticed a few times that Uri looked puzzled and raised his eyebrows at Abe.

The formal dining table was more than large enough to accommodate everyone, and the Victorian enhancements in the room felt like traveling back in time. Siofra, Evelyn, and Erin, a bit shellshocked from the goblins, had spent lots of time in their rooms, but they came down for dinner. Zoë was enjoying a break from her frequent shifts at the Audubon Zoo. The new gang member, Eli, was there, never being found too far from Lâmié. Even Yarielis had moved from her usual perch in the parlor to join the dinner party.

'Tit Boudreaux began bringing dishes from the kitchen to the dining room.

"Alright, everyone, this might be my greatest work, provided it tastes good. I wanted to make an international meal in honor of our friends here from India, Beast Stalker from the Cherokee Nation, Abe from Israel, and Veronica from Boston, along with all y'all from right here in New Orleans. So, allow me to present…"

After he had made several trips to and from the kitchen, the table was overflowing with dishes. In honor of Uri and Abe, there was gefilte fish with *chrain* and red chrain; stuffed beef *holishkes*; *borscht* with sour cream; falafels; and hummus with flatbread.

To honor Swami Maitra, Apada, and Iraj, and especially their loyalty in remaining in New Orleans to help, he served *macher jhol*, a fish curry; *kosha mangsho*, a lamb curry; *Kolkata biryani*, a delicately-seasoned rice dish; and *katla kalia*, a fish dish with rich, complex spices.

In honor of Beast Stalker, their faithful fellow warrior against evil, he offered blue corn grits; fried green tomatoes; venison stew; fry bread; and *kanuchi*, a special pâté made of nuts. For Veronica, he presented Boston-style clam chowder. Finally, for himself and the other locals, he brought out gumbo, jambalaya, and Oysters Rockefeller.

"Holy. Fucking. Shit." said Paul. "Marcus, mate, this is more than amazing."

"Oh, how delightful and considerate!" said a jolly Swami Maitra.

"Just like home," added Beast Stalker.

Veronica said, "Man, I've never seen anything like this. Thank you!"

"*Yet he did not stretch out his hand against the nobles of the sons of Israel, and they saw God, and they ate and drank!*" screamed Skink, causing everyone to jump. "And I shall now say grace!" he insisted. Uri rolled his eyes but remained quiet.

Skink stood up and raised his hands melodramatically up to the sky, closed his eyes hard and scrunched up his wrinkled, leathery face, then began to pray so loudly in his reed-like, high-pitched voice that several people had to cover their ears.

"Oh, God, father in heaven, we do thank you so for this bountiful feast! Please bless it to the nourishment of our bodies! And thank you, God, for the gift of life and that of death! Just as your son Jesus willingly gave up his own life unto death, let us follow His heavenly example! Amen!"

Several of them, annoyed yet shocked by his bizarre and suicidal prayer, muttered *Amen*, but the others simply looked uncomfortable.

"*Bon appétit!*" Lâmié said in an attempt to end the awkward silence. It worked.

As 'Tit Boudreaux made the rounds between his own bites of the meal to refill everyone's glasses, the wine flowed, the food charmed and delighted, and the conversation was warm and cheerful for about an hour. After that, however, Pierre knew he had to steer the conversation toward the demonic.

Preparing himself, he downed a full glass of Torgiano in one gulp. He felt pleasantly buzzed and outgoing. "So, Abe," he began. "Uri said you spent time in Israel before this. That's very interesting. I've visited Jerusalem. Amazing city. What did you think about it?"

"Very interesting indeed," agreed Abe.

"Such a long and ancient history," continued Pierre. "There must be lots of Hasidim there?"

"Oy, so many!" answered Abe.

Uri added, "You see us everywhere!"

'Tit Boudreaux stood up again, opened another bottle of the rare Italian vintage, the 1990 Torgiano, and made the rounds topping off all glasses in need.

"I've always been curious about Orthodox Judaism," said Pierre. "I hope it's alright if I ask some questions, just to satisfy my own curiosity?"

Abe nodded with a smile.

"The main thing I've always wondered is if the Hasidim take the *Tanakh* literally. Like, the stories, Moses, all of that."

Abe looked at Uri and answered, "I think Uri and I would give the same answer. We believe that parts of the Bible are meant to be taken literally, as actual history, while other parts are meant to be metaphors, moral lessons, or musings on wisdom."

Uri nodded in agreement but purposely remained silent so Pierre could talk specifically to Abe.

"Something else," added Abe. "We believe the Torah, the law, was given to Moses in written *and* spoken form. So, the spoken law has been passed down, and the rebbes have interpreted both the spoken and written over the millennia. We call that commentary the *Talmud*."

The meal was so abundant that everyone was still eating, although several were having to slow down as they became overstuffed.

"Very interesting. Thank you," said Pierre.

'Tit Boudreaux walked to the kitchen and returned with a massive dessert tray that everyone could choose from. First, there were grape dumplings in honor of Cherokee cuisine. Then, as a nod to the Kolkata guests, 'Tit Boudreaux served *malpua*, sweet and syrupy coconut pancakes. Next, for Uri and Abe, there were perfectly formed rolls of chocolate *babka*. For Veronica, of course, there was Boston cream pie. Finally, representing the locals, he brought out bread pudding with rum sauce, baked Alaska, and pecan pralines.

"Oy!" said Uri. "Diabetes it is, then!"

As they set into the dessert course, Pierre turned to Reverend Skink and asked, "As for your faith, Reverend, is it similar to many Protestant churches in that you take the Bible to be the inerrant word of God and do not accept oral tradition as binding?"

"It is as you say, my child!" said Skink with a broad, greasy grin, bits of crumb and butter smeared on his chin. "We believe in *sola scriptura*, only the Bible, the *complete* Bible, both testaments!" He glanced at Uri with that comment.

"Then I have a question for both of you if you do not mind. What are your thoughts on this rumor of increased demonic activity in New Orleans?"

Abe opened his eyes wide, and his already-pale face seemed to blanche further. He looked at Skink, who was stuffing pie into his gustatory hole, seeming quite indifferent.

"Demons, you say?" said Abe. "Yes, well, we had the, um, that break-in at the synagogue. Just terrible."

"Yes, quite sacrilegious," agreed Pierre. "And that sigil found around town. But, you know, I have a little background in demonology. I recognized it immediately as the sigil of Moloch. Do you know about Moloch?"

Abe stared at Pierre, and Skink stopped chewing and did the same. Pierre allowed the slightest trace of a smirk to cross his lips, using that classic French understatement to send a subtle message with plausible deniability.

Abe composed himself and asked Uri, "Moloch. That Canaanite idol that required children to pass through the fire, isn't it?"

"The very one," said Uri.

"The horror!" cried Skink. "*Suffer the little ones to come unto me!*"

'Tit Boudreaux stood up and cleared the table, then reappeared with several bottles of rare vintage Port wine, aged several decades. He poured everyone a glass while Pierre continued the discussion.

"My own demonological research indicates that Moloch has the power to grant great abundance and wealth, and to some who dare offer mass human sacrifice, even…eternal life."

Skink stood up and raised his hands, preparing to make some ridiculous declaration. Everyone sighed.

"Eternal life!" he began in a wavering, high-pitched, cartoonish voice. "It is the very purpose of God's creation! For, my children, we were meant to live forever in paradise! But sin! Oh, that horrid sin that doth beset us at every turn! That sin has brought death unto the world!"

Pierre yawned and gave a classic French *bof*.

"Children, just as Jesus gave himself up to death voluntarily and did achieve eternal life, so must we offer ourselves up to death to receive eternal life!" He sat down, coughed gently, and returned to eating his pie.

"Er, yeah," said Pierre. "So, Reverend Skink, you seem to be endorsing, what, suicide? Human sacrifice?"

"*A little yeast leavens the whole lump of dough!*" replied Skink.

Satisfied with his reconnaissance, Pierre steered the conversation toward more mundane and quotidian—and sane—topics.

++++

Later in the evening, Lâmié invited everyone back into the grand parlor for a nightcap of Lagavulin Islay Scotch. Then, after a few minutes, Abe stated that he needed to get to bed for an early start on the morrow, and Skink followed him. Once Lâmié had closed the door behind them, he spied on them for a minute through a front window. *Odd*, he thought it, that they walked and talked like old friends rather than two strangers who had happened to have dinner at the same place. He passed this information along to the others.

Chapter 42

Roch Hard

The interior of the chapel at St. Roch's Cemetery No. 1 at midnight usually mimicked the mausolea around it: dark, quiet, and still. However, this night, while the chapel was indeed dark as the night around it, it was neither quiet nor still.

Instead, it was packed with the pale forms of vampires, their gaunt eyes and smooth, porcelain skin reflecting the little moonlight that shone through the windows.

The atmosphere was exciting, energetic, and joyful in a morbid, vampiric manner. They had inverted the crucifix above the altar and had attached an enormous clay penis to the statue of Saint Roch.

Behind the altar stood Ophelia, a dark anti-priestess in cold contrast to the saintly images all around the chapel. Her crowd of undead subjects stood on the other side, a devilish congregation waiting to receive its anti-sacrament, which was currently struggling inside a burlap sack.

"My children!" began Ophelia as if she were beginning an evil homily.

The other vampires became silent, their anticipation filling the atmosphere with dark energy.

"As you know, I have returned from the former Ushaville. To see that once-great city, that bastion of our kind, of undeath and blood, that asylum for our kind—to see it again as only a pile of ashes and rubble tormented my spirit. Such loss! Such sadness! The stench of the charred remains of our brethren still hangs in my nostrils, and the collective wisdom of the Old Ones in the tunnels beneath, those sages now only dust, haunts me every day and night. I swear revenge!"

The vampires roared in angry applause.

"But, alas, all is not lost, children! In Ushaville, I forced Chief and Beast Stalker to reveal the amulet's location, and I am glad to report that..." She held the amulet, now glowing bright red, above her head. "...I have the amulet! The world is ours, brethren!"

The vampires cheered and chanted, "Our world! Our world! Our world!"

"Things are going to change in New Orleans, children, beginning now. The humans are ours now. With this amulet, and the secret of its use as revealed to me in Ushaville, we no longer have anything to fear from the hordes of humans: they will be our food and our slaves. I know how to recite the words on the amulet, and when I do, I will be imbued with unimaginable power, and you with me."

The vampires cheered and howled in delight.

"Queen Ophelia?" asked a vampiress in the front of the crowd. "When will you activate the amulet?"

"Patience, child. We have another situation to deal with first. Most of you are aware by now, but I will tell you officially. There is a demonic uprising in New Orleans. As usual, it concerns the Gravediggers and their stupid friends."

The crowd hissed and spat at the mention of the band. Then, outside, from somewhere deep within the cemetery, two crows called to each other.

"Queen, are we not all demons within?" asked a vampire, a new convert.

"We are, child. Demons, and a fragment of the person we once were. However, the demons in New Orleans are powerful demons straight from hell. To them, we are as useless and inferior as humans are to us. With the demons, and their possession of the humans, we will be in competition to take New Orleans, and we have no power against the princes of hell."

Ophelia casually paced back and forth behind the altar, in front of the statue of Saint Roch, until she stopped, took the clay phallus in her hand, and mockingly stroked it while she spoke.

"And so, we must devise a plan. We must force the Gravediggers to fight the demons in our stead without their realizing it. In fact, my spies tell me that they may already be planning such a thing. We must be ready to strike immediately once they have defeated the demons."

She broke off the clay penis.

"Oops. That must hurt. Anyway, beware that the Gravediggers have enlisted a powerful demonologist who takes the name *Pierre Lascif*. There is more to him than meets the eye; I suspect he also knows us and our kind very well. He will be the first to die once I activate the amulet. And now, children, my bloody congregation, it is time for the sacrament."

The crowd moved with excitement and anticipation as Ophelia ripped the burlap sack off of a naked, muscular young man who was looking around frantically. With the ease of the strength of a vampiress thousands of years old, she lifted him onto the altar and lay him supine. Then her assistant vampires tightly bound his wrists and ankles with a strong rope.

"What the hell is this?" he cried in panic, but he saw Ophelia and said, "Is this some kind of kinky sex club? I've heard about these!"

His erection pointed at the vaulted ceiling. Ophelia nodded and smiled as she began to slowly stroke him. Then, she took him into her mouth and sucked him for several minutes before mounting him.

She rode him as if she were a Mongol upon the warring plains, and as they achieved a powerful, mutual orgasm, she leaned over and plunged her fangs into his neck. He shrieked in shock and fear, but it was too late. The crowd of vampires set upon him, sinking their sharp fangs into every part of his body and drinking his blood eagerly, orgiastically, until he was a flat husk of tissue.

Back in New Orleans, everyone gathered in the Grand Parlor after Abe and Skink's departure from the dinner party.

"Well, mate?" Paul asked Pierre. "What'd you get out of that, besides that Skink's batshit crazy?"

"Indeed he is," agreed Pierre. "What a bizarre and ridiculous man. But yes, I have my thoughts. Let me sleep on it, please. Tomorrow, I suggest we reconvene, and I will tell you what I think is happening and how I think we should proceed. Also, I think we should try to remove the curse of the wishes from Aaron and Amos first thing tomorrow. I suggest everyone get lots of rest."

They retired to their bedrooms, Mary notably sleeping in her own room instead of with Paul. Isabella and Varco still shared a room, but Isabella felt a deep dread and sadness: Varco had clearly been flirting back with Veronica.

Early in the morning, everyone woke up and shook off the wine hangover with 'Tit Boudreaux's eggs and bacon and grits, along with several cups of very strong Colombian coffee.

Poor Aaron and Amos still went through most of their days with duct tape around their heads and over their mouths, terrified of accidentally saying something that would activate the burdensome, accursed wishes.

After breakfast, everyone gathered around Pierre in the grand parlor to hear his summary of everything.

"First," he said, "I learned many things from the dinner conversation last night. Abe and Skink are certainly in cahoots, and it has everything to do with Moloch. In fact, I would go so far as to say that they are behind the sigils and the synagogue desecration."

"But why?" asked Uri. "Why put the sigil on my house in particular?"

"To mark you. He senses that your association with the Gravediggers is an obstacle to his plans, so he wants Moloch to kill you. It's that simple. As for the synagogue? It's the same reason that the Romans when they took Jerusalem, sacrificed a pig on the altar of the temple: to be a grotesque insult to God and his people."

'Tit Boudreaux went around and refilled everyone's coffee cup. He handed a Bloody Mary to Paul. Isabella, Varco, and Veronica were sitting on the same loveseat, Varco in the middle, as was the new standard. They were all wearing shorts, and Isabella was being eaten alive with jealousy because Varco's and Veronica's bare thighs were pressed against each other.

"What's their goal, Abe and Skink?" asked Uri.

"It's like I said at dinner. Moloch grants power, abundance, and eternal life. The pure, innocent life force of the sacrificed children is used to add to the worshiper's own life, allowing him to basically live forever."

Uri began tugging on his payot. He was clearly distressed at the thought of sacrificing children.

"What is it, Uri?" asked Lâmié. "I know it means you're doing some heavy thinking when you pull on those things."

Uri drank a sip of his strong, black coffee and replied, "Last night before dinner. I was talking to Abe in Hebrew, just to practice. If you don't use it, you lose it, that sort of thing. Well, he used really weird words and phrases a few times."

"Weird how?" asked Pierre.

"Well," said Uri, "at first, I thought it was just some sort of slang or dialect that he had picked up in Israel. But after I pondered it more, I realized that he was using verb forms and other words and grammar from ancient Hebrew, the kind spoken in the Old Testament. No modern Jew would speak like that. In fact, many of us don't even know the grammar too well."

Pierre rubbed his chin and said, "Hmm. Are you thinking what I am?"

Lâmié said, "I sure am. He and Skink are planning something to do with eternal life. Maybe he's speaking in Old Hebrew to sort of get in the mood? I cannot imagine any other reason. Uri, could a modern Hasid study the old language and learn to speak it like that?"

"Oh, certainly! It is readily accessible in books."

Lâmié nodded as he sipped his coffee.

"Well," surmised Paul, "I don't know exactly what's going on, but Skink and Abe are weirdos with evil plans, and they have something to do with Moloch. No matter what the details, it's our job to stop them."

"We need a solid plan for sure," agreed Pierre. "But first..." He looked over at Aaron and Amos, all wrapped up in duct tape. "...we need to help these guys."

"Then the pertinent question," said Lâmié as he drained his coffee cup, "is *how the hell do you banish a djinn?*"

CHAPTER 43

Bottle Up Your Feelings

Imam Mohamed Riyad sipped tea in the grand parlor of Lâmié's mansion. Father Woodrow sat next to him, and across from them sat Rabbi Shlomo Cohen. Joining them were Swami Maitra, Apada, Iraj, Lâmié, Pierre, Paul, Mary, Matt, Uri, and 'Tit Boudreaux. The others were either working or in their rooms. Aaron and Amos, mouths taped up, sat across the parlor staring at the religious leaders.

"Thank you so much for coming, Imam, Rabbi," said Uri. "I hope you don't mind, but we have a sort of *situation* here, and your expertise is needed."

The sunlight coming through the windows was an eerie shade of green, the color that precedes tornados in the Midwest. It was otherwise a bright, clear day without a could in the sky.

"What, Uri?" retorted Rabbi Cohen with a wink. "You think I'd refuse a chance to see inside one of these big Garden District mansions?"

"Happy to help," said Imam Riyad. "This is an excellent tea, by the way."

"It's a special black tea from China," said 'Tit Boudreaux. "Glad you like it."

Riyad nodded and smiled. He was clearly a man who had learned good manners as a child and had carried them with him throughout his life.

"So, um, Rabbi and Imam," began Uri as he broached the subject of the supernatural. "I'm not sure you'll believe me, but I give you my word that what I'm about to say is true, alright?"

The two men nodded their assent.

"What do you know about djinns?" Uri asked.

"Djinns?" repeated the imam. "As in, the supernatural creatures?"

"Oy!" exclaimed the rabbi. "Those demons from the Middle East?"

"Those are the ones!" said Uri with a goofy smile. "What if I told you that we've encountered one, and it's causing lots of trouble?"

Imam Riyad took a sip of tea, then leaned back into his chair and rubbed his bearded chin for several moments while Uri told the weird encounter that Amos and Aaron had had with the djinn...and the even more bizarre consequences.

"Yes, yes," began the imam after Uri finished the tale, "djinns are real. The belief in djinns, and human interaction with them, predates Islam and comes from Arab cultures. Djinns, you see, are not exactly equal to Christian demons. Rabbi, you can correct me, but they are similar to some types of Jewish demons."

A crow landed on the outside windowsill and cocked its head, watching the activity in the grand parlor.

"Djinns are not all evil," continued the imam. "Some are, of course, but some can also be helpful to humans, some can be neutral, and some are trickster spirits. The djinn you found in the bottle sounds like an amoral trickster spirit acting only by its own sense of whim and amusement. By granting you three wishes, as I assume it did, taking your words literally and to the extreme, it is amusing itself. By making the wishes, you have temporarily set it free, but don't worry, there's a catch."

Aaron and Amos nodded their heads frenetically and made excited, muffled sounds from behind the duct tape. They still wore their black slacks, white shirts, and Mormon Elder nametags.

"Likely, the djinn led you to believe that, once you made the three wishes, it was now free of you and the lamp. Not so. You are now the masters of the djinn, and it can be forced back into the lamp. I assume you still have the lamp?"

The brothers nodded with wide eyes.

Rabbi Cohen said, "This has something to do with mirrors, I

assume? It's very similar to the Jewish method."

The imam nodded and said, "We're going to need some iron, and some mirrors, say, four mirrors, and the lamp, of course."

Lâmié stood up excitedly and said, "Oh, I know! I have a ton of old stuff in the attic. I'm certain I can find some mirrors and iron. Give me a few minutes!"

He bounded out of the parlor, up the stairs, and into the attic. The others made polite conversation while they waited, but the undercurrent of jealousy and desire flowed through the room.

Paul and Mary had not sat together or interacted much since Paul's porch confession, and it was killing both of them. Perhaps it was easier or more natural for Paul to put up a wall of toughness and hide behind it, but Mary was barely holding on. She wanted pure, brutal honesty.

She did not know yet if she was ready to forgive Paul or even if she would forgive him. She understood the context, that the Indian girls had not been real, and that he had been under tremendous stress and fighting a demon after all. Still, it showed his intent and desire, proving that he *would have cheated* if given the chance.

While her feelings roiled in her stomach, Lâmié returned from the attic holding four medium-sized, square mirrors.

"How's this?" he asked as he held up a mirror to Imam Riyad. "The frames are made of iron!"

The imam smiled approvingly and said, "Perfect. Even better. We can do it all at once."

Rabbi Cohen raised a finger of warning and admonished, "We must be very, very careful. You see, a mirror forces us to look at ourselves as we really are. It is the most brutal way because it neither lies nor hides flaws. Djinns cannot bear to see their true nature.

"Now, djinns will turn away from a mirror, especially one with an iron frame, because iron is an ancient, earth-element metal that repels evil. So what we want, and please correct me, imam, is to position the mirrors so that the djinn has nowhere left to turn but back down into the lamp."

Imam Riyad finished his tea and said excitedly, "Yes, yes! This is correct! But we must be careful, as you said, because it is always possible for the djinn to jump into a person and possess him instead of the lamp. This is why I will be reciting from the Holy Quran while we summon the djinn."

"How do we summon it?" asked Uri.

"Well," explained the imam, "the brothers, Aaron and Amos, remember, they still have control of the djinn, even though he lied to them and tricked them to believe otherwise. So they only have to speak the command, and it will come."

Swami said, "Very interesting! We have a similar concept in India: spirits who cannot face themselves."

Half an hour later, after they had rehearsed the plan a few times, everyone was in position. The lamp sat on a side table, on each side of which Aaron and Amos stood. Around the table, one on each side, stood Imam Riyad, Rabbi Cohen, Swami Maitra, and Paul, each hiding a mirror behind their back. Plus, Apada, because of her natural ability to repel demons, and Pierre, for the same reason, stood behind the others, ready to intervene if necessary.

"Everyone ready?" asked Lâmié.

"What could possibly go wrong?" asked a sarcastic Mary.

"Alright. Aaron, Amos, take the tape off your mouths and summon the djinn!" said Lâmié.

The brothers looked at each other with fear in their eyes but peeled off the duct tape.

"Um, you do it," said Amos.

"Alright, I guess," agreed Aaron. "Um, hey, djinn! I, um, we, we command you to appear before us now!"

Immediately, the sound of a rushing wind filled the grand parlor, and a puffy cloud of black smoke sailed in through the kitchen door. It hovered right in front of Aaron and Amos, then materialized into the djinn, fez hat, and all. He crossed his arms and frowned.

"Curses!" the djinn said. "You little bastards have figured out my secret. How did you know that I still have to obey you?"

Aaron and Amos just shrugged. The djinn looked around at everyone else.

"Hey, wait a minute here. I sense a trap! What's going on here?"

Imam Riyad began to recite the *Surah An-Nas* portion of the Quran. At the same time, he, Rabbi Cohen, Swami Maitra, and Paul pulled their mirrors from behind their backs and pointed the glass at the djinn, who furrowed his brows in rage.

"No! You've tricked me! I can't bear it!" cried the djinn.

"Now, Aaron!" yelled Uri. "Command it back into the lamp!"

The djinn turned from mirror to mirror, holding its head and spinning around. "I won't go back into that infernal lamp! It's a prison! I will not!" he shrieked.

"Djinn!" said Aaron loudly. "I command you to return to the lamp!"

"No! Not again!"

The djinn turned and spun like a dervish, and like in a cartoon, all the others could see was a sort of blue cloud of motion. It thrashed about so violently that it slammed into Paul's mirror, screaming in pain but also shattering the glass and knocking the frame onto the floor. The force knocked Paul onto his butt with a grunt of pain.

The djinn flew up into the air and stopped spinning. It looked down at Paul.

"You bastard! I'm going to possess you now for trying to trick me!"

Paul scurried back like a crawfish and pressed himself against the wall. There was nowhere left to escape to. The djinn growled and flew across the room toward Paul.

"No!" yelled Mary. She picked up the silver teapot in which the Imam's tea had been brewed.

"Paul! Hold it in front of you!" she screamed while hurling the teapot across the room to Paul, who managed to catch it.

At the very last moment, before the djinn was ready to enter his body, he held up the teapot, and the djinn saw its reflection in the shiny, polished silver. It screamed and backed up, but it was no use.

Aaron ran to the djinn and held the lamp under him, while Imam Riyad, Rabbi Cohen, and Swami Maitra ran with their mirrors and shoved them toward the djinn, forcing him into a sort of box of mirrors.

Riyal recited the *An-Nas* as Uri and Rabbi uttered prayers in Hebrew and Aaron commanded the djinn to do his will. Apada uttered prayers in Hindi as well.

"I command you, djinn! Get back into the lamp and stay there!" yelled Aaron.

The djinn screamed, roared, and growled as it was slowly sucked back into the lamp against its will and struggled in vain to pull itself back out. Then, in a matter of ten seconds, it disappeared back into the lamp.

Paul stood up, brushed himself off, and everyone else returned to the chairs and sofa. Aaron carefully carried the lamp over with him.

"That was fucking close," said Paul. "I guess, like, thanks,

Mary."

She tried to hide her smile and folded her arms.

"That was a close one!" said a relieved Aaron.

"Boys," asked Rabbi Cohen, "what lesson did you learn from this ordeal?"

They looked at each other and thought for a few moments.

"Be careful what you say!" said Aaron.

"And stay away from demons!" added Amos.

"You know, we Jews have a saying," concluded Uri. "Be careful what you wish for because you just might get it!"

Pierre sighed, holding the silver teapot in his hand and turning it over and over as he thought.

"Well, that's three tasks down," he said. "We've exorcised Madame Who, figured out that Skink is behind the demons and is planning a mass suicide, and solved the djinn issue."

"Boys, I suggest you give the lamp to me," said Imam Riyad. "I have a good place to keep it safe and secure."

"Yeah," said Paul as he opened a can of beer. "Now, all we have to do is stop a Prince of Hell! It should be fucking easy." He shook his head and sighed.

CHAPTER 44

Torch of Love, Porch of Betrayal

The evening after the djinn fiasco, Apada and Iraj were sitting on a porch swing on the front porch of Lâmié's mansion. The sultry, naughty night air caressed them with warm hands.

"Such a crazy trip!" said Iraj.

"And a crazy life! You know, it's not easy for me to accept that my purpose in life is to fight demons," replied Apada. "This is only the beginning." She bobbed her head gently from side to side.

They swang gently forward and backward, and with each swing, the rusted, iron chain attaching the swing seat to the haint blue porch ceiling squeaked and complained a little.

"What do you think of these people?" asked Iraj. "The punk rockers, and all their friends, you know?"

"Well," answered Apada, "they take some getting used to, I would say. They look a little weird, but clearly, they are good people inside because they are on our side against evil."

A cricket hopped across the porch in front of them, and Apada tried to touch it with her bare foot but could not reach it.

"That Paul fellow," said Iraj. "He's quite an...*interesting*...character, isn't he? He can come across as a little mean and vulgar sometimes."

Apada looked down, and her cheeks turned a gentle, rosy hue.

"Oh my God!" said Iraj. "You have a crush on Paul!"

She remained silent and looked at her fingernails.

"How could you?" he huffed.

Apada looked up, surprised. "Why do you care?" she asked. "I'm close to his age, sort of."

"It's not fair! I've known you all your life, and you just met him and, and—"

She put her hand over her mouth. "Oh my God. Iraj, you have a crush on me?"

"I don't want to talk about it!" He stood up from the swing and stormed back into the house.

Apada stood up and slowly went inside. Iraj had stomped up to his bedroom, so Apada took a seat in the grand parlor and started reading a book about the history of New Orleans.

After a few minutes, Varco and Veronica walked out onto the porch and sat on the swing together. They had been in the grand parlor talking about Romania, as Veronica was obsessed with learning about foreign cultures and people. Isabella was finishing up some investigation inside.

They swang and watched people walking by on the old, cobblestoned sidewalks. Despite the city being full of demonic activity and possessed people, New Orleanians were showing their true fortitude and indomitable nature: the willingness, nay, the determination, to dine and drink even while the world was going to hell around them.

"This is such a cool city," said Veronica. "As, like, an emo, you know, I feel so much at home here. Not so much in Boston. Everyone there's obsessed with their jobs and money. They literally only talk about work."

Varco smiled and said, "In my town in Romania, no one is obsessed with working. Instead, they are more obsessed with eating, drinking, and avoiding work!"

They both laughed.

"You're a really cool guy," she said. "I'm glad I met you and Isabella. I think the Mean Girls would've really screwed me over psychologically, and I'd just be a loner and a loser on campus. But now I have friends! Not only friends but this whole insane group of people and the amazing things we do!"

Someone from a bar down the street was arguing loudly with someone else, but the crickets, with their chorus of chirping, were trying their best to drown out the fight.

"So, Isabella told me about your friends who died. Like, Martina and Blake were their names, right?"

Varco looked down and winced. He had not heard those names in a while. Sure, he thought about them, but he had walled off the pain of their loss inside. Plus, his guilt for being with Blake's former girlfriend was overwhelming.

"Yeah, Martina and Blake," he replied. "I miss them. They were really cool. Isabella and Martina were best friends for a long time. It really hit her hard."

"You poor guy," said Veronica. "People think we emos are obsessed with death, that we like it or something, but it's not that. I mean, we're all gonna die. The more we can accept and embrace that in life, the more we can appreciate living. But death sucks. It really, really hurts."

She leaned against Varco and put her head on his shoulder. At first, he tensed up, but when her straight, raven-black hair brushed against his cheek, he relaxed and just let it happen. His guilt was overpowered by the warm spices and vanilla fragrances of her perfume, the soft warmth of her shoulder, and, after a moment, the way that her hand slowly slid onto his leg, gingerly testing every millimeter for any sign of resistance, but finding none.

Against everything in his logical prefrontal cortex screaming at him to stop, his mammalian brain forced him to put his arm around Veronica. She looked up at him, her eyes brimming with anticipation and self-doubt. Varco felt the tingle in his stomach, that familiar tingle that accompanies infatuation and physical attraction. He knew then that there was no hope, no possibility for him to control himself.

He leaned in and kissed her, and as she responded, they kissed sweetly and romantically, with open mouths but without the aggression of their tongues. Veronica softly moaned, not in sexual eagerness but in a loving way.

The front door opened, and they quickly sat straight up.

"Oh God…oh God!"

It was Isabella's voice.

Varco stood up and whirled around. "Izzy! Wait, no, it's not—"

"Don't you call me Izzy, you cheating pig! How could you? Of all the guys I know, you were the last one I would suspect of being a typical dog!"

"Wait, Isabella, it's my fault," said Veronica. "I'm so, so sorry. I was vulnerable and confused, and—"

"Shut your mouth, whore! I should have known after the way you two've been flirting lately. Fuck. I just cannot believe this. Leave me the fuck alone!" She turned and stomped back into the house.

Varco said, "Veronica…"

"I'm so sorry! I…yeah, I've really liked you since the first time I met you in the cafeteria."

Varco rubbed the back of his neck and exhaled. "Look, Veronica, I guess I'm confused. I like you too, but I have a history with Isabella. But there's a darkness in you…and I don't mean that in a bad way. It's some kind of a mystery, and I crave to uncover it. So let me try to smooth things over with her, and then you and me, we can talk, alright?"

"I guess that's the best I can get right now. I hope she can forgive me eventually."

Varco walked back into the house like a death row prisoner walking to the gallows. Veronica walked to the back garden to think about the situation.

On the other side of the house, on another porch swing, Lâmié sat next to Eli, the helicopter pilot. They each held a mint julep and swang in that silence that is perfectly comfortable between old, lifelong friends who simply had not seen each other in years.

"I guess I made a hell of an entrance back into your life," said Eli.

Lâmié laughed and said, "I wouldn't want it any other way. That's always been my life, our life—absurdity and operatic trouble."

They sipped their drinks and listened to the crickets serenade them, with the occasional bass punctuation of a bullfrog.

"Do your friends here know about our history?" asked Eli.

Lâmié laughed and said, "Oh, hell no. No one knows but you, me, and the *Troisième Régiment Étranger d'Infanterie* of the French Foreign Legion. Well, a few locals in Kourou, French Guyana, probably know, too."

They laughed heartily for a moment or two.

"And I want to keep it that way," added Lâmié. "No one else needs to know that we're technically French Foreign Legion deserters."

"Come now, Lâmié," said Eli after a sip of the mint julep. "Extenuating circumstances. We did our duty in the rebellion, but we just couldn't do what Sergeant LaPierre commanded us to, that bastard. And I'd already taken a bullet for that asshole. He actually wanted us to execute civilians!"

Lâmié put his hand on her shoulder and said, "Ancient history, Eli. Ancient history. Believe me, with all the shit I've seen here, that seems like no big deal anymore."

"The supernatural stuff?"

He nodded.

"I want to hear more about all that soon," she said. "I mean, I believe you, especially after that night in Kourou, but we can't dredge that up now. Not tonight. It's too nice out here." She leaned her head onto Lâmié's shoulder. "What ever happened to *us* anyway?" she asked.

"I've often asked the same question," he replied. "In the moment, back then, day to day, I'm sure we had reasons, complaints, disappointments…but when I look back now, all I see are the laughs and the love."

"Maybe me coming back into your life wasn't just a coincidence," she suggested.

"Well, you do own the only civilian Sikorsky X2 in the world. Who else would have come?"

She laughed and playfully slapped his leg. "I *used to* own the only civilian Sikorsky X2 in the world. It's now rotting in the middle of a swamp. And you know what I mean."

"Yeah, I do. I really do."

She looked into his eyes, and he leaned in to kiss her.

On the back porch swing, overlooking the lovely back garden filled with blooming roses, sat Evelyn Fogelberg alone with a cold can of beer, mostly still full, in her hand. She rocked gently on the swing, contemplating how much her life had radically changed since her move to New Orleans. From sheltered, nerdy Yankee to New Orleans monster fighter—could anything have been more surprising?

She heard the back door open and heavy footsteps on the wooden porch.

"Oh, sorry, Evelyn. I didn't know you were here. I don't want to disturb you."

She looked behind her. "Beast Stalker, hi! Don't be silly! I can always use some good company, don'tcha know! Come sit! I have an extra beer, too!"

He looked down and rubbed his neck, unsure what to do, but decided to sit beside her on the swing and accept her beer gift. He awkwardly tried to use his feet to help swing, but he could not match Evelyn's rhythm, and the swing wobbled and moved from side to side in a weird figure-eight pattern.

"Are all Indians as awkward and reserved as you?" she asked.

"I—"

"I'm just teasin' ya, Beast Stalker, don'tcha know! But you are really reserved, ya know. You don't show lots of emotions, and you speak carefully. But what am I saying? I guess to you, I talk too much and act too emotional, don'tcha know!"

Beast Stalker took a sip of his beer and replied, "Not at all. But, to be honest, yes, we Indians can be reserved. It's not in our culture to openly display our emotions. Of course, we feel them like everyone, but it's just a cultural thing."

"Oh, I see! Well, I must be a real weirdo to you then!"

He shook his head and allowed a small smile to appear on his lips. "Actually, Evelyn, I find you very refreshing and fun and exciting. My culture is very reserved, but sometimes it gets to be too much. Sometimes, I just want to open up to someone, relax, and be more emotional. I feel like I can do that with you, to be honest."

She slid her arm around his muscular bicep and said, "Oh, you've got muscles, Mister! And you're not so hard on the eyes either, don'tcha know!"

He chuckled and looked at her, and she, at him. Then, without warning and without that long-lasting, loving gaze that movies portray, Evelyn yanked his face to hers and kissed him hard on the lips. At first, he recoiled in surprise, but then he gave in to it as they kissed the night away.

A few minutes later, Mary walked onto the porch alone and sat on the swing. A glass of Bordeaux in her hand, she swang slowly, listening to the crickets and crows, the diners and drinkers, the lovers and losers, the sounds of New Orleans at night.

She heard the front door open and the clap of combat boots. She knew it was Paul. Without a word, he sat next to her. She scooted away from him.

"I guess I deserve that," he said.

After several moments of silence, Mary asked, "Paul, what does *punk* mean to you?"

He took a long swig of the cold beer in his hand and thought about it for a minute.

"To me, it's always been about being an outsider like in Iggy Pop's song, *The Passenger.* You know he wrote that while he was touring with David Bowie? Iggy said he watched the world through the bus windows and felt like an outsider to the world."

Still looking at the street ahead, not yet able to bring herself to look at Paul, Mary replied, "You feel like an outsider, huh? Yeah, I know. That's a big part of your personality, you know? Your parents abandoned you in a sense, and you were bullied at school. An outsider."

"Yeah. People think punk's about all sorts of things, but it's really not that complicated. Musically, it's a return to pure rock and roll, like, a guitar, a bass, and drums. Three chords and a chorus. Rock and roll started out anti-establishment, countercultural; I mean, it was just *cool*. It was a big middle finger to the fifties' conformity, racism, and bullshit. Then, somewhere in the sixties, rock and roll got off-track. It became one with the establishment. Punk just wanted to get back to the roots."

A couple walked by the house. The girl was giggling and drunk, and the man was making her laugh.

"So, being an outsider?" prodded Mary.

"Right. Being outsiders, society's outcasts, punks find others to become a family with. Punk means that, and it means not putting up with the authoritarian bullshit of society. But it doesn't mean being a bad person."

"You know," said Mary, "this is the Paul I fell in love with. The honest Paul, the real Paul. This is more punk than all your drinking, Mohawks, leather, and raunchy jokes. This is you, Paul the outsider, connecting with another outsider."

He shrugged, a little embarrassed and not sure how to reply. Mary scooted back over toward him and put her head on his shoulder.

"I think," she said, "I think I might eventually be able to forgive you if you sincerely apologize. No excuses, no defenses, no explaining. Just a plain, simple, sincere apology."

He opened another beer and guzzled half of it. "For courage," he explained. "Mary, there's no excuse for what I did. I don't want to lose you. You're the best thing that I've ever had, maybe the only good thing I've ever had. I'm so, so sorry for giving in to those girls. I really am."

Mary tried not to cry. She took a deep breath and sighed, "Well, I guess I can forgive you, you idiot."

CHAPTER 45

Fly by Night

After the sacrament had been dispersed to the crowd of vampires in St. Roch's chapel, letting it lie on the altar like a cob of corn that had been shucked and drained, Ophelia stood behind it. She motioned for the other vampires to compose themselves.

"Children, things are coming together in New Orleans. The Gravediggers will be holding a show soon. I suspect they plan to draw the demons to their bar and deal with them there. We will be there, of course."

The vampires cheered.

"Before that, I want to assert our dominance in the city. I want to provoke the demons and the Gravediggers, bring things to a boil and see what happens. I know, children, that we have had to hold back lately. We have had to hide in the shadows, but this will soon change. For now, tonight, I send you out into the city, into the darkness! Feed! Any humans you find, drink their blood! Feed on them and create a massacre! Let their blood flow in the streets! Do this for one night only, and then we will cement our plans for the showdown tomorrow night. Now, go!"

The vampires needed no more encouragement. Hissing and growling, they filed out of the chapel and flew into the air, into the night, and into the city.

That night, from Metairie to the Central Business District, from the Faubourg Marigny to the French Quarter, from the Warehouse District to the Garden District, from Uptown to the Mississippi River, and all across the old city, dark and pale figures were seen whispering through the air, down the streets and alleys, into the restaurant and bars and nightclubs.

Somewhere on Carondelet Street, a young girl rose from a fitful sleep to tapping at her window. She looked at the figure outside, nodded as if in a trance, and opened her window.

Somewhere on Rue Ste. Anne, a drunk tourist was stumbling back to his hotel when a dark, hooded shape stepped out of an alley and thrust its fangs into the man's neck.

Somewhere in the kitchen of a trendy restaurant on Burgundy Street in Marigny, a lithe figure slipped into the employees' entrance, and before the chef could react, fangs were plunged into his veins, and he was drained of his gourmet blood.

At the exact moment, at someplace near Tulane University, a young girl was walking home from the library after a late night of studying. A handsome but pale young man stepped out from behind some bushes and smiled. She blushed, and he flew at her with superhuman speed and tore open her neck.

All over New Orleans, bodies drained of blood littered the streets, alleys, boulevards, sidewalks, homes, bars, and restaurants. Barillo started receiving calls, and before long, he was overwhelmed with frantic reports of murder most foul.

That night, the vampires made their presence known in New Orleans indeed.

In the afterglow of the blood-orgy, Ophelia remained alone in the chapel with the desecrated statue of St. Roch. She stood facing away from the back of the chapel, the inky shadows behind the altar. She was tense as she awaited the inevitable call.

"Ophelia. Come." The voice from the shadows was that of a man, full of authority, malice, and wickedness.

She obeyed silently, entering the shadows and kneeling

submissively. She waited for the voice to speak.

"I will admit that I am impressed. You really found the amulet. Now, when you do take New Orleans, and I am confident that you will not fail me, then, as I promised, I will establish you as the Queen of the city."

"Thank you, your Excellency."

"Before you thank me, be very sure that this depends on your promise to me to kill Paul and his friends. I will not seat you as Queen of New Orleans unless you accomplish that. But, if you fail me in that, I will also destroy you. Is that understood?"

"Clearly, your Excellency."

"Good. Now leave me."

With that abrupt dismissal, Ophelia walked away backward to not turn her back on her superior, much in the way that people used to exit the throne rooms of kings and queens. Then, she left the chapel and flew off into the night.

CHAPTER 46

We Walk the Streets at Night; We Go Where Demons Dare

Paul should have been thrilled that Mary had forgiven him. Still, all he felt was a wave of fomenting anger without a rational origin. In fact, their conversation about being an outsider had only made him feel like more of an outsider, which had led to him withdrawing inside his shell even deeper.

When Mary went inside to get some sleep, Paul remained on the porch swing, promising her that he would be there in a bit. He cracked open another beer and watched the street life. He leaned his head back and felt like he was falling, not into sleep, but a new sense of being.

He raised his head and said, "Oh shit!"

Everything had changed. Yes, he was still on the porch swing of Lâmié's mansion on St. Charles Avenue in New Orleans, but still, everything was different. The world's natural colors had melted into a delicious, brightly-hued, psychedelic oil painting, as if he were on the best acid trip in history.

All the people walking past the house transmogrified into most curious creatures, still human, yet, they had grown limbs, legs, horns, wings, and even soft cocoons around themselves. It was as if Paul could see their real, true nature in graphical form, as if these changes were not really a part of their physical forms but a sort of spiritual second person made visible.

The cars, buses, motorcycles, scooters, and streetcars on the avenue retained their shape but also took on the spirit forms of ghastly chariots made of bones and pulled by rotting, undead hell-horses.

A woman walked by with her dog, and as it looked up at the punk man, it grew into a ferocious hellhound and then returned to a simple dog. The entire world around Paul was showing him its true nature in vivid color.

The sounds of people talking, chatting, and laughing transformed into unworldly horn blasts, moans, bass string tones, and the ringing of bells.

"What the fuck?" Paul asked, his own voice carrying along with it the unmistakable sound of a young boy weeping.

Then, it was as if his emotions switched poles. The happiness and delight at the beautiful colors became bitter to him, the thought of Mary's forgiveness and love like a searing acid on his heart.

This caused him anger, and the anger swelled to rage and wrath, enveloping him in madness and ire. The anger strangely became warm, safe, and pleasurable, even causing an orgasmic tingling all over his body. Good was bad, and bad was good; up was down, and down was up.

He felt his aura, his inner self, expand from his physical body, so he looked up to see. Flowing from his head was a misty, white cloud, but the white somehow angered him, and as the anger grew, the mist turned dark red, and two black spirit wings grew from his back.

He understood. He intuitively knew. He was experiencing the world as demons did and he never wanted to return to the dull, normal *good* way.

He was one with all other evil things: the demons in hell below and those roaming the earth. The delicious, satisfying rage and hatred and malevolence were the bonds that held them together, not just as a group, but as one evil. He finally understood what the goddess Durga meant when she said that there was only one.

"Are you coming in, Paul? I couldn't sleep."

It was Mary's voice. With a booming sound and the feel of a physical jolt, Paul was sucked back into his ordinary world, and everything that he had experienced disappeared.

"Dammit!" he cursed. "It was so fucking good!"

"Um, what?"

"Shit. Sorry, Mary. I was…like, hallucinating or something…I dunno. Yeah, I'm coming in."

"Good, weirdo. We need to wake up tomorrow and plan the show at The Gutter. I found some bands."

They retired to bed and made love, but Mary noticed that Paul was much more intense than usual.

"Mary, Paul said you found some bands for this weekend?" asked Titania. "Do tell."

"Alright," said Mary as she sat next to Paul on the sofa in the grand parlor.

All of the housemates were there that morning, even Barillo on a rare day off amidst all the confusion and crime. Varco and Isabella were sitting on opposite sides of the large room, and Veronica was trying to keep a low profile in a small chair in the corner. Apada was sitting on the loveseat where the three college students usually sat, and Iraj had strategically positioned himself next to her, yet he was still too embarrassed to do much talking.

"Wait," interrupted Barillo. "Some bad news. Looks like the vampires went on a killing streak last night. Tons of dead bodies drained of blood. Everywhere."

"Shit!" declared Mary. "Shit. So, in addition to the damn demons, we have to deal with the vampire shit. Bad timing, Ophelia."

A collective sigh of exasperation filled the parlor.

"Well," continued Mary, "one thing at a time. We're having this fucking show, even if the whole fucking city explodes!"

No one seemed to dare to argue with her determination. Barillo shrugged and exhaled, so incredibly weary of dealing with the supernatural crimes of New Orleans. He sipped his coffee and held his aching head.

"Here's what I got," said Mary. "First, a local punk band called *Severed Sex Organs*."

Yarielis, who was knitting in the corner, tsk-tsked.

"They've agreed to do a full set. I said we'd play a few songs here and there. They seem cool. I've only communicated with the second band through email, but they're a hardcore punk band called *Fratricide*. They said they'd play a set after us."

"Do both bands know the, well, *interesting* history of The Gutter Bar?" asked Lâmié.

"Severed Sex Organs do. They thought it was a plus, so yeah. Fratricide? No idea. They never mentioned it."

"Well," said Lâmié, "the bar's just about ready. With Titania's help and the contractor I hired, it's looking pretty good. But that's sort of not even the point. We need a plan for the, well, you know, the demons. Oh, and now the vampires. Dammit."

'Tit Boudreaux brought homemade biscuits and coffee from the kitchen, then handed Paul his customary Bloody Mary. "I have a basic idea," he said. "So, we know Skink will probably try something stupid soon, and Abe won't be far behind. Those two snakes are working together; I just know it. Now, instead of waiting passively, let's invite those two to the show. And on top of that, let's invite Skink to hold another tent revival in the parking lot. That'll force his hand. If he's behind all this, then surely he'll try something there, no?"

Varco waved to Isabella from across the room, but she just frowned and looked away. Veronica sighed, frustrated at the pain she was causing but also longing for Varco.

"Wait, wait," said Matt. "We can guess that Skink and Abe, if they're really working together, are going to, like, conjure Moloch, or whatever it's called. They want him here for the sacrifice. What about all the people around New Orleans who are possessed? We can't possibly exorcise them all!"

"Maybe once we stop Moloch, the possessions will end," said Paul. "It's all one evil anyway."

He twitched a little.

"You alright?" asked Mary.

"Yeah, yeah."

"I like the idea," said Lâmié. "We force their hand. On top of it, I say we invite Rabbi Cohen, Father Woodrow, and Imam Riyad as well. Their presence will provoke the demon, especially if they pray."

"Shit!" said Matt. "Don't forget that Baptist preacher dude, the one who followed Skink when he performed that so-called miracle at the religious street fair."

"I think he's in Skink's cult now," said Lâmié. "Add saving him to our to-do list."

The coffee cups were emptying quickly, sending poor 'Tit Boudreaux on a refill frenzy. Caffeine seemed like the one, good thing left in their messed-up lives.

"Yeah, so once they conjure Moloch, what then? How do you stop a prince of hell? Whatever form he takes will attract all the demons and possessed people in the city to The Gutter, all at once," argued Matt.

Lâmié giggled, then tried to stifle another giggle.

"Oh, no," said Matt. "Oh, God. Lâmié. Does your attack of the giddies have anything to do with a souped-up Microbus? You always giggle when you do that."

Lâmié could not suppress his ridiculous, childish grin. "Yes, and there's more!" he announced. "Everyone, to the garage!"

The others groaned but followed him into the kitchen and through the door that led to the massive, multi-car garage.

"Fuck. Me." said Matt.

"Allow me to commence with the Microbus itself," said Lâmié in a mock professor's voice, "and then I shall proceed with the other equipment. First, you will note that the basic structure of the Microbus has not changed. The tires? Bulletproof and all-terrain, and it is still four-wheel drive. The body armor persists, and still, there is a layer of salt and holy water between the layers of metal. Nothing unclean can pass through that sort of armor, nor can physical bullets."

He walked around the van, pointing out the various features like a father breaming with pride at his son, and the others were trying not to laugh.

"The armored turret atop? Reinforced and completely covered, and with bulletproof glass in the windows. Now, a couple of changes: the suspension is now military-grade, so the van is able to climb over rocks. It is also completely convertible into a boat. Upon entering the water, the wheels become flotation, and a propeller is extended into the water in the rear via an electric motor. It is fully navigable."

Paul opened a beer and took a long swig while the others stared dumbfounded.

"You will notice the new cannons extending from every side. These shoot holy water, which explains the new armored tank on top: it is filled with fifty gallons of holy water. I've added more silver spikes all around to deal with physical threats, with a few amenities inside for the comfort of the passengers and driver. But that's just the van."

Several moans and curses came from the others.

"The obvious change is the mobile cannon attached to the van as a trailer. It is an extraordinary, custom-made weapon, made just for us specifically, by a weapons group whose identity I am not allowed to reveal."

Matt just shook his head while Mary facepalmed.

"Just tell us, Lâmié. What's the cannon?" said Matt.

"This is a military-grade sentry gun that rapid-fires alternate rounds of salt shot and holy water bullet packets that burst upon impact, not too different than a paintball bullet packet. But this cannon fires at a rate of seven-hundred rounds per minute, alternating rounds. Here's the best part: it's a sentry gun, so we can set it to detect motion and fire at anything that moves!"

"Good Lord," said Matt. "This is fucking ridiculous."

Lâmié could not control himself from giggling in delight like a schoolgirl. The one person who was genuinely impressed beyond merely the ridiculousness of the equipment was Eli the helicopter pilot. She walked around the van and the cannon, touching them gently like they were babies, admiring every angle and every feature. She looked at Lâmié with raised eyebrows, whistled, and nodded in approval.

"Thought you would like it," he said, beaming with pride.

"This is absolutely ridiculous, beyond ridiculous, and that's why I love it," said Barillo. "Now excuse me. I gotta get to the precinct. More calls about murder, rape, and possession. Are we doing this show Saturday night? That might be the best night. We have two days to finalize everything. I'll track down Skink and tell him he can hold his tent revival at The Gutter. When I talked to him last time, I got his license information, which shows that he lives somewhere in the Warehouse District. Gonna pay that weirdo a visit."

Uri, who was still staring at the Microbus in wonder, added, "I'll get Abe to go to the show as well."

"Wait, wait!" said Mary. "Before everyone leaves, you know, we have this tradition of naming the Microbus every time we face a new enemy. So we gotta do it now."

They all set to thinking for several minutes.

"The Microexorcist?"

"The Microdemon?"

"The Microhellion?"

"Wait," said Uri. "What was the name of that priest in the movie *The Exorcist*?"

Matt, an aficionado of horror movies, immediately answered, "Father Merrin."

"Then," said Uri, "what about the Micromerrin?"

Everyone laughed and agreed.

"The Micromerrin it is," said Mary.

Paul christened it by pouring a splash of beer onto the hood.

Chapter 47

Police Truck

Saturday morning, the day of the big show and the big showdown, began like any other standard, peaceful day. Everyone except Barillo, who was at work, was sitting in the grand parlor of Lâmié's mansion.

Paul and Mary, having reconciled, sat together. Most certainly not having reconciled, Varco and Isabella sat on opposite ends of the room. Veronica, who could neither hide nor resist her burning desire nor Varco anymore, sat beside him, making him very uncomfortable. Iraj, still too shy to do anything about his crush but sit by her, was next to Apada, and Lâmié was happily next to Eli. Beast Stalker and Evelyn sat together, drawing everyone's curiosity,

"You two a thing now?" Paul directed the question to Lâmié. "Sleep with her yet?"

Mary slapped him. "Paul! Stop! Sorry, Eli. He's a moron."

'Tit Boudreaux was serving a Chinese breakfast of fried yeast sticks to be dipped in a spicy and flavorful soy curd. "Let me know if you like it!" he said. "I learned this one from a girl I once knew from southern China."

As they enjoyed the exotic and savory breakfast with tea, Lâmié said, "Tonight's the big night, y'all. I guess we should get to The Gutter a little later this morning and make sure everything's set."

HELL'S BELLS: A PUNK ROCK DEMON STORY

―――――― ·•◆•· ――――――

At the New Orleans Police Department precinct, Detective Barillo could hardly handle all the phone calls. In fact, every officer and every detective present was juggling several phone calls at once. The sounds of the various conversations filled the station.

"Murder? Where?"

"Please slow down, Sir. You saw what?"

"You saw a demon? What? Is this a prank call?"

"A pterodactyl? Please, Ma'am, come on."

"Your son is possessed? Please call a priest!"

"What do you mean, there's a demon in your toilet?"

Barillo, who was dealing with all sorts of horrifying and ridiculous phone calls of his own, looked out of a window in frustration. His eyes grew wide, and he just hung up the phone in the middle of a conversation.

"Uh, guys?" he said. The other cops kept on with their phone calls, ignoring his voice among the many. "Guys?" he said more loudly. The conversations continued. "SHUT THE FUCK UP!" screamed Barillo, and there was instant silence in the squad room. "Look out the damn window!" he said, and they did.

The sound of the phone calls was replaced with gasps and curses as they let their phones drop from their hands.

"What the hell is going on, Barillo?" asked Detective Guillot.

"I…I don't fucking know, but I know it's trouble. Everyone, take a window and get your weapons ready in case!"

Horrible creatures surrounded the police station. First, the humans among the crowd looked like they were barely hanging onto life, with pale and yellow skin, thick drool, and sunken eyes. These would have been terrible enough, given there were dozens of them, but the others were the real problem. For a vast crowd of unearthly, demonic creatures encircled the station.

They looked like the pictures in a demonology handbook had come to life. There were Hindu demons with multiple arms; Native-American wendigo wolf-men; Jewish half-men, half-snakes; traditional, Christian demons that looked reptilian with long tongues, red, scaled skin, wings, and tails with pointed ends; Japanese corpse-demons with their mouths cut in a slit from ear to ear; ancient Egyptian human forms with crocodile heads; as well as countless other demons from whatever unknown and unrecognized cultures they came from.

Some looked like giant bats with one enormous eye in the middle of their foreheads. Others were ferocious dogs with three heads, and still, others were indescribable, fanciful but fearful monsters from the demented mind of Hieronymus Bosch, wicked and hellish things that should never have existed.

The host of demons and possessed humans simply stood and stared at the police station, particularly at Barillo.

"They're here for me because of Paul. Shit," he mumbled.

"What'd you say, Detective?" asked a uniformed cop.

"Nothing, just…everyone listen! I know what these are and how to stop them, but you gotta trust me. Have I ever let you down before?"

No one said a thing.

"They're real, and they're dangerous," he continued. "But they're here for me. I'm gonna call some friends, and they're gonna rescue me, and these things will chase me and leave you alone, but you have to trust me. Look, don't open fire, alright? Some of them are people out there."

Not knowing what else to do, the other cops had to agree as the demonic throng began to descend upon the station.

Back at Lâmié's place, the phone rang. Lâmié answered it.

"Oh, hey Barillo, did you…what? Wait, what?" He listened for a few moments, then replied, "Shit! We're on our way! Hold tight!"

"What is it?" asked Mary.

Lâmié answered, "Demons and possessed people attacking the police station! They're after Barillo! Come on; we must rescue him and get all to The Gutter! To the Micromerrin!"

"Hold on there, Batman," said Paul. "We can't all go."

"How about the Gravediggers, me, and 'Tit Boudreaux? Paul, you drive, and Beast Stalker, you're pretty experienced on the turret gun."

The other friends listened and struggled with what to do. Eli said, "Look, the rest of us can hold the fort down here. They might attack this place, too. The rest of us will get ready in case of an attack here."

"Got it," replied the Cherokee as Lâmié led them all back into the garage to the Micromerrin.

Paul, drunk as always, sat behind the wheel while Mary sat in the passenger seat as the navigator. The front windshield, replaced with bulletproof armor, had small viewing slits like military tanks. A fully-rugged GPS device was attached to the dashboard in front of Mary.

"Christ, Lâmié! This is like military technology!"

He giggled.

"We dragging the fucking mobile cannon along?" asked Paul.

"I say yes," replied Lâmié. "I mean, the cannon unit's tires are fully rugged and bulletproof, so it's virtually indestructible. It's loaded and ready to install and use. Oh, it floats too." Lâmié reached for the comm system's microphone and spoke into it. "You all set up there, Beast Stalker?"

"Um, Roger," replied Beast Stalker. "Wait, am I supposed to say Roger? Roger Wilco? Just Wilco? Anyway, I'm ready."

"Matt, Uri, Marcus? Each of y'all man a holy water gun back there. To the police station, Paul!" shouted Lâmié.

"That's something a punk never likes to fucking hear," answered Paul as he turned on the engine, which growled and roared to life, causing the entire vehicle to dance to the rhythm of the twelve cylinders.

"Holy crap," said Matt.

"Oy vey!" called Uri from the back.

Lâmié clicked a remote control, and the garage door opened. Paul slid the van into gear and hit the gas. The tires peeled out with a screech, and they heard Beast Stalker curse from above.

As the Micromerrin made its way around the Garden District and Uptown, people on the sidewalks, restaurants, and bars turned to stare, point, and either comment or laugh. Several obviously possessed people watched, sneered, and hissed at them as they passed by. Just for fun, Matt took a few pot shots at the possessed, and as the holy water blasted them, they shrieked and howled, and their skin smoked.

"Cannons work!" said Matt. "And it's real holy water!"

As Paul took them on his wild, drunken ride, the Micromerrin careening dangerously from side to side and screeching around corners, Uri became nauseated but held it together.

Finally, they were on the police station's street. Paul saw what was in front of them. He slammed on the brakes, causing the van to shudder, everyone inside to be thrust forward, and Beast Stalker in the turret to launch into a series of curses.

"Look at that shit!" exclaimed Paul. "What the fuck?"

The precinct building was swarming with demons and possessed people. They stamped around the flat roof; they climbed the walls; they pounded on the walls and doors. The occasional cop would fire a shot at a demon, doing about as much damage as a feather might have done. Wicked black shades rose from the ground around the station, spirits from hell flooding the earth.

They saw Barillo through a window with his pistol drawn and looking horrified. He saw the Micromerrin, and relief flooded his face.

"How do we do this?" asked Paul.

"I'm calling him now!" said Lâmié. He spoke to the detective on the phone. "Barillo! Shit, are you alright? Yeah? You think they're after you, right? Wait, are you sure? Yeah, good point. Alright, stand clear, buddy! We'll get you out of there!"

He hung up and said, "He wants us to just ram the fucking wall down!"

"Uh…" said Paul.

"Don't worry," explained Lâmié. "The bullbar on the front of the van's military grade. It's made for battering walls. Give it the gas, Paul! Beast Stalker? Hold on up there! Here we go!"

Paul revved the engine twice and then cranked it into gear. The tires squealed on the pavement as the Micromerrin lurched forward like a drag racer, pinning everyone back against their seats while poor Beast Stalker bounced around the turret, out of control.

As the police station loomed larger, the van hit fifty miles per hour and kept increasing velocity. The demons on and around the building, and all of the possessed humans, turned and saw the van wildly speeding toward them. The possessed humans opened their eyes and mouths wide and tried to run or dive out of the way, and the demons, sensing that Paul was there, moved toward the van, but it was too fast and too late: the Micromerrin slammed into the brick wall of the police station and made a Microbus-sized hole.

Paul hit the brakes, and the vehicle shrieked to a quick stop, filling in the gap of the hole in the wall so that the front doors of the van were inside the station, but the rest of it was outside.

"Open up the guns, boys and girls!" shouted 'Tit Boudreaux.

The holy water cannons in the back section of the van began to spray and soak the demons and the possessed. Their skin hissed and crackled, and the black smoke of charred flesh rose and enveloped the entire area.

"*Yotta-hey!*" cried Beast Stalker from inside the top turret as he opened fire on the demons and possessed, creating an even thicker cloud of smoke.

The Gravediggers and friends watched with concern as the demons began to surround the Micromerrin, their demonic speed and intelligence allowing them to start to dodge the cannons. The people inside the van simply could not keep up with the sheer number of them.

"Time to activate the sentry gun!" said Lâmié with a sparkle in his eyes, barely able to hide his excitement. "Paul, see that green button on the dash? Would you do me the honor of pushing it?"

Paul groaned and pushed the button. The mobile cannon behind the van extended a stability tripod and began to turn from side to side and beep as it detected the movement of the demons.

"What about the possessed people out there?" asked Mary.

"Looks like they've run away!" said 'Tit Boudreaux.

The sentry gun found the pattern of demon movement and began to fire. The explosive sounds it made caused the cops inside to look as it sprayed out alternating rounds of salt shot and holy water bullets seven hundred times per minute.

The screams and shrieks of the demons made everyone hold their hands over their ears, so shrill and deafening it was.

"Fuck yeah!" yelled Paul as he opened the driver's door. "Get the fuck in, Barillo!"

The detective needed no further encouragement as he climbed in over Paul's lap and squeezed into the back with the others.

"What about the other cops?" asked Mary. "I don't like cops, but they're still humans."

Barillo shook his head and said, "The demons'll follow us, meaning Paul. They want him."

The sentry gun still roared and delivered its biting gift to the demons, round after round. The black cloud of smoke from their burning skin engulfed the van, so they could see nothing from the windows.

"I have an idea!" said Lâmié. "One of the features I installed on the van was like a James Bond rear smokescreen, but with salt! Paul, drive, lead them somewhere out in the open."

"Fucking where?" he asked as he pushed the green button to stop the sentry and threw the van into reverse.

"I know!" said 'Tit Boudreaux. "Remember Tu's family's Vietnamese restaurant in New Orleans East? There's this huge cement lot near it. I think it used to be a factory or something that got torn down. It's wide open."

"That's across the river!" argued Paul. "It's too far!"

Lâmié giggled, and Matt said, "Oh, shit."

"Yep!" said Lâmié. "Remember I told you the van's convertible into a boat?"

"Fuck," said Paul with a chuckle. "I gotta see this."

He stepped on the gas, and the van thrust backward. He put it in drive, then made a beeline for the Mississippi River along the streets perpendicular to St. Charles Avenue. As Barillo had predicted, the crowd of demons followed them, angrier than before at the beating they had endured from the sentry gun.

They were approaching the levee and the bulkhead that kept the great river away from the great city, and Paul did not slow down. They were almost at the levee, and Mary had her hands over her eyes and was squealing. Beast Stalker was screaming in terror from the turret, and everyone else was holding on to their seats with white knuckles.

They were right at the levee! Paul mashed the accelerator even harder and screamed, "Geronimo!" The van hit the levee, traveled up its sloped side, and zoomed off the ramp into the air like Evil Knievel.

"Woohoo!" yelled Paul as the others screamed in mortal terror. The van sailed through the air and landed in the river with a giant, jarring splash.

"Blue button, Paul! Blue!" yelled Lâmié.

Paul slammed his hand onto the blue button, and the van metamorphosed. The tires tucked themselves under the van to cause it to float, and a powerful propellor extended from the back. A rudder lowered from underneath the van's rear, and a small keel did the same from under the middle.

"You drive the boat just like the van," said Lâmié.

"This is badass!" said Paul as the others slowly opened their eyes.

"Well, I'll be damned!" exclaimed 'Tit Boudreaux. "It's a damn boat!"

Looking in the rear-view mirror, Paul saw that the mass of demons was still following them. The demons had no problem floating across the river behind the van.

Paul began seizing, his arms and legs shaking uncontrollably.

"Shit! Paul? Paul?" cried Mary.

The world changed again for Paul as it had on the porch, and the vivid, clear colors of everything were enchanting. Everything was interconnected and gloriously wicked. Paul looked again in the mirror at the demons following them and felt a delicious, angry brotherhood. He determined to stop the van and let the demons take them all.

Mary slapped his arm and yelled, "Paul! Come out of it!"

He returned to his reality, and the feelings of rage and evil faded but did not completely disappear. Again, he was with his friends on a mission, and he felt love again for Mary. He stepped on the accelerator, and the Micromerrin sailed across the churning, swirling, dangerous waters of wide Old Man Mississippi.

After several minutes, they reached the other side, and the rugged tires became tires again as the powerful engine pulled them up the levee and down to the other side.

'Tit Boudreaux gave Paul directions to the cement lot he was talking about, and as they passed Phở 88, he felt pangs of loss and nostalgia. He remembered Tu as he had thought she was, as the cute and sassy little Vietnamese girl, rather than the monster that she truly had become in the end.

"Listen, y'all, here's my idea," he said as the Micromerrin approached the vast, open, cement lot. "Lâmié, you open up that salt smokescreen in the back. Paul, you start making giant circles in the lot, like do doughnuts; drive this bastard around like you're ruining the lawn of your worst enemy. The demons'll follow us and, hopefully, get trapped inside the salt circle. Then we'll have time to set up the show tonight."

"Will that work?" asked Mary.

"It's our best chance," said Lâmié. "I mean, we kind of know that Moloch's the main demon. Maybe if we stop him, these other demons will go back to hell too. Or, if they eventually escape the salt circle, then at least we'll have time to be ready. Hit it, Paul!"

Paul opened a can of beer he had brought along, and before anyone could protest his drunk driving, he downed it in one sip.

"Fuck yeah! Woohoo! Let's trap these bitches!" he shouted. The dark part of him, the part that must have entered him in the dining room in the form of the black cloud, still struggled to make him give up and let the demons win. Still, his human part forced it down like it was cheap American beer.

He mashed the accelerator pedal, and the van roared forward like an angry dragon. The demons followed. Paul, yelling in dangerous delight, jerked the steering wheel to the left, and the van began to slide.

The tires sounded like a chorus of furious crows as they howled and squealed across the cement.

A scream of terror and a series of curses in Cherokee came from the turret above.

As the van drifted and slipped around, Lâmié climbed to the very back of the van and pulled a small lever. This opened a sluice gate that had been holding back an enormous reserve of rock salt. The salt began to stream out of the back of the van, creating a thick line behind it.

Paul drunkenly steered the van in a vast circle, the sale line obediently following behind. Because of his inebriation, the ring was more of a collapsed spheroid, but it connected back with itself, which was all that mattered.

Lâmié closed the salt sluice, and Paul slammed on the brakes just outside the salt circle. The demons rushed toward the van, but at the last second, the salt stopped them as if they had slammed against an invisible wall.

"Fuck yeah! It worked!" said Matt.

"Now there's something you don't see every day!" added Uri. "Oy vey, that was one wild ride!"

"We need to get to The Gutter and pick up everyone at my place along the way," said Lâmié. "And I mean *everyone*. I want to ensure everyone is together in a safe space, or at least as safe as possible."

"Yeah," said Barillo, who looked green and sick from the ride, "can we take the bridge this time?"

CHAPTER 48

Idol Hands Are the Devil's Workshop

Across the river in New Orleans East, a couple of hours before the show at The Gutter Bar began, Abe knocked on the corrugated aluminum door of a nondescript brick building with no sign or street number.

After a minute, a small panel near the top of the door slid to the side, revealing a pair of eyes.

"Who are you?" asked a voice with a thick, Vietnamese accent. "What do you want?"

"I'm Abe. Thuc is expecting me."

"You wait."

The panel slid closed again, and Abe heard male voices speaking Vietnamese from inside. Finally, the door opened, and a young Vietnamese man gestured him inside.

"Thuc see you now. This way."

He led Abe past a small, cluttered sort of office, through a hallway, and into an expansive main room. The room was crowded with Mardi Gras floats in various stages of construction and decoration. A mountainous form was covered in a corner with several thick, opaque construction tarps. Abe gazed upon it with eyes replete with lust.

He felt a flood of sadness, anger, elation, nostalgia, and abject terror. The stream of memories, of his history with the demon, was at once both absurd and eternal. He was inexorably intertwined with the demon, really fused to it in a spiritual sense, and it was far too late to try to change that. He had pushed away his regrets hundreds of years ago.

He had chosen the pseudonym *Abe* precisely because it led others to believe that his full name was Abraham and not the true Abijah. Abijah was such an old-fashioned Hasidic name, and it would arouse suspicion. After all, living for thousands of years did tend to teach wisdom and caution.

His first encounter with Moloch had been, of course, when he had sacrificed his son for a good harvest. Starvation and poverty can drive people to do insane things, and he was no exception. He winced as he remembered how his son has screamed as he had burned alive. Worse even than seeing his precious son's flesh shrink and bubble and blacken, and worse even than seeing his son's face catch fire and his eyes erupt, was that final look of betrayal from his son as the flames had begun to lick his feet, that face of understanding that his own father would do such a terrible thing. And, unlike with Abraham and Isaac, God had not intervened at the last moment.

He returned in his mind to the scene of his trial, to the terrible pain of the stoning that the hypocritical elders had condemned him to undergo. There, in the New Orleans East warehouse, he felt as if he were back there again, so many centuries before.

Unbearable pain pounds him as the stones strike his torso, his face and head. He feels each stinging blow and his mind can think of nothing else. Hot blood rushes down his face in rivulets, and he can feel his skull being bashed open, the bone fracturing and rupturing. Hot brain matter splatters the back of his neck, and the world begins to turn brown, then black. Death is a welcome pleasure for him, compared to the pain of stoning.

He is in blackness, still sentient and aware, but without a body. He experiences neither heaven nor hell. What does that mean? Have his life, his people, his religion, all been a lie? Is Sheol *mere darkness for eternity?*

Now, he hears deep, booming voices from an impossible distance, from somewhere in the inky void. They are terrifying voices, the voices of creatures so large that they could fill the heavens. They grow nearer, and with them comes a glowing orange-and-red haze, the first color he has seen in the beyond.

Then he sees the source of the voices.

Incomprehensible is the size of the beings. They are horrible to gaze upon. They are a jumble of eyes and limbs and horns, each larger than the world itself. He knows in his being, in his instinct, that they are coming for him, to take his soul away to a terrible place of torment and torture.

This will be his fate, then – an eternity of pain with terrible beings. Does he deserve this for what he did to his son? He only wanted a harvest so the rest of his family could survive.

Another entity appears before him, and he instantly recognizes it as Moloch, as the real god behind the idol in the valley. Moloch is the size of the other beings, but much more definable with his bull's head, man's torso, horns, and hooves. It speaks to him in the Hebrew tongue rather than that of the Canaanites.

"Abijah, you sacrificed your son to me, proving your devotion and loyalty. I grant bountiful blessings upon those who worship me with the offering of their own children. The priests and elders of Israel have unjustly killed you. Therefore, I offer you a choice. You may choose to remain in death, and to suffer forever, or you may choose to accept the favor I grant you: to live forever as a human on earth, in exchange for devoting and sacrificing children to me regularly. Should you fail to do so, I will return you to this fate! You must make your choice now."

He does not need to think about the decision for even a moment.

"I choose life! I will provide you with children!"

At the speed of thought, he is back in his physical body, back in the world. He is in Jerusalem again, but time has passed, and no one knows who he is anymore. He begins his new life by finding a dwelling and beginning his search for children to offer unto Moloch his savior.

Abe's contact, Thuc, looked up from his work on a float, saw him, and walked over. "Abe, it's ready. You have payment?"

Abe handed over a bag filled with one-hundred-dollar bills. "You can count it if you want," he told Thuc.

"No. I know Hasids honest. You don't steal. Come on; I show you."

Phuc walked to the large form and pulled off the tarps, revealing Moloch's colossal bronze idol. He was glorious. The torso, that of a man, towered sixty feet or more into the air, and the bull's head that topped it extended that height another ten feet.

The two long, curved horns with sharp tips tilted forward like those of a longhorn steer, and the spacious, oval nostrils were pierced with a golden ring. Moloch's two arms extended forward, palms upward, beckoning the burnt sacrifice of children, and his legs were backward-jointed like those of a bull and complete with two thick, cloven hooves.

"It's on rolling pallet," said Thuc. "Like we agree, I have boat ready to take across river."

"Thank you," said Abe. "It's better than I even imagined it would be. So, let's roll it out and—"

Thuc held his hand up, palm facing Abe, and waved it back and forth in the Asian gesture of strong contradiction.

"Wait. We make prayer. This idol? Very evil. Must clear warehouse of evil spirits. You should be careful too!"

Thuc called out something in Vietnamese. The young man who had answered the door and a middle-aged Vietnamese woman joined him. They walked to a corner, where a small shrine stood, inhabited by a statue of Buddha. Thuc lit some incense, and the three placed their palms together and, hands under their chins, bowed several times and said a Vietnamese prayer.

"Alright, we take to boat now."

Abe, the idol again covered and riding a trailer behind the truck he had rented, arrived at the parking lot of The Gutter Bar about thirty minutes before people started arriving at the bar and Skink's tent.

Skink and three muscular thugs met him, and the five men managed to roll the idol inside of Skink's enormous tent and place it at the front, behind his altar. Abijah and Skink stepped back outside to observe the people arriving for the revival.

Chapter 49

Old Punk

Mercifully, Uri's parents and sister were in New York visiting relatives, which meant that Uri did not have to worry about their safety in New Orleans. Everyone else in the city, however, was in real danger. Nevertheless, the Gutter Bar, as Lâmié insisted, was a relatively safe place to be for the big show and showdown, so Lâmié made several trips in the Micromerrin, transporting all of the friends from his mansion to the bar. Finally finished, he conducted a mental headcount of those present.

He saw Paul, Mary, Matt, and Uri, the Gravediggers. There were the core friends who had been through such much with them: 'Tit Boudreaux, Beast Stalker, Zoë, Barillo, Titania, Varco, Isabella, and Yarielis.

Then there were the relative newcomers and the brand-new friends, which included Judy Felix, Siofra Fay, Evelyn Fogelberg, Erin Drasiedi, little Grimbil, Miss Annabelle, Madame Who, Aaron and Amos, Swami Maitra, Apada, Iraj, Pierre, Eli, Veronica, and, of course, the two indomitable cats who had defeated the goblin king, Baozi and Pidan.

Three out of the four members of the New Orleans Interfaith Council were there, who were Rabbi Cohen, Imam Riyad, and Father Woodrow. Reverend Don Malbrook remained in the brainwashed clutches of Reverend Skink and the People's Family of the Divine Blessing.

Skink, who had accepted Barillo's parking lot offer, had his crew putting the finishing touches on the giant tent for his revival. Then, in the late afternoon, when shadows were becoming longer and people's work ethics shorter, men, women, and children, all in their Sunday best, began to file into the tent. Skink himself was at the entrance in his trademark mortician's suit and hat, his greasy smile greeting each entrant. Abijah stealthily slipped into the tent as well.

Around seven o'clock that evening, the first band, Severed Sex Organs, arrived. They looked similar to the Gravediggers: spiked hair dyed in unnatural colors, black leather jackets with metal spikes and band patches all over them, plaid pants, black painted fingernails, and combat boots. The band consisted of two guys and two girls. Mary greeted them.

"Hey y'all, thanks for coming!"

The singer replied, "Yeah, this seems like a fun gig, but I have to ask—"

"The tent revival meeting in the parking lot?" said Mary laughing. "Yeah, just…long story. Just ignore it. Have all the free beer you want; obviously, the stage is over there. Can you start around eight?"

"Sure thing. You did say free beer, right?"

As usual, Lâmié had stationed Varco, Barillo, and 'Tit Boudreaux in the front as security and to take cover charges. Beast Stalker would walk around in an intimidating manner to stop bar fights. Titania would make the rounds working her magic if necessary, and the bar would be tended by Zoë, Siofra, and Isabella and Veronica, between whom was a tangible cloud of mistrust and anger.

Everyone else was either sitting behind the bar observing or helping out in one way or another. As the band began their equipment check, a line formed at the door. The parking lot was divided by a line of punks, goths, and emos on one side and a line of well-dressed religious nuts on the other.

Inside the bar itself, the ratty booths had been restored to nouveau-ratty, and the high-top tables for drinking still persisted, covered in graffiti. On the walls hung graphics of famous monsters.

Veronica needed some fresh air, so she stepped just outside the door into the parking lot for a few moments. She walked back inside, tapped Varco on the shoulder, and pointed. The Mean Girls had paid their cover and stepped inside the bar. They saw Veronica and Varco and walked over to them.

"Oh my God," said Anna. "What are *you* losers doing here?"

"I do *not* want to be seen out with those losers!" said Rose.

"Um, Varco and new girl? Don't think for a second that we're hanging out with you just because we're here," added Lucy.

"Don't flatter yourselves," said Varco.

The Mean Girls walked off toward the bar in a huff, chatting and gossiping among themselves. Isabella, who had watched the brief interaction, was crying inside, the bitter sting of jealousy and the deep cut of loss consuming her thoughts and emotions.

Paul, who was leaning against the back of the stage, looking frail and unsteady and unnoticed by the others, began to dissociate again. The colors and spirit bodies of everyone around him were intoxicating. That familiar rage and desire for destruction rose in his body, from his feet through his spine and finally into his brain. This time, it was much more difficult to press it down, although he did manage to teeter on the edge of the real Paul and the demonic Paul.

Mary took the stage at eight o'clock and looked at the overly-full bar. She felt a squeeze of tingling excitement in her stomach. Punk was back!

"Welcome, you fuckers!" she said into the microphone, rousing up a great cheer from the jovial crowd.

"The Gutter Bar's seen some shit, that's for sure. Murders, stampedes, massacres…but one thing's for sure: punk never dies!"

The customers shouted with glee and stomped their feet, shaking the entire structure.

"Alright, you bastards! We have a very special band for you tonight. From right here in our fucked-up city, please welcome Severed Sex Organs!"

The crowd's yelling and cheer were immediately drowned out as the band started right into their first song, named *Who's the Real Demon?*

> *Cops in the streets, blasting open heads,*
> *Can't commit a crime if they're already dead!*
> *Fat rich judges, life sentences for pot,*
> *Too much competition for the dispensary they got!*
>
> *Who's the real demon? Who's the real saint?*
> *I'll tell you who it is, and I'll tell you who it ain't!*
> *It's not the little guy trying to get by;*
> *It's the big guy who doesn't need to try!*
>
> *Prison for profit? What a fucking idea!*
> *He's guilty as fuck! Didn't I make that clear?*
> *The corner where he used to deal and sling,*
> *Now gentrified with legal pot shops profiting!*
>
> *Who's the real demon? Who's the real saint?*
> *I'll tell you who it is, and I'll tell you who it ain't!*
> *It's not the black man serving life for stealing smokes;*
> *It's the white man getting away with snorting coke!*
>
> *I got friends in high places; that's the way this country runs!*
> *I'll never go to jail, 'cuz I know all the rich ones!*
> *Got a badge? Got some dough? You can get away with crime;*
> *Down and out? Poor and struggling? You'll do hard time!*

They stopped abruptly to loud yells and applause. A few songs later, the crowd loved them. They took a break, and the Gravediggers took the stage to play one of their own songs. When Uri mounted the stage, there was a moment of silence as the crowd wondered if he was a joke. But as Paul counted in the song, they quickly changed their minds.

As Mary started jamming her wild guitar chords and Matt battered his drums to set the fast-paced rhythm, Uri joined in on his bass. His fingerwork was flawless, and the song's rhythm enthused him to spin around at a nauseating speed and jump high into the air so that he was a long, blurry cloud of hair, hat, and coat. The crowd yelled their approval and formed a mosh pit as Paul started into the lyrics of

HELL'S BELLS: A PUNK ROCK DEMON STORY

their song, called *You Don't Belong*:

Hey boy, you can't play football like us,
So you don't belong!
Hey girl, you don't lead cheers like us,
So you don't belong!

You don't belong with the people who matter;
You're not as pretty and much much fatter!
We cast you out; we ostracize you,
We'll never let you in or romanticize you!

Hey young man, you didn't go to my university,
So you don't belong!
Hey young woman, you didn't join a sorority,
So you don't belong!

You don't belong with the rich and the smart;
You just wanna play music and just wanna make art!
We cast you out; we ostracize you,
We'll never let you in or romanticize you!

Middle-aged dude, you don't have a wife, kids, you're not a moneymaker?
So you don't belong!
Middle-aged woman, you don't want be a barefoot homemaker?
So you don't belong!

You don't belong with the pillars of society;
You're a punk of quite another variety!
We cast you out; we ostracize you,
We'll never let you in or romanticize you!

The song stopped, and Uri stopped spinning. Drunk with dizziness, he stumbled around on the stage as the crowd laughed and cheered.

"Never say that Hasidim can't rock!" he said into the mic.

The Gravediggers played another song, and then Mary got on the mic to announce the third band.

"Alright, you freaks, the next band's called Fratricide! I'm not sure they're here yet, but I know they're on their way, so hang tight while we bang out some tunes on the jukebox, and remember to tip your bartenders!"

She scanned the crowd but didn't see anyone who looked like a band. She also realized that she did not see Paul anywhere.

Paul stood in the very dark, remote area behind the stage, struggling with his own soul. The demons' world was so seductive, so beautiful in its inverse, wicked way. He remembered the words of the goddess Durga:

Pain is pleasure, Paul. There is no difference. It is all Brahma. You are different because you have a purpose. Have you not known that evil has always been at your side like a thorn in the flesh? Has evil not always tried to stop you? Vampires, werewolves, zombies, goblins, demons—they are all the same, Paul. And your purpose in this life is to fight against them. That is also my purpose, which is why I am with you, Paul.

Would it be so evil, then, to give in to the temptations of demons, flesh, and emotions? The rage and hatred were sexual and orgasmic.

He saw Mary looking for him, and the pang of doubt stabbed him again. She was the one thread holding him to his reality. The love he felt for her within rivaled the attraction of the demonic world, even trumped it, or at least he hoped.

Mary was becoming a bit nervous about the no-show band. Then, just as she was about to make another announcement and suggest that the Gravediggers finish the night, she gasped into the mic, causing everyone to turn to look at what she was staring at.

The Reverend Methuselah Skink, in the flesh, had entered the bar, followed by Abe. Skink, having shed his black suit, fedora, and patent leather shoes, was now wearing no shirt, with his pale, almost-translucent, wrinkled old flesh covered partially with a leather punk jacket, covered in patches of various Bible verses.

The few remaining wisps of hoary hair upon his bald head had been fashioned into a ludicrous imitation of a Mohawk. He wore plaid slacks so tight that they defined the slithering garter snake between his legs. His black combat boots with platform risers were so large and heavy that the ancient, oily man could barely walk. Upon his face were his usual lizard grin, decaying teeth, and wet, lapping tongue.

"What. The. Fuck." said Mary, not caring that she was still speaking into the mic.

Behind Skink, the entire congregation of the People's Family of the Divine Blessing, still in their finest clothing, pushed their way into the bar, far too many and far too forceful for the few bouncers to do anything against. In a few minutes, Skink and Abe—in full Hasidic garb—had taken the stage along with two parishioners. The Gutter was stuffed from wall to wall with punks, goths, emos, and Skink's congregants.

Skink took the mic from a protesting yet stunned Mary's hand. She tried to tell him no, but he smiled as some large congregants carried Mary off the stage. Abe picked up Uri's bass guitar, and the two suited men behind them took over Matt's drum set and Mary's guitar.

Skink, accentuating every hissing, slithering, sibilant sound, spoke into the mic: "Good evening, punk rockers! We are the band Fratricide! Yes, it is we whom Mary has booked for this fine rock and roll concert this evening!"

"Oh, fuck me," said Matt.

Having been snapped out of his demonic dissociation by Skink's appearance, Paul came to his senses and said, "What the ever-living hell?"

Normally, he would have climbed onto the stage and dragged Skink off, but there was something so uncanny, so unnatural, so jarring, and—to be honest—so damn comical about seeing Skink dressed like a withered old punk that he just stood and beheld the disaster of a spectacle.

"Our first song, young rockers, is called *Get High With Us!* We hope you enjoy it!"

The congregants and Abe began to play what might have been, in another world, somehow distantly related to music. As Skink began to sing? the lyrics, the bar's customers looked around in confusion.

> *Get high with us! It's oh, so fun!*
> *Not beer and drugs! No, from those run!*
> *I tell you, friends, of another way,*
> *A way to get high forever! Yay!*

HELL'S BELLS: A PUNK ROCK DEMON STORY

Jesus is the way, the way to get high!
I don't mean drugs; I mean heaven, when you die!
Who doesn't want to live in paradise?
So, follow me now, and take your own lives!

Jesus gave himself up to death,
And when he gave his final breath,
He rose from the dead forever,
To be in paradise with God, to die never!

You like to drink, young punks?
Like to get absolutely drunk?
Well, I've got a brand-new drink to give;
Drink the Kool-Aid cup, and forever you'll live!

The train wreck of a song managed to eventually stop, and while the punks, goths, and emos were silent out of pure bewilderment and disorientation, Skink's congregants began to pass out little cups of Kool-Aid, both to their brethren and the bar customers.

Mary yelled at the crowd not to drink the Kool-Aid, but Skink's voice was too loud over the microphone, encouraging them to drink it. The church members began. Almost in unison, they emptied the little cups in one sip. Many bar customers followed suit, but several others threw the Kool-Aid on the ground or just held the cup without drinking it.

"Yes, children! Yes! Drink! Drink the cup of salvation! Give up your life to God, and he will lift you up! Drink, and join me and Abijah! Oops...I mean, Abe!"

"I knew it!" yelled Uri. "It's not Abraham, it's Abijah!"

At the mention of his real name, Abijah rose into the air, arms extended, and his face changed into something horrible and wicked.

"Drink, everyone!" boomed Abijah's voice above the din. "Drink and live forever! Praise Moloch, king of kings! Become eternal, like me! Your lives for Moloch! Your lives to pave the path of eternal life...for me! I have lived for thousands of years by the power of Lord Moloch! Praise him!"

Matt climbed onto the stage. Abijah did not see him below because the ancient demon worshiper was hovering above and looking out into the crows. Matt shoved the frail old Skink away from the mic. The drummer and guitarist congregants moved toward Matt, but the threatening look he gave them turned them off, and instead, they drank a cup of Kool-Aid.

Matt yelled into the mic, "Stop! Don't drink the Kool-Aid! It's poisoned! Stop! Barillo, call for backup! Repeat: do not drink the Kool-Aid! It's laced with poison!" He turned around and grabbed Skink by the throat, pushing him against the back wall. "What'd you poison it with, you rat?"

Skink just laughed and smiled.

Matt slapped him hard in the face, and Skink quickly gave in.

"Conotoxin! Beautiful, glorious conotoxin from Australian poisonous snails, in huge amounts! It's the best! Drink up!"

Rabbi Cohen, who had been behind the bar just observing the horror, saw the Baptist Reverend Don Malbrook raising the little cup of Kool-Aid to his mouth. Then, with the dexterity of a man half his age, the Hasidic rabbi leaped over he bar, knocked the cup out of the preacher's hand, and hugged him tightly.

"My friend, my brother, don't do this! You know this is heresy! It is suicide!"

"But…the truth…Skink…he…"

Malbrook fell apart and bawled, and Cohen hugged him more tightly.

"It's alright, brother," soothed the rabbi. "Even the saints are misled from time to time. Come back to the light."

The rabbi gently led Malbrook, arm in arm, back behind the bar to safety. Pierre was also behind the bar. He held the Catholic Rite of Exorcism in his hand, prepared for the arrival of the demons that he knew were coming.

The crowd was panicking, stampeding toward the exit, but the people who had drunk the poison one by one began to show the symptoms. With drooping eyelids, they stumbled around confusedly, some fainting and falling onto the ground. Many of them were vomiting everywhere, causing a revolting, slick layer of vomit all across the floor, which in turn caused everyone to slip and slide and fall into the puke.

Some people were bleeding from their eyes, nose, ears, and mouth. After only a minute or two, everyone who had drunk the Kool-Aid was on the floor, twitching and struggling for breath. They looked around in agony with their eyes and their bodies paralyzed completely. Across the putrid bar floor, people's lungs became paralyzed, and they asphyxiated. The floor began to be covered with dead bodies, thick as the flies that would soon be there to take advantage of them.

Abijah landed on the ground and stomped through and among the dead bodies with as little care as if they were potato sacks.

Paul, Mary, Matt, and Uri gathered on the stage, stepping over the dead drummer and guitarist and looking out over the sea of corpses. The bar-goers who had not drunk the poison had made it outside and were mulling about in the parking lot, trying to come to terms with the latest massacre. Lâmié joined them on the stage.

"You'd think we'd learn one of these days," he said.

"Yeah," said Mary, "this is beyond ridiculous. But, wait, what the hell are those two doing?" She nodded toward Skink and Abijah, who were in the bar's entrance, kneeling facing Skink's tent and praying."

Uri tugged his payot and said, "Whatever it is, it can't be good. They're praying in ancient Hebrew. I can barely make it out, but I sure did hear the name *Moloch* in there."

A great roar exploded from outside the bar, in the direction of the tent. Then they heard—and felt in their chests—a series of thudding, pounding sounds that shook the entire bar, sounds that seemed a bit too much like gargantuan footsteps to be comfortable.

CHAPTER 50

A Load of Bull

The Gravediggers and friends rushed to the entrance of The Gutter. Abijah and Skink had arisen and were walking toward the tent vibrating with each colossal boom. The poles, beams, and ropes holding up the tent were shaken loose with each pounding shudder, and finally, the tent fell down like the House of Usher. The tent fabric covered a towering figure that began thrashing, leaning, and struggling.

Two enormous, brazen fists punched through the tent fabric like it were plastic food wrap, followed by two brazen, muscular arms and then a head: the bovine head of Moloch.

The idol had come to life!

The people in the parking lot stared up, necks straining, trying to comprehend what they were seeing. Moloch looked down at them and roared, and black smoke poured out of his nostrils. As he walked, slow and gargantuan like Godzilla, his cloven hooves crushed cars and people, flattening them into putrefying discs of fat, flesh, blood, and squishy gore.

The demon's resounding, baritone voice shook the ground as he spoke: "Come, children, and give yourselves to me! Come and lay down your lives, and let me feast upon your souls! Where is my servant, Abijah? Bring the children and the people to me!"

Abijah and Skink were doing their own forms of damage. Abijah held an ancient, Hebrew sword in his hands, and in the confusion of the idol, he was running around the parking lot, slicing up anyone he came across. Skink, contrarily, was loping about, trying to force the poisoned drink down the throats of anyone who was weakened or confused. As he succeeded, people convulsed and fell to the ground.

The black smoke from Moloch's nostrils became fire, and when he spewed it out, anyone in its path caught ablaze and shrieked as the flames charred their skin and melted their fat, killing them in the most agonizing way possible.

"Get back into the bar!" yelled Mary to the group of friends. They began to head toward the entrance. Moloch stamped around and neared Yarielis, but the old Voodoo queen was not going to just lie down and die.

Moloch's hoof headed right for her, but the determined, wiry old woman grabbed onto his ankle and rode it as the idol walked around the parking lot. She was screaming curses in Spanish as the massive leg swung her around, covering a huge distance with each pace. Moloch turned and spun around, throwing her off his ankle and right into Mary, who padded Yarielis' fall and saved her life. Mary pulled her into the relative safety of the bar.

Exhausted, Mary returned to the parking lot to try to help some more. She saw Siofra running from the looming hooves of Moloch. Titania saw this, extended her gossamer wings, glowed green, and flew across the lot toward Siofra. She reached her and shoved her out of the way, then quickly pointed her palm toward Moloch. A green shield of light surrounded her. Moloch's hoof hit the shield and crushed it partially, but the shield held temporarily. It was buckling, however, and Titania knew that she could not hold it forever. She had nowhere to go in the time that it would take the hoof to crush her. It seemed grim for the green fairy.

Then, she remembered something.

"Siofra!" she strained to cry out. "Remember? You're a changeling! Remember what Efnysien said! Help me! You can do this!"

Siofra had always remembered and pondered Efnysien's words. She was a goblin changeling, and though she looked and felt human, she was of the otherworld.

"That means you have power, too!" grunted Titania. "I can't hold this forever! Help!"

Siofra carefully approached Titania. Moloch was focusing on breaking through Titania's shield, so he paid Siofra no attention.

"But what do I do? I don't know how!" protested Siofra while she desperately watched Titania's green shield shrinking and denting from the enormous demon hoof.

Titania strained her arms and winced as her power deflated more and more.

"Focus, Siofra! Focus on my shield. You're not a fairy, but we can work together. Hold out your hands like I'm doing, and imagine a stream of protective magic flowing out of your palm. Do it! Hurry!"

Siofra followed Titania's instructions. Holding up her palm toward Moloch's hoof, she closed her eyes and trusted the magic. She envisioned a beam of light shooting from her palm up at the hoof. For a few moments, nothing happened, but then she felt her palm heat up and vibrate. She opened her eyes and saw a beam of pure, green light emanating from her hand. Unlike Titania's emerald green, Siofra's was more like a sickly, gangrenous green, but it worked anyway.

With Siofra's help, Titania regained some strength, and their joined protective shield held fast. Moloch tried in vain to stomp them. He realized that it was not going to happen, so he pulled his hoof off of the magical shield.

Siofra felt elated. She could really perform magic! This would change everything! She smiled and looked at Titania.

"Run, Siofra! Run!" shouted Titania, but it was too late. Siofra's complacency allowed Moloch to look down at her. The idol smiled a thin, wicked smile, opened its mouth, then breathed fire down upon Siofra. Titania screamed as she watched her friend being consumed with hellfire. Poor Siofra stood no chance – she fell to the ground and was burned to death within moments.

Aaron and Amos, dressed in their Mormon Elder suits, complete with nametags, had knelt to pray. They called out to God to save them, for the help of the Prophet Joseph Smith. But God helps those who help themselves, and they should have been running instead of kneeling. The two brothers looked to see the brazen, cloven hoof of the demon Moloch coming down upon them. After only a brief moment of excruciating agony, their young souls were taken up into heaven.

Paul stared up at Moloch, and the world melted away again. The oil-paint colors seemed especially rich and creamy, and the auras of all the people seemed closer to solid and real than ephemeral and illusory. It was Moloch, however, who was the most stunningly beautiful.

The Great Bronze Beast looked angelic, its golden aura spreading out in the pattern of multiple, glorious wings. Swirling around his splendid bull's head were countless dots of light, more numerous than the stars in the sky, each little orb the soul of a child sacrificed to the Beast. How beautiful was each innocent sacrifice, each pure little life plucked away at its flowering infancy in the most painful way possible!

Moloch looked down upon Paul and smiled. The man was feeling at one with the demon.

"Oh, that's just what we fucking need," said Matt, pointing across the street. Everyone looked and saw Ophelia's pale, wraith figure leading her kingdom of vampire subjects. They were watching the massacre from a safe distance, Ophelia with a smirk on her face.

"She's waiting for us to fight the demon, and then she's going to activate the amulet," said Mary. "I know how her demented mind works by now. And what the hell is Paul doing? He's just looking at Moloch like a lost puppy!"

Pierre, no longer behind the semi-safety of the bar, climbed onto the bar's roof to view the scene. He climbed back down to rejoin the Gravediggers in the parking lot and said, "It is as I feared. In the dining room, when the demon appeared and that black cloud went into Paul's mouth, it partially possessed him. It's the demon inside of him. It's drawing him to Moloch. I'm putting it all together. This must be what is happening."

"But why?" yelled Mary over the screams of the crowd.

"Paul has some kind of special ability. I have felt it since my arrival. I cannot define it, but the feeling is strong, and I am never wrong when it comes to demons. I think whatever demon in inside of Paul wants him to go to Moloch so that Moloch can kill him and end whatever that special power is. So we have to save him!"

Mary did not think twice. She sprinted off from the group as Matt called in vain to her to stop. She ran right to Paul, who was on his knees staring up at Moloch, the idol directly above him. She reached him and pulled his arm.

"Get up, you idiot!"

Paul shook her off his arm. He was enamored of Moloch and would neither tolerate nor abide anyone trying to take him away from the object of his besotted fascination and worship.

"Mary! Mary!" said Moloch, and his booming voice put her into some sort of daze. "Do not resist me, Mary. Like Paul, you are rejected by this world. Like Paul, you were mistreated as a child. None of your friends really like you. You do all of their dirty work! You put yourself at risk. You have always been the weak victim, Mary, who could never stand up for herself. Now is your chance to finally be powerful! Do you remember?"

The world around her glimmered, then faded, and she was back in her childhood room. *She did not have time to look around and wax nostalgic, for her father burst into the room. That familiar old reek of whisky, so sharp and acrid, pelted her nose.*

"Your mother told me you were in here," he slurred.

A pang of betrayal flooded her, bringing both fear and anger. Her mother? Had she not always considered her mother also a victim of her violent, alcoholic, abusive father? Her mother knew that her father came into her room for only one filthy reason. Why would she have done that?

Her father pushed her back on the bed, her frail child's body unable to resist. She tried to dissociate to another place as he pulled off her shorts and underwear, then his, revealing his horrible thing. The pain was sharp, like she was burning from the inside, and she hated the world and life. How could her own father do this? How could her mother help him?

She saw her mother standing at her bedroom door with a malicious grin of satisfaction as she watched her husband rape her daughter.

"See, Mary?" growled Moloch, and she snapped back into the real world. "You had no chance, even from your childhood! You were always just a doll, a plaything, an object to be manipulated, a ragdoll to be tossed about the world. Even Paul betrayed you for the Indian women! Don't you see? Come, Mary, and join us. We are not truly evil. We are those who make our own way in the world, who refuse to bow down to our abusers. We are powerful, and we stand up for ourselves."

Mary paused and thought. Was Moloch really wrong? Demon or not, he made good points. Her father had abused her; that much was true. She must have forgotten the memory, but her mother had apparently been an accomplice all that time…her parents, the ultimate betrayal.

"He's right, Mary," said Paul. "No one else loves you, loves me. Our friends are all hypocrites. They use us. They make us do all the dangerous things! All along, the real monsters we were fighting were other people. Look at him, Mary. Look at Moloch and behold his glory!"

Mary raised her head and gazed up at the brazen idol. He sparkled with the gleam of a million stars. His arms reached out, and his upturned palms beckoned Paul and Mary like a loving father, not stern, but gentle, safe, and warm.

Mary took Paul's hand in hers, and they both stood up. They walked toward the mountainous idol. Moloch smiled lovingly and reached down to take them in his arms forever.

Then, Mary realized something.

Her mother had *never* helped her father rape her. It had never happened. On the contrary, her mother really *was* a victim, just like her. All of the late-night beatings, the sound of her mother weeping in the kitchen, the way her mother would wince when she heard her father come home.

She remembered something that Father Woodrow had said at Madame Who's exorcism: *Do not, under any circumstances, engage the demon in conversation. Do not reply to it, and do not react to its taunts or mockery. The demon may reveal personal things about you, things that are embarrassing or humiliating and private. Ignore these. It only mentions these to tempt you to react and to engage it in conversation...Jesus called Satan the father of lies. Assume everything the demon says to be a lie, even accusations.*

It was all a lie!

She returned to reality and cried, "The father of lies, Paul! The father of lies!"

Paul turned to her with a puzzled look on his face. Moloch roared. Mary slapped Paul hard, not out of anger, but to bring him out of his demonic revery, and it worked.

"He's a liar, Paul! Remember what Father Woodrow said! Everything the demon says is a lie!"

Paul wavered.

How could the beautiful world of the demons be a lie?

He looked into Mary's eyes, and it all flooded back. Her love, his love for her, all of the things they had been through together, the possessions, the evil, the killing—they all came back to him like

Mary's slap in the face.

That snapped him out of his daze, and he returned to the present, to his reality. In anger, Moloch bent his brazen brows and reached down to swipe at Mary, but he missed. Paul and Mary ran back toward the bar, and Moloch pounded after them, but much to their luck, the Moloch idol was distracted by something that did not bode well for the Gravediggers: the mass of international demons that the Micromerrin had trapped with the salt circle had managed to break through and were marching down the street right toward the bar.

"Christ, this might be the biggest clusterfuck ever!" said Mary.

Pierre stepped forward calmly and said, "Please bring Rabbi Cohen, Father Woodrow, Imam Riyad, Reverend Malbrook, Swami Maitra, and Apada to me."

The Gravediggers ran back into the bar and found the people requested. They stood in a group before Pierre as the towering idol ran amuck and slaughtered people in the background.

The Mean Girls were backed up against a tree, terrified and confused, as they had no idea that the supernatural even existed, much less a giant, demonic idol come to life. But, unfortunately, that idol had them in his sight.

Moloch stomped over to the tree, his profound and bass footsteps shaking leaves and twigs out of the ancient oak. Anna, Lucy, and Rose screamed, held hands, and closed their eyes tight as Moloch reached them and raised his giant leg above them, ready to pulverize them.

"Hey, Moloch! Hey, you overgrown statue! You bronze piece of shit! You stupid old demon!" yelled a girl's voice behind the idol, causing him to stop and turn around. It was Veronica.

"That's right, you ugly ass cow! You're full of bullshit! Come get me, coward!" She backed up, and Moloch followed her.

"Run! You three, run! Get out of here!"

The Mean Girls were frozen in fear, but hearing Veronica's voice snapped them out of it. They ran as fast as possible in the other direction.

"Veronica! No!" yelled Varco, but he could not help her. Moloch had backed her up against a pickup truck that the idol had flipped onto its side, and there was nowhere to run.

She looked back at Varco as the idol reached her and yelled, "I always loved you, Varco! I always will!" She turned her head in the other direction and found Isabella. She looked her in the eyes and yelled, "I'm so sorry, Isabella! I never meant to hurt anyone!"

Moloch raised his leg, and the brazen hoof quickly ended Veronica's life.

"Listen carefully," said Pierre to the six other exorcists in a loud voice to overcome the screams of terror all around them. "Each of us here has a special ability and duty to fight the demon. Apada and I were born with the skills of the exorcist, as was Swami Maitra, who's passed it down to Apada. You other four? You are men of God, religious leaders. You have faith! I need you to reach down and find that faith right now. The seven of us will conduct the biggest, baddest, interfaith exorcism in the history of the world. Are you ready? Are you with me?"

They all looked at one another and somberly nodded their inclusion in the plan.

"Then come on, *allons-y!*"

CHAPTER 51

En Garde!

The Gravediggers and friends watched with anger and sadness as Moloch raised a hefty, bronze leg and smashed it down right onto the roof of the Micromerrin.

"No!" screamed Lâmié. "You son of a bitch!"

The armor held valiantly against the juggernaut's leg and hoof, but it was a simple matter of physics. As the cloven hoof crashed through the van, the layers of salt and holy water built into the armor sizzled against the idol, and it screeched, but it did not stop. Instead, it stamped all over the vehicle with both feet until the glorious Micromerrin was just a flattened mass of metal, rubber, oil, and memories.

"Get some salt, Lâmié! Hurry!" yelled Pierre.

Lâmié returned from inside the bar with several boxes of Epsom salt.

"Come on!" said Pierre, handing the boxes out to the others. He led them toward the idol, who was distracted at the moment by a group of fleeing punks behind him.

"Make a circle! Hurry!" shouted Pierre as the hooves crushed the punks into a pool of gore. One bodiless head lay in the pool of blood, its Mohawk still holding solid.

The friends ran around Moloch, laying down a thick line of salt in a circle and closing the loop. Moloch tried to push his way across the salt line, but it held, at least for now. So, he could not cross it.

Pierre joined hands with Cohen, Woodrow, Riyad, Malbrook, Maitra, and Apada, forming an unbroken circle.

"Do *not* break the circle, whatever you do!" instructed Pierre. "The union is our strength! Now, I want each of you, right now, at the same time, to conduct an exorcism however your faith does it. The combination of faiths will be powerful! Now start the joint exorcism!"

Father Woodrow began the Catholic Rite of Exorcism from memory, while Rabbi Cohen loudly began his Hebrew prayers. Riyad prayed the prayers of exorcism in Arabic while Reverend Malbrook forcefully recited Psalms and the Lord's Prayer. At the same time, Maitra and Apada said Hindu prayers against demons, and Pierre firmly commanded the demon to depart, also citing parts of the Catholic Rite of Exorcism.

It began to work. Moloch backed away to the far side of the circle of salt and roared in pain. They all prayed and recited louder, and the giant idol thrust his bronze hands in front of his face as if to block them. He violently shook his head around, the pain of the combined divine forces unbearable.

Paul, who was still beside Mary, felt the demon's call again. The demon from the dinner still possessed him, after all, and it would not let go without a fight. For Paul, the world morphed *again* into the demon world. He looked at Mary and saw that her spiritual self was a yellow haze with multiple arms protruding from it, the center mass, and an external, beating heart.

However, he also looked up at Moloch and saw pure, energetic evil and rage. The demon was under assault from the exorcists, and with each prayer-arrow hurled at the idol, Paul himself felt the ripping, tearing sting in his own body. This incited his own anger, and he marched away from Mary toward the salt circle. Mary immediately recognized what was happening.

"Paul, no! You don't know what you're doing! Not fucking again!"

It was too late.

He kicked a large hole in the salt circle. Moloch noticed it immediately and, with an elephantine blast of his nostrils, stepped outside of the circle and walked around it toward the exorcists. They quickly ran into an alley that was too narrow for Moloch, saving themselves.

By this time, the entire city was in a panic. Demons were manifesting everywhere, so many that even Ophelia and her vampires were hanging back, unsure how to proceed.

Unfortunate Madame Who had lit some candles in the parking lot, a little way out from The Gutter, and was loudly calling out to her ancestors and the spirit world to banish Moloch. This served only to attract the demon's attention and draw his ire. With a swipe of his great bronze hand, he stomped over to her and smeared her into the cement before she even recognized what was occurring.

"Oh no!" cried Miss Annabelle from just inside the bar. "If I hadn't been possessed, she never would have had to get involved, and she'd still be alive!"

"No, no," said Titania, also in the bar, desperately trying to summon some more fairy magic to help. "You didn't choose to be possessed. None of this is our fault! Now, let's see what I can do here. I'll make my magic work, or die trying!"

The Gravediggers, except Paul, who was still in the parking lot lovingly admiring Moloch on his rampage of death, were also in the bar for cover. Mary nervously watched him, waiting for an opportunity to steal him away from the Great Beast yet again. Did women always have to do everything?

"Can fairy magic do anything against that thing?" asked Matt, who had decided to hang back for now and look for an opportunity to get Paul away from Moloch.

"Not sure," she replied. "Remember, demons are ancient, older than humankind, but fairy magic is ancient too! I managed to stop his hoof from crushing me with my magic, so there's every motivation to try again."

She stepped outside the door, closed her eyes, and focused on reciting a spell in the ancient fairy language. It sounded like chimes and wind. Then, she glowed bright green, a radiant ball of light larger and deeper than anything the Gravediggers had ever seen. Her silver, sparkling wings extended from her back, and she rose a few feet from the ground.

She thrust her hands forward, and a thick, green bolt shot out of her palms toward Moloch. The light struck the demon, and a green, fiery ball engulfed him. He roared in pain and fell to his knees.

Titania did not have the energy to hold the spell, though. She fell to the ground in exhaustion, and the wounded idol stood back up.

"I...failed..." lamented Titania. "He's just...too...strong..."

Mary rushed to Titania's side and said, "Get her some water, someone! Titania, you wounded him. I think you weakened him!"

"When the magic connected, it opened me to his inner self, to the feelings of a demon. Such tragic sadness and remorse and hopelessness and rage! Such hatred for everything good!"

The entire area around The Gutter Bar looked like an alien landscape because the whole parking lot and the streets immediately surrounding it oozed with human gore. Flesh, fat, organs, and crushed heads piled several inches high canvassed the ground, and each step of Moloch squished down into the mess, sending it flying in all directions and smearing the people who were still alive.

The crowd of demons who had broken through the salt circle in New Orleans East were staging their own massacre, and they had spread out into the neighborhoods around the bar. Trails of massacred corpses and, in some cases, possessed people, marked their paths.

Barillo, who was inside the bar with the others, had simply turned his phone off. There was nothing he could possibly do to help the remaining police force, the cops who had not been killed or possessed by the demons, and it was no use answering the hundreds of phone calls flooding his phone.

Pierre and the other exorcists had resumed their prayers and rites, directing them at the unbound Moloch, but as the idol stomped around and killed, they were able to do nothing more than slightly weaken him.

The situation was without hope.

Paul, who was following Moloch around, gazing upon the massive, brazen form with adoration, felt pure hatred for the demon, which, in the demonic world, was like pure love. He was indeed a part of the demon.

Moloch looked down at Paul and snorted, fire and smoke pouring from his nostrils. Then, he reached down and picked up Paul with his large, bronze hand.

"Shit!" said Mary. "Pierre said Moloch wants to kill Paul, to stop whatever his special ability is. We have to do something!"

Moloch lifted Paul to the level of the idol's face, and Paul stared into his red, furious eyes. Mary ran to Moloch's feet, caring nothing for her own safety or life. Instead, she shouted up at Paul.

"Paul! Break the spell! He wants to kill you!"

Paul looked down at Mary and yelled, "You are wrong! We are one! I finally understand what the goddess Durga meant! All is one! All is Brahma!"

At the mention of Durga, Moloch roared, the deep vibrations of his voice almost shaking Paul off of the giant hand.

Paul was still seeing the world through the demon's eyes, but a rift appeared in the smeared, color paint of reality. Through that rift, Paul saw the darkness of infinity, and then a bright light appeared in the dark, and that light came forward: it was the goddess Durga. She floated in front of him, her many arms extended with palms open, giving Paul the gifts of wisdom and free will.

Paul! Paul! called Durga in his mind. *Why have you chosen the path of death and destruction?*

He answered back in his mind: *You said that all is Brahma! It's all the same! There's no good or evil!*

But there is choice, she answered. *Death and destruction are necessary and fundamental to the universe. Such is Shiva. But there is also light and love and good! So look down, Paul, and make your choice!*

Durga drifted back into infinity, and the rift closed.

Paul saw both realities at once: his ordinary reality and the demonic reality. He looked down at Mary and then back up at Moloch—two opposites, two poles of the same magnet, two sides of reality, of Brahma.

The darkness in Paul desperately wanted Moloch, even if that meant death, destruction, or hell. But the goodness in Paul wanted Mary, wanted her humanity and flaws and frailty and love and warmth and loyalty. He wanted to be a part of someone, and each choice offered supreme union.

The draw of the demon was great, as it not only tapped into Paul's own darkness but the demon inside of him, the demon possessing him. He looked down once more at Mary, so vulnerable beneath Moloch. One small footstep would snuff out her life instantly. Then the answer came to him.

Mary would give her life for you.

As he thought that, the demon inside him raged and roiled, wracking him with intense pain, but he knew the choice he had to make. The world returned to reality.

"Mary, run!" he yelled. "Run away fast and hard! Trust me!"

She had no choice but to trust him. She remembered the times he had come through despite everything, so she sprinted back to the bar.

Paul stood on Moloch's bronze hand, wobbling back and forth, only a foot away from a deadly drop.

Then something from outside of this world, white and bright and ancient and untold and *good*, entered Paul. His chest swelled with understanding and the wisdom of old. He knew that love, plain and simple love, was the entire universe and the very reason behind it. Creation, life, death, good and evil—they all bowed down before love, and Paul loved Mary.

As if not even under his own control, feeling like he had turned into metal, he stood firm and uttered, "Moloch, you ancient serpent, you prince of hell, you prince of liars, I command you to leave this place and this world! I speak from light and love, and I order you to leave us and return to the fiery pits of hell where you belong!"

He felt the demon inside of him thrashing and furious. His chest and organs burned as if with fire. He could barely remain conscious through the pain. He knew, though, that the pain meant that his words were working.

"Paul, you fool!" bellowed Moloch. "Have I not shown you love? Have I not brought you in as my very child? Do you now betray me?"

Paul tensed every muscle in his face and replied, "Mary would die for me. You would not!"

As Paul spoke, black smoke poured out of his own mouth: the demon had left him. His strength and understanding had exorcised it from his body. He felt like good old Paul again.

Then, something unique happened. Moloch roared and shrieked in defiance and defeat. Paul had aligned with the forces of good, and together with Titania's magic and the faith of the religious ones, the power had been so great as to overcome Moloch, that demon of old.

Moloch shook, and Paul fell off the idol's hand. He raced toward the ground, his life flashing before him, but at the last moment, something good and invisible slowed him down and landed him gently on the ground. Whatever forces controlled the universe, whether the God of the Bible, or Buddha, or Shiva, or Durga, or something else entirely, they had seen and heard his and Mary's struggle, and they had finally come to help him.

Mary and the others raced out to greet Paul, and they all looked up at Moloch. It was over for the idol. The brazen, living idol was burning up from the inside out, its bronze melting and falling onto the ground and on whoever was unfortunate enough to be standing too close. Several bar customers were burned to death by the molten metal, and as it hardened, it formed human-shaped bronze statues, testaments to the slaughter that had occurred there.

"Over there!" yelled Uri to the others. "Skink and Abijah! We have to stop them, or they can just do this again, conjure him back!"

An amorphous glob of liquid molten bronze formed on the melting idol's shoulder and drooped tenuously over Mary, who did not notice it. Uri saw it, and as it began to detach from the idol's shoulder, Uri realized that it would fall on Mary and kill her.

"Mary! Watch out!" he screamed as he ran toward her; his payot bounced with each step, and his hoiche hat flew off. The dangling drop of deadly liquid metal detached from the dying idol and fell quickly. Mary looked up and understood what was happening, but it was too late for her to run. At the last moment, Uri reached her and pushed her out of the way. He looked at her and smiled, as if to say, *You would have done the same for me.*

The molten blob hit Uri with the force of a large piece of bronze, with enough heat to liquify it. His initial scream of pain was stifled as molten bronze ran into his mouth and down into his stomach and lungs. Then, his chest burst outward, splaying his ribs and shooting out blood, organs, and bits of hardening bronze. The others ducked to avoid the same fate.

"No!" yelled Mary. "Uri, no! Oh, God!"

"Oh damn!" screamed Paul. "Why him? He was a harmless Hasid! Mary, he gave his life for yours."

Amid the shock, loss, and trauma, the remaining Gravediggers still had to deal with Skink and Abijah. After all, Uri had been right. Unfortunately, nothing was stopping them from simply conjuring Moloch again or doing something even more wicked. Sometimes, however, the winds of misfortune change direction.

Skink and Abijah had been kneeling, bowing, and praying to Moloch, but as they saw the idol begin to self-destruct, their faces turned to fear. Moloch swayed this way, then that way, slowly twirling like a drunken ballerina, until it finally teetered in the direction of the two worshipers.

The colossal idol fell in one crashing motion, simultaneously bursting apart and exploding, and it fell directly onto Skink and Abijah. Abijah, still in the eternity of unchanging youth, sprinted out of the way, but Skink was old and creaky, and he had no chance. The slimy death cult leader was instantly reduced to a burning pile of gore and ash.

Abijah looked at the lifeless, fallen idol and the bits of Skink that had been squished out from under it. Sword still in his hand, he rushed the Gravediggers and friends, his eyes red with fury. Like a berserker, he swung his sword around him manically.

Pierre ran into the bar and re-emerged quickly; he held the metal microphone stand in his right hand. The microphone was still attached to the top of the stand. He drew his left hand back and over his head and stood in a fencing stance.

The others watched him with smirks and eyes of curiosity. What the hell was he doing?

"All French boys study fencing!" he yelled. He turned toward Abijah and yelled, "*En garde!*"

Abijah stopped and looked at the odd little Frenchman with the microphone stand in his hand and laughed.

"What? What do you think you are going to do? Drink wine, smoke a cigarette sarcastically, and fiddle about with that mic stand?"

With a wide grin on his bearded face, Abijah pointed his sword at Pierre and lunged. With the deftness of a bullfighter, Pierre sidestepped, and as Abijah ran by him, he swung the mic stand and hit Abijah in the ass.

Abijah howled in pain and fell to the ground. He pulled himself back up, recomposed himself, and faced off yet again against Pierre.

"*Fils de putain! Con! Viens donc!*" shouted the Frenchman.

Abijah made the mistake of charging first again. This time, Pierre feigned a sidestep to his right. Abijah, planning for the step, jabbed his sword at Pierre's righthand side, but Pierre lightly stepped back to his left, and as Abijah stumbled yet again, he bashed him on the back of his head with the mic stand.

Abijah cursed in Hebrew and rubbed his head. Blood was pouring down his hair and his payot.

"Never, ever underestimate a Frenchman!" shouted Pierre with an arrogant twist to his voice.

This time, Abijah faced Pierre, sword in front of himself, but did not lunge. Instead, he cautiously stepped forward in a sword fighting stance.

He approached Pierre and carefully thrust his sword, which Pierre parried with the stand. They went back and forth, thrusting and parrying for several minutes as both men became tired.

Finally, Abijah skillfully feigned and avoided Pierre's parry, then flanked him quickly. He thrust the sword, and it entered Pierre's side. Blood immediately poured out, and Pierre fell to the ground. He dropped the microphone stand and held his wound.

"Well, it looks like my millennia of sword training has outdone your few years of fencing. You have fought bravely, though, and so I shall afford you a warrior's death."

He strode to Pierre and held the sword above his head.

"One, swift stroke, and off with your head!"

He tightened his muscles, ready to deliver the death-slice.

During the fight, Paul had rushed inside the bar and had returned with a bottle of strong, London Dry gin.

"Not so fast, asshole!" yelled Paul, causing Abijah to turn for a moment. Paul shook the bottle and splashed the gin into Abijah's eyes. He shrieked, dropped the sword to the side of Pierre, and grabbed his burning eyes.

Pierre wasted no time. Suffering through his pain and blood loss, he picked up Abijah's sword and sliced deeply into the man's calf. Abijah fell to the ground amid a series of Hebrew curses. He was now blinded and wounded.

"Hand me the sword, Pierre," said Paul. "I want to be the one to take out this son of a bitch."

Paul took the sword from Pierre.

"You could control a demon," hissed Paul, "but you messed with the wrong punks! Punk's not dead, but you are!"

With the rage of a man wronged, he did not hesitate to plunge the sword into Abijah's heart. The ancient Hasid quickly died. As they all watched, his body began to disintegrate, to decompose. No longer under the demon's power of eternal life, he was reverting to himself when he had died so, so long ago. He became a corpse, then bloated, then decomposed, then nothing but a skeleton, then a pile of dust. Abijah was no more.

"Well, shit," said Paul with a sip of gin.

The demons all around New Orleans, the instant that Moloch, their prince, was expelled and sent back to hell, writhed and shrieked as they were pulled down through the sidewalks, streets, cobblestones, and dirt back into the fires of hell.

All the possessed people fell to the ground, flopped around, became rigid, and screamed, but their demons were released at the end of the struggle. New Orleans was filled with perplexed people lying on the ground and wondering how they had arrived there.

CHAPTER 52

I'm Gonna Get You, Sucker!

Ophelia smiled. The demons were gone, and it was finally the Era of the Vampires. Across the street from The Gutter Bar and the carnage in its parking lot, the ancient vampiress turned to face the bloodsucking horde.

"Now is our time, children! Now is the age of the vampires! Come, I will activate the amulet, and we will take this city and the world!"

The vampires roared in approval, and the roars, like those from a group of lions, shook the buildings around them.

Ophelia held the amulet up in front of her and in front of the horde. It glowed red. She beheld the sparkling, ancient runes and read them aloud, having long ago in Ushaville memorized the correct words to bring the amulet to life for her wicked purposes:

Seven demons from the land, air, and sea. Seven demons come from below to trouble us above. They drink our blood. They steal our little ones. They take our life, and they live forever. I, Asarial the wizard, have learned the secret of killing them. I, Asarial, have created this amulet to contain the power of their death.

The words took force as the amulet shook, and the red glow intensified to a deep, sanguine ruby hue.

"Yes! The power! Oh, God, the power!" she screamed. "The

power of the vampires through the ages is now manifest in me, Empress Ophelia! Come, children, take the city! The city is ours!"

The vampire rushed forward toward the bar. As they came across any straggling survivors, they tore them apart and totally drained them of blood.

"Christ, look!" shouted Mary.

The sight of the pale horde flying at them was not encouraging. The unfortunate Judy Felix was standing at the wrong spot.

Judy, who had been holding Baozi and Pidan in her arms, placed them down on the ground and said, "Run, my babies!" They seemed to understand her intent, and the two cats ran inside the bar, barely escaping death.

Judy turned and faced the vampires. She pulled the holy water gun and crucifix out of her pocket—Pierre had insisted that they come prepared. She took a long, deep breath, and decided to honor the memory of Dr. Handler by going down fighting if she had to.

"No more!" cried Judy. "No more fear! No more hiding inside! No more avoiding the outside, and what is real! I am Judy, bitches! I am a tiger now, so come hear me roar!"

She knew that she was overwhelmed, but dammit, she was going to take out as many bloodsuckers as she could before she left this world. She opened up the holy water gun, and the holy liquid sprayed out as if it were in a machine gun. The vampires in the front of the flying horde were hit and dropped to the ground screaming and holding their sizzling faces and skin.

"There's more of that!" yelled Judy as she emptied out the gun's entire magazine. She had dropped about three dozen vampires. She threw the empty gun to the side and held her crucifix out in front of her. The vampires that had overtaken the ones with burning skin flew back hissing and screaming as the shame of the holy cross made them confront what they really were. As if she were Moses parting the Red Sea, Judy held the cross firm and the horde of vampires broke in half and went around her.

Ophelia saw what was happening and ordered her children to flank Judy. They did, and Judy swirled in a circle while holding out the crucifix, making a sort of whirlpool of retreating vampires.

She could not do this forever, and as she became exhausted, a male vampire swooped in and lunged for her neck.

"Not so fast, asshole!" she yelled. She produced an ashwood stake form her pocket and held it out in front of her. The surprised vampire sailed right into it and disintegrated into a puff of dust. Judy coughed.

Ophelia was beyond pissed at this, so she herself dive-bombed Judy from above. Judy did not see her coming. Ophelia knocked Judy to the ground, growled like a tiger, and plunged her fangs into Judy's carotid artery. Blood blasted out, coating the ground around her as Ophelia guzzled her life force until she was drained. Ophelia looked up at Paul and Mary with her blood-smeared lips and grinned. Her face was transformed into that of the demon that lived inside her.

Unlike her cats, poor Judy Felix did not have nine lives.

"You bitch!" yelled Mary. Then, she turned to the others and cried, "What the hell do we do?"

"Shit. No more Microbus and we weren't counting on vampires," answered Lâmié. "We don't have enough stakes or holy water left for that many vamps! We can hold them back for a minute or two, but then what?"

"Everyone, stand back," boomed a voice from behind them all. The group parted in the middle, and a tall, proud Beast Stalker strode to the front of the group and faced Ophelia.

"You again?" she taunted. "Can't Cherokees ever take a hint? I have the amulet on my side now, Beast Stalker. There is nothing you can do. I have unlimited power, and I can feel it!"

"You are forgetting Cherokee magic," he replied calmly.

"What is that supposed to mean? Vampire magic is more ancient."

"Not by far, Ophelia. Keep in mind who the amulet was given to first. It was not for vampires but *against* vampires. It was not to vampires, but to my people."

"Well, good for *your people*. The fact is that *I* have it now, and it serves *me*."

In an instant, she leaped across the space between her and Paul, restrained him with his hands behind his back, and, with perfect control developed over the millennia, placed just the tip of her fangs against his neck, not quite piercing the skin, but pushing dimples into it.

"Get off him, you bitch!" cried Mary, but Beast Stalker gently raised his palm to her.

"Don't feed into the fear," he said. "Ophelia, you do not know it, but you are making a huge mistake."

She pulled back from Paul's neck and laughed. "My only mistake was not taking the amulet sooner. I can feel the glory of a thousand moons, the wicked will of countless demons coursing through my veins. I am power! I am evil!"

Beast Stalker lowered his head and began chanting something in the Cherokee language.

"Final prayers before you die?" mocked Ophelia. "Fine. That goes for everyone else too, especially you silly religious men with your silly hats," she said with a gesture toward the interfaith group. "Whatever gods you pray to, and the rest of you as well, go ahead and say something to them. I will grant you that one last grace. After all, we have quite a history, don't we? So, what's one last little mercy before I completely ravage your bodies and engorge myself on your blood?"

Some of them did indeed begin to pray, desperate little petitions to the invisible ones in the sky to take their souls up to heaven. Then, the vampire mob moved in toward them. Things looked terrible.

Beast Stalker continued to chant in Cherokee, louder and louder, and faster and faster.

"What the hell?" shouted Ophelia.

The amulet's color had begun to change from red to a dark purple, then to less purple with a touch of blue, and then to a full, dark, brilliant blue. As Ophelia held it, the skin on her hand began to sizzle, melt, and char. She shrieked with surprise and pain and anger.

"The amulet was given to my people," repeated Beast Stalker. "It has always served my people. It has strong, ancient protection magic inside of it to prevent its misuse by demons and vampires!" He thrust his large, ruddy hands in front of himself and opened his palms, and the amulet soared through the air and into his grasp. "You never could use the amulet, Ophelia!" he cried triumphantly. "Chief put Cherokee magical protection in it so it will not bow to your wicked will!"

Ophelia wailed and shrieked furiously.

"No! It can't be! I've worked so hard for it!" she bemoaned.

"And that was your mistake, you fool!" answered Beast Stalker. "Your lust for power and control clouded your judgment and knowledge! Now begone, or I will turn the amulet against you and all your children!"

The amulet pulsed blue, building up energy and power. Ophelia snarled at Beast Stalker like a cornered wolf, but she backed up. The fury on her face turned her corpse-pale skin to a light crimson.

"Come, children!" she screamed. "Save yourselves! This is *not* over, Gravediggers! Amulet or not, I am going to kill each and every one of you! One by one, I will find you when you are not under the protection of the amulet! I will hunt each of you here in New Orleans. You cannot all have the amulet with you at all times. I'll guzzle your blood! I vow it! When you are least suspecting it, I will swoop down from the sky like the terror of the night!"

The vampire hoard took to the air and flew off toward Metairie Cemetery like a murder of crows aloft.

"Why didn't you kill them?" asked Mary.

Beast Stalker turned sheepishly and said, "It probably would have taken out a few, but it hadn't built up enough power to kill them all. So I made them think it would. Thank goodness Ophelia didn't call my bluff, or we would all certainly be dead right now."

"You clever fucking Cherokee!" said Paul. "Good fucking work!"

"Yes," agreed Beast Stalker, "but nothing truly stops her from taking us out one by one, like she said. One against one, we are no match for the vampires. This means that we must always stay together. We cannot risk venturing into the city alone or even in pairs at night. So we have to stick to the daylight until we figure out what to do."

CHAPTER 53

Hey Little Girl, I Wanna Be Your Husband

One Month Later

"And do you, Beast Stalker," said Father Woodrow, "take Evelyn Fogelberg to be your lawfully wedded wife?"

"I do," said the Cherokee.

"Then, by the power vested in me by God, the Roman Catholic Church, and the state of Louisiana, I hereby pronounce you man and wife. You may now kiss your bride!"

Evelyn took the lead in planting a big, wet kiss right on Beast Stalker's embarrassed mouth.

"We're married, don'tcha know!"

Everyone laughed and applauded as the couple turned around, walked back up the aisle, and led the others to the grand parlor of Lâmié's mansion. Lâmié had hired wedding planners to decorate it beautifully, using traditional Victorian wedding decorations to match the furniture. Bows, flowers, and ribbons tastefully adorned the room.

"Well, I guess opposites really do attract," said 'Tit Boudreaux.

Beast Stalker, wearing a traditional Cherokee wedding outfit, laughed for once. "Yes," he said, "who would have thought that a stern Cherokee man and a Yankee with an annoying voice would fall in love?

But we did, for sure. Some things are simply mysteries."

Lâmié had paid for Eli to rent a helicopter and fly to West Virginia to transport Chief Cloud Mountain and his wife to the wedding.

He had also hired the Gravediggers to play the wedding reception, only after forcing them to swear to play more traditional music. Paul looked ridiculous in his tuxedo on stage, and he twitched and scratched as if he were wearing someone else's skin. Mary had washed and combed his Mohawk so that he looked like a complete mockery of the idea of *formal*.

"Oh God, I can't believe I'm saying this," said Paul over the mic, "but we're going to play some nice pop music for you to dance to and…you know what, Lâmié? I can't say all this. So I'll play the stupid music, but you can do the speech, dude."

Mary slapped Paul on the arm. Lâmié just laughed.

"Fine, fine," he said. "By the way, you look so handsome in that suit, Paul!"

Paul flipped him off.

"Attention, everyone!" said Lâmié to the crowd. "I know this will embarrass Beast Stalker, but I just want to say a few words here. Everyone here has been through, excuse my language, some really messed up shit together. Beast Stalker has been with us since the beginning, since Ushaville. Evelyn has also put in more than her fair share of time in the field.

"The Gutter Bar's seen so much sadness and destruction, but this wedding is something new and happy, and, well, it feels like a new beginning, not just for Beast Stalker and Evelyn, but for all of us. So, everyone, please take your glass of Champagne, and let's raise a toast to the newly married friends!"

Everyone clinked their glasses around with the others and took a sip of the very rare and exclusive vintage of Dom Pérignon that Lâmié had splurged for. Lâmié nodded to Paul to start playing, and, with great shame and frustration, he and the Gravediggers broke into a non-rousing, unenthusiastic, very non-punk version of *My Sharona*.

While everyone danced and the Gravediggers languished their way through pop wedding songs from the 1970s, 1980s, and 1990s, the bride and groom were not the only ones trying to spark romance.

Iraj and Apada had walked into the back garden and sat on a stone bench between lovely rows of blooming magnolias. They sat for a few minutes in silence. Iraj was wringing his hands, and Apada was studying a flower very closely. Iraj finally forced himself to break the silence.

"Apada, I'm, I'm sorry about the other night, okay?"

"It's alright. I was being immature too."

She turned to face him.

"So, I guess you still have a crush on Paul," he said.

"Oh, you boys are so ridiculous! I said he's cute, and he is. It's just a silly crush. It means nothing. That's not the point."

He raised his eyebrows and asked, "Then, what's the point?"

"Oh, you silly boy! The point is that *you* have a crush on *me*!"

He looked down, not sure what to say.

"Well, don't worry, Iraj. Paul's just a silly crush. But I've known you for so long. Maybe you and I have a future together. We'll talk to Swami about it when we return to India."

Iraj blushed but took her hand in his, and she did not pull hers away.

Both Varco and Isabella, shocked by Veronica's self-sacrifice, were not talking or interacting. Isabella felt that she had a very long journey ahead of her if she were to forgive Varco, and she was not at all sure that she would. He would probably go back to Romania, so what would be the point anyway? Yet, her heart throbbed when she stole a glance at him from across the room.

Lâmié, an impeccably gracious host, had invited even the Mean Girls to the wedding, as they had been a part of the traumatic experience with Moloch. Of course, they had accepted, and each of the three had individually and personally apologized to both Isabella and Varco for their bullying and hazing. Obviously humbled by their experience with the Gravediggers, they sat quietly with their heads down.

Lâmié and Eli took a break from dancing and from laughing at Paul and the Gravediggers, who looked so ashamed to be playing a wedding. However, he was paying them a hefty fee, so they were suffering through it like almost champs.

"Well, it looks like everything worked out well this time," he said.

"This time?"

"Eli, if you only knew. Demons are just the tip of the supernatural iceberg. Imagine what we went through this time, and multiply it by a hundred, then stretch it out over the years."

"Well, damn!" she said as she took another sip of the

Champagne.

"Yeah, if you stick around, you'll be caught up in the same crap."

"If I stick around?" she asked with a coy smile.

"Oh, I mean...just...well...you know...I was just..."

She laughed and said, "Relax, Lâmié. I'm actually glad we ran into each other again. The days in the Legion were weird and terrible and wonderful, but we were just two immature kids, running from life and responsibility. But, of course, we're more mature now."

"Speak for yourself!" he joked.

She took his hand and said, "Well, I suppose I could stick around for a while if that's what life has in store for me, for us."

Paul interrupted them on the mic: "Um, ladies and gentlemen, Beast Stalker wanted to dedicate this next song..." He looked down at the notecard that Beast Stalker had handed him. "...to his beautiful, lovely...oh hell, I can't say this corny shit. Beast Stalker, sorry buddy, but you can tell her yourself. Anyway, here's freaking *Lady in Red*, for God's sake."

He looked miserable as the band started the ballad. Eventually, he had enough beers in him to relax a little, but Mary could not stop laughing at him through the night.

The following day, 'Tit Boudreaux prepared a full English breakfast for everyone, along with Bloody Marys and mimosas to assist their Champagne hangovers.

"Cherokees don't really say thank you among family and friends," said Beast Stalker to everyone in the grand parlor. "We consider it too distant and formal, like you might say to a stranger. Well, you are all my family now. There is no question about it. Evelyn feels the same way. So, instead of thanking you, I will just say that I had an amazing time at the wedding, and you really went out of your way, especially you, Lâmié, to give us the best wedding we could imagine."

"I'll drink to that!" said Paul.

"Wait," said Beast Stalker. "I also want to remember the ones we lost. So, let's raise a glass to our friends who perished at the hand of the demons: Aaron, Amos, Siofra, Veronica, Madame Who, and Judy Felix. And especially Uri, who gave his own life to save Mary's."

"I guess that slimy Reverend Skink was right about one thing:

giving your life for others is a great, noble act," added 'Tit Boudreaux.

They heard a scratching at the front door.

"Oh, Lord. Not something else," said Lâmié. "Hold that thought. I'll get it."

He made his way down the main hall to the front door and looked out of the peephole. He saw no one. He turned around and heard more scratching.

"Oh, for God's sake," he muttered.

He opened the door, and Baozi and Pidan meowed once, then strutted in like they owned the house. They trotted to the grand parlor and jumped up into Mary's lap.

"Oh, poor babies!" she said. "You found your home! Oh, poor things. They're going to mourn the loss of Judy. Cats do that, you know. Oh, come here, babies. I'll take care of you."

Everyone smiled that, despite all the deaths of their friends, the two innocent little souls had made it back alive.

"Now," said Lâmié, "I agree. So here's to the ones we lost. May their memories be blessings."

They all took a drink.

"Another thing," added Barillo. "Most of the New Orleans Police Department was wiped out. We'll rebuild, but at least this time, I don't have to make some ridiculous story to explain the destruction. There are almost no more cops to even care. There's heavy rain in the forecast, too. It'll clean up the, well, the parking lot at the bar." He grimaced at the thought of the gore.

"Say, Lâmié," said Paul, "are we gonna open up The Gutter Bar again? I mean, shit. We stopped demons. What more could there possibly fucking be? Vampires, werewolves, zombies, goblins, demons…I think we've emptied out the supernatural monster bin."

Everyone turned to Lâmié to see what he would say.

"Well," he began, "I think you have a point, Paul. It felt different this time, like, once you stop demons, that's it. So yeah, I think we will re-open the bar once things calm down in town. It'll be nice just to have some punk shows that end with a last call rather than a massacre. By the way," asked Lâmié as he turned to Pierre, "what are your plans? You're more than welcome to say here as long as you want."

"*Merci, mais non,*" replied the Frenchman. "I did my duty. *Alors*, I'm going back to Mexico, far away from demons and cities and the Vatican and all of that. I plan to relax the rest of my life away, but if you ever need me again, well, I'll see."

Paul nodded and said, "Well, I'm gonna head down to the liquor store and grab some beer. I wonder who's working there now?"

He stood up, winked at Mary, then walked down the main hall past the grand staircase, through the foyer, and then out the front door. The warm morning sunlight soothed his face.

He felt enormous relief. Whatever so-called special abilities he had no longer mattered. He had stopped Moloch, stopped the demons. It was time to retire from monster hunting and enjoy being a punk lucky enough to live rent-free in a mansion with the girl he loved.

With an uncharacteristic spring in his step, and his Mohawk freshly spiked and gelled, he headed toward the corner liquor store but did not make it. Instead, as he drew closer, he saw a group of people standing on the sidewalk. More of an angry mob than anything else, they held knives and even pitchforks.

"What the fuck?" he said. "Who the fuck has a pitchfork?"

One of the mob members saw Paul and pointed at him, yelling something to the others. They all turned and began to run toward Paul, who froze in place, confused.

"There he is!" yelled one of the men. "He's the one who conjured the demons!"

"Wait, no! No!" protested Paul to no avail.

"He did it with black magic!" yelled a woman. "He's a witch!"

"Witch!"

"Get the witch!"

"Kill the witch!"

Paul did not need any more time to think. He swirled around on his heels and sprinted hard back to Lâmié's mansion. Reaching the house in enough time to beat the Medieval-style peasant mob, he ran inside, slammed the door closed, and locked it behind him. Finally, he took a few panting breaths before trotting into the grand parlor. Everyone looked up at him.

"Well, guess the fuck what?" he said.

Made in United States
Orlando, FL
01 November 2023